'Gets you like a punch to the throat, tough, character-driven—a gripping ya.... .... you'll read this year.' —BEN HOBSON, author of *Snake Island*

'Chalmers is a strong new voice in Australian bush noir. *Conviction* is everything you thought about Queensland in the 1970s, corrupt, harsh and desperate . . . a skilfully drawn study of desolation and vice. Fast-paced and brilliantly executed.' —MICHAEL BRISSENDEN, author of *Dead Letters*

'In *Conviction*, Chalmers has distilled rural noir down to its hard, bitter essence. Stylishly written with poise and savage insight, *Conviction*'s fierce vision will stay with the reader long after the final page has been turned. A brilliant debut.' —DAVID WHISH-WILSON, Ned Kelly–shortlisted author of *True West*

'*Conviction* is where *Wake in Fright* meets *The Moonlight State*. With his gritty, authentic, taut and elegant prose, Frank Chalmers draws a terrifyingly evocative Royalton—a very Australian place where racism and violent misogyny are as pervasive as the guns and the crooked cops . . . and all of those broken hearts behind closed doors.' —PAUL DALEY, bestselling author and *Guardian* writer

'Gritty, hardboiled and immediately compelling; *Conviction* is a crime thriller drenched in atmosphere. Its sense of character and place are so vivid you'll swear you can taste the outback dust. A brutally confident debut that will seize your attention from the first page and dare you to look away. Don't miss it.' —GABRIEL BERGMOSER, bestselling author of *The Hunted*

'An atmospheric outback thriller which winds up from the mistaken official premise that exile was the way to deal with both the police too corrupt to keep around the capital and the police who wouldn't look the other way.' —PHIL DICKIE, Gold Walkley Award–winning journalist

FRANK CHALMERS is a graduate of the Australian Film, Television and Radio School. His academic background is in philosophy and he has taught at high school and university. He began his writing career on scripts for linear and interactive drama, documentary and educational media, and moved to conceptual/interaction design for websites and games. He merged all of these skills to work for museums and interpretive centres. He now writes novels.

CONVICTION

FRANK CHALMERS

ALLEN&UNWIN
SYDNEY•MELBOURNE•AUCKLAND•LONDON

First published in 2022

Allen & Unwin
83 Alexander Street
Crows Nest NSW 2065
Australia
Phone: (61 2) 8425 0100
Email: info@allenandunwin.com
Web: www.allenandunwin.com

A catalogue record for this book is available from the National Library of Australia

ISBN 978 1 76106 532 3

Set in 12/17.5 pt Sabon LT STD by Midland Typesetters, Australia
Printed and bound in Australia by Griffin Press, part of Ovato

10 9 8 7 6 5 4 3 2 1

For Julie, who made this possible

1

Ray jerks awake, sucking air as if he's burst from a bottom-less, dark-green pool, fingernails gouging his palms. He gapes at the compartment's two long, leather benches, his facing the future, the other the past. Empty. Also empty, the corridor outside, running the length of the carriage.

His blood pulses with the clatter of the train. What woke him? He stares out at eroded gullies, escarpments, stunted trees on red-brown plains rocking by. The first Monday of the new year, 1976. Heading west into desert, Brisbane must be two hundred and fifty miles behind already. Noon heat gone, shadows returning.

The percussion of the train soothes him until all in a rush the world comes back. Transferred. No, exiled, self-inflicted. He presses his forehead against the vibrating window and resists the urge to press hard, to push, shatter it. Imagines slivers of glass flying, cutting. He sits back.

That morning, waiting to board, no one to see him off, all he owned at his feet: a suitcase and small canvas knapsack, the sum of himself. People were quiet with the pale vulnerability of early-start travellers. He watched a woman about his age, maybe thirty, lick her fingers and use the spit to glue a defiant curl onto a little boy's forehead, the boy's head rocking under the pressure. The boy stared at Ray, enduring it, as kids do.

The train arrived in a wall of clamour and power. The woman took hold of the boy's upper arm, steering him into their wooden carriage. Ray stared at her tight grip, jolted by an image of his own mother pointing at him and laughing. It was doubly rare: her laughter and Ray thinking of her at all. It stopped him, causing ripples of discord among the throng of passengers pushing to board.

Ray stares out at the parched world filling his carriage window. She came from out here, although he has no idea exactly where. Expelled under circumstances, she would bitterly describe, that prevented her bringing photos, clothes, mementoes, anything of her family. She was killed when he was twelve in what cops called an 'unnecessary' car accident.

His mother's eyes had Medusa's intensity, her weapon. She knew all about exile, her truest home. He shakes himself, realising that her roots, which never mattered to him before, apparently now do. His transfer to this piece of country has needled him, as if the anonymous clerk who picked it knew, was twisting some spiteful knife. He puts his forehead back against the rattling glass, enjoys the buzz spreading through his head.

The landscape jumps like a badly loaded old movie. Fifty miles more without a bend. The train is a mail run, stops everywhere, stays nowhere, takes forever.

He snaps alert at the muffled sound of someone lurching into a wall. Muscles flex in his neck and arms, which is how it starts, the build of dark, violent energy that has pushed him through the ropes into the ring so many times. He hears a gravelly curse. Out of sight in the external corridor, something heavy crunches into a wall again. Another curse. Hairs on his neck move. His body knows.

A large man weaves into view, his round, sweaty face tight with frustration, arms out against the sway of the train. He slams back the sliding door of Ray's compartment, twists big shoulders through the doorway and half falls onto the opposite bench, buffeting Ray with grog fumes. The man winks and raises his eyebrows. Ray lifts his eyebrows in tepid response as the man heaves himself along the bench to the window until he is opposite Ray, shading bleary eyes from the fierce sunlight. He stretches his legs, hits Ray's, grunts, and jams his boots under his own bench. Ray gazes out his window.

The man is drunk but big enough to do harm. In his late twenties, face shining and greasy, crew-cut hair, wary brown eyes. Stained jeans, ex-army shirt, battered boots. He looks Ray over, burps. His top lip and one cheek are red and raw as from a blow, skin freshly broken. He produces a bottle of rum. Ray shakes his head. The man shrugs in disgust, joking maybe, lifts it in salute.

In a high-pitched voice, as if his words are starved of air and only escaping by stealth, he says, 'Gives you breath like a brewery horse's fart.' Leans in towards Ray, blowing hot air. 'My old man used to say that. Your old man say that?'

Ray shrugs, turns back to the window.

The man shakes his head, drains the bottle, pulls a face. He lifts the window off its hook, drops it with a crash and hurls the bottle out. Burps again and holds out a giant hand, too close to Ray's face, maybe from the roll of the train.

'Name's Burt. Not Burp. Burt.' Snorts at his wit, his lip bleeding a little.

Ray shakes the sweaty paw. 'Ray.'

'Ray? Ray what? Ray of sunshine, eh?' Stares too long. 'Where you headed?'

'End of the line. Royalton.'

Burt lets out a squeaky giggle, odd from such a big man. 'Arsehole of the west. Royalton, not you.'

Out the window is a tall green crop, row after row after row to the horizon. After all the ruthless red-brown, it looks hand-painted.

There's a bellow in the corridor. 'Burt! You ugly bastard, where are you?' Clear as a starting bell. Ray keeps his arms limp as a second man eases into the compartment. More grace than Burt, and more venom. Burt delivers the punches but this is the prick who sends him to do it.

'Whyn't you answer me, cunt?' He flops onto the far end of Ray's bench. Looking at Burt but snapping his head at Ray. 'Who's your poofter mate?'

Ray waits. Bastard's already earned the hurt that's coming. Same age, same clothes as Burt, but underfed. Thin, wiry arms knotty from the grind of manual work. A lean face, skin tight over cheekbones, beady eyes of uncertain colour. The corner of his mouth curls.

'Ray of sunshine, my mate Jimmy. Jimmy, this's Ray.'

Jimmy turns to Ray, makes his judgement, and lifts his boots onto Burt's bench. Exit blocked. Burt tries to grin but it hurts his lip. Ray stares out the window but watches Jimmy from the corner of his eye, ready if he moves.

Jimmy takes his time, sliding his legs along the bench till he leans in close to Ray. Brewery horse's fart alright. Ray holds up a hand and Jimmy jerks back, vibrant with mock outrage.

'Fuck! You going to hit me, you bastard? Yeah?' He flicks a teasing open hand at Ray's head.

Ray leans out of range.

Jimmy's lips set in an irritated line as he swings a backhand at Ray's face. Ray sees it, savours it, slips his own right under the loose arm to chop Jimmy's throat. Effortless, cruel. Jimmy spasms, eyes bulging, he leans forwards choking. Ray cracks a vertical right arm hard on the side of Jimmy's face, shoving him away, waits for the recoil, then slaps him backwards with the back of his right hand.

Over in a flash, stinging, insulting. Jimmy's eyes fill with tears and he coughs, unable to speak.

Burt growls, drags himself up and at Ray, arms wide in the narrow space, coming to crush. Ray stays seated, contemptuous, and lazily shapes up. He enjoys the satisfaction in Burt's eyes, before going southpaw, to tease. Hits a vicious jab to a bulging gut. Burt makes an explosive sucking sound, a boot coming out of deep mud, and sags, shocked face leading the way down. Ray hits him with a thudding right on his sore cheek, then takes his time for a snapping left to the other cheek. Burt groans, driven back, tears showering. He covers his face, doubles over onto his bench on top of Jimmy's boots, pinning them.

Ray stands, sways away from Jimmy's wild, seated swing, comes over the top and crunches his right elbow onto Jimmy's nose. Jimmy groans. His blood spurts across the floor. Ray lifts his boot to smash Jimmy's knee, make a cripple for life, but stops. Shakes all over like an animal then kicks the thigh instead, hard and painful enough to jolt Jimmy's legs free and off the bench, dropping him face first onto the bloody, grimy floor, where he whimpers, huddled.

Ray stands there, wanting more, fists and boots ready. Got to be more. The urge to hurt surges through him. But these two are done. He gives a low, rasping moan, clenches and unclenches his fists. Cheated, and hates it.

Faces crowd at the windows to the corridor. As usual, what seemed silent was a racket of pain and anger. Hoarsely pulling in air, he makes himself sit. As ever, shame comes creeping in. The shocked faces retreat. He closes bulging eyes, balances his breathing, applying years of post-fight practice after the rush of the ring.

Ray's eyes open to a beer-gutted, middle-aged man in dark-blue uniform and round peaked cap in the doorway. His cap's metal badge gleams CONDUCTOR.

'What the hell's going on here, son?' Jerking his chin at Ray as he takes in the bloke on the floor. 'Shit, Jimmy?' He recognises Burt too, which gives him pause.

Back to Ray. 'You alright, mate?'

From the man's sweaty uniform, Ray smells the dense odour of fear, sees his mother ironing his serge school shorts, same pair, night after night. Brown paper sprinkled with water for the creases, the iron hissing. Same wet smell. Her unnecessary road accident came almost a year to the day after his father died in an accident too, just as unnecessary but more freakish. Tripped over the fucking dog, then crashed down stairs, breaking his neck and skull. Tripping on a dog then falling to his death—a joke to tell at the pub, while toasting the dog.

Ray recalled shivering with rage beyond words at his dad for letting it happen, and even more so at his mum for provoking it, a rage that sank deep, and stayed, lying in wait, ready, useful or not; a feeling like drowning, thrashing in the dark, kicking the wall beside his bed. Trembling fury at the bad luck of it all, if that's what it was and not stupidity or gutlessness.

To stop the anger from eating him, to try to make it work

for him, he took on all comers, first behind the school dunny, then, after leaving school, behind the pub, fighting everyone's battles till a local copper shrewdly pointed him to boxing. Gave his dumb brawling a shape, and legal cover. Brought some relief, not enough.

The conductor asks again, 'Mate? You with us?'

Ray nods, mute so an unsteady voice won't betray him.

The conductor teeters in his highly polished boots and peeks at Jimmy and Burt for signs of life, then relaxes.

'What'd they try on?' He tilts his head like a bird, as if sharing a gleeful secret, and slyly holds up a fat, soft fist. 'Should've invited me. Give me enough curry over the years.' He chuckles, a conniving sound. 'You want to go official?'

Ray produces his police ID, intent on hiding any tremor in his hand. 'I'm a cop.'

The conductor, wide-eyed, nods feverishly. 'Ah, good-o, they're off next stop anyway. If they can get up!' Rubs his hands together, can't get away fast enough. In the corridor, ordering people back. 'Nothing to see here. Bush justice, all over. Seats please.'

Ray shuts his eyes, breathes very deliberately. The two on the floor wheeze, grunt—maybe there's even a sob. No effort to rise.

Time passes in that coming-down, post-adrenaline way, the train clicking and clacking.

Jimmy elbows Burt, spits blood. Burt burps, then rises, gripping his stomach, eyes on sticks. His boots lumber all over Jimmy, who yelps, contorts, can't get out of the way. Burt reels out of sight. Ray listens to the rolling roar as Burt vomits out a corridor window amid indignant yells. Burt yells something unintelligible, voice fading as he heads away.

Jimmy pulls himself up onto the far end of the opposite bench, hunched, shivering. He tentatively wriggles his nose, flexes his leg, close to tears of ferocious frustration.

'Fucking copper piece of shit.'

Ray watches, expressionless. Ready.

'Going to fucking book me?'

'For what?'

Jimmy absorbs this, then says, 'Usual shit. Assaulting a copper. Drunk in a public place. Public fucking nuisance. Obscene fucking language.'

Ray offers a wry grin. 'Nope.' Anger subsiding, a sandy cliff collapsing into the sea. He looks out the window at desert country. It's as if his earlier rage belonged to someone else.

Jimmy swigs whisky, snorts blood. Silence grows, deadens the space. The train rattles on, talking to itself. As a kid, Ray hunted for words to fit the pattern of train sounds. Going-away, going-away, going-away, daddy-game, daddy-game.

One time, he was maybe five, with his mother on a train, she said they were playing a game, away from daddy, making daddy find them. Daddy needs a lesson. How to behave, treat mummy. Not to worry, not to worry. Squeezing his hand, her eyes scary. How far did they get that time? At a station down the line his father was there puffing like he'd run the whole way. Ray rushed to him, happy to end the game, his mother following slowly. Then in the car going home, his mother stiff, hard. His dad giving her quick looks, Ray in the back seat humming, not understanding. No talking. Windows down, air whooshing in. Home for supper.

After his dad's death, Ray learned how to cook. His mum swung between attacking his late father for endless failures and lamenting his absence, then cursing him for both. And always drinking. Life never returned to any equilibrium, then his mum's death ended their old life altogether.

Neither his mum's family nor his dad's came to either funeral. Ray once asked his dad why he had no grandparents like other kids and his dad said it was revenge for his own and his mother's loud, bold resolve to dump their pasts and start entirely new lives. Owe nothing, no baggage, clean and free, was the idea. Not the hollow grind it became. Ray understood none of that, then.

The morning after his mum died, the local cop, shuffling his boots, came to the empty house and told Ray no family member was stepping up to take on a wordless twelve-year-old. So, Ray had to come down the station soon as, and get onto getting adopted. Instead, Ray rode his bike five miles out of town to his schoolmate Mark's, where Bill and Virginia McDonald, stolid canefarmers, let him stay. And that was that. Maybe Virginia signed something, he never knew.

Jimmy looks at what's left of his Scotch and holds it out. They slide along their benches for the handover. Ray has a swig, pulls a face, hands it back.

Jimmy swigs more, nurses the bottle against his thigh. 'You one of Kennedy's new dickheads?'

'Who's Kennedy?'

Jimmy considers him. 'Chief dickhead detective. Been at the Royalton copshop for fucking years. Fucking owns it. How come you don't know him?'

'I haven't been there yet.'

'New boy? Poor bastard.'

'Why's he a dickhead?'

Jimmy fidgets but it hurts. 'Chucks us in the clink, fines us. Locks us up for shit he does himself. Fucking cops, eh, all do what you like. Who'd you fuck over to get sent out here?'

Ray returns to the landscape. 'The wrong people.' Feels his mouth twist. A corrupt cop, even out here? So much for a fresh start.

Burt reappears, seriously pale. Jimmy offers the bottle but Burt shakes his head, and hangs onto the doorway, head down. Ray inwardly shakes his head at them. Aggressive as they are, they always end up whipped. Flogged by life. Jimmy is maybe smart enough to read the signs but likely it'll only make him more bitter.

Ray indicates Jimmy's bottle. 'You celebrating?' Goading and knows it.

Jimmy stares at him too long. Ray wonders if the glint in his hooded eyes is tears. 'Fuck you, cunt.'

Burt says, 'Bank's taking his place tomorrow. Thirty thousand acres some ten mile south of here.'

Jimmy aims angry eyes at Burt, who clamps his mouth shut. Points at Ray. 'You coppers come and help, eh? What you fuckers do best. Back the bank.'

The rattling changes as the train slows, jerks and jolts. Burt holds on and Jimmy gets up, swaying.

'See you later,' Ray says.

'Not if I fucking see you first.' He elbows Burt aside and vanishes.

Burt gives a cheery wink and follows.

As the train grinds away from the bare concrete slab that passes for a station, Ray sees them at a battered red ute, heavy with bull-bars, bristling with aerials, tossing bags into its back.

The remains of a large cow or bull are on a rise near the tracks, desiccated, torn hide trailing loose from its jutting skeleton. Too dry even for crows. An endless dried-up land.

Checks his knuckles. No skin broken.

2

Ray emerges from the standard brown and cream-coloured train station onto a dusty footpath. He faces a broad main street softened by a late-afternoon golden glow. In a place this size the copshop won't be hard to find. Nothing is. He walks easily, an open air, but his movements are sharp and measured. He's cruiserweight, that awkward zone, neither light nor heavy. Amateur boxing has left minor facial legacies, a protruding, bony ridge under his eyebrows has webs of tiny scars. Now knocking thirty, crow's feet are starting in the corners of watchful, deep-set eyes that shift from brown to green in the light. His hair is honey-blond surfer. His nose curves left from inept salvage work after a teenage street scrabble and cheap mouthguards have left small scars around his lips. Ears fine, no cauliflowers. He never took that much of a beating. He said no to turning pro; that's a scar that doesn't show.

On the far side of the main street, the Athos Café is a restaurant plus fish and chip shop plus pizza takeaway. A newsagency doubles as post office. The grocer is also a fruit and vegetable market, the chemist a gift shop and hair-dressing salon. A service station sits on a huge apron surrounded by growling semi-trailers and serves meals twenty-four hours. And there's the copshop, a dusty concrete bunker with an unsealed carpark and three tired gum trees out front.

On the train side of the road is a butcher, and the two-storey Prince of Wales hotel, with long verandahs and cast-iron railings, a motel tacked onto its side. A narrow, second-hand book shop and a bakery proud of its pies. The street runs east–west, putting all the shops side-on to the late sun. They look secretive under awnings of odd heights, casting dense, slanting shade, paint peeling, leaning on each other like worn-out soldiers from old wars.

Utes and semis roar by. The main street is also a highway. He read somewhere main streets were made wide enough to turn ox-trains. The pub is next to him, the copshop looks a long way across that road. He's not expected to start till tomorrow. Tough choice.

Ray enters the copshop. The reception area is small with a simple desk and empty chair, no posters or signage. No people, no bell. Ray drops his bags. A single, closed door labelled STAFF ONLY NO ENTRY leads further inside.

It swings open and a woman appears.

'G'day. Thought I heard someone.'

Ray guesses mid-thirties. Stocky, a battleship. She enters and hovers, clicking a biro. She is in a basic dark skirt and blouse; no uniform, support staff.

'Detective Senior Constable Windsor, reporting for duty.' He smiles to soften it.

She points her pen, pleased. 'Ray? Ray Windsor? You're early.'

A man in short-sleeved shirt, jeans and grubby boots appears behind her and saunters, definitely saunters, to stand behind the desk. The woman manages to maintain her welcoming expression but slips back to stand against the rear wall. He clicks his fingers at her, and she disappears back behind the staff door.

He offers a smirk, not his hand, not his name. 'Good timing. Copped your first case already, mate. Welcome to the desert.'

His manner says it, cock of the fucking walk. Must be Detective Kennedy. Late forties, receding hairline, red-faced, beefy arms and brawny shoulders tipping from hard-muscled to slack. Thick lips curled.

Ray feels the push and shove of being sized up, wonders if he ought to turn around so Kennedy can smell his arse. Or the fight on the train has pushed up his own aggro. Ray produces a smile, which at least seems to confuse Kennedy, the smirk slipping a little.

'Grapevine says you're a bit of a boxer,' Kennedy says, and snorts.

Ray lets nothing show. News travels. Question is, how much news?

The woman returns with a manila folder and hovers. Kennedy clicks fingers, again, again not looking at her. She hands him a sheet of paper from the folder.

'We're more pub brawlers.' Gestures to own the whole region. 'Age-old question, who's gonna win, boxer or brawler? What do you reckon?'

Ray shrugs a lazy shoulder, face closed. Lots of fights are lost before the first punch is thrown. Knows Kennedy smells resistance, a gift they share.

Kennedy holds the page out as if for Ray, then taps its edge on the desk and drops it there. 'Been this far out before?' He leans his knuckles on the desk, stretches like a man with nothing to do. 'Nah. You got that glazed, dead-eye look.'

He puts out his hand to the woman, again not acknowledging her. She hands him what looks to Ray like a school
exercise book. Kennedy flips it onto the desk too. 'This's
our trip book. Bit different to your townie copshop. You go
anywhere, bung it in here first. You get lost, which's fucking
likely, we'll know where to look. Even if we'd rather not. On
your Pat Malone out here. Only copshop for hundreds of
miles.' Kennedy stares at Ray. 'You with me? Course you are.'
His black eyes are hard.

Ray holds the stare. He came in braced for the usual aggro
banter of any copshop but this is beyond that.

Kennedy sniffs, waves a hand in dismissal. 'People die out
here. Petrol, water, radio, fucking trip book.' Taps his forehead
as if to a simpleton. 'Alright, that's your orientation done. Sweet.'

Another man comes through the doorway and hands
Kennedy a sheet of paper. He's shorter, heavily tanned, lean
in loose jeans and faded, short-sleeved checked shirt revealing
stringy arms. He fixes a calculating stare on Ray, hollowed face
inert. Ray estimates late-thirties, mouth set to aggrieved. Eyes
icy blue, almost transparent, looking up from below as if he's
ready to bolt anywhere he can get to. Shades of Jimmy and
Burt: a bullish resentment of wrongs prolonged but unspecified.

Kennedy hands the page to Ray. 'Here. Your first cold one.
Body's still there. Case notes by Happy here'—jerks his head
at the second man—'so careful what you say. Investigation
so far's pretty much fucked.' Ray takes the paper as Kennedy
turns away, saying, 'Off you go, son. Detective Laming'll run
you out there.'

Kennedy walks away, eyes narrowing at Laming. Ray reads
venom in it. Or how Kennedy treats everyone. Laming stays
impassive.

Ray looks at the sheet of paper. It has the barest details of the discovery of the body. Looks like beaten then strangled. Doctor's report to follow.

Ray tells himself it's a gift horse, real detective work. He looks up to see the woman sit at the desk, hunching over, her dark, lank, shoulder-length hair framing her face, which, like her arms, is marked by red splotches, maybe anxiety.

Ray steps up, hand outstretched. 'Pleased to meet you.'

She startles and takes his hand. 'Kaye. Yeah, pleased to meet you.' Ray has to lean forwards to hear her.

Laming walks past them, twirling car keys. 'Move or walk.'

Ray doesn't know what to do with his bag and suitcase. No help from Kaye so he takes them with him and follows Laming. So much for the trip book.

Laming drives the police Land Rover at bone-jarring speed. They're soon past the clutch of homes that make up the town, onto a corrugated dirt road through rocky country. The sun is close to the horizon, rays hitting the earth and flashing up in dazzling display, dull oranges to fiery reds punctuated by trees that are almost khaki-coloured. Reminds him of the army. He licks parched lips. The open windows and so-called cooling fan blow burning air. Sweating into his shirt, feeling it drying.

Laming skids to a halt at a dry, shallow gully framed by spiky acacias beside an ambulance and another police Land Rover. A tall, solidly built, dark-complexioned constable stands next to two male ambos carrying a stretcher. As Ray and Laming approach, he signals the ambos to wait. They stroll to the back of the ambulance, a converted panel van, to smoke. Ray, holding the single page, nods to the constable who offers a scant chin-up. He's late middle-aged, dark eyes deep in sockets under bushy, greying eyebrows, watchful, lived long enough to not be rushed. Ray notes nothing warm passes between the constable and Laming.

The constable holds up a small camera. 'Got the shots we need.'

Ray says, 'When will I get them?'

'Newsagent's shut now. He'll take a day or so.'

Ray braces, breathes, turns to the slender body on the bare earth. 'Jesus, she's a kid.' He pulls back the sheet covering her body. She is naked, early teens, body and face distorted and swollen from the heat—and a beating. Heavy bruising discolours her pale skin, especially around her neck, tiny breasts and almost hairless mound. Dead almond-eyes stare back from a round, bashed face with broad cheekbones, a Chinese face? Ray swallows dismay, pulls the sheet back up to cover her again. 'Who'd do this to a kid?'

Laming leans in, not actually looking, hands in his pockets, says, 'Upset someone. What's she doing out here on her own? Didn't walk here.' He nods at a small bra, torn skirt and tie-dyed T-shirt heaped at her feet. 'Well, well. Looky here.' Ray sees it's a performance. 'No knickers. Like I said.' This aimed at the constable, who shows no response.

Ray says, 'What've you said?'

Laming gives him a surprised look as if he'd forgotten he was there, then at the constable, then juts out his jaw, looking at the sky. 'There was another one, couple of months ago.'

The constable looks at Ray. 'Same age, sexual assault. But suicided. Named Diah. *Di-ah*. Not hard to say.'

Laming drops his chin to his chest, sullen. 'She was raped at Petersens Dam and left there. Then walked into the dam and drowned herself. Fourteen.'

Ray exhales, says, 'Another kid.'

Laming is breathless. 'These foreign chicks're not bloody kids. No way.' Cringing like a dog, expecting a kick but snarling too. 'Get around no knickers on. You see any knickers?'

The constable's voice is patient, dogged. A sense of having said all this already. 'Diah was raped. We had to drag her from the dam. A mess.'

'No knickers, they're asking for it. Parents're supposed to look after them, bring them up right.'

Ray sees the constable stare at Laming, sees his effort to remain calm. Ray turns to Laming. 'You looked at her? Not a kid, you reckon?' He dangles the sheet of paper, the case notes, at Laming. 'How do you know what she wasn't wearing? Who'd you talk to? Is it here?' Waves the sheet of paper again.

Laming doesn't look, sniffs. 'What do you know? Been here two fucking minutes. Foreign chicks're like the boongs, mature faster than white chicks, everyone knows that. Sexual fact, heat or something.' He takes a breath, hikes his belt. 'Your case, new boy.' Laming stalks back to his Rover, tosses Ray's bag and suitcase onto the dirt and fishtails away in a swirl of dust.

Ray watches him go, feels the constable's gaze on him. Lifts a shoulder, quizzical. 'Am I getting special treatment or is he always like that? Him and Kennedy?'

The constable gives a soft grunt, assessing him.

Ray stares at the case notes, folds the page, folds it again. 'Name's Alice? We know her at all?'

The constable pauses, maybe noticing that *we*. 'No police record, if that's what you mean.'

Ray reaches down to touch her clothes, the rips in the skirt. 'Why's he on about knickers?'

The constable comes closer, still wary. 'Diah and Alice were both physically and sexually assaulted.' He half turns away. 'Diah drowned fifteen mile that way. Both girls found with no knickers. Like it must be their fault. Some blokes get excited just saying a girl's not wearing any. If she's foreign, even more so.'

'Foreign? Wasn't she local?'

'Some here'll tell you one cancels out the other.'

Ray swallows against his throat clamping. Still feels the constable measuring him up, the distance between them in more ways than one. 'So, what do you reckon?'

'Some blokes keep trophies.'

'Find the knickers, find the killers?'

'You're the detective. Bugger all else to go with.'

Ray looks again at the half-page of typed notes. Bugger all, alright.

'She ready to be moved?'

Ray nods, signals the ambos. When they come over he introduces himself, shakes hands, relaxed smiles and promises of beer all around. Ray steps away to let them get on with it.

He turns to the constable. 'Both girls—foreign?' The word, saying it, sounding foreign.

'Alice, Chinese. Diah, Indonesian.'

'Alice's family know yet?'

'It was Detective Laming's case.'

Ray waits for more. 'You saying he won't have?'

The constable lifts his eyebrows to say that's what he means.

Ray says, 'Doctor's report?'

'Take a while. Doctor might come from Tyborg or the body goes to him.'

'So we can get started. I'm no doctor but my read is badly beaten about face and body, looks mostly inflicted with fists, maybe boots too. Extra emphasis on genital area. Cause of death, strangulation. You?'

'Yes.'

They watch the covered body on the stretcher being put in the ambulance. One ambo nods to Ray and the constable, who both nod back.

'How come Royalton's got an ambulance?' Ray says.

'Tiny hospital too. Same bloke who gave us the vehicles. Big landowner. Loves his town.'

Ray nods at the departing ambulance. 'Handy. We need someone to ID her.'

The constable says, 'I know her. Knew her.'

'Her parents too?' Ray watches him take time to answer.

He nods. 'I can tell them, soon as we're back.'

'My case. You don't want me to do it?'

'They mightn't want to meet you,' the constable says, bluntly, watching Ray in the silence that follows. 'Nothing personal. The last time, they—'

'Did Kennedy or Laming meet the previous parents? Diah's?'

'Laming made out he did. I did it.'

Ray looks at the darkening plain, sun delicately balanced on the horizon as though on a wire, ready to roll along it. Birds are silhouettes, high and far.

'I'll ask them if they'll see you. And when. Let you know.' The constable looks to the sunset too. 'Helps you're a new face.'

'Christ, isn't this hard enough already?'

'Bit harder for them, I reckon.'

Ray shuts up, meets the man's steady gaze. His eyes travel around the constable's face, which the constable catches.

'No, not a blackfella. Not quite.' His mouth twists, more in weariness. Sick of it.

'I wasn't thinking blackfella.'

'Bit foreign but, eh? Hard to place?' Tired tone. 'Armenian. You heard of Armenia?'

Ray nods. 'Mass killings. Genocide. Near Turkey.'

The constable lifts bushy eyebrows. Ray opens his mouth to speak but the constable steps up and offers a large hand. 'Arshag. How come you know Armenia is near anything?'

'Ray.' They shake. 'Bloke I boxed in high school was Egyptian Armenian. Told me a bit.'

Arshag absorbs this, looks at his deeply sun-tanned arm. 'Could be a touch of the pyramids here too. Plus a lifetime of local sun.' Then, done with it, looks at Ray. 'You been a bad boy, ending up out here?'

Ray smiles more broadly. 'Just my big mouth.' He looks around. Three sixty degrees of twisted trees and a huge sky, orange and brilliant red in the west. Ray recalls a yarn about Japanese tourists on an outback bus tour. Driver stops for a photo op, middle of nowhere, suggests the tourists stretch their legs. They get out, take a couple of steps, and scuttle back onto the bus. Too scary, all that space.

'Get up on higher ground, you can see the earth curve,' Arshag says.

Ray grins. 'Really? Higher ground, out here?' Thumbs west. 'That orange is intense.'

'Dust storm. Puts grit in everything from your jocks to your corn flakes. They usually wear out before they get here.'

Ray says, 'My first time this far west. The Outback.'

'Nah, this isn't the Outback. Outback's a whole other thing. This's the edge.'

Ray stares at the ground of the gully. What's left to show of what was lying there? Ants have already taken care of any blood. 'Anything special about this spot?'

'Does the job. Shows hate for anyone dumped here.' Arshag kicks the ground. 'Kennedy put you on this right away?'

'Soon as I walked in. Thought I'd be in the pub by now.' Watching Arshag watching him. 'You and me work on this?'

Arshag takes his time. 'Sure.' But holding back. Then says, 'Get ready for the Diah case to get dumped on you too.' Meaning, no one else wants it. 'I'll see about the parents.'

Ray nods.

Ray tosses his gear into the vehicle. Arshag drives them back to town. Ray looks around the Rover. 'Having one of these's pretty handy for a bush copshop. Let alone two.'

'Gifts. Same bloke, local station owner,' Arshag says.

'Must be flush?'

Arshag shrugs, nods.

Ray says, 'And the copshop's a bit flush too for this far out. What do you call a crowd of detectives?'

Arshag laughs. 'A suspicion? The Inspector's got a bit of clout. Word is, the place was pumped up for him.' He falls quiet. Ray stares at the passing, relentless country, seeing it soften a little in the dusk.

They come into town with the dark, the main street buildings looking sullen.

'Where're you living?' Arshag says.

'Same place as the last bloke, I hear. What happened to him?'

'Quit. Out of the blue. Something did him in.' Arshag looks away, not elaborating.

'Desert wore him out and he escaped back to the surf?'

21

Arshag laughs, points west. 'He went that way.'

'Shit. Did he go bonkers?'

'Townies. You all think that way when you arrive. All reckon you're temporary. Then somehow you never leave. The place works on you. Better watch out for that.'

———

Before the night absorbs all colour, Arshag leaves him at a large, high-set, wooden house on tall stumps, surrounded by zealously mown brown grass and a few determined pot plants, three blocks from the main drag. Ray drops his suitcase and bag at the bottom of the stairs up to the front door. Under the house is enclosed by fibro and Besser blocks. As he starts up the steps, a naked electric bulb lights at the top, the door opens and a woman appears, late thirties, barefoot, wearing shorts and halter top. She has a long face with a strong chin under a full, generous mouth, long brown hair in happy disarray.

She grins, breathless. 'Thought I heard you. The new copper? Been expecting you. Ray, isn't it?'

Ray reaches up and shakes her hand. 'Sorry, didn't know you were waiting.'

'No worries. Waiting's what we do around here. Waiting for rain, for pay day. Waiting for life.' She gives a full-bodied laugh and holds up a key on a ring with a length of braided multi-coloured plastic. 'You're down there.' Points below the stairs to a door.

'Handy,' he says. 'I can walk to work.'

'Whoa, what? No one here walks. Bit extreme, that.' She laughs. 'Need me to show you round? Not that there's much to see.' She laughs again, a tinkling sound this time. 'Whoops,

I shouldn't say that!' She gives him the key. Her arm is lean and tanned and she's wearing turquoise bracelets.

'Nah. I'll sort it.'

'Beauty. Travel light, I see.'

When she laughs again, Ray can't help grinning.

'G's a hoy if you need anything. I stocked the fridge so you don't have to shop right away.'

'You're Dorothy, is that right?'

'Oh, sorry, yeah, Dot.' She reaches out and they shake again, laughing together.

A male voice inside says, 'Dot, what're you doing out there? Tea's getting cold.'

She winks at Ray and grins. 'First time I heard it called that. Sink a beer soon, eh? Tomorrow night? Good.' She is gone, giggling, door closed before Ray has recovered.

His flat fills most of the space under the house except for a walled-off garage. Grey bricks all around with one bevelled-glass window in each wall. Bathroom and bedroom partitioned off in thin plywood. Spacious, furnished, basic, painted mostly a washed-out blue; paint must've been on sale. An air-con thing he doesn't know how to use. In the busily humming fridge are steaks, potatoes, onions, butter, milk and a six-pack. He takes two beers and flops into a chair at the laminated kitchen table. Drains the first stubby, opens the next. Leans back, eyes closed.

Farther away from home now than he's ever been, he's ambushed by thoughts of family. His first home with his real parents until they died. His second home, the cane farm of his adoptive parents, Bill and Virginia McDonald.

Conjures up images of Bill and Virginia still there. Bill always working, never speaking if silence will do. Virginia, full of talk, always her own person. Ray grins. She was what the locals called a handful. Not one to knuckle under, an expression she savours.

Mark, their only son, turned out to be no farmer. As far as Ray knows, he's teaching in Brisbane. Ray and Mark started out inseparable but Mark became more Beatles and Beach Boys; Ray, The Who, the Stones, Dylan. After finishing school, Ray became an apprentice electrician while Mark escaped the place altogether.

Ray counts five or six years since he saw Virginia and Bill. She always threatened she'd leave Bill as soon as the boys left. Maybe she did, although it was always a poor bet to guess Virginia's next move. Ray often thought it a shame his mum and Virginia never met; would've been an explosive combo.

He drains his second beer, thoughts on his mother now, maybe finding where she came from out here. He was six or seven when she told him most stories of her life growing up on a cattle property. With no photos or anything else, Ray daydreamed any images he wanted.

A wealthy family, a governess instead of school. Her own horse! He believed everything she told him. How she met Ray's father at a dance in a decked-out community hall. They'd whirled around, drinking spiked punch, eating lobster and crab trained in from the coast, both aching for more from life. She told Ray his father was magical then, brought a rush of the thrill life could be. He came west as a reporter for the local rag, next stop a real journalist on a big-city paper. Had she seen New York? Did she want to? Or Paris or London? She'd never before grasped she could just go. All that mattered was wanting it badly enough.

Her parents had distrusted him. All words and wind, her father said, no heft. Then, her eyes shining, she told Ray how the local paper went broke and Ray's dad was returning to the coast, daring her to come with him. They'd be fine. He'd always get another reporting job and his novel was coming along. So they eloped! Outrageous! Her father cut her from his will. She didn't care at first but then there were no more jobs. His dad became a proof-reader, joked how he'd gone from writer to reader, but what he felt as humiliation, the rotting weight of a failed novel, poisoned him, she'd whisper to Ray. After a few years, he turned mostly silent.

Life as a housewife was alien. Wouldn't cook or clean. Ray's dad did it as Ray watched his mum harass his dad, round and round the house. About money, having nothing, being ashamed. Saw his dad trying to stay out of range, tuning her out till she smashed things. It shames Ray still to remember he tuned her out too. Change the station, his dad'd say, all we can do. He recalls her being drunk, when she'd leave him feeling he'd done wrong by being born.

He dredges up her family name. Rogers. She rarely mentioned it. Then one hot afternoon, she was dead. Replaced by some sort of hole in his chest.

He hears a thump above his head. His low ceiling is not soundproofed. The thump becomes a rhythmic beat. He grins, beats a tattoo in time on the table. Toasts his new home. Even got a phone, installed for the copper here before. Ray leans back and closes his eyes. You never know where your big mouth will land you.

3

Next morning in the copshop, Ray meets the two other uniforms. He's been in enough copshops to read quickly how things work. Constable Ernie Baxter has been a copper forever, only in the regions. He's heavy-set, taciturn, close to retirement. Handles routine work for Kennedy and Laming. Constable Louise Wiggins, in her twenties, is overweight, lacklustre. Did typing at school so she types for everyone at the station but not well; a source of tension with Kaye, who has to correct her work and increasingly sees official records as her job. Louise rarely ventures outside officially. Her first posting, and probably, Ray thinks, her only one. Kaye, general admin, part-timer but always there.

He waits on a hard chair outside the Inspector's office. After thirty minutes, Kaye brings him a second folder. Diah's case notes, as slim as Alice's. 'From Detective Kennedy,' she says. And the *Tyborg Times*. 'Have a read, our window on the world. Not a big window. Tyborg's next town west.'

Ray opens the Diah folder. One sheet of paper again. He takes the newspaper. 'There used to be a local rag. The *Royalton Pioneer*?'

'You know about that?'

'My dad was its reporter for about a minute.' Feels her pin him with an intense stare. 'He told me about Royalton versus Tyborg. Two towns at war!' He gestures dramatically.

Kaye is unimpressed. 'War we lost, obviously. Tyborg's twice as big as us these days.' Ray can tell she's calculating something. She smiles, preoccupied, and marches off, something on her mind.

Ray opens the paper but is interrupted as the Inspector almost sidles to his office door, but stops dead, seeing Ray.

Ray guesses late forties, tall and lean with a long, soft face and small, weak mouth permanently expressing distaste. With his short back-and-sides haircut and grey eyes darting about, Ray would've pegged him as an anxious priest. Or failed teacher. Ray stands to introduce himself but the Inspector says, 'See Detective Kennedy. Kennedy fixes whatever needs fixing.' He continues into his office and closes the door.

Ray finds Kennedy and Laming playing darts in the spartan lunchroom. He asks for Arshag as offsider for the two cases.

'Shaggers? Sure, get him out of my hair. Kaye give you the rape of the other chick? Forget them for now, it's duffing season. Big city bloke like you know duffing has a season?'

Laming sniggers as if it's a joke. Maybe it is. He lights up a roll-your-own, the brackish smell off-putting. 'Ask him if he even knows what duffing is.'

Ray lets that pass.

Kennedy throws another dart, with added force. 'Joe Carmichael's place just lost forty head or so. Your mission, get them back. It's a big country out there, but—'

Laming says, 'Big fucking country.'

'—we all know you're up to it.'

'And the dead girls?'

Kennedy faces him, hands on hips, as Laming takes his turn at the dart board. 'Well, sonny Jim, there's not a lot to find there except dead-ends, as Detective Laming's case notes show, if you'd read them. Unless you've got any clever ideas about new leads?'

Laming turns to face Ray too.

Ray holds up the page of case notes on Diah. 'You talk to family and friends? Who saw the girls last? Times, places?'

Laming slumps into a chair at one of the formica tables and folds his arms, trying for bored, finding something more menacing. 'This pup's telling me how to piss on a pole. Interview family? I'll tell you how that goes—short. Out of those who'll talk at all, fuck-all people saw fuck-all.' He winks at Kennedy. 'Besides, report's easier to do when you work out who did it. Fill it in after.'

Kennedy chimes in, pointing a dart at Ray. 'No useful clues, wet body or dry. But go ahead and solve it, Sherlock. Make a big impression. Meanwhile, in the real world, duffers. Fucking cattle are probably at least still alive. Shaggers knows the drill.'

Ray stands there.

Kennedy throws a dart, it goes wide. He turns to Ray. 'You still here?' Delivered with a hard, empty grin.

Ray stalks out onto the packed red-earth apron in front of the copshop as Arshag parks a patrol Land Rover and approaches, carrying hubcaps. Semi-trailers hurtle past behind him, whipping up dust, litter and thunder.

Ray gestures at the hubcaps. 'You a collector?'

'Pick them up along the highway. Send them to Vinnies. They make a few quid.'

Ray shuffles his boots as if to scrape off dog shit.

Arshag says, 'What?'

'We're off the girls' cases, chasing cattle.' Ray waits to share the outrage but Arshag says nothing. Ray says, 'Two rapes, a suicide, a murder, and we're chasing cattle? No one's on fire about this?'

Arshag drops the hubcaps with a clang at the copshop steps, and points at the Land Rover. 'I was coming to get you.'

Arshag drives them around Royalton's town blocks, his expression keeping Ray silent. The houses are mostly timber-framed, low, modest. Ubiquitous air-con boxes sit squarely on top of tin roofs. Dogs, sheds, utes, a couple of brilliant-blue above-ground pools. Cyclone-wire fences separate identical bare, sunburnt lawns.

Arshag says, 'He won't help investigate the girls.'

Ray looks at him and waits. 'He?'

'Kennedy.' Looks at Ray. *Who else?*

'What about the Inspector?'

'Inspector doesn't count.'

'Doesn't he run the place?'

'Pretty much absent even when present.'

Ray exhales. 'They're girls. Just kids.' Watches another street roll by. 'Place ought to be up in arms.'

'Won't be. Look, how do I . . . They're the wrong colour.' His mouth twists.

Ray shuts up to absorb this.

Arshag adds, 'A bit like corn-fed instead of grass-fed.'

'Corn what? Grass what?'

'Corn-fed versus grass-fed?'

Ray shakes his head.

Arshag says, 'Grass-fed is country gentry, the big property owners. Fly themselves to the coast to shop. Corn-feds are your mob.'

'My mob.' Ray manages a tight grin, knows where it's going.

'Townies—generally white but you'll never own your own plane. Then us coloured types, below you. Guess who gets the attention?'

Ray sees a taut challenge in Arshag's mouth and eyes as he holds up a hand to indicate levels.

'Grass-feds up top. Next's corn-feds. Then my lot, reffos, a step below your lot. Then down again, so low they're hardly human, the boongs. Not my word.'

'Haven't seen a lot of them.'

'Funny that, eh?'

'Reffos!' Ray says. 'Haven't heard that since I was a kid. Okay, you're Armenian, the victims're Chinese and Indonesian, very multicultural. So? Most small towns I've seen are the same, including where I grew up.' But somehow it stays one of those know-but-don't-know secrets. Afghans out west. Maltese, Eyeties up north. Russians. Lebanese, Dutch and Germans and Greeks. Couldn't lock them up fast enough during the war. 'Rape's still rape. Murder's still murder.'

Arshag turns into a street that at first looks to Ray the same as the last. Same houses, aircon boxes, brown lawns.

'Where are we?'

'Massacre Row.' Arshag points. 'Every house a different wog, a different foreigner. A different massacre drove each of them here. All in one street.'

Ray looks more closely. Now sees difference. More trees,

more struggling gardens, and what might be greenhouses, covered in dark canvas and shade-cloth. 'Why pick here? Edge of the bloody world?'

'Maybe big sky, space, infinity is what they had to have.'

'Is one of these yours?'

'I live in the bush. I get enough people at work.' He pulls over and stops.

Ray shifts in his seat, looks straight ahead, says, 'So. Dead white girls, big deal, big case. Otherwise . . .'

'Diah and Alice?' Arshag says their names gently, lifts his eyebrows. 'Said it yourself. Don't their parents care? Well. They care.'

Ray hesitates. 'Enough to meet me?'

'Men only.'

Ray absorbs that. 'Mothers might know more about their girls than fathers.'

'Not my rules.'

Ray exhales heavily, waves a hand to push frustration aside.

Arshag nods ahead to the last house.

Ray says, 'Right now? Shit, lucky I didn't say bugger off.'

'Might've been tricky.'

———

Arshag ushers him into a sun-heated, enlarged porch shut in by lace-curtained louvres, a clumsy add-on to the front of a modest, low-blocked timber house. Three men sit in cane chairs in a small arc. Homemade biscuits, cups, saucers and a highly ornamented, heavy porcelain teapot sit on a tray on doilies on a round, glass-topped cane table. No more chairs; Arshag and Ray stand.

The first man is slight, balding, with watery eyes and a gentle handshake. He half-turns his face away. Ray guesses he's in his fifties, with the ropey muscles of the lifelong manual worker.

Arshag holds a formal pose as he says, 'This's Intan, father of Diah. Intan's a navvy. Works on roads, all over. Like his old man and mine used to, eh, Intan?' Hard to know how much of Intan's nut-brown is natural and how much is from the sun. 'Third generation on the roads.' Arshag and Intan exchange friendly nods.

During a gentle shake with a hard, bony, hand, Ray nods to Intan. 'Sorry about your daughter.'

Intan nods sharply.

Arshag turns to the second man. 'Cha Fou Lin. He's fine to be called Harry. Harry was Alice's father.'

Harry nods slowly, makes no move to shake. Ray nods again, says sorry again. Harry's face doesn't change.

'Harry's a driller, for water. Maybe oil and gas soon? Knows the land, real bushman. Couldn't get lost if he tried. Knows about water divining too.' Harry is maybe forty, stocky, with hard eyes and a fleshy mouth that signals a steely politeness atop seething anger. He bows slightly to Arshag and dabs his eyes with a white handkerchief.

Arshag gestures to the third man who is elderly with a leathery, pockmarked complexion and an old, pronounced scar on his right cheek. He lifts a hand to Arshag, nods brusquely to Ray. 'I am Nick. I own the café.' Ray recalls the Athos Café, fish and chips and pizza.

Nick's shake is soft, gentle. 'You have inherited the deaths of our girls.' A measured nod to Intan and Harry, who don't move.

Ray hears sour sarcasm but also genuine feeling. Worries his own unease shows.

Nick says, 'Well now.' Purses his lips, a decision made. 'Welcome to our N-Q-W club.'

Everyone looks to him, startled, at each other, then at a baffled Ray, all in a moment.

Nick bobs his head, defiant. 'Let's not waste time. Any more time.'

Ray feels their jolt of nerves as Arshag stares at Nick in surprise. *What just happened?*

Intan's thin lips tremble and twist, perhaps in resentment, certainly anger. Harry's eyes gush with tears of such quick force he takes a moment to detect his wet cheeks, then dabs them away. He nods grimly to Nick.

Ray feels their shock as a buffeting. Looks to Nick who is stiff with haughty hostility. Ray says, 'N-Q-W?' This's a fucking minefield. He'll tear strips off Arshag later for dropping him in it.

Nick says, 'Arshag tells us you may have a sense of humour?'

Ray glances at Arshag, who is firmly impassive.

Nick says, 'N-Q-W. New Queensland Wildlife.' With a low, bitter laugh.

'Sorry, wildlife? You look for new wildlife?'

'We *are* the new wildlife.'

Intan says, 'N-Q-W, Not Quite Welcome.' His half smile is fed by nervous defiance, surprising himself.

Harry raises a finger. 'Not Quite Wanted.'

Nick flicks off imaginary dirt. 'Not Quite Washed.'

Ray says nothing. The gatecrasher.

Arshag takes pity on him. 'Not Quite White. Our local joke.' Gathers himself to continue. 'They believe the fate of their daughters'—bows slightly to the fathers—'doesn't matter to the police.'

Ray feels the force of that said out loud. Even dark humour vanishes as desolate, controlled breaths crowd the overheated space.

Before he can stop himself, Ray says, 'Now Quite Wary,' then freezes at his big mouth.

Nick claps with a kind of respect, maybe relief, and inclines his head towards Arshag. 'Oh, very good.'

Harry sobs gently, face covered.

Intan puts a hand on his shoulder but stares at Ray as he says, 'We need someone brave enough to look at his own backyard. His own people. Strong enough.'

'I know how to do my job,' Ray says. 'Do it properly. But with your help. Talk to me. The girl's mothers too.' He looks to Arshag, who has folded his arms.

Nick stands, rocking gently till he finds his balance. Harry hands him an elaborately carved, dark-wood walking stick which Nick wields more as accessory than necessity. 'We welcome good intentions. We wish to cooperate.'

—

Ray and Arshag exit, the door closing behind them. Air in the yard is cool after the overheated porch.

Ray turns on Arshag. 'What the fuck?'

Arshag shrugs. 'They said they just wanted to meet you. See for themselves.'

'Did I pass?'

'Well. First time anyone's said N-Q-W to outsiders. All my years here they've expected nothing. But with Alice as well as Diah . . . I've never seen them like that with anyone'—he searches for the word—'from outside.' Pointing at the sky.

Ray rubs his eyes, crosses the brown grass footpath on the empty street. Locked houses, parched yards, desperate gardens. Nods at the garage-sized wooden frames draped with heavy cloth to block at least some of the heat, some foliage visible inside. 'What do they grow?'

'Tomatoes, chilli, capsicum, ginger, beans. On the goldfields, the Chinese always knew how to grow vegies. Used human shit. Resourceful buggers.'

'Enough anger here to burn this town to the ground.' Was N-Q-W in his hometown Caneville too? Had to be. Is it still?

'Guess they hope it's bad enough now for a real copper to do something.'

'A real copper. As opposed to . . .?'

Arshag lifts his eyebrows, playing at non-committal.

'Shit, Arshag.'

'Pretty much.' The silence sits there.

'You've got their hopes up. What'd you say about me?'

Arshag grins. His face softens as his eyes fold up a little, show a glint of fun. 'Stuff I heard Kennedy telling Laming, out on the copshop back verandah. I'm inside, window open, they didn't notice. Or care.'

'About me?'

'Kennedy made a call to find out about you. Didn't like what he heard. Hears you're a stirrer, says don't send you. Doesn't want you.'

'You told them here about it?' Nods at the house.

'Yep.' Arshag grins even more widely.

Ray swallows. 'You know your town, this whole place. Your bloody turf. You've got no idea who for the rapes or the murder? No names at all?'

'People out here drive a hundred mile to go to a dance or for a beer. Mightn't be a local.' He pauses, gives Ray a searching look, looks away to speak. 'Might have a name. But saying it, aloud, you know . . .'

Ray gets the message, puts a forefinger across his lips. 'For sure.'

They hear the Land Rover radio, return to it but ignore its static as Arshag drives them away. He takes them across the concrete bridge at the western end of town, swings off the highway, down a two-rut track into an empty traveller rest area with huge ironbarks. Pulls up on a grassy outcrop above a brown river maybe thirty feet wide. The level is low, the flow sluggish between thick reeds. A family of ducks paddles in the paltry shade of tall gums. Erosion of the clay banks has exposed the large, tangled roots of the big trees. Looks unstable.

Ray waits.

Arshag says, 'You heard of The Train? From up north, sugar-cane country?'

'Some kind of nasty initiation.' Sugar-cane country, like his own.

'Local young blokes had a club. At a dance they'd pick a virgin, one bloke'd coax her outside, then the pack inside'd make the sign.' Pumps his arm up like pulling the cord of a train whistle. 'Then these red-blooded country lads'd whisk her away, hold her down in the dark and rape her.'

Ray has heard about it but not till long after he left home. He'd wondered then, and now, if it went on in his own town and he was too dumb to notice.

'Whole town up there knew,' Arshag says. 'Knew but didn't know. Not a soul spoke up. Not the girls. Parents. The boys. Priest. Or the local cop. Nothing said, not even after a reporter wrote it up. Southern reporter, not a local. It was going on a few years.' Arshag looks at Ray. 'How's that happen?' Truly wants to know.

Ray rolls down his window, smells sour mud, dank water. Piss-poor river. Move any slower, it'll die. 'Knowing but not knowing? Some would've shut up in case their own boy was in on it.'

'Let someone's daughter get sacrificed? What about the parents of the girls? What about them?'

Ray lifts hands in defeat. 'Not always in the girl's interests to speak up. As you'd know. Some would've shut up cos they'd get shunned. Small towns know how to do that.' Edge in his voice. Defensive, out of his depth. He stares at those tangled roots. 'You saying there's a rape club here?'

'Grab one, get away with it. Grab another one, get away with it. Get a taste.'

'But kill as well? Jesus. Well, you know the local boys.'

'I don't move in their clubs.'

Ray purses his lips. 'Kennedy ought to know.'

Arshag says nothing, starts the car.

Ray nods at the tree roots. 'Those trees'll come crashing down one day. Land on top of us.'

The radio crackles into life. Arshag looks knowing, folds his arms.

Ray answers it, hackles already up. 'Windsor.'

Kennedy. 'Where the fuck're you? Is Shaggers with you? What the fuck're you pair of poofs doing?'

'Constable Arshag's introducing me to locals. Building community relations.'

Arshag manages a wry grin.

'That right? I can guess. You forget the duffers? I give you a bloody job, you do it. Get back here, get a map and get your arse out there on real police work. And in case you don't fucking understand, that's a fucking order.' The radio pops and fizzes loudly into silence.

Arshag weaves among the ironbarks as he drives them back to the highway.

Ray shakes his head. 'Diah first. Names? Hints?'

'You met Barb at the pub? Ask her about Peter, Paul and Mario.'

'You're kidding. If only I had a hammer. I'll bring them a hammer?'

Arshag shakes his head. 'They've heard all the jokes. I'll come if you want, but me being there might get in the way of what they want to say.'

'Cos you're not quite white.'

Arshag offers a cold wink of approval.

Ray nods to himself. Learning.

4

Arshag stops the Land Rover at a crossroads. No road signs, no human habitation. Ray checks the map, tilts his head at the narrower road.

Ray says, 'So Kennedy's plan is, grab whoever knocked off Carmichael's forty head, right? Rolling up here in broad daylight?'

'Yep.'

'Down that excuse for a road? In a semi?' The narrower road is badly potholed with broken bitumen.

Arshag says, 'Coopers Road's in better nick.'

'We wait over on Coopers, and miss them, he'll eat us alive.'

Arshag grins. 'You're the boss, boss.'

Ray rolls his eyes, checks the map again. 'I'd break my arse driving a semi down that shit-house road. Coopers it is.' Ray points, and Arshag drives off.

Ray says, 'Pretty blatant, moving stolen stock during the day.'

Arshag lifts a lazy eyebrow. 'Maybe tells us something.'

Ray exhales an angry hiss, unhappy.

Coopers Road bisects a baked, fiery orange landscape, both directions. Ray parks at an angle, blocking both lanes.

He opens the bonnet, props it up. He and Arshag slide into an eroded gully alongside, skirt the ant nests and settle in for a hot wait.

Ray looks around. Must be nearly forty degrees. Country you can die in—from heat, thirst or hunger. No useful shade and total silence, not even crickets. Midday heat and dazzling light pins everything down: birds, trees, people. Their vehicle roasts in full sun. Sparse vegetation sags in red dirt under a hard blue sky. Ray watches the tall white gums tremble as their branches shimmer, vanish, re-form. A distant mirage of water glitters and teases.

How does anyone end up here? The heat is alive, hostile. Arshag on his right, slumps forward a little, head bowed, eyes closed. Ray shakes himself, envious. Shuts his eyes too, soaks up the silence.

He hears a low rustle to his left and looks up lazily, expecting an equally lazy lizard.

A brown snake, a yard away, slips gracefully into the gully, looking straight ahead. Ray gulps, a sharp sound startling himself, his right arm nudging Arshag.

Arshag whistles softly. Whispers, 'King Brown. Stay still.'

Ray commands his body to remain inert but shaking starts deep in his guts. The snake turns his way, head up, and stares at him, eyes black, tongue darting in, out, in, out. Jesus Christ, what's it looking at? It looks ahead again and resumes its controlled slide to the dusty floor of the gully, then, unhurried, across to the far side where it calmly searches for a path up through the meagre greenery. Its dull body at its thickest is not quite the size of Ray's wrist, its full length now exposed, about six feet. It pulls itself up smoothly, powerfully, and with a flick of its tail disappears.

Ray dry retches, clenches his fists for control. 'Fucking snakes! I'll dream about it.'

Arshag stretches out his arms. 'Leave them alone, they usually leave you alone. You get occasional bad-tempered ones.'

'Just about the most venomous snake in the world. Seen enough of the bastards.'

Arshag laughs again. 'Close, eh? Beautiful, but.'

Ray shivers, forces himself to breathe deeply. Silence returns. The far end of the road in each direction is lost in a flame-like shimmer against purple hills. Behind the gully giving them cover are twisted mulga trees a nuclear blast couldn't kill, trunks black as if from fire but it's the everyday sun that burns them.

Ray pulls his gaze away from where the snake vanished and checks his watch. Arshag shrugs. Emus and wallabies come to inspect them, then trot or hop to cover under the sparse ghost gums. The white trunks are aglow against deep red earth and burning blue sky. Stark colours made starker.

Ray says, 'When you left Armenia, did you know you were coming to desert country?'

'I was two, I knew nothing. This's as far as my father could make himself go. Got here, off the train, just stopped. Quit. He married Dymphna, daughter of a grass-fed.'

'A reffo and a grass-fed? How'd they get away with that?'

'Nearly got them shot. Dymphna was a terror, upset everyone. Made my father laugh.'

'What'd he do here?'

'He was an engineering student in Armenia until the killings and had a bit of English. Talked his way into work at a silver mine, used to be near here.' Points vaguely south-west.

'That closed, so he got into building roads. Away a lot, all over the place.'

'Still around?'

Arshag shrugs. 'World War Two come along, he signs up in a flash. Hot to kill Turks. Silly bugger, so out of touch he didn't know they'd switched sides, thought they were still the enemy.'

'For him they were, maybe?'

Arshag shrugs one shoulder. 'Went back to Armenia instead. Never came back. Good on him.' Arshag crumbles a handful of dry, red earth. Ray sees something tender in how he handles the dirt.

'What about Dymphna?'

He pauses. 'Died three years ago.'

'And you're still here.'

'Moving on never seems worth it.'

Ray looks along the road, still empty both ways. Hits the heel of his boot on the cracked earth. Iron-hard. Sulphur-crested cockatoos droop on scraggly branches like scraps of white paper snagged by high wind, except there is no wind.

On the cane farm near the coast, at noon cows stood bowed under the grudging shade of tall gums in a sticky, liquid heat. But the heat here, hundreds of miles inland, is a whole other beast, deadly, searing.

Ray tosses stones at crows tearing at roadkill, the bloody remains of a wallaby. They look at him, keep eating. Contempt.

Ray says, 'You in the war?'

'Not till forty-two. My father gone made it hard to leave Dymphna. I did stock work, got paid as an Aborigine. Funny that. Rubbish money but every quid helped. Dymphna's family had cut her off but ended up giving us a bit. So I signed up.

Sent to New Guinea. I thought about never coming back too, but for Dymphna. Coming out of the army made joining the cops easy. Even for a not-quite-black bastard.'

Ray shakes his head. 'Twenty-five years later I did Nasho for two years, then signed on for two more for Vietnam. But I missed out when our troop pull-outs got underway. War cancelled till further notice. Missed my war, eh?' He shrugs it off. 'Anyway, after that, yeah, turning into a copper seemed natural. No bloody imagination, that's me. Whole world out there and I pick this.'

Arshag lifts a hand, nods at a ball of dust from the western end of the road. They check their matching police-issue Model 36, Smith & Wesson revolvers.

Ray crosses the track bent double and drops into a parallel eroded hollow. The crows retreat to watch.

A few minutes more, and the distant growl of an engine grows to shatter the silence. A semi grinds up, gear-box protesting, and stops at the car.

Ray and Arshag emerge each side of the Land Rover, weapons aimed. 'Police!'

The driver roars the engine screamingly loud as if to ram the Land Rover, faces in the cabin invisible behind a reflective windshield. Ray fires a shot over the truck. The engine whines down, and wheezes to a halt, slowly, as if cursed never to start again. The silence presses in again.

Two men climb out, one each side. The driver is in his mid-thirties, the other younger, looking alike. They saunter forwards to lean against the grille, arms folded or hooked in torn jeans. Got to be brothers. Grubby flannel shirts, cracked boots. Both look malnourished but cocky, too needy to care about much at all. Ray feels the hair on the back of his neck move. They want aggro, he can do that. He walks past them, along the side of the load.

Its high, slatted sides hold crowded, lowing, shuffling, stamping, pissing cattle. He returns to the front, pats the truck's huge mudguard. '1968 Ford F8000. What scrap heap'd you find this on?'

The truckies look surprised.

Ray assesses them. Desperation blues. Offers a sour grin. 'Where're they from?'

'Where's what from?' The older one, the talker. The younger tries hostile poses like he's still practising them.

'The cattle.'

'I seen no cattle.'

'Whose are they?'

The older one aims his chin at Arshag. 'Shit, look, a boong with a gun. Hey darkie, give it to a white man who knows how to use it, eh?'

Ray comes in close, sticks the barrel of his handgun into the man's chest and pushes. 'The cattle.'

'What cattle? Ain't got no cattle. You on drugs, copper?' The younger one erupts in high-pitched laughter as his mate says, 'Shift your heap of shit or we'll run over the top of it. And you. And your suck boy.'

Something in Ray shifts. He drops his shoulders, then stands tall, rigid.

Arshag yells, 'Ray!'

Ray steps back, holsters his weapon, then swings around and explodes, attacking both, the older bastard first, Ray's fists like iron. They are unprepared, too slow, too weak. He thrashes them till they lie doubled and moaning on the bitumen and the melting, burning, tar.

Arshag pulls Ray back and cuffs the men, hauls them bleeding into the back of the Land Rover, then carefully approaches Ray who's staring out over country.

'What the hell was that?'

Ray's breathing is too intense, too erratic to speak.

'Them having a go at me? That set you off?'

Ray still doesn't answer.

Arshag comes in front of him, stands close. 'I did fine before you turned up. Don't go doing that sort of harm thinking you're saving me. Got it?'

Ray looks at his scraped knuckles as his breathing calms.

Arshag says, 'You ought to know better.'

Ray nods to the semi. 'I'll take the truck.'

Arshag sighs. 'You can drive that thing?'

'Did it in the army.' Ray won't look at him.

Arshag waits till Ray gets the truck started, then drives off.

Ray follows, shame settling in the truck cabin.

———

Kennedy's mouth and eyes are twitching. Ray reads it as excitement at signs of violence, like front-row fans at fight night. Blood-spatter range. The semi sits parked on the highway outside the copshop. Arshag stands guard over the cuffed, bashed duffers leaning against the mudguard. Kennedy stares at the semi, its load, the duffers, then Ray.

'Hope for you yet, sonny Jim.' He snorts. 'Fuck-ups deserve all they get. They need ambos?' He calls to them, 'Hey losers, you going to live?' Arshag brings them in ahead of him and they stand in front of Kennedy, faces averted.

Kennedy seems awkward with them, and he jerks around as if he caught Ray's thought. 'So what the fuck were you doing on Coopers?'

'Way to go if I was driving a semi.'

Kennedy belts his own leg like a jockey whipping a horse. 'Lucky you, eh? Lucky fucking you.' Ray gets the accusation but watches Kennedy shuffle something in his head. Something wrong here.

Kennedy forces words out at Arshag. 'Whose stock is it?'

Arshag's impassive, says, 'Carmichael's brand on most of them.'

Ray points casually at the truck. 'Have to unload them to do a count.'

'Put them straight in the big pen.'

Ray looks blank. Kennedy juts his lower lip, exhales, shakes his head, and speaks slowly. 'The pen where we put stock that's stolen, or wandering on the highway. Till the magistrate lets owners retrieve them. Right? Got it?'

Ray holds his ground. 'I know what a stock pen is. I'm wondering about the cattle already in there.'

'They're Taylor's we found on the highway. He's collecting them tomorrow. Quit whinging and get on with it.'

Ray looks at his boots. Bit obvious. Mix Carmichael's stock with Taylor's. Taylor collects his but can also take any of Carmichael's unbranded, for free. 'Why do this Taylor any favours?'

Kennedy bristles. Which Ray enjoys but hides. 'You got lucky ignoring my orders today. Don't expect to stay lucky. Do what I tell you. Day one—you trying to be a country copper.' He glares at the bloodied faces of the duffers, and says loudly, 'Not your fucking day, eh?' But it seems like Kennedy is berating himself. And Ray.

Kennedy jerks his thumb at the duffers and pushes them as they stumble into the copshop. Nods at the semi. 'Move that shit,' then follows the duffers inside.

46

Ray spins about to Arshag. 'Doesn't everyone brand their stock?'

'They mean to. Not a fun job. And some brands're easy to alter to look like someone else's.'

'You see his face when we drove up? We're the last thing he expected. Who's Taylor?'

Arshag half-laughs, a bitter sound. 'Ian Taylor. Property owner on the rise. Been the local state MP forever.'

Ray kicks at the dry, dusty earth. A road train roars by, its swaying double trailers whipping up a whirlwind of dust and stones and noise. He wipes the back of his neck, his hand comes away wet. 'Kennedy ever stop the angry act? Or is he just shitty about everything all the time?'

'Got to break you in first.' Arshag grins.

Ray pulls his shoulders back, does the whole pose except raising his fists. 'How long's it take?'

Arshag wags an unsympathetic finger. 'Up to you.' Points at the semi and its cattle. 'We going to do this?'

'I'm not mixing the stock. Put this lot in the side pen.'

Arshag nods. 'Fine. He'll come after you. After us. But fine.'

Ray snorts at the semi. 'No way I can reverse that ugly bastard. Where's the pen?'

'Without reversing? One block that way, left, two blocks. Left, down the slope.'

'Barb on today?' Angles his head at the Prince of Wales across the road.

'Usually.'

'Time local people got to know me.'

'What makes you think they don't already?'

Ray starts up the semi and grinds it away.

———

Ray steps into the cool dark of the public bar. All men except the barmaid. Four drinkers lean on the bar, more or less separate from each other. Close enough for occasional chats, far enough for brooding. A table beside a window to the main street has four more. Rugby league paraphernalia dominates every space. Buzzing and ringing spills into the bar from two poker machines in an inner hallway. Ray signals the barmaid to the end of the bar.

'I'm Ray, the new detective. Arshag said to ask you about Diah.'

'Course you are. I'm Barb.' She's in her forties, rangy, taller than most, bottle-blonde hair coiled atop her head. Sharp features, and a small mouth mostly pursed. Her light, lacy apron matches her easy manner, but there's steel not far below.

She tilts her head. 'I knew Diah. Your timing's good. See them back there?' Tilts her head to the table of four blokes towards the front of the bar. She pouts in contempt and her voice is tight, low. 'Night of the attack—that gutless attack— they come in late, strung out. Like they'd done something sly, but not, like, cocky, you know. More shell-shocked? I heard stuff while I was pouring. Nothing concrete. All of them except Benny. The bald one.'

'In front of you?'

'Drinkers don't see me. Invisible except for my tits. Them saying *she-this, she-that, bitch, slut.* It was like one's about to blab something, and his mates're telling him to shut up. All I had was a feeling, okay?'

'Better pour me one.'

'Watch out for Ginger Meggs. Real prick.'

Ray crosses to their table with his beer and makes a lot of noise dragging up a chair and flopping into it. The guys are in their early twenties, in facing pairs, Ray at one end.

The first on his left pushes his broad-brimmed hat high on a freckled, sunburnt brow. 'Who the fuck invited you?' Ginger hair sticks out from under the hat.

Ray grins, angry and primed. Leans back in his chair till its two front legs are off the ground and rocks it. 'Detective Senior Constable Windsor. I invite myself to all the parties. Who's who?' Ray points at Ginger. 'What'd your mum decide to call you, carrot-top?'

Ginger scowls. 'Peter.' Nods at the others. 'Paul.' Smothers a grin. 'And Mario.' The big in-joke, which Ray ignores.

Mario is built like the classic brick shit-house. Short, squat, huge arms in a tight short-sleeved shirt. He jabs his thumb at the man beside him. 'We think that's Benny. Didn't invite him either. He hangs round. Fuck off, Benny.' Benny waves like the Queen and grins, impervious.

Ray brazenly checks them out as their unease rises. They're all grubby from work.

Mario shifts in his seat. Ray looks at him. 'Italian or Maltese?'

'Maltese.'

'You making grappa?'

Mario takes his time to answer. 'It's illegal, mate. Don't want to get in strife with the law.' He gives a hollow laugh, large brown eyes flicking to Peter. For approval?

'Yeah, yeah, but you making any? Love the stuff.'

Mario shrugs, sulky. 'And where're you from?'

'Cane farm outside Caneville.'

'Yeah I know Caneville. Got cousins there.'

Ray looks at Paul. Opposite Mario, he's tall and lean, with long arms and large, almost delicate hands despite fingernails black with grease or oil. His fingers are flexing, tapping.

49

Ray says, 'I'm after a motorbike. Know anyone who's got one?'

Paul sniggers, looks wide-eyed at them all. 'After one? Why? They run a red light?' They roll their eyes and groan and Paul basks in the thin appreciation, mouth nervous.

Ray joins in, sips his beer. 'Been wondering about fun around here a bloke can get a piece of?' He holds Mario's gaze as Peter and Paul swap glances.

Benny says, 'Horses and cars. Cars and horses.'

Ray says, 'No girls?'

Benny says, 'Nah. Horses come when they're called and cars you start and stop with a key.' Looks around the table for approval.

Ray says, 'No wonder you prefer cars and horses. They all you can get?' Peter, Paul and Mario laugh too loudly at Benny's expense.

Benny pretends he's affronted, dignity bent. He drains his beer and pushes his chair back. 'Got to go to work.'

Peter says sharply, 'You haven't got a job?'

Benny leans in close to Peter. 'Wouldn't you like to fucking know?' He strolls out, swinging car keys around his fingers. Ray decides Benny is his own gang.

'So, what do you do for fun around here?' Again Ray holds Mario's eyes as Peter tries for scorn and Paul keeps tapping away. Mario's gaze slips away to the street. Ray switches to Paul.

Paul grimaces, scratches light stubble. 'Lou Ricketts's got a motorbike, never rides it.'

Ray nods in thanks. 'Come on. Fun?'

Peter laughs. 'Fun, out here? You joking? You don't know shit.'

Ray examines him, the one to be wary of. 'Just wondered.' He indicates the all-male bar. 'Where're all the good sorts? They're sure as shit not here.'

Peter says, 'In hiding. Their old man hides them.'

Peter's hostility almost physically buffets Ray. Not even a veneer of affability. Ray notes Peter's glances to Paul and Mario score grins. Leader of the pack, vroom, vroom. He is average height but solidly built, tanned, lots of freckles, dark eyes deep under shaggy, reddish eyebrows. Lank, reddish hair hangs over his sweaty collar and is stuck to his forehead. His full top lip curls back, exposing uneven teeth in a thick square jaw. 'Keep them safe from bad bastards like us.'

Ray says, 'Bad? You lot? What'd you ever do that was bad? Wheelies in the main street on Saturday night?'

Each one shifts in his seat, the silence combustible.

Peter leans in towards Ray. 'Come along, see if you can keep up.'

Ray raises his glass. 'Great, when?' All three snort in noisy disbelief, and laugh, showing teeth. But from Peter, pulses of resentment, fed by deep, swirling anger.

Ray smiles as his shoulders bunch and relax, bunch, relax. He lazily spreads both arms to grab his corners of the table, taking up space. 'Tell me, where were you on the night that poor schoolgirl got raped? Diah. So disgusted by what was done to her, by who touched her, she drowned herself. Preferred to be dead.'

Silence. Each of them looks up from under heavy brows. Glances whip around the table.

'You ever thought how hard it'd be to drown yourself? Keeping yourself down there, your whole body screaming to come up?'

Shifting in their seats. Thought about it alright.

'We were at a fucking dance.' Peter spits out the words.

'All of you? In a pack?'

Ray considers egging Peter on right now. Too easy. Not every push deserves a shove. *Oh yeah?* a sardonic voice in his head answers. He stands quickly, which gives them a small shock. Uses his boot to tap his chair hard into the table, forcing Peter and Mario to shift their knees.

'You play touch Sunday mornings, right? Might see you there.' He leans in for his beer and drains it, eyeing each of them, daring them to say he's not welcome. Nothing. He turns on his heel, takes his glass to the bar, winks at Barb and leaves whistling. But he's seething. He did that badly, needs to walk it off.

One thing is clear: Barb's info is solid.

On the street, he turns at the lumpy rumble of a V8. A 1964 Cortina GT, nearly every panel a different colour, is parading slowly by. It's been modified, and not only the engine. The tail is low, probably sandbagged, the tyres too wide for the wells. Ray notes that's illegal then grins at the outrage he'd provoke by fining him. The car is held together by the love and passion of its driver. Benny, at the wheel, blows a klaxon horn he must've nicked from a truck. Hoping the bugger is as innocent as he seems, Ray slow claps and Benny's face bursts into a big smile. Any attention is good attention.

5

For the rest of the week, in between Kennedy's infuriating diversions—different jobs called urgent that turn out not to be—Ray tries to keep the rape and murder investigation moving. He meets both Diah's parents, then Alice's, occasions crowded with baffled anger. Neither girl mentioned threats or problems with friends or strangers. Diah was snatched at dusk walking home from Alice's, following a late after-school visit. Her assailants must have taken her past several homes but no one saw or heard anything unusual. Alice vanished riding her bike home from school, dusk again, after a piano lesson. The bike was found in a gutter on the edge of town. Again, no witnesses.

Arshag suggests Ray make his first visits alone as a fresh face around the community. 'The cake rule'll tell you how you're going. Everyone offers cake the first visit. If you get no cake on your second visit, you're not welcome.'

Whoever he meets, Ray stays alert even to hints of parallels with that Train case up north but detects nothing, which draws him back to following up on the obvious: Barb's trio.

He decides to start with Paul, the most vulnerable, and drives out to his parents' property, a hundred acres of pasture with virtually no remnant bush, where they run cattle. They're clearly struggling. Ray has visited homes on several properties surrounded by meticulously watered, green yards of trees, lawn, vegetables, flowers, but here whatever was green is now brown. Bore-water here is good so this smacks of neglect—or loss of faith.

Ray frames his visit as part of his getting-to-know-you rounds. Paul stares at the floor, barely speaking. Dally Nixon, his mother, is also virtually mute, busying herself with tea and cakes. Reg, his jaundiced father, gripes about ungrateful children. Paul lives at home helping his ailing parents keep the place viable, but the older two have flown the coop for far-off Brisbane. A common enough tale. This inheritance sounds more trap than gift. Ray asks but can't get a straight number of how many cattle, sore point maybe.

The next day, Ray corners Paul outside the service station where he puts in a few hours as a diesel mechanic. Paul's answers to Ray's questions about Diah only highlight that Paul is owned by fear, of his father, his mates, and something more. Amid such pervasive defeat, it's hard to know what weighs most heavily. He has a trade and a job but Paul's spirit seems doomed not to rise. Asked if he's looking forward to taking over the property, he laughs bitterly.

He swears, face averted, he was at Tyborg dances the days those girls were grabbed. Peter and Mario will back him up. They do just about everything together. Ray leaves, worried not only about Paul's possible guilt but for his whole future.

His visit to Mario's parents goes largely the same way. Now in their sixties, they built their rambling, grey, wooden house themselves decades ago. It's ringed by mature, whispering she-oaks, the usual leaning, crowded sheds, and lots of machinery.

He introduces himself to friendly dogs, then to Mario Senior and Alyssa. Enjoys excellent coffee and almond cake with a nervous, mostly silent Mario sitting in—the dutiful son who leaves before Ray can talk to him separately. Like Paul, Mario faces unwelcome pressure to take on the family farm. He also works for the pumps, pipes, and plumbing business in town, usually in the field, installing and maintaining equipment or digging irrigation channels.

That afternoon, Ray meets him at that shop, muddy and soaked from a bad day at a failed pump, and gets familiar answers. Peter'll back up wherever he was those days but, unlike Paul, Mario is hostile throughout. Fucking ages ago, how's he supposed to remember where the fuck he was? Peter'll know, he was with Peter. Mario stamps off to his ute, boots squishing with water.

Peter lives on the edge of Royalton in a large, dusty, brown, grassless allotment the size of three or four ordinary urban properties with many acacias and mature, bark-bedraggled gums. He lives in one long metal shed like a railway carriage. Another accommodates three cars, and a third has two sad tractors unlikely to pull a plough again. It's unclear what a six-foot cyclone-wire fence and three emaciated cattle dogs are there to protect.

The residence shed has multiple dents. Rocks hurled at it? Its few windows are covered in sagging, blue plastic. Heat'd be bloody awful in there. Ray already knows Peter's parents live on a large property south-west of Royalton, where the land is even drier and poorer.

As Ray drives in, Peter is in the yard with an ex-army SLR rifle, taking pot shots at crows who seem indifferent.

Ray climbs from his vehicle.

Peter says, 'I got a fucking licence for this. I earn a quid shooting foxes and ferals.'

'I never asked.'

'What do you want then?' Another shot, another miss.

'When you're ready.'

Another shot, another miss. Peter faces him, holding the wandering weapon more or less down.

Ray points at it. 'Handle that bloody thing properly or having a licence won't help.'

'What do you know about it?' Sullenly turning the barrel away.

'Four years in the army helps.'

'Where'd you serve?'

'Here at home.'

'Waste of time, eh? Didn't go nowhere.'

Ray asks his questions, names the dates. Peter grins and cavorts in his version of a ballroom dance with rifle. 'Dances with the team in Tyborg. Not even in Royalton. Even got the tickets somewhere.'

'Keep tickets, do you?'

'I keep everything.'

Yeah, Ray thinks, especially grudges. 'You and your mates all made a few calls, have you? Got your story well lined up.'

Peter laughs. 'Reckon there's a fucking phone in this dump?'

Ray pauses to breathe. 'Did you know those girls?'

'Nah.'

'You heard stories about them? Maybe told some yourself?'

'No knickers. Everyone knows that.'

'How do you know if you didn't know the girls?'

'Foreigners. Bring their habits with them.'

Ray resists advancing on Peter but can't keep his mouth shut too. 'Dirtying up your superior ways, are they?'

'Pretty much, yeah.'

Ray steps forwards. 'Get the tickets. Bring them to the copshop soon as. Since you might all hang together on them.'

He drives away. On the road he hears a shot and wonders about the bullet. Hits the wheel in frustration.

———

Ray arrives on a motorbike, no helmet, bouncing over rough ground past parked trucks, jeeps, utes and two small planes. Only been here a month or so, feeling a little like a local even if he isn't, which makes him grin. He pulls up beside a sagging, hand-painted sign: SAVE OUR ROYALTON RODEO!

Another hot Sunday afternoon outside Royalton. After recent no-shows—he was off riding his bike getting to see country—Kaye informed him these barbecues are practically compulsory, most Sundays, or for births or marriages or sport events. The barbecue is on level ground above a scoured gully and a barely flowing creek. Two temporary toilets stand on trailers. Ray looks around. Sparse vegetation over red and black earth to the edge of the world whichever way he looks. Human insignificance.

Ray drops a bunch of cash in an Akubra next to another SAVE OUR RODEO sign and greets anyone who greets him, waving and nodding like a local. Claims a beer near a happy queue at a forty-four-gallon drum halved-lengthwise and filled with wood, all mounted on a homemade steel frame. Flames lick the wood below a steel verandah railing serving as a grill. The air is steeped in the heady aroma of smoke, frying beef, sausages and mounds of onions.

The road runs alongside the area then rolls on, infinity to infinity. Ray feels the whole event as alien, risen intact from beneath the earth, mid-conversation and fire burning, to return down there when darkness comes. Or the beer and steak run out. Recalls a cartoon of a gate sitting in a huge desert. No fence, just a gate, yet everyone uses the gate.

Couples arrive together, then men cluster by the fire while women form a circle on folding chairs in the paltry shade of a large river gum. Ray sees Kaye and Louise sitting there together.

He walks along the bank, following cheering and yelling, to an open space where two five-man teams are playing touch football. He flinches to imagine hitting the baked ground at speed and never getting up. Touch replaces tackling players with only touching them, meant to outlaw tackles on ground so hard it jars and thrums when you hit it. But who can resist knocking a bloke over? Ray hears his name. A player from one team is limping off and Peter, in the opposing team, is gleefully calling Ray to replace him. With malice. Ray points at his unsuitable motorbike clothes—they are all in shorts and T-shirts—but others, including Paul and Mario, take up Peter's cry. Change behind a ute if he's that bloody shy. He yields, puts on the sweat, blood and dirt-stained shorts and shirt of the player leaving, nursing a bleeding elbow, knees and chin and grinning at Ray.

Ray joins in and eyeballs his opponents—a man whose name he forgets, one he hasn't met, and Peter, Paul and Mario. No bloody surprise if he cops more than touches. He fields his share of crunching collisions but stays upright, mostly, losing only the usual flesh from elbows and knees. He uses every evasive boxing trick, slipping and ducking to dodge the worst hits. His team are no slouches and Ray's skill or luck, reluctantly at the centre of the action, gets them the ball often enough to tip the score their way. His team wins, if he can call the pain he already feels a win. Paul and Mario offer hand-shakes, not a sulking Peter. Ray rinses in a bucket of brown creek water, towels dry, and returns to his own gear.

Piling his plate with the makings of a serious steak burger, he considers crashing the circle of women but doesn't risk it, instead crossing to the pugnacious, brittle solidarity of the men. Mario, still in footy gear, finishes an anecdote, saying, 'So, what are you, you bastard, a spaz?' Some laugh but Ray feels strain in the air. Another man in the circle, shorter, wiry, strides across to Mario and hits him sharp and hard in the midriff. Mario's plate of food flies skywards, he folds to the ground gasping. Ray is slow to recognise the hitter is Laming. Paul helps Mario, who is doubled up, coughing in the dust. No one speaks as Laming stalks away, face a mask.

The man beside Ray says, 'His fucking kid, dipshit! Jesus Christ, Mario!'

Paul says, 'He fucking forgot. Doesn't mean king hit him!'

Ray holds up a hand in query. The man next to him says, 'Laming's kid's a spastic. Or some fucking thing.'

Ray stares at his steak. Laming's got a kid? Spastic? Bastard carries himself like he's got no one.

Mario stands with help, takes a beer. 'Good fucking steak wasted.' Manages a grin. 'Better get another one.' Makes his unsteady way to the fire.

Ray feels sly attention swing onto himself. Copper and newbie. Double fucking trouble.

He says, 'Anyone else here own a motorbike? I'll need some spare parts soon for the rattler I just got from Lou.' He holds out his stubby at Lou Ricketts across the circle. 'Calls it the Black Bomber.' Lou leads the circle in an easy laugh. It's enough, the circle resumes, the pushing and shoving, the declarations of opinion carved in stone, lewd comments about women that aren't the wives.

Ray can't see Kennedy but wonders if he'd fit in anyway. Which precipitates a familiar feeling, keeping himself remote as a horizon. He looks around to escape. Alone atop the bank, an older, white-haired man perches on a seat that folds into a walking stick, facing away across the gully.

The man beside him laughs. 'Bloody Pom. English lord, would you believe? Baron something. Everyone calls him Lord Billy, not to his face. He owns this land we're on and the big place, Millabunda, hundred mile north. Few thou square miles.'

A lord? Ray laughs. A real fish out of water. Half expecting to be dismissed, he approaches Lord Billy who gently shakes his hand, while remaining sitting.

'William Wallace. A Pom with a name like that, quite ridiculous, I'm afraid.'

Ray smiles at an accent fruity enough for a Christmas cake. He tries to squat but it hurts so he stays standing.

William says, 'Do you know British history? No reason you should. William Wallace was a Scottish rebel at the end of the thirteenth century.' He laughs, and nods at the sweep of the country. 'I say thirteenth century in Britain and it's quite intelligible. Say it out here and it can't help sounding odd. Did they tell you not to call me Lord Billy? Silly buggers.' Said affectionately. Thin, longish, straw-coloured hair protrudes from his straw hat. His pale complexion glows red from the sun. He's wearing long sleeves and pants, only his hands exposed.

'You must be the new policeman. Sorry, detective. Fresh blood, what a good thing.'

'Ray Windsor.'

William laughs. 'Windsor. Another touch of England. You colonials. Never understand why you didn't throw us out years ago. And you box! Even better.'

'You're well-informed.'

'Hard not to be in this part of the world. Locals call it the Royalton Radio. Reliable, word-of-mouth transmission, or it's mystical somehow. You'd think our vast distances out here would work against that but oh no.' He shapes up in mock boxing pose. 'Not much scope for boxing here. Proper Queensbury rules, I mean.'

'Hard to get passionate with a punching bag.'

'Indeed. One needs a live opponent to keep that edge alive.'

'You've ended up a long way from home.'

'You might think it to look at me, but no, this is my home. My true home.'

Ray hears irritation in his voice.

'I could not live anywhere else. I tried,' William says. He waves at the guests. 'In Africa, we used to call these types of outings sundowners. The whites, I mean. Colonials are the same all over the world. Look at us. Huddling together in the middle of all this.'

He winks, stands and folds his seat. 'Now, any time you want a chat on the gentlemanly art of pugilism, let me know. I used to box myself, you know, and I'd enjoy it. I can collect you, take you out to the spread, as the Americans call it.'

'Sure, that'd be great.'

'Excellent. I must be off before the sun sets me on fire. Much as I like it here, I'm not built for it. Like life, perhaps.

See you soon, I hope.' He ambles off with a slight limp, waving vaguely.

Ray sees a woman he knows detach herself from the circle to refill her white wine at an esky. Stella is about his age, wearing the standard broad-brimmed hat, moleskins, elastic-sided boots, all looking new. Both unattached, they have already found themselves partnered by default in tennis and various games at functions. A casual arrangement that so far suits them. Ray feels some pressure to advance from casual, wondering if she does too. He joins her, collects another beer, and smiles. They turn as the engine of one of the planes, Lord Billy's, splutters then roars into life. The plane rocks and trundles along the road, awkwardness smoothing as it gathers speed. It leaps into the air, rises, and disappears into the blue. The drone of its engine is the last to go. They turn to each other, and something unsaid passes pleasantly between them.

Ray nods towards the plane. 'Nice work if you can get it.'

She half-smiles, preoccupied, turns to the circle of women then back to him, resigned. Ray realises she's teasing, like he's the least bad choice, showing she knows what they're doing. He smiles too.

She says, 'Life of a detective keeping you busy? Exposing society's seedy underside.'

'Still haven't arrested any dangerous crims.'

'Slacker.'

He grins. 'How's your contribution to society?'

'Still babysitting rambunctious teenagers. Every teacher's delight.' She winks.

They pause for mutual assessment. She's lean, same height, mouth mocking, holding her glass aside so he can get a better look.

Embarrassed, he fixes on her face. 'Next question?'

'What do you do for kicks?'

He laughs. 'You as bored as you sound?'

'What've you got to offer?'

'You ride a motorbike?'

'Is a pig's arse pork?' She laughs at his startled expression. Gotcha.

They ride off, no helmets, aware that behind them women are raising eyebrows, men simulating hip rolls. The couple that brought Stella exchange nods. Mission accomplished.

Stella calls out, over the noise of the engine, 'Where'd you dig this up?'

'Lou Ricketts, you know him?'

'I teach his daughter.'

'Saw it sitting in his shed, all dusty and sad. We did a deal.' He guns it for effect. 'It's a heap but it goes.' He pats the tank in apology. 'Reliability matters out here.' They settle into the ride. She hugs him just tightly enough. He enjoys how they move as one on the corners. Casual is as casual does. As long as it lasts.

At his flat, sweaty, determined sex follows, around his aches and abrasions. Not to be outdone, bed-banging starts soon afterwards upstairs. Ray laughs, for which Stella gives him a mock slap on the arm. Lying there in the rattling gale of the air-con, Stella tells of her transfer to Royalton High School six months earlier. Calls it a self-inflicted wound— she told her previous principal she was bored—but she's recovering. It's a precarious posting. Low student numbers and always threatening to go lower. Never know when the government might close the school. Bad for the whole place if that happens.

She says, 'So what was your sin?'

He shrugs. 'I refused a superior officer's order to knock a bloke down and arrest him for doing nothing bad at all.'

She stares at him. 'Impressive. I tell my classes the police are your friends, they'd never knock you down or arrest you if you're not being bad.'

'Guess I'm their friend then.'

'Good. Guess we both gave people the excuse to get rid of us. Careless.'

'Doesn't make it right.'

She rolls in closer and kisses him. 'What's right?'

A question he gnaws at, maybe too often. He leans back to see her better, smiles at the defiance in that uplifted chin, enjoys her bright blue eyes surrounded by dark make-up. Cropped, dark hair and thick fringe down to her eyebrows frame a pale, freckled, round face. Pursed lips and a set mouth are a warning to anyone tempted to take her for granted.

She thought teaching bush kids'd be easier but finds a desperation or grimness in them that alarms her. 'Makes them older than their years. There's always ones with that cowed look kids get from bashing going on at home. But this's different.'

'Could be they've sussed they'll quit school with bugger-all to keep them in town, and not a lot to help them get anywhere useful.'

She shivers for them, sympathetic. 'This's the last place they want to be. Older brothers or sisters lie around at home all day, no jobs, living with parents forever. I had a brain to get me out, and a scholarship. What'd you have?'

'Boxing. Maybe wouldn't hurt these kids too. Then I got a sparky apprenticeship. Bought a motorbike, happiness. Even had a girlfriend.'

'Yeah but girls, you know, can be tricky. Can't get her pregnant cos if she's up the duff, you've got to get married. Lost a couple of friends that way.'

'I saw a shotgun marriage that had a real shotgun. Meant as a joke but no one laughed.'

'But you're not an electrician.'

'Got called up. Two years conscription in the army. Rolled with it.' Always his way, even then. That thought, unbidden, feeds sourness into his tone. 'A way to see the world. They lied.'

'Vietnam?'

'Too late.' Pulls his lips down. Is he going to feel crappy about this for the rest of his life? He knows she's seen it. 'After Nasho, I signed up for two more years, then into the cops. And here I am. Driftwood.' He hears himself and is irritated. He wants to be a copper. He just hasn't worked out how to handle the shit that comes with it. How to live when the rules keep shifting and everything gets murkier every year.

Stella says, 'You don't have to be driftwood here.' Her sharp tone surprises him. 'We didn't choose it but it's dumb not to try to make it work.'

He leaves that alone, drinks his beer. 'Get many drugs at school?'

She laughs. 'You want some, or asking as a cop? Grass and weird pills sometimes. A hippie travelling salesman drops off a mix occasionally.'

'So what else do you do for fun?'

'I sing. I'm in this a capella group but two of the girls are pregnant, they'll probably quit. Come along. We could use a fella.'

He laughs. 'That'll be the day.' His mother had had a crystal-clear voice, in the kitchen singing songs from *Oklahoma*. He'd forgotten loving her singing.

Stella says, 'My first day here, I panicked. Christ, that main street! Brissy girl dumped in a desert, thought I was gonna die. I'd fallen off the world. So right away I took up French by correspondence. I've since discovered there's something in the air here that makes French sound weird. I swear it turns it into noise. *Commorn voo-uppeley voo?* But I'm hanging in there.'

He can tell, a strength of hers. Soft slimness barely conceals a hardened core. Bit like Barb at the pub.

She gestures. '*Et vous?* Or, *et tu?*'

'I play touch football, because I'm bored. Never play cricket. I run.' He sits up. 'All these pissed-off kids. Maybe they'd like a boxing gym? I could teach them a few moves. Made me feel more okay about a shitty world.'

'So they could beat each other up better?'

'Cool huh?'

They lie in silence. He's thinking, *This is working*. Maybe she's thinking the same. They make love again.

At the next barbecue, they arrive together, split up like the others and leave together, this time for her place. Become a couple, seen as that already. It changes his sense of belonging. So far.

6

The travelling magistrate runs his temporary courtroom in the old Masonic Hall down the western end of the main street. Ray marvels at the ponderous drama of the hall's frontage: local pink granite, heavy 'classical' Greek columns backed by thick, square blocks of the same stone. Too grand for so modest a town. Like it's bluffing. Four stalwart Masons still meet behind locked doors every three months.

Behind the façade is a prosaic, tongue-and-groove meeting room where the court sits. A shallow stage sits at the far end, although this magistrate elects not to use it. The only decorations are leadlight windows and a small honour board of the Masonic dead from World War One.

The first charges are public drunkenness, an attempted assault, and driving a car on the footpath while under the influence. In answer to why he was driving on the footpath, the accused says that in his shameful condition, he believed it was safer than driving on the road. He gets a twelve-month good behaviour bond.

The next case is the captured duffers who are indeed brothers: the Randalls. To Ray's dismay, Detective Kennedy advises the court that due to problems with the collection of evidence, these charges have been dropped. The accused pair claim they found the cattle loose on the road. Kennedy apologises and notes in passing that an added complication is the arresting officer is accused of 'undue and excessive force' in making the arrests. The magistrate sighs, maybe at the tortured implausibility, taps his gavel and calls for a dismissal of all charges. The brothers stride out, grinning in disbelief, giving Kennedy openly admiring looks.

Ray is stunned. He follows Kennedy from the hall. He did attack the brothers, but withdrawing the case? He catches Kennedy on the main street. 'What's going on?'

Kennedy offers a supercilious grin and eyes Ray up and down as if stupidity is visible. 'You mingled them. Left the gate open and in they all wandered and got mixed up. Classic newbie can't close a gate. No problem if they're branded but, gee, what do you know, not everyone keeps up with that. Have I got to spell it out? We can't say which cattle came off the semi.'

'You told me to mingle them. I didn't mingle anything. I shut the gate.' He stops, distracted, recalls Kennedy's shock that day seeing the Randalls at all. Nothing to do with Ray thrashing them. More about something wrong in catching them. And being on the wrong road, which turned out to be the right fucking road.

Kennedy steps closer, points a finger at his chest.

Ray braces. He'll never control his rage if that finger makes contact.

Kennedy looks around, maybe for witnesses. 'You better hurry up and learn how shit works here, mate.'

'Like a murder you think isn't worth investigating? That the shit you mean?'

Kennedy shakes his head. 'Jesus. How'd you survive the fucking army?'

'If we'd stayed on your road we'd've missed them.'

'No, you would've followed fucking orders. Where do you reckon me and Laming were? Down where Coopers Road joins the fucking highway. We had them whatever you did. You think we trusted you pissants to do the job? The B team? Tell you what. Just go. Fuck off. Quit. Leave.' He flourishes his folder of court papers. 'Or maybe you'll never get out of here, like your mate Shaggers.'

Ray hears a yell from across the street. The Randalls hold up cans of beer and carry half cartons, catcalling and mooning.

Ray turns to Kennedy. 'Better go collect your reward, eh?' Said before he thinks.

Kennedy jolts, deeply hostile. Ray stops himself shaping up in a defensive crouch and strides off, boots jarring on the pitilessly hard ground, raging against himself, his big mouth, but also thinking, *What price am I prepared to pay to stay a copper?* He's so far on the outer, no way back in.

At the copshop steps he stops. Were Kennedy and Laming really at that highway intersection? What if the Randalls weren't meant to be caught? Forget Kennedy grifting a few cattle to Taylor in a mingled herd, that's beer money. But cattle knocked off by the truckload?

Arshag emerges from the copshop and comes down the steps in a hurry, checking his handgun, passing Ray at the bottom of the steps. 'Feral dog at Callaghan's. The kids trapped it in a shed. Big bugger's been taking their chooks. Now they don't know what to do with it.'

'Someone doesn't know what to do with a feral dog?'

'The dad's away. Aren't you in court?'

'Kennedy got the case dismissed.'

Arshag stops dead. 'What?'

'I'll come with you.'

Arshag drives the Land Rover out of town. Ray briefly explains Kennedy's tale about Ray leaving the gate open so no one can prove which cattle came off the bloody semi and which were already in the pen. Mostly what stands out for Ray now is Kennedy's lack of enthusiasm for proceeding.

Arshag puffs his cheeks, exhales slowly, unimpressed. 'Him and Taylor are good mates.' As if that's all that needs to be said.

Ray says, 'I need to know more about duffing.'

'What's to know? Sneak your truck onto a property. Sort the stock you want. Hope no dogs get a whiff. Load up, hit the road, drive god knows how far. Unload. All in secret. Then deal with branding.'

'Piece of cake.'

Arshag says, 'We could call in the stock squad but Kennedy won't. It's his turf, his copshop.'

'*His* copshop.' Ray snorts. 'I could call the stock squad myself.'

Arshag laughs hollowly. 'Go outside the line of command? They'll call Kennedy anyway.'

'And I get crucified.' He shifts uncomfortably. Every copshop, every team, a world of their own. 'Been there. Not ready for that again.' Yet. He thinks about it. 'Can we figure out who's been hit, try to work out who's next and ambush the bastards?'

Arshag shakes his head. 'How much time you got? Even if we pick the right property, we could be off about *where* on the property. Stock squad's set up for stakeouts and long waits. Not us.'

'The Randalls are off the hook. Maybe they'll be hot to go back to work?'

'They'll clear out, get a job in another region. There's a network.'

'Nice to know they get steady work.' He dislikes his own bitterness but can't stop it.

Arshag looks at him, then away. 'When there's nothing else around. Older Randall's got a wife and two little kids on a bush block out south-west. Everyone needs food on the table.'

The radio snaps to life. It's Wiggins: Lorraine Callaghan shot the feral dog. Arshag grins and shakes his head before slowing into a U-turn. 'Good on ya, mum.'

On the way back they come up behind a beige panel van. Ray grins. '1969 XW. Ford Falcon.'

'Petrolhead.'

'Two kinds of men where I grew up, Holden men and Ford men. You had to choose.' He looks closer. 'This one's seen better days. Riding on its axles. Overloaded to hell. Get alongside, I'll pull him over.'

Arshag looks over in surprise.

Ray points as the van wanders a little out of its lane. 'Look at that.'

Arshag shrugs, pulls alongside and Ray leans out, signalling until the driver stops. Arshag parks behind him.

Ray walks to the van, followed by Arshag who has a casual grin. The driver erupts from it, slams the door. He's in his late forties, muscular but with a beer gut. Wearing a torn dark-blue shirt that Ray sees has what looks like blood splattered on it.

Ray steps back and pulls out his pistol. 'Hold it, hands high.'

The man continues to advance and bangs the side of the van with a fist. 'What is this? You fucking kidding me?'

Ray points to the rear of the van with his gun. 'Open up.'

There's what seems to be more blood on the man's faded shorts and Ray flicks a glance at Arshag, who looks curiously relaxed. The man belts the side of the van again but opens the rear door. Ray peers inside. Full of racks of metal trays containing big pieces of ice and parcels of butchered meat. Cuts he's seen in butcher shops.

Ray exhales. 'Illegal butchering. Against health regulations.'

The man paces, too outraged to be still. 'So? You gonna take food from my kids' mouths now, eh?' He hovers, unsure what to do with his hands.

'Who owns this meat?'

'That'd be fucking me. Or Con, now it's bagged.' He turns to Arshag. 'You going to help out here?'

Arshag holds out a calming hand. 'No problem, Barry. This's Detective Windsor. Ray, this is Barry Slater. Barry, you can go on your way.'

Barry steps up too close to Ray, who is working at staying loose. 'The new bloke.'

Ray decides to stay quiet.

Arshag says, 'He's learning the ropes. Why don't you get on to Con's? Have a good one.'

Barry spits on the road, eyes on Ray. Then he rocks back in his mud-caked boots and returns to the van cabin, slamming the door.

As he guns it away, Ray says, 'What the fuck was that?'

Arshag starts back to their Land Rover. 'For some local industry we cut some slack. Barry's on a dying property. Even his bores've given up the ghost. Buying water these days. Only way he's making a quid is selling meat on the side with Con the butcher.'

'Con with the butcher shop in town? Selling illegal butchered meat?'

'Barry started it, small, few bob on the side, for family, few friends, then it grew. Con got involved, tidied it up healthwise. He's the butcher so it's not hurting anyone. Con's got guys who'll drop it around to your place, offer you a good deal. Good meat.'

'How is this legal? And that bloke Barry's a loose cannon.'

'A desperate man.'

'We let it happen?'

'I buy his meat.'

———

Ray is heading home to his place when he recalls Stella is making dinner, already a regular Wednesday night arrangement. Too regular for his mood.

They kiss in her kitchen. She asks him what's wrong. He shakes his head. Bad day, he'll get cleaned up.

He emerges clean, changed. She greets him on her verandah. He toasts his beer with her gin and tonic, feeling her wariness. Knows his mood's doing it. He samples the beer, mock-approves it, crosses to her and kisses her. 'Calming down now.'

She says, 'I told some kids at school about your boxing gym idea.'

'My what?'

'A boxing gym. You should set one up, it's what these kids need.'

'How? It'd cost money.'

'The kids went on about it, they love the idea. All over Royalton Radio by now.'

Ray sighs. 'I wouldn't even know where to start.' Antennae on alert: another way to tie him here.

She laughs, oddly. He knows she knows he's struggling with something but has no sense of what. He doesn't share his work.

She points her gin and tonic at him. 'You have to do it now. These things get a life of their own. It's how life happens. We're here so let's be here. And doing it for each other. You're my soft landing zone.' She wriggles her arse like a bird settling into its nest. He laughs, playing at ogling, but he's uneasy.

He says, 'On our own, we talk about leaving. Not staying.' His voice sounds hollow.

She offers a lazy thumbs-down. 'Leaving? Escaping? Like kid-talk from school? Please, miss, when's real life going to start? We're here. This's it. What's wrong with it anyway?'

He's angry. 'What about using your French by going to France?'

'I don't know why I bother with it. I suppose I could teach it.'

They sit watching the sky lose colour. The evening star appears.

He says, 'What's for dinner?'

She shakes her head in mock horror. 'That was close. Lucky you didn't say, what's for dinner, missus?' And laughs at his shocked face. Him thinking the smallest things make him feel like he's been here forever.

———

In the copshop, Ray checks the trip book for the day they caught the Randalls. He and Arshag are there. Not Kennedy or Laming. But everyone's slack about the trip book. Ray slaps it shut and marches into what passes for the lunchroom. Kaye is eating a sandwich with Constable Louise Wiggins. She gives a tentative wave, with her sandwich.

He gets a can of drink and joins them and looks at her lunch. 'You giving away sandwiches?'

Kaye looks at her sandwich, then, baffled, holds it out for him.

He holds up both hands. 'No, no, I was kidding. Eat up. What's new?'

'Actually'—she puts her sandwich and lunch box aside, holding up a finger as she thoroughly chews and swallows—'I want to ask you about your family.'

'Really?' *Here we go.*

Louise shuffles her feet, scrunches up waxed paper from around her own sandwiches and leaves without a word.

Kaye lays a hand on his arm. 'You know I do family trees?'

When Ray doesn't answer, she says, 'Cos you're new I was hoping you wouldn't mind if I asked you about your family.'

'I don't know, Kaye. My family's chockers with thieves and child molesters.' He looks at his watch.

Kaye pales, covers her mouth with her hands. 'Oh no! I haven't looked yet. Truly, I haven't.'

Ray thinks, looked where? 'No, sorry, hey, it's fine.' Has to remember: no jokes.

'Well, okay. See, your name's Windsor and I was telling my mum you'd started here and she said that name rang a bell and of course I said that's probably because it's the queen's name but she said no, no.' Kaye is in full flow. 'My mum remembers a very exciting time here thirty years ago, before I was even born. Mum remembers all that stuff. It's a gift she's passed on to me, I guess.'

'My mum ran off with a reporter, my dad.' Interested in spite of himself.

'Yes!' Kaye is wide-eyed. As vital as if it happened yesterday. 'And, of course your mum was Ann-Louise Rogers.'

Ray can't help himself. 'Is the Rogers place around here?'

'Fifty mile east.' She points east, to a wall of the lunchroom.

'That right?' He sits back. A load shifts, surprising him. Matters more than he'd allowed. Recalls his mother's intensity in cutting herself off from her family. Damning them for damning her. Not using her name in stories she told him. Inventing fairytale names all the time until Ray was sometimes unsure what the real name was. Which was her intent, her rage undiminished. He tests the name to himself: Ann-Louise Rogers. Beautiful. He pushes himself upright, stirred, but pinned in Kaye's fierce focus.

He keeps his voice as casual as he can. 'Still there, the property? Who's there now?'

'Yes, it is. Oh no, hang on, it's sold. Recently. Your mother's parents are both dead, of course.'

Ray looks startled.

'Didn't you know?' Her eyes widen. 'But they were your grandparents!'

'Who was there before it was sold? Any living Rogers?'

'Well, your cousin Jimmy. Jimmy Rogers.' He watches her wrestle with the utter wrongness of not knowing your own immediate family. Ray realises with dismay she may feel she needs to take him under her wing, make him her newest project. She points to the dead and the living in the air as if on an invisible screen. 'Your grandparents, Harry and Myrtle Rogers, had Ann-Louise, your mum, and Gary, your uncle. Gary used to run the property but he got bad flu and died and so did his wife who was a Norton from Chinchilla. They had one child, Jimmy. Bit of a troublemaker. Seen him here a few times, sorry to say. He sold to Ian Taylor after going broke and the bank stepped in.'

Ray stares ahead, stands, almost hearing steel bars click into place. The fight on the train. That Jimmy. His bloody cousin? Invisible threads tightening around him.

Kaye wriggles with excitement. 'I can do your family tree. For free, for the love of it. Louise makes the diagrams with boxes, all neat and spaced out properly. Then you add to it from your photo albums and letters and newspaper cuttings. You can mount it on your wall for everyone to see where you came from and who you are.'

Photo albums, letters, cuttings? He has none. He's sure he's backing away but he's standing still. 'How about I get back to you?' Kaye may still be talking as he heads off. 'Talk later, okay?' And escapes.

———

Near the end of day, when it's supposed to be cooler, Ray goes for a run. A rattling ute that has seen better days rumbles by, a large black dog loose in the back, head poked over the side of the tray, barking wildly. Ray halts, afraid it will jump out. The ute screeches to a grinding halt, blocking the road. Ray braces for attack.

A hulking, unkempt male of indeterminate age leaps out, fists in the air, and confronts the dog. 'Shuddup! Shud-the-fuck up! Sick of hearing you. Sick of fucking telling you! You got to fucking shuddup!'

The dog sinks from view below the side. Ray approaches warily, like he is intruding.

The man turns to him. 'She's been barking for fucking years.'

'G'day.'

'What the fuck're you doing anyway?' He points back down the empty street.

'Going for a run.'

'Fuck me.' Puts out a grimy hand. 'Don.' Don keeps looking at him hard, as if he knows Ray but has forgotten his name.

Ray shakes his hand. 'Ray.'

The dog's head appears over the side of the ute to eye-level. Don, mouth set, points at her and she sinks from sight again.

Don looks at Ray. 'Dunno you, do I? You the new cop?'

Ray nods, watches Don absorb this. He is forty-ish, muscular in what's left of a shirt with torn-off sleeves, greasy shorts and curling-up boots with much knotted laces. With a wild black beard and head of hair, intense black eyes under raised eyebrows, and a dark tan, Don looks a lot like his dog. Or vice-versa. 'How you finding it?'

'Okay. Yeah. What do you call your dog?'

'Mongrel. Eh, Mongrel!' Mongrel lifts her head, gets a pat. All forgiven. 'Just can't keep her fucking quiet. You want a watchdog to fucking bark but, Christ on a bike, she never fucking quits. Pat her. See if she likes you.'

Character test. Ray carefully offers the back of a hand, which Mongrel sniffs. Ray pats her.

Don says, 'There you go. You're okay. Good cop. Not like that prick Kennedy, eh?'

Ray stays neutral.

'Anyway. Running, eh? No bastard out here runs, mate. Why Jesus invented cars.' He laughs.

'I like running.'

Don shakes his head. Takes all kinds. Gets back in the ute as Ray reads part of the sign on the door: EARTHMOVING! LAND CLEARING! DAMS! Don drives bulldozers. Perfect. He guns the

78

ute away. Mongrel starts barking. Don leans out of his window. 'Shuddup! Shud-the-fuck-up!' Mongrel is undeterred.

Ray thinks about Kennedy. No one mentions Laming. Even when Laming's around it's as if he isn't there. His dry throat turns sharp, painful. He stops, swallows hard for moisture that won't come. Desert dryness. A man sitting on his front steps lifts a beer. Ray waves back.

'You the new cop?'

'Yeah.' Doesn't matter how long he's here, he'll be the new cop.

'Don't stop. You look like you're just starting to enjoy yourself.'

He erupts into a deep laugh that becomes a rolling, smoker's cough. Ray turns for home, reduced to a slow jog. Bring a bloody bucket of water next time. He passes kids on bikes on and off the road, hanging round. Laughing at the dumb runner. Nothing to do, nowhere to go. Ray pounds on, swallowing hard for spit. Too hard. Stops. Looks back at the kids. A boxing gym might even work.

He sits at his kitchen table to unlace his running shoes when loud knocking crashes into the room. A man's shape fills his doorway, silhouetted in the afternoon sun.

'G'day bastard. I just heard the weirdest fucking Royalton Radio yarn.'

'Jimmy?' How bloody speedy is Kaye?

'Your fucking cousin! How the fuck'd that happen?' He steps in, laughing, a six-pack in each hand and a bottle of rum somehow tucked into his jeans. He unloads it all onto the table and holds out a calloused hand.

'Pleased to meet you properly, cuz!' He slaps his thigh, sits opposite Ray, opens a beer each, toasts the air. 'Here's to Aunty Ann-Louise who I never met but heard a lot about.'

Ray opens a beer and taps Jimmy's bottle in a toast.

Jimmy laughs, a full-bodied sound. 'Now we're rellies, you ought to quit that fucked-up copshop. Come work with me and Burt.'

'Best offer I've had all day. Nah.' Taps his chest. 'Born copper, me.'

Jimmy shakes his head in mock sadness. 'Too many belts to the head, mate. Yeah, Kaye says you're a boxer. Should've warned me, you bastard.'

They sit in silence. Ray lets the beer unstick the insides of his whole body.

Jimmy starts his second stubby. 'You been out the old place?'

Ray shakes his head, hoping any flash of anxiety doesn't show. 'Sold now, isn't it?'

'Sold but still empty. Taylor's a prick, only wants the water and land, not the house. He'll use it as a barn.'

Ray feels a jolt which he guesses didn't show, as Jimmy exhales heavily and continues.

'One minute he's broke as me, or so he tells me months ago, next thing I know he's got the moolah to buy me out. Crony of bloody Kennedy. Fuck them.' He drains his beer, 'Listen, I left family stuff in boxes in the shed out there. I'll give you a hoy when I head out to pick them up, you can come along.' He stands to go.

'Hang on, what about all this?' Ray points to the grog.

'Leave it. So I know there'll be shit to drink next time I drop in. Cuz!' He laughs at what Ray knows is his alarmed face. Family, closing in.

7

Ray wakes in his bed to a strange smell. Knows it but can't place it. It's from outside so he goes to his door.

Dot, halfway down her stairs, leans over to greet him. 'Gets you up, doesn't it?'

Ray looks into the yard. The gentlest rain he has ever seen is falling.

She laughs and inhales, deep and loud. That unmistakeable, heavy, slightly sour scent of rain after a long dry spell. 'That smell. It's got a name, you know? Petrichor.'

Ray says, 'Petrichor.' He puts out a hand, feels the rain land lightly.

'Make the most of it.'

———

Ray pushes the black bomber through Dot's yard, leaving for work. The sky is blue and cloudless. What's left of the rain on the lawn no more than a heavy dew. He stops to look at her Banksia rose plants growing steadily along the fence. Dot's making sure they get water. Two months since Kennedy handed him Diah's and Alice's case notes and he's added precious little. He starts the bike, guns it away.

The new day brings more jobs Kennedy deems urgent but are more of the same. Faces change but what happens to them stays remarkably similar.

At a highway collision, no one is hurt but a ute is a write-off and a bus is stuck in Royalton for two nights for repairs. That'll please the town. Trapped visitors need food, grog and beds.

After a firearm incident, Ray interviews victims in a noisy ward in the spartan Royalton hospital. A ten year old got hold of the family twenty-two rifle, accidentally shot his dad in the shoulder, and himself in the foot. His ex-nurse mother did everything right, looked after them on the spot, then drove them to town, yelling at her husband the whole way.

The husband is plainly proud of her but she is grim. 'Dumb bastard. Need this like a hole in the head.' Knows the extra work she's in for till her man recovers. 'No money to hire any-bloody-one.'

Her husband is embarrassed, silent. The boy's wound is more serious, bones shattered. Need X-rays to know what the future'll look like.

The rifle was not locked away. 'Course bloody not. Never. Take so long to get it out, what you had to shoot has gone home.' No answer to why the rifle was loaded or why the boy reloaded it to shoot himself. Ray lays no charges, promises visits to ensure compliance with home safety firearm regulations. With tea and cake. On his own farm, growing up, there'd been an ex-World War One rifle, three-oh-three. Never locked up, but never loaded. Never saw any bullets for it.

Too many days bring pleas for help from domestic violence that the caller denies by the time he arrives, despite signs of assault dismissed with unlikely explanations. Coppers can usually read what's going on, less often find a way to help, and leave expecting to be back next week or month. Ray hates seeing kids lurking, trying to be invisible. Cops visited his parents' home when he was a kid, called by neighbours. Nothing came of those visits either. The usual cases are murky enough but his parents weren't usual. The cops never grasped it was his mum who was the abuser. Emotional lashings, her tongue a razor, his dad mostly inert, taking it.

On the way to any domestic violence call, Ray fears his own anger will overwhelm him, never trusts anything he can do will help. He lets the rage flow by and over him till it's exhausted itself enough so he can do his official job. Till next fucking time. Hates the people, the wounds, even the houses where it happens. Every call threatens every cop's dread, family murder-suicide including children.

And the suicides. Young, old, male, female. Not every day but not rare. Gun. Hanged in a shed. Gas. Single-vehicle road smash. Attempts to make sense of them cite old age, alcohol, relationship breakdown, fatal illness, bankruptcy. Maybe a roo burst onto the road leaving no tracks, that's why they swerved head-on, full speed into that tree. Absence of skid marks, like his mum.

Ray writes them up, trying for neutral, but thinks anyone who wants to die should be let do it. Someone has to check on those who succeed, and those who don't, but a cop walking in feels like invasion of privacy. He's seen his share of corpses working murder and suicides in Brisbane, has been first at ghastly car accidents. His long, hard look at a suicide comes from wanting to ask them why. Now you've done it, did it do the job? Telling family and friends the bad news leaves Ray silently, angrily, regarding the suicide as a coward. Or bloody something. Bloody tell those who matter, then fuck off and do it. Don't leave it to a stranger. God knows how that'd work. Mostly he wonders if his inner wrangling is because something inside him is drawn to it. Start out asking how to live, then has to fend off that the real question is how to die.

One afternoon, as he drives alone back towards town after an ambiguous shooting incident where no one was hurt and nothing revealed, he recognises a crossroads and on impulse takes the road to Petersens Dam, site of Diah's rape and suicide.

He parks beside it, rolls down a window, listens to the silence. Always struck by how traditionally beautiful it is, unlike where Alice was found, which is ruthless Australiana. This is a large body of water with pristine edges, no trampled mud or bovine corpses. Cattle kept out. A couple of pumping stations deliver water to distant troughs and channels. Ti-trees stand in a clump on a stretch of bank. Farther back, stone barbecues and three sheltered picnic tables sit among casuarinas, acacias, patchy grasses, children's swings. He drives between two shelters. The rape was here. No sign now, but Laming's report described refuse from a drinking party, torn-up ground from raging tyres, earth trampled by boots, and a partly burnt mattress.

He drives to the edge of the dam. Waterbirds, herons, even huge pelicans. Are they migratory? A faded sign pocked with bullet holes announces the dam is stocked with fish. It's assumed Diah went into the water in the ripped remnants of her clothes because that's what she was wearing when she was pulled out. A poor swimmer, Fang Su, her mum, told Ray. Likely she made herself keep going, then didn't have the strength to get back, then drowned. Nothing easy about drowning yourself. Recalls a case in France, a drowned man found with ankles tied together and a rope to a slipknot on his wrists tied behind his back. The case, not unique, was judged suicide, not murder. As a note confirmed, the slipknot ensured that if the man struggled, it pulled the slipknot tighter. No way out. Taking the pressure off the decision. How'd the bloke feel as he tied the knot?

He climbs from the car to walk around, missing where red earth gives way to glutinous black clay. As he walks, his boots gather thickening layers of sticky mud, forcing him into clown-like high-stepping. He high-steps back to the car and uses sticks to clean his boots as best he can.

Irritated, he starts to leave, carelessly reversing into more black clay. The car founders as its wheel-wells clog with mud. Takes an hour of scraping it out to escape. On the drive home, pieces of mud fly off the tyres and pound the undercarriage, sounding like the car is being pelted underneath with stones. What's left of the clay will make it plain what's happened when he gets back. Newbie Numbnuts.

He corners Arshag in the copshop carpark, a favourite space for straight talk, although they can see Kennedy at his desk watching them. 'So, Laming did a lousy interview with the parents, I get that, but he missed Barb's info too? She didn't tell him?'

Arshag uses his right hand to force back the fingers on his left, stretching them. 'Three years ago, Laming bailed Barb up in the pub storeroom. It got heavy. I asked her about her bruised face but had to drag it out of her. No way she'd report it. To Kennedy? Not on. Got stuck into me when I said I would. She'd've lost her job, would've had to leave town. On her own with a kid, and not young, so that was that. Laming and Barb don't talk.'

'He knows you know?'

'Things get around.' He holds up a warning hand.

'Royalton Radio.'

'Everything's personal here. Look, the government was going to open a domestic violence advice office on the main drag but it never got off the ground. Like anyone was going to walk in that door in broad daylight?'

Ray says, 'Royalton Radio'd be right onto it. Okay.'

Arshag shrugs. 'Not always a bad thing, a bush telegraph. Also useful to know what it's not talking about.'

'Like Diah and Alice.'

Arshag spreads his arms in agreement. 'Too scary?'

'They're treated like ancient cold cases,' Ray says. 'Beyond solving. Well, I don't think so.' He wipes away sweat from what is laughingly called autumn. 'Putting heat on Laming won't hurt. Let him know I'm on the job. Maybe he knows more than he's letting on.'

Ray collects Diah's folder from his desk in the office where everyone is in earshot of everyone else. He walks past Kennedy to Laming, hands him the single page with Barb's information added. 'You miss this?' And waits, standing.

Laming scans it, flicks it back at Ray. 'Bullshit. She can pull a fucking beer and that's it. You spoke to these three bozos?'

'For alibis.'

Laming shakes his head at Kennedy and leans back, looking at Ray. 'They got any?'

Ray shrugs.

Laming says, 'This you, big city detective on the case?' Ray slips the page back into the folder, and goes to his own desk, noting Kennedy's jaw working hard, saying nothing. Laming stamps out.

———

Day's end, a tired Ray enters the pub's main bar and falters to see Kennedy drinking alone at a table, summoning him with an open hand. Ray reluctantly walks over, stays standing. Kennedy leans back, beefy arms folded, face sweaty, waiting as Barb delivers a jug of beer and a glass for Ray and takes Kennedy's empty jug.

'Where the fuck've you been this arvo?'

'Redman's. A call from the wife. Unexplained discharge of firearms causing damage to a kitchen. No fatality or wounding. Warnings issued. No charges laid.'

'Redman's been shooting pigs, and his kitchen, for years. The only thing keeping his arse out of fucking jail for murder is his missus learned to shoot too. Wears her own gun, keeps him in check.' He laughs, it's genuine. Points at a chair.

'I noticed.' Ray sits.

'I reckon they fuck wearing their guns. Kill each other one day. Bush fucking justice.' His mouth shapes a grin, he pours beers but his eyes stay hard. Ray wonders, is this an offer of friendship? Kennedy the larrikin, full of bad behaviour but lovable if you dig deep enough? Needles you till you lose it, then grins, says, Can't you take a fucking joke?

If friendship were on offer, Ray knocks it back. 'I had another look at Petersens Dam, where Diah drowned.'

Kennedy puts down his glass, grabs the table with both hands. The sides of his mouth pull down in a deep grimace, his face whitening. Ray braces for glass, fists, or boots, and watches Kennedy's eyes flare, knuckles whiten. 'I know where she fucking drowned. Jesus, waste of fucking time.'

'I'm investigating the kid's rape.'

'Kid? Fuck me.' He has to stop, stares wide-eyed at the tabletop. Places his hands flat in the wet rings of condensation, swirls them around, spreading the water. Closes his eyes, breathes out noisily, wipes wet hands on his shirt. Lost in some distant place.

Ray says, 'Laming's notes don't say much.'

'That tell you anything? Nothing at the crime scene, no witnesses, etcetera, etcetera.'

'You gave me the cases, I'm doing them.'

'What are you doing? Tell me. Talking to people? Helped, has it? Fucking blow-in.'

Ray combines a wink with a wicked grin. 'Who're you calling a blow-in? I got rellies here. Haven't you heard?'

'You and Jimmy Rogers. Ace fucking match.' Kennedy splashes his glass half-full, drains it, slams down the glass and waves to the barmaid. 'Hey Barb, don't give this prick any more. He can't hold it.' His aggressive swagger is all back as he walks out.

Ray turns to Barb who shakes her head, eyebrows raised, mouth pursed, like she just saw a traffic accident near-miss. Then she surprises Ray by joining him, sitting where she can keep an eye on the other drinkers.

Ray says, 'Does he have any other life?'

'Not a lot. Not married. Lives with his mum.'

'Really?'

'More of a holy terror than him. She's in a wheelchair. Can get up but needs it to get around. She came with him when he was transferred from up north. Sits for hours every day on the back verandah, abuses any nurse silly enough to come, won't let them near her.'

'He tell you this?'

Barb laughs. 'I live nearby. For my sins. It gets better. She packs a gun.' Slaps her thigh.

A drinker holds his empty beer glass aloft and she gets him a refill. Ray watches, enjoys the economy of her movement, the understated style she brings to it.

She rejoins him. 'Yeah, the gun. Keeps it cleaner than herself.'

'Does she use it?'

'Her devoted son put a holster on the chair and she shoots at crows in the bush behind her place.'

Ray laughs. 'She ever go out?'

'He pays Elsie Clarkson up the road to take her shopping now and then. Least she leaves the gun at home. She yelled at me one day that the only way she'll ever leave the house is in a casket. So till then Kennedy's going nowhere either.'

Ray's face contorts into a misery mask, but for himself. Barb laughs.

———

The sun is a giant, orange fireball slipping in slow-motion to earth when Ray parks his bike at his door. As he kills the engine, he hears a distant roar which quickly becomes the bellicose, clattering engine of Lord Billy's four-seater plane. It swoops by and lands on the street, U-turns at an intersection, then trundles back to Ray's.

The noise draws out Dot, who pulls a funny hoity-toity face at Ray. 'Who'd you kill to score this? Whoops, better not say that to a copper.'

'Might slap the cuffs on you.' He laughs as her eyes light up in mischief.

'We tried that already.' Nods at the plane as the passenger door flops open. 'Maybe you're the son the poor bugger never had.'

Ray heads for the gate. 'See ya, Mum. Don't wait up.'

Ray clambers into the cramped cockpit. He buckles up beside William, who isn't buckled, and shouts hello. The engine noise peaks as they roll along the street, weaving slightly, giving new meaning to road signs before leaping into the air. Ray braces, on the lookout for electricity wires.

'Been in a small plane before?'

'Not this small.' He grins, both of them yelling. In front of him is half a steering wheel, a copy of William's.

William nods at it. 'When we get up higher, you have a go.'

He tilts his stick and the plane banks over the town. Ray stares down at a mess of dark, square and oblong shapes, the highway an impossibly straight black cable, trucks and cars tiny, slow-moving boxes. 'It all looks different.'

'Pilots out here used to navigate by watching the ground, following roads, telegraph poles, creeks. Whatever worked. I'd like to be buried up here. Scatter my ashes all over. Some would never land.'

Roads are narrow lines. Corrugated-iron roofs shine inside oases of green, dams are as blue as the sky, creeks are glittering ribbons. All glowing in end of day. The larger landscape looks empty but Ray has been here long enough to know there is no empty down there. Empty land is a delusion.

The wings shudder. Ray looks at lines of rivets on the plane's metal sheath, so frail. William lifts his hands from the controls and gestures for Ray to take over. Ray grips the stick as if his life depends on it, then laughs because it does. The whole plane thrums through his hands, up his arms, into his gut, his dick. He cautiously pushes the stick and the plane's nose dips. Pulls it gently back, the nose lifts. He whoops. William laughs and takes control again. Ray exhales for probably the first time since take-off.

William says, 'First time I saw it from up here, I wanted to protect it. Shape it, make it strong. Save it from itself.' A more passionate William but with rancour too. 'You're police, you know. Always some who're blind to the good you try to do. Can't comprehend a vision, an idea. What else can you do but roll over them?'

Ray hears the grim tone but the world outside is crowding his senses. No clouds, no way to gauge distance, and soon the sky is glowing red, the blazing sun feeling dangerously close.

William taps his temple and speaks as if coming from deep in his own thoughts. 'You have to think long term, a lifetime. Be strong yourself.' Taps his chest hard. 'But I can't do it alone.' A harshness pulls Ray's attention back.

He glances at William but can't read him. Why invite him out here? 'You already do so much.'

'Not enough. Not enough. I need help, you see. Everyone's got their part.'

'What's mine?'

'Being a good cop.'

Ray winks in support of that but is confused. Lets silence return and settle. He has no idea how long it's been when William points ahead. 'Home sweet home.' It takes Ray a moment to find a jumble of buildings below.

They circle, then William lands on the road to the house and taxis into a large open-sided metal shed. They climb out and he ties the plane down. 'Wind gusts. If it's not tied down it'll end up against the wall or blown away.'

The three-storey house is large and square. A tower-like structure rises above the main entrance topped by an incongruous widow's walk. Hundreds of miles from any ocean, though these plains once lay under an inland sea. On the lower two levels the house is circled by verandahs.

Ray points to a solitary round garden bed six or seven feet in diameter, greenery and flowers in shocking contrast with the brown plains. William's face collapses into what Ray reads as sadness. 'My wife. Her doing. You've heard I assume?'

Ray shakes his head.

'No?' William is clearly surprised. 'After ten years here, one day she upped and disappeared. Shot through, as they say. I thought we were happy. I pay good money to keep that oasis alive in her honour.' He strides towards the house, holding out a welcoming arm for Ray to follow.

William pours two generous whiskies as they sink into deep, canvas chairs on the verandah overlooking the garden bed. On their left, the sun shimmers as it slips from view at a horizon so remote, Ray thinks, it might as well be the edge of the earth, which of course it is. The light is softening.

William says, 'My favourite time of day. The light is vaguely soft enough to remind me of home.'

'You miss home?'

William laughs almost to himself. Waves his arms. 'No. Everything here's so—outsize? It fills me up.'

'You don't get lonely?'

'Everything is as it should be. And if it isn't, I make it so.' He laughs, so Ray does too.

Ray submits to the vista. It permeates his skin, deep into him. His mother grew up in this scale of things, then faced the dense closeness of semi-tropical Caneville, jammed with green high and low, water everywhere.

He and William face north but look west, nothing between

them and the glowing horizon but flatness. A massive, empty, still-radiant sky waits for the evening star. No building is in view this side of the house. Relentless brown plains roll on forever. He recalls Arshag's warning, those who swear they'll never stay but never leave. 'Can you see the curvature of the earth from the top verandah?'

William marks out an exaggerated arc in the air. 'I can see it from here.'

With the sun gone, desert evening chill moves up and around them like a prowler. Venus appears, splendid. More and more stars fill the emptiness with glowing points of light. Somewhere nearby, a generator kick-starts in a low drone. An electric lamp inside the house gleams through a coloured leadlight-glass window behind them, lighting their faces in blue, red and green.

'How long you been here?'

'Thirty plus years. Came in the forties, about your age. The delightfully understated Constable Arshag predates me as a local. Detective Kennedy has been here six years or so. Laming about ten.'

Ray quails inside. Years and years.

'How are you fitting in with them all?' William says.

'Only way to fit in with Detective Kennedy is don't try not to.' Big mouth, words out too fast.

William lifts bushy eyebrows. 'Those poor girls. Your cases now I hear?'

'Diah and Alice. Plodding along. Seems it isn't a priority.' Not sure he should say it but does anyway.

William sips his whisky. 'The invisible Inspector, how do you find him?' A disapproving tone.

Ray sits forwards. 'Rarely. Mostly absent. Mystery man.'

William's mouth sets hard till he speaks. 'Brisbane imposing this fellow on us remains an insult. Changed my views on a number of things.' Ray notes William's tone is sharper, there's intense feeling here. He waits for more but William sits up and clears his throat. 'You know I'm mayor of our bustling region?'

'Yep. Although I'm buggered if I know what a mayor does here.'

'Oh, very little, very little. Take petitions to state government about the region's needs. Once a month, I set up a folding table and chairs in the Masonic Hall and invite locals to tell me how they're doing. I help if I can. I know a little about who pulls the strings, who doles out the meagre funds, and I grease the wheels. A mayor can breach a minister's office but it's a whole other know-how to make them hear you. I'm part-time, unpaid, get a pittance for expenses and no one else wanted it. Aussies being odd about being the front man. You're ex-army, you'd know a volunteer's chosen by every other bugger stepping backwards.'

Ray smiles. 'Lord Billy of Royalton, right?'

William tilts his chin up, defensive. 'My wife used to joke about being a commoner. I called her Duchess. Didn't help.' They laugh but Ray again hears William's voice tighten, breath constricted.

'Was she a local?'

'No, another ring-in. We met at a governor's garden party in Brisbane. She was the pianist for the event, tinkling away, nobody listening. We got talking. She was a dreamer. Obviously all this was too much for her.'

William drums his fingernails on his glass in a clinking tattoo, looks to the sky. Ray feels the point of his invitation here is looming.

William says, 'We face extreme conditions out here, they're our normal. We need police we can trust. And our current senior officers are not, dear me, held in high regard.' He sits up. 'The Inspector arrived under a cloud that hasn't dispersed. Kennedy behaves like a despot. Or thug.' He looks away.

Ray sees William's hand holding his glass gently tremble. What's Kennedy done to him?

William says, 'Detective Laming I did respect, but he was lost the day Kennedy came.'

Ray hides his surprise. Laming?

William purses his lips. 'I do not wish to put you in a cleft stick over loyalty. It's the top that needs reform. No news to you, I'm sure.'

'The Inspector's under a cloud?'

'Dumped on us to evade scrutiny for corruption in Brisbane. An illegal casino. Imagine you could indulge yourself, build something worthwhile, what would you pick? Casinos? So here he is. Exiled to our Siberia till the dust settles, like a Russian novel. Well, the dust here never settles. He shows zero respect for us. Zero. Brisbane's a corrupt world, you're well out of it and we should be too. Corruption is a poison. Seeping out.' Shudders.

Ray glances at him. Not just the whisky talking.

'You've seen how well you're set up for a remote copshop? It was boosted as a sop to the Inspector. Biding his time till he goes back and takes up where he left off. Let Brisbane do to itself what it wants. But the contempt for us made me realise . . .' His voice fades.

He shakes his glass sharply, the ice tinkles. Shakes himself too, and the anger and dispirited demeanour vanish. His

energy is back. 'The good news, however, is this is an opportunity for you, should you choose to grab it.'

'Me? I never know what's going on. Slack for a detective.'
Tries for a smile, confused.

William is not to be distracted. 'This is politics. Different.
My point is, concerned people asked me to convey their
appreciation to you.' William lifts an open hand. 'They wish
to remain anonymous. But you are not alone, should events
turn against you.'

Ray is stumped. The generator completes a cycle and dies
with a whisper. He stares into the night as silence settles. Ray
can't hear another sound.

'I don't know what you want me to do.'

William looks irritated, perhaps with himself, then sighs
and pats him on the shoulder. 'Feel supported, that'll do. Feel
supported until the moment of test arrives. It always does.
You see . . .' He laughs nervously. 'I see you as a fellow seeker.'

He puts his hand on his heart and looks sharply at Ray.

'How to live! That's the question, hey? You think it's the
whisky talking.' He gives a self-conscious laugh, with a bleak
undertone. 'When official authority fails, the enlightened
have a duty to step up. We can make *this* a centre, around
Royalton, its own centre. Protect it. Save it.' He laughs, the
same trapped gurgle. 'Enough! Enough.' He stands, rubs his
hands together. 'Nice and chilly now. Let's dine, yes?'

He holds out both arms to embrace a moonless but spark-
ling sky, faces Ray with an uncomfortable expression. Ray
braces for another hand on his shoulder but William half-
smiles. 'Do you know how to spot a satellite? Pick it from a
meteor or falling star? I'll show you later. Come along.'

Ray follows him inside, startling himself with the thought
that he's already had two fathers, doesn't need another one.

Inside is almost cavernous, with high ceilings of pressed-metal patterns of roses and vines and Greek urns. Not that he's ever seen a Greek urn. The whisky is hitting. They pass through a room with what looks to Ray like a grand piano, its dark wood gleaming. On the piano is a photo of a youngish woman, head and bare shoulders in an ornate silver frame. She is dark-haired, wide-eyed, with a warm, playful, beguiling smile.

William says, 'The former lady of the house.'

'What a smile.'

William walks on. 'She gave it to everyone.'

They sit at one end of a ten-seater table of heavy dark wood, its legs ornately carved like, yes, miniature Greek columns. Roast lamb and vegetables, served, unnervingly for Ray, by a buxom woman in her mid-thirties, solidly built. Her long blonde hair is curled and pinned in a kind of tower on her head, with something like a lace tiara pinned across her forehead. She wears a dark, short, tight skirt, dark stockings and high heels. A very white long-sleeved top is cut low to expose copious cleavage. The intended effect appears to be that of a formal maid with sexiness bursting out all over. Does William offer this show for all his guests? Christ, hope he doesn't offer her.

She seems aware of her own performance, brazen but avoiding eye-contact, practised. Ray stares at his plate. William is offhand. 'Shirl is my live-in housekeeper. Wonderful cook.' Shirl does a limited curtsy, eyes downcast, thick make-up masking any expression. The food is good.

Late that night, lying in a large iron bed upstairs, Ray watches the revolving sky through open French windows. Hears the grunts of sex elsewhere in the vast house.

Breakfast is stilted, William is terse, preoccupied with some property issue to fix after returning Ray to Royalton. They speak little during the flight. William doesn't elaborate on what Ray's opportunity might be. Ray doesn't ask. The plane lands near the railway station and they part with formal jollity.

8

It's the start of what's called winter. Heat of the day is still virulent, even more parching, but the nights are freezing cold. Leaves stay on most of the trees. Eucalypts lose their bark instead, decorticating. As a kid in the bush, Ray loved to stamp on the stiff, fallen bark so it crackled underfoot, saying over and over in step, *De-cor-ti-ca-ting, de-cor-ti-ca-ting*, enjoying its sound.

He stands inside a long, corrugated-iron shed once used for repairing furniture. Windows along its sides are broken and massed cobwebs hang in sheets like lacy hammocks from high, exposed rafters. Royalton's first boxing gym is being born. The space gets as hot as the Hobs of Hell so an old tea urn has been filled with water and plastered with hand-painted warnings to stay hydrated. Wooden fence posts cemented into holes drilled in the old, undulating concrete floor and slung with scrounged ropes turn into two improvised boxing rings. The bells are hubcaps, provided by Arshag, hit with tyre levers. Heavy punching bags are made of long, ex-army canvas kitbags hanging from the rafters, stuffed with stamped-down, old clothes and the odd brick.

Arshag enters amid the dust and buzz of a working bee. 'Heard you're having a fundraiser? Exhibition bouts? Really?'

'Lord Billy's idea, not mine. All in fun.'

Arshag laughs. 'Locals get to hit you for free? Free belts on a copper? Sure.'

Ray has declared the club is for boys and girls, and adults can come for basic gym workouts. On sign-up day, he arrives at the warehouse early to find a sprawling, squirming line of kids waiting with a few parents. He sits at an old school desk and records details in an exercise book. Excitement and energy are in the air though some are disappointed he can't train them as ninjas.

He lines up a baker's dozen, aged eight to sixteen, nine boys, four girls, gets them shaping up, orthodox or southpaw. Tells them to check each other's stance, which they do as if they've been boxing all their lives. Shows them what 'Keep your guard up!' means, which he repeats a lot. Works along the sometimes too-spirited pairs, demonstrating how defence works, and how it doesn't. They love how he can tap or tickle their noses so fast they hardly see him do it. Gets them chanting over and over, 'Straight left! Right cross! Left hook!' as they throw the stock punches, southpaws contrary as ever. They love the rhythms and thrash their worst, invisible enemies.

To Ray's delight, Lord Billy appears with a free towel for each member, then enjoys offering tips here and there on stance and footwork. Word is spreading.

Ray quickly spots a favourite. Cassie is a hyperactive four-teen year old, bright-eyed, rangy but strong like a whip. Olive complexion and straight black hair worn short. A natural, she fights boys too, against the rules. Ray tries to stop her but she is so quick no one can hit her anyway.

In a rare, quiet one-on-one with Ray, she reveals her old man is a Scot and a drunk. Some years ago, he started beating her mum, so her mum left him, and Cassie. No word since. Ray can tell she is still waiting for her and wouldn't be caught dead admitting it.

If it wasn't for food and other help from her uncle, life would be a lot harder. Ray realises he's met her uncle on his runs, the big wild-man yelling 'Shud up!' at the big black dog on the tray of his old ute. So, Shuddup is Cassie's Uncle Don. Cassie wants to be in the Olympics doing whatever she ends up best at. Taking on the world.

Stella explains later that she teaches Cassie. 'Her mum left before Cassie could learn about her family. All she knows is she's descended from an Afghan camel-driver from further west. Her Afghan name is Homa but her father hates it so now she's Cassie.'

'What about Uncle Shuddup? He'd pass for Afghan. Or Armenian.'

Stella smiles. 'Nah. He'd scrub up white if he ever had a bath.'

'Is he really her uncle?'

'Sure. Her dad's brother. Better class of Scot. More to him than meets the eye.'

'I've met Mongrel. You knew her mum?'

'Pardida. Very briefly. Where Cassie gets her strength.'

'She ever coming back?'

'Cassie hasn't given up so I won't either.'

'Does she want to be called Homa?'

'Hasn't worked it out yet.'

Two weeks later, William joins Ray watching the line of flailing punchers. 'You better work up to a tournament or they'll explode. Weight divisions, champions, whole kit and caboodle,' William says.

Ray pales.

William pats his arm. 'The exhibition bouts are a good start. Let a few locals test you out. Wallop your local walloper, as they might say.' He laughs as Ray's face expresses pain.

———

Exhibition day is on a Saturday morning at the gym, set up like a fete. Ray is braced to spend the day being everywhere, doing everything, but finds it fully volunteered and lively. Stella is helping too but refuses to stay to see Ray thumped.

Col, a teacher colleague of Stella's, sells sizzling sausages between slices of bread, cooked on a steel plate over a fire in a rusty, halved kerosene tin. Trestle tables display home-made biscuits and cakes, plastic and metal jewellery, knitted beanies and scarves, trash-or-treasure arrays of old tools, bits of machinery, odd crockery, wooden toys and breadboards, even pet rocks. Two mothers offer boxing singlets hand-embroidered with *Royalton Boxing Gym*. Ray is moved by it all.

William walks up and down banging a tyre lever on a hubcap, announcing the bouts with an affected snarl. Excitement rules. Everyone crowds around one boxing ring. Ray, striving for eagerness, emerges in shiny, red satin shorts and his own, gifted, embroidered singlet, gloved up. He climbs through the ropes to whistles and applause, embarrassed even as he feels the familiar thrill of coming combat. Warning himself to stay well inside the limit of an exhibition.

He keeps moving as William lines up opponents. Arshag is time-keeper and bell-ringer. Ray tells himself it's all in fun, which becomes harder to believe when he sees Laming and Kennedy. He's braced for them to challenge but they don't, and he's suddenly disappointed.

Six hopefuls line up, including Peter. His cheer squad of Paul and Mario are punching and ducking and weaving, trying to dance like Ali. Ray recalls fights behind the Caneville pub when he was eighteen, doing his sparky apprenticeship. Bare-knuckle, bloody events. Mostly his rash, often drunk opponents did the bleeding but sometimes he did too. Matches often turned dirty. He learnt the tricks. Then one night, the local copper took him to the Caneville copshop, walked him into a cell and slammed the door. Told him this was his future. Or fucking hospital, come out a cripple or brain-dead. 'Reckon you can fight? Get in the ring. Get some fucking class instead of trash behind the pub.'

Ray is unsurprised to see Peter push to the front, driven by some engine of anger. Mother's fucking milk, that. Ray often sees him, Paul and Mario around town or on the road. They're avoiding him. He's making sure they know he's watching. Finding useful clues about Diah is unlikely, so he needs one of them to open up. Pick one and isolate him. Alice is on his mind too as time runs on, sand through his fingers. Looking like he's doing nothing.

William does stilted pre-fight patter for Ray and each challenger, charging it all with mock fight-night energy. The gym kids are wide-eyed. One three-minute round each. *Only three?* say the uninformed. He can't see Stella. She said she'd want to kill anyone who hit him. He laughed, reassured her it was in fun, but she said no.

The first bout clangs into life. Peter is first, roaring across the ring, head down, an angry bull, swinging but hitting air. Ray pops up inside his thrashing arms and even beside him to tap him on his nose, then is gone again. Peter's rage soars, his swings grow wilder and worse. He ends the round sagging and panting, his frustration ready to turn mean. Ray sees him stalk off, shoulders tight, his mates offering bogus consolation.

One challenger, Wayne, whirls his arms, a windmill in a cyclone. Ray is delighted he's turned up, knows his father gives him a hard time. Another challenger dances like Ali till Ray hits him. The next clowns about, keeping a safe distance, playing to the crowd, no eye contact with Ray and precious little other contact either. Ray enjoys confusing him with feint after feint, till humiliation becomes too apparent. The man quits amid friendly howls from the crowd.

The fourth, Ray belatedly realises, is Benny, trying to pose as a bold fighter, mouth set, hitting one glove into the other, but fear showing through despite raucous taunts from Peter, Paul and Mario. As Ray approaches, Benny throws out punches too early then futilely tries to cover his face and body with the gloves, scarcely punching at all. Ray feels bad hitting him. After an eternity, the bell goes and Benny strides back to his corner, flexing like a champion.

The last, like Peter, arrives angry, is furious when he misses, astonished when he's hit. The crowd happily cheer and boo every challenger and every blow, successful or foiled. Ray's easy superiority shows. He even enjoys it.

In mock betting around the ring, Kennedy raucously backs every challenger. Laming stays at the back, arms folded tight, rocking on his heels. Ray sees William exchange brusque nods with Laming and Kennedy, followed by an intense, deadpan stare between the two detectives that to Ray carries the same venom he saw on his first day in town; but perhaps he imagined it. Shuddup lets Cassie demonstrate finer points. Ray is grateful he didn't challenge. No sign of the Inspector. Louise and Kaye drop in between calls away. Kaye cheers everyone loudly. Constable Baxter, as usual, prefers to monitor communications at the copshop.

The day is a success. Masses of sausages sizzled, many items sold, another six recruits and ninety-two dollars for the gym's kitty. William announces he will match that, which earns a cheer. More small donations drop into an old felt hat passing through the crowd. Ray declares he'll invest the lot in gear and is clapped extra loudly when he says a large box of gloves from Brisbane is arriving soon. Gloves had been too expensive for most, and Ray has been improvising cloth-wraps. The gift was meant to be anonymous but William is outed as the culprit.

The event peters out. Arshag is called away, Kennedy and Laming vanish. Ray enjoys a drink with William who elaborates on his lineage. At his birth in Portsmouth, he became the eleventh Baron of Twyford but on his twentieth birthday, appalled his family by abandoning his estate and duties to seek a freer life around the world, finally settling among barbaric Australians. He travels mostly alone by private plane, even for grocery shopping all of three hundred miles and more east in Brisbane. Bypassing local shops infuriates some but William sloughs off all that.

He is adopting the gym and can help defray costs. He can occasionally come to watch training and maybe recall enough from his own distant experience not to make a fool of himself.

William shapes up at him. 'Seeing you in there, you're good. Why did you quit?'

'Not good enough. You have to be so good to be any good at all.'

'What do you get out of it?'

Ray laughs. 'I can hit people legally. It helps.' He feels William looking at him, assessing what gets helped.

Ray knows his sheer pleasure in fighting is clear. Does it show in his eyes? The eyes of his opponents get a faraway, wide-eyed look when they know they've lost. What does the savage joy of winning look like? Is the look there all the time? Is it why some fights are lost or won before a punch is thrown. Is it there now?

William says, 'Have you thought any more about what I said?' He's fidgeting, unlacing gloves. 'Fact is, I need an offsider, someone across the bigger picture.' He stops, stuck, irritated at the struggle to find the words. 'I have a vision for this place. This whole place. I want to shape it, you see? Give it a future, save Royalton from itself.' Tries to laugh a little. 'Repeating myself.'

'Like here, helping me?'

William is intense, managing to be hard-edged but vulnerable. 'Unlike here, trying to help isn't always welcome, as any cop knows. You know what's needed, they don't.'

Ray sees agitation and passion as William points at the air, struggling for words. 'I want to be able to rely on the police. And unlike some others, you have authority, don't deny it. Obvious everywhere today! You'd be a huge help. Unofficially. Nothing can be official if the official authority's corrupt.' A rush of anger reddening his face forces him to stop again. 'The right people have to take responsibility. Grab power and use it.'

Ray half-laughs, doubtful. 'Not vigilantes?'

William waves urgently, then pauses and abruptly smiles, confident again. 'The law's a blunt instrument. Every keeper of the law learns that. Hard cases need wisdom to win the right result. The letter of the law is for simple minds, simple cases, not real life. A true keeper of the law needs their own internal compass.' Ray stays composed against the strong flow of words. Thinks of the copper who shoved him into that cell.

William nods at the ring, the gear. 'You've got it and people respect it.' Ray sees William stare at the gloves, restrain himself. 'This place, you know, the whole region, it's worth the fight, isn't it?'

Ray nods. 'Yeah. It's beautiful here.' And means it. At least they share this.

'A kind of purity is possible. And necessary, to beat corruption.' William slaps his thigh and erupts into a higher-pitched laugh than usual. 'Next I'll be saying you have to be cruel to be kind. I'm on my hobby horse now.' Points at their empty stubbies. 'It's this blasted beer. Paint stripper, I call it.' Claps Ray's shoulder. 'Damned if I talk like this with anyone else on the planet.'

Ray hears an abrasive edge in William's voice, sees resolve in the set of his mouth, but hardness is often brittle too. Deep frustration is working in this man, pain mixed with his love for this place.

And it's not as if Ray doesn't know about creeping corruption spreading like a fucking disease.

They sit in silence till Ray winks. 'You are an old-style lord of the manor. Here in an Australian desert.'

William laughs, pleased, restored. Drops the gloves and laces back in their box. 'See, that old feudalism's not all bad. For the right lord, the right attitudes.' He stands, squeezes Ray's shoulder. 'We'll have dinner again soon. Talk all about the lord of the manor, and his samurai. Every lord needs a samurai.'

'Ninjas too?' Ray laughs.

William tries a smile but a flash in his eyes marks flippancy as unwelcome. 'Good-o. Well, great day but a dust storm's coming, tricky for a plane I can tell you. Think about it.' He marches off.

Ray silently asks the boxing ring, was that a job offer? Keeper of the law for the lord of the manor? As a samurai, knight of the round table? Or has the baron of Royalton had too much sun? No wonder people tease silly Billy, Lord Billy. Maybe loving the place is making him crazy. Deserts do that.

Ray arrives home, sore but not sorry. Dot is tenderly weaving new growth of the Banksia rose plants along the fence.

He grins. 'Lucky you're not the obsessive type.'

She steps back, proud. 'Like basket-weaving we did at school. Sticking out my tongue helps.' She brandishes a watering can. 'Checked you out at your gym today. Put a quid in the hat. You've got a hell of a left hook, if that's what you call it. This idea of yours'll work.'

He laughs. 'If that enthusiasm lasts.'

'Reckon it will.' She winks. 'And perfect timing, a mini-show's coming to town. Got a boxing tent, right up your alley.' She shadow-boxes with the watering can and grins.

He shudders. 'Shit no. They're a bloody racket.'

'I'd come to watch. Stir my old blood. Your Stella came by.'

Ray checks his watch, pulls a face. 'I got held up.'

'Said to tell you dinner's on at her place.' She winks.

'Guess I could get used to this.'

'The general idea. Hubba-hubba.'

He laughs but some tiny bell tinkles inside him.

—

The pub is dark and cool. The door and windows facing the street glow white and gold from the glittering heat and glare outside. A TV in one corner runs horse races for one glum drinker. Ray and Jimmy stand at a bench as Burt brings beer. A shared lift of glasses, the mandatory, ruminative sip.

Jimmy says, 'Barb heard Kennedy here the other day badmouthing you. You're getting up his nose, nice one. Thought he'd steamroll you like everyone else.'

Burt holds out huge arms. 'I'd like to steamroll Laming. Sit on the pipsqueak and fart.'

Ray drags his thoughts away from the image. 'Early days. That what you wanted to tell me?'

'Wanted to tell you about the fucking vulture who now owns the Rogers family property. *Our* place.' Gesturing to include Ray. 'Ian Taylor. Fucking vulture. He owns a few properties now.'

Burt says, 'Too bloody many.'

Jimmy says, 'Sucks them into his empire when others fail. Don't know how he does it. I was making no money and I don't see how he is either but he keeps getting bigger. Turning into a fucking tycoon. Big as that Lord Billy bastard, the way he's going.'

'Where's Taylor live?'

'East, alongside mine. What was mine. Fucking levitating on a magic carpet above a debt swamp that drowned me. How?'

'Shitty. Cashing in on people's troubles,' Ray says, and means it. Remembers Bill's fists, tight mouth and bottomless rage when he thought the cane farm was lost. Sees Jimmy appreciating that he gets it but feels a tingle of warning, something coming.

Jimmy says, 'There's more. Except as a fucking cop, you'll say I got no proof.' He's defiant, his jaw setting the way Ray saw on the train.

'Try me.'

They drink, Jimmy gathers himself. 'Down the bottom of my property that isn't mine anymore—or yours, right?— this road runs onto my place near the south-east corner.' He draws in the air. 'Runs along inside my border there across to my western edge, then out the south-west corner, to Taylor's.' He has to stop, breathes hard, drinks.

'Where's this road come from?'

'Down from the highway, doesn't matter. What matters, it's handy for Taylor to get to his place. We never minded him using it. Good fucking neighbours.'

Burt says, 'Long as the prick closes the gate.'

'Long way round for him but handy in the wet cos he's got black clay. Anyway, one night I hear trucks. Hard telling where the noise's from. Highway's up the front of my place, north side, and noise carries all over.' Jimmy stretches both arms to indicate vast spaces. 'But these're sounding like they're on my bloody road.'

Burt says, 'Ground down there's hard as iron, leaves no mark.'

'I'm hearing trucks, over several nights, okay? One night, can't sleep, sick of it, I go down the back. Two trucks coming through, towards Taylor's. Load of fucking cattle. Bit of a fucking giveaway. Next day, I front up, ask him, whose are they? He says fuck off, they're his, bought them off Ed Thomasen.'

Burt grunts. 'Should've locked that gate, kept him off your road.'

'Well, that'd be bastardry, Faulkners use the road too. I say I saw the cattle, reckon it looked and smelt like a duffer's load, I'm going to the cops. That cattle was some poor bastard's life's savings. He laughs! Go for it, he says, I bought them fair and square. But I can tell he's not happy. At all.'

'And you know he didn't—buy them fair and square?'

'I saw Ed Thomasen at a sale at Tyborg a month earlier. Just that day he sold the last of his stock, Ed rethinking his whole future. Had no fucking stock left to sell anyone. I front up to Kennedy. He hears me out, says, You done now? Like I'm boring him. I stamp out and Laming's at my ute writing tickets for busted tail-lights and bald tyres. See? Get it? I thump him, of course, but fuck. Can't win that shit. That started Kennedy coming after Burt and me for fucking breathing. Then I start to notice my stock's getting nicked too. Not a lot, enough to notice when I pay attention, eh. My place's going down the gurgler anyway, debts I can't pay. So, cut a long shitty story short, now he's got my place. Thank fucking god my dad and mum are dead, eh? Don't even mention my grandparents.' He winks, without humour. 'Yours too. And your bloody uncle and aunt.'

Burt laughs, pointing at Ray too. 'Who fucking knew?'

Ray looks mock-horrified, he hopes. Says to Burt, 'Shit, I'm not related to you too, am I?'

'No one's related to me. Fucking safe this time, copper.' It's a joke but Ray hears an echo of sadness there.

'What's your story, Burt?' Ray says.

Jimmy punches Burt on his arm. 'Yeah, arsehole, what's your story? Hanging round like a bad smell.'

Burt directs a thumb at Jimmy. 'His mum found me in a basket on their doorstep one day—'

'Like fucking Moses.' Jimmy laughs.

'—and they figured if they fed me up, I could keep this walking, talking disaster here out of jail. I do my best but jeez it's a shithouse deal.'

Jimmy nods. 'His mum and dad didn't want him and I'm bloody stuck with him.'

He and Burt launch into a well-worn routine of punching and wrestling each other, laughing. Burt drains his glass, Jimmy's is empty. Ray waves away more as Burt returns to the bar.

Jimmy says, 'Taylor. What're you going to do about it?'

'Take a closer look. I'll let you know.'

'That the best you can do?'

'I'll have a look. Let me do my job, okay?' He means it but winks to soften it as Burt brings a new jug, does the honours. Ray puts his hand over his glass but Burt pours beer over it anyway and Ray gives up. 'So what're you two doing? You swaggies now?'

Jimmy lifts empty hands. 'Maybe gas and oil drilling up north? Might be oil in the top east of Lord Billy's. The rich get bloody richer, eh?'

'If you promise to quit picking fights I can put in a word for you with him.'

'Quit fighting? Fuck, why?'

Jimmy and Burt start wrestling again and Ray rolls his eyes in mock despair.

Jimmy shrugs. 'Fuck the Pom. I went to him at the Masonic Hall, him at his little desk, and asked for help. Nothing. Failed some secret test.'

Ray walks home, thinking about that back road on Jimmy's place. His lost place, his mum's place. 'My mum's place.' Says it aloud to test it. Owning land, how would it feel? He'd never expected any share of the cane farm—Bill and Virginia had their own son. But owning land then losing it? Putting a hole in Jimmy's soul.

—

Ray stands at the edge of the paddock next to the railway station, watching a boxing tent setting up, and six stalls for food and games. He's not pleased to see it. The annual circuit of omnibus, travelling shows enlivening country towns is faltering. Not delivering the returns it once did. End of an era, if true. Big ones breaking into smaller. He doesn't know the name on the boxing tent. Thinks no more about it till William phones, suggesting Ray challenge a tent fighter. 'Good publicity for the gym.'

Ray pulls a face. 'The gym doesn't need publicity. How big's it supposed to get? And I'll get my arse kicked. You know how these show-tents work?'

'You can out-box a brawler without raising a sweat.'

Ray smiles. Bloody Billy just wants to see a punch-up. Imagine that.

Later at the gym, Cassie and other kids come to watch his own training session and make the same suggestion. Sure, they saw Ray in the exhibition bouts but that was for fun. Be great to see him in a proper fight.

'Boxing tents don't have proper fights. They're rigged so the tent fighters win.'

'You'll beat them. We want to see you really box.' Ardent, even misinformed, requests from kids carry mysterious weight.

113

'They won't let you in. It's illegal,' says Ray.

They cheer.

———

Ray stands on the sawdust-covered grass in the ring of the boxing tent. The word is out, a crowd of locals is there, calling his name, offering free advice. Ray eyes his opponent, unsurprised to see a scarred, humourless man with dead eyes. What the Yanks call a slugger. No boxer with hopes wants to be just a slugger. The rigid shell of his opponent's face and body renders him ageless. Tattoo, ex-army. Jesus, whose bloody idea was this?

Stella is here, wide-eyed. She felt silly missing the exhibition bouts, afraid they'd be blood-soaked, then so many people said what fun they were. Hardly any blood. So she feels safe today. He'd told her it was likely to be blood-soaked this time, but no, she wants to support him. He breathes deeply, trying not to notice a quivering in his arms. Too long since he did this.

The bout begins as it continues—bitter, crude and punishing. His opponent knows it all: illegal hits, swinging elbows, head-butting, maybe something coarse on the glove he scrapes across Ray's face. Ray fights to hold his temper but the urge to hurt this bastard surges and he flares with wild punches. The crowd gets it as Ray ferociously delivers and takes thudding abuse beyond anything he's done for years. Chants of 'Blood! Blood!' turn into 'Kill! Kill!' amid splattering blood, loud whooping laughter and pushing and shoving, feeding energy to the boxers till an infinity later a bell clangs and it's over.

Ray makes it to his corner, stands, leaning back on the post and ropes, full of the rush, the smell of blood and sawdust. He sees awed faces, Kennedy's and Laming's too, his violence a revelation. Why the fuck not? Revelation to him often enough. What do they know about him anyway? Fucking nothing. How he likes it, defiant, even as adrenaline seeps away, pain leaching in to replace it.

Both fighters weave with exhaustion but are upright and shaking as the kill fever rushes through their bodies. Ray looks through a swelling eye, savouring that at least he forced emotion from his adversary. Jesus, his punches hit like bricks. Probably some inside his gloves. He looks around the charged crowd. No Stella.

The tent judge declares the tent fighter the winner. The crowd yells, aggressive, rolling boos. All part of the show. On to the next bout, a new challenger.

Ray stumbles into dazzling sun and finds Jimmy and Burt. As he evades their thumps on his shoulders, Jimmy swears Ray won and fuck the judge. Ray shrugs that off, over it.

Jimmy bristles as Kennedy, Laming and a man Ray doesn't know walk by. Jimmy looks ready to attack all three, but Burt casually wraps a friendly arm around Jimmy's shoulder, using his heft to hold Jimmy back.

Ray sees through a red tinge that Kennedy is subdued, evading eye contact. Rethinking Ray as threat? That'd be fucking good. Even so, Kennedy snorts at Ray, enjoying eyeing his wounds. 'You lost, you weak prick. What are ya!'

He looks for approval from the third man, who doesn't respond, only licks his lips, nods, nervous, and speeds up to pass. Laming hovers then peels off, leaves. Kennedy hesitates then struts after the other man. Jimmy shrugs Burt off, holds up empty hands to concede.

Ray says, 'Who's the other bloke?' Thinking, *Taylor. Ian Tayor, for sure.*

Jimmy's mouth works as he struggles to speak. Burt opens his mouth to speak for him but Jimmy raises an urgent hand and Burt shuts up.

'Taylor. You might've heard me mention the prick.' Jimmy's lip curls. He shakes all over like a dog. 'We're going to the pub. You coming?'

Cassie and other gym kids crowd in, all talking at once, full of how Ray really won, re-enacting his best punches. He grins though it hurts. 'How'd you get to see it? You mob aren't allowed in there.'

Cassie says, 'Pulled up the flap on the side, snuck in. No worries.'

Ray laughs. Some things never change. He nods to Jimmy. 'Talking to my fan club here.'

Ray's opponent emerges from the tent in a worn, blue satin robe, bass drum on a strap over one shoulder, and starts beating out a relentless, two-hit rhythm. He stares in Ray's direction but, Ray thinks, sees nothing.

Jimmy nods at the man, says to Ray, 'You ought to work for these bastards.' It's meant as a compliment.

9

At his flat, Ray sits at his table as a distressed Stella checks his swollen eye and welts, cuts, bruises. He advises on the repairs, mocking himself, mug enough to fight there at all.

Her thoughts are clear. 'I'll never come to see you fight again.'

'Tent fights are the worst. No art to it. It's brawling, not boxing.'

'Art?'

He sees what may be tears in her eyes.

'I don't know who you were in there. Never seen him before. Or again, hopefully. Crowd's chanting "Kill! Kill!" and you, ready to do it! Why in god's name do you do it?'

'There's no god I know of.'

'You know what I mean!'

Rowena, a woman he liked a lot in Brisbane, asked him this too but took the next step: quit or she was gone. Off she went. Too sore now to sugar-coat it. 'I like fighting. And I'm good at it. Aren't I supposed to find what I'm good at and go for it? Be true to the real me?'

'Why do you like it?'

'Boxing's an art. With special skills.'

'How to hit and hurt people.'

'It's the way you do it. Tent fighting's not boxing! I was stupid, showing off, serves me right.'

She sits opposite him, puts down the bloody cottonwool, her mouth a thin line. 'You couldn't wait to get stuck into him. I could see it. I don't care if boxing's something special. You knew it'd be a brawl. You wanted it.'

Ray is silenced.

She leans back in the chair, pushes the cotton wool away. 'Have you ever really hurt anyone?'

'Not that I know of.'

'A lawyer's answer. You going to keep doing it? I don't mean just tent fighting.'

'Boxing? I'm too old and not good enough.' Spits that out with more anger than he expected. 'You think I'm bad to teach it to the kids?'

'Not with how you talk to them about it.' She looks at her own hands, makes fists, opens them. 'I'm talking about you. You ever look at me with the face you had in there, I'm gone.'

He sighs. If he ever did, she'd be better off gone.

'I still don't know why you like it.'

He lifts weary arms in defeat. No words. Knows this road.

The sounds of sex start above them.

'Not the sounds of silence,' Stella says, pouting.

They set up a bed-pounding rhythm themselves, despite his wounds. Ray thinks they have the same pace as his former opponent drumming outside the boxing tent.

Afterwards, they lie in bed, Ray propped on pillows. He recounts first meeting cousin Jimmy, in a fight, and she rolls her eyes. 'Kaye's got her bulldog teeth into your family, cousins and all. Your bad dad sneaking off with your bad mum, a scandal goldmine.'

'I don't want to answer her questions.'

'Make stuff up. Didn't you say one time that's what cops do? Okay, some cops, not you.' Offers a wicked pout.

He changes the subject. 'Lord Billy's story is pretty amazing.'

She lifts her eyebrows at the blatant segue but lets it go. 'You know he's a fraud? Lord of the Lies.'

Ray straightens too fast, which hurts. 'What?'

'Calm down, copper. Nothing illegal, I don't think. I got students to do a project on histories of locals. Even got Kaye in to do a talk, which she loved, surprise, surprise. A couple of kids picked Lord Billy, wrote to England. It's all rubbish.' She ticks off points on her fingers. 'His supposedly illustrious ancestor came from Manchester, not down near Southampton. Only became a peer of the realm after World War One. But our William reckons he's, what, the eleventh baron? Since the 1920s? Bit quick. Maybe he poisoned a lot of them to speed things up. Don't look so shocked!'

'Who knows about this?'

'Everyone, I guess.'

'Does he know everyone knows?

'Who knows what Lord Billy knows? He knows we call him Lord Billy.' She laughs. 'Live and let live. He wants to tell us a fairytale, no worries. Sad about his wife, though.'

'He called her a dreamer.'

'I hear she played piano at a school concert one year. Someone said there was something fragile about her, like precious, thin pottery always on show. Not someone I imagine getting by easily out here.'

'Locals've voted him mayor how many times?'

'Yeah, we like having a lord. So leave the poor bugger alone.'

Ray notes the *we* but lets it go, laughs instead. 'Where's his money from if it's not his inheritance?'

'He talks about Africa. Maybe he robbed African banks.' They laugh. 'Too polite, I reckon.' Points her hand as a gun at Ray. 'Can't you see him? *Excuse me, sir, I've brought along this bag and I'd rather like you to fill it with money. Please? By the hair of your chinny-chin-chin.*'

Stella leaves at dusk for her a capella group. He switches his radio on, a talk-show, turns it down to background drone so he can't make out what's being said. Pulls a six-pack from the fridge, sits at the table to work through it. Shares jokes with the wall, whether grog stops numbness and pain or brings it on. Angry again that he took on the tent fight. Stella is right. It was a freebie he couldn't pass up. This lean into violence is his own doing. Can't blame his father or mother. Well, not for the physical kind. They had a grip on other kinds.

Unsure if he's asleep or awake, he sees himself, all of eleven, in their Caneville house, peering out through the back flyscreen door into the gloomy dusk, mesh against his nose. Smells its acrid dust as his parents circle each other out there on the deck, yelling for the whole street to hear, punctuated by flat barks from Ginger, their ancient, agitated, blue cattle-dog lumbering upstairs from the yard.

Ray knew the ritual. Whatever sparked the hate and rage was long lost, if he even ever knew—lost in attack and counter-attack, stuck in a familiar, degrading path as fixed as ruts in a dried mud road. This night was as bellicose as ever—the noise and strutting and gesticulating—but with something extra in his father's fists and advances on his mother. It stirred Ray to go out to protect her, standing small between them, facing his father whom he loved but who frightened him with those eyes hard as metal.

Ginger, bewildered, circled, barking, barking, eternally barking. Both parents drunk, usual for his mother, not his father. Ray gaped at his father's eyes, burning in a face so twisted it was hardly his father's at all. Then, moments seared into Ray's brain as this balding, slight, trembling stranger came at him, fist and arm rising, maybe to hit him, who knew, when a thud and cry behind Ray revealed his mother fallen backwards, spread-eagled deep into a deck chair, its weathered canvas ripped, tangled in it, jammed.

Her mouth half-covered, voice muffled, shrieking, 'Ray, help me!' Her laughter raucous as she twisted and called to the darkening world, 'The road to hell is paid with good intentions.' Ray sensed it was a peace offering, a pantomime, a chance to quit the raging.

But his father scrunched into himself, and spat out with bottomless anger, 'Jesus Christ!' He lashed such a hopeless kick at Ginger that even the old dog dodged it. 'Shut up, Ginger! Shut up!'

Ginger crawled off in retreat, still barking, then in confusion shuffled back, barking and barking. Ray's father, spittle on cheeks and shirt, turned to kick again at the cringing dog but stumbled over it, fell from the momentum of the kick, and crashed down the stairs, tumbling with a dreadful crying out, thumping on every step till he hit the concrete path. Ray, at the top of the stairs, heard the crunch as Ginger slunk by to slump on his blankets, silent at last.

Ray recalls his terror, swamped by a menacing, abnormal nothingness, a void. Staring all around to find the edges of the sudden stillness, to make it visible so he could escape it. Daring a sidelong peek down at his father's inert body, then at his mother as she tore the canvas and writhed to extricate herself, weeping or laughing viciously at some secret absurdity, nursing bruised arms and shoulders. Then, upright at last, stamping her foot, still unaware.

Ginger barked and she turned on him. 'Shut up! Shut up! Shut up!' till the dog jammed its nose into its blankets. Ray recalls his mother halting, sensing absence, face collapsing in on itself, lurching to the top of the stairs, leaning on Ray to breathe, then whimpering at the crumpled body below. She might have fallen too had Ray not hauled her back, wrestling her lumpy weight. He recalls a brackish mix of perfume, alcohol, sweat, can still see himself drape her on the railing and sidle down the stairs, not looking directly at the body. 'Dad? Dad?'

Noel and Beryl from next door appeared in the yard. Noel ran to the body. Beryl grabbed Ray in a suffocating embrace, her apron a cloud of flour. Ray's mother peered over the railing, only half her face visible. 'I didn't mean to get it wrong. We do our best, Ray, my baby.'

Ray rocking stiffly, face in Beryl's apron, flour caking his tears. Noel standing up, face saying it all, body cringing away from the dead man. Ray understood then. No idea when his mum understood. He and she kept Ginger, who only lived a few months more. Then his mother died too, in her maybe not-so-accidental accident. As the cops never came right out and said.

———

Next day, Ray again feels numbness that may or may not be grog-induced. He patrols alone over uncompromising country. In a kind of daze, approaching a bridge over a creek overflow, its bed dry as a bone, he feels himself drawn, definitely drawn, to one of the bridge's thick, concrete pillars, the vehicle starting to veer. He gives a guttural animal moan, resounding in the closed cabin, full of shock. He wrenches the Land Rover straight, crosses the bridge and pulls over on flat orange clay, panting for breath. His mother drove full throttle at a rock wall but instead T-boned another car passing by. Killed herself, and a mother and child in the other car. Ray shivers. Maybe he did it as a test, see how close you can get and still pull back. He looks out at emptiness matching his own. Torpor beyond heat and grog.

Late that afternoon, as the falling sun offers a little relief, Ray heads out to run, carrying water. Counting the days of Jimmy's shift. Ten days on, then ten off when they can visit his mum's place.

At the last house on a street he slows where the road narrows to head west into the mulga. He turns for home, stops, turns back. So far he has only run circuits of the town's few residential streets. He's patrolled this way, no houses for a few miles. Feels promising. He sets off out of town.

Crossing a fairly open section of road, he hears the rough noise of an engine behind and moves to the right-hand edge of the bitumen.

It comes closer, engine growling, bloody loud.

Speeding up.

He glances back to see an old Toyota van heading right for him, wrong side of the road. At the wheel, the older Randall brother grinning like a wolf. His brother in the passenger seat belting the outside of his door with manic joy.

Ray hears a yell. 'Prezzie from Laming!'

He leaps sideways as the van whips by, so close he feels the wind like a fierce breath, lands on broken mounds of clay and scraggly bushes, loses his balance. An ankle twists, he lets himself fall and roll to protect it, hitting iron-hard ground, sharp pain in his shoulder. The van thunders ahead, heads off-road over low bushes and turns back.

Ray gets up, ankle stretched but holding. He runs and limps across open, flat, rough ground. The van roars and rattles behind, the brothers whooping. Ray zigs and zags but can't sustain a lead. Acacias form a rough line across his path ahead. He aims for them, breaks through the line of low trees at full pelt, the van sounding dangerously close.

His feet flail in empty air. The tree line marks a dried, eroded creek bed a yard or two below. He hits sand, sprawls face first, mouth clogging, sour smell and taste, then rolls wildly to get out of the van's path, sure he is yelling too. He hears a crash right behind him and loud bawling. He turns as the van smashes down the trees, and thumps hard, nose-first into the sand, jams there, and tips forwards, slow-motion all the way over onto its top. The engine screams louder, then splutters and stops, steam or oil or petrol spurting, wheels spinning. Ray scrabbles backwards over the sand, braced for an explosion. Waits. No sound or movement from the cabin.

He timidly checks each limb, spits out foul sand, wipes it from his face, works his jaw. Jesus, he'll be sore. But intact. He climbs to his feet, hobbles. His ankle hurts but takes his weight. He edges up to the vehicle, bends to peer into the cabin. The driver is unconscious, or worse, head at an odd angle. No seat-belt. Ray reaches in, turns off the ignition, takes the key, avoids contact with what he fears is a dead man. He goes around the buckled, hissing front of the vehicle to the passenger door.

The younger brother is moaning, crying, staring fearfully at Ray who smells urine and shit amid engine fumes. 'We didn't mean nothing. He made us.'

Ray tries opening the door but it is jammed, crushed out of shape. He returns to the driver's side, feels for a pulse on the driver's neck. Nothing. Looks around. Reaching carefully into the cabin again, he presses the horn, hoping it still works. Its loud aggressive blare makes him jump, which hurts. The other brother goes into spasms and wails harder, his body hunched into the roof. Ray presses the horn again, holding it on, the noise awful, violent, hurtful, until the live brother screams for it to stop. Ray slumps to the ground, closes his eyes.

An unknown time later, he opens his eyes at voices. A girl and boy about twelve are pushing through the trees on bikes. They stare wide-eyed, point-two-two rifles slung across their shoulders.

Ray recognises them. 'G'day kids. Stay back. Petrol every-where here.'

'Is it going to explode?'

'Who's in the cabin?'

'Bloke in there needs help.'

The girl says, 'We'll go, we'll go. Mum's at home. We've got a truck.'

Ray watches them pump away towards a shining iron roof on the far side of the creek bed, quarter of a mile away. Shaking violently, he sinks to his knees, head ready to explode. Throbbing in his brain. *Prezzie from Laming!*

Laming, not Kennedy? He can maybe see Kennedy dele-gating murder, murder as this sort of joke. Yet Lord Billy has faith in Laming. Someone's getting conned. He lies down, stares at an empty sky. Works to calm his breathing. The engine's stopped hissing. Hears birds, bush sounds. Whimpering from the van, then a wail. Live brother discovering dead one.

A truck stops at the far tree line. A woman climbs out with a small canvas bag, a first aid kit. The kids in the back move to get out too but she stops them with a throaty roar and comes to kneel beside Ray.

'G'day, Ray. How are you? You alright?'

Ray knows her, she drives the school bus, can't find her name. She looks at his running shoes, then the van, shakes her head. 'How the hell'd these jackasses end up here?'

Ray sits up. 'They missed.'

'Bugger me. Kids said one of them needs help.'

He indicates the passenger side. 'Passenger's alive, maybe need jaws of life to get him out. Driver's his brother, dead.'

The snout of a police Land Rover pushes through the trees beside her car. She nods their way. 'I give them a call.'

Arshag and Laming appear. A moment of accusatory eye contact shared between Ray and Laming. Then Ray doesn't know what to do, so he does nothing.

Arshag puts a gentle hand on Ray's shoulder.

Laming snorts. 'What've you bloody done now?'

Ray opens his mouth to reply but the woman beats him to it.

'You blind as a bloody bat and twice as stupid, or what? Come and make yourself useful!'

Ray nods he's alright to Arshag. Laming can't budge the door but Arshag opens it enough for both of them to drag it fully open. The younger Randall falls out, cut and bruised, blubbering. Peed his pants. The ambulance arrives.

Ray thinks about it, what he can prove, what he can't. Ignores Laming, turns to Arshag. 'Can I go?'

Arshag, puzzled, looks to Laming but Laming turns away.
Arshag nods. 'You want a lift?'

'Rather walk. Shake it off.'

Arshag lifts his eyebrows, looks Ray up and down.

Ray shrugs, scales the eroded bank, slowly walks towards
the road, feeling Laming's eyes on his back despite the trees
between them.

He walks along the dusty road towards town. Can't decide
if he's blessed or cursed. Manages a smile as he waves away
an offer of a lift from a passing acquaintance. The sun in the
west is at his eye-line, hiding that whole side of the world
behind a dazzling painful sheen.

Kennedy, or Laming, making it explicit, that's what this
is. Make it look like a dumb accident; stupid townie running
down the middle of the road, too easy. Ray recalls his first day
here, bouncing into the copshop for a new start. Kennedy's
aggro full on right away. Up till now he's assumed it was a
reaction to his history back in Brisbane. Kennedy hearing he
was a troublemaker, so making sure to let him know he had
no friends here. But to run him down? Jesus. Is he a threat
somehow? To Kennedy? To Laming?

There was a story he'd had to read in school, about two
soldiers from the nineteenth century, with swords and uniforms,
and one hated the other on sight. They fought for decades,
duelling whenever they met, a slow-motion struggle to the
death. No room on earth for both of them. Does he have to kill
Kennedy before the bastard kills him? His gut clenches, breath
jams. He stops, has to pull air in and force it out. Was Laming
the messenger boy, or trying to impress Kennedy?

His eye catches a solitary flower bursting from a small cactus
in the red soil beside the road. A startling, violent purple with

a centre as yellow as the sun. He bends closer, staring, defying pains already strong. Feels the flower's perfection, its sheer, pointless beauty there in the dirt. Something passes from it deep into him, and he starts crying. Straightens, looks around, desperate not to be seen, tears streaming. Then as sharply as they began, the tears stop. He wipes his face, streaked with sand and dirt and sweat and some blood.

Stoic again, bone weary, he tries to jog but his ankle aches, and he is afraid. Of Kennedy, who is all fire, and Laming, who is all ice, but more than that. Too much of his life already lost, trying to work out how to do anything, just how to live. He's a seeker, Lord Billy said. Cursed, more likely. Thorn in his brain. Getting it out, getting through this, how to live, that's the real fight. The real duel. The real deal. He laughs. He wanted something to shake him out of his torpor.

He turns to the sun, breathes deeply, freely. Day's end heat is a cleansing burn on his face. He breaks into a clumsy jog, reaches houses on the street, waves to familiar faces.

———

Two days later, Ray is at his copshop desk, none the wiser about what to do. Laming said write it up. But why would he? He'd be starting a feud—him versus Laming—with added spice because cops wear guns. With no real evidence, no one'd want to get involved.

He loses sleep, sees himself smashed, dead on the road. A neat hit and run, Randalls with a grudge to settle, Laming cued to turn up fast, cover up whatever, plant whatever. Or Ray not dead but unable to describe his attackers. Not so hard to imagine. No witnesses, so Laming could have left something incriminating from a different sort of vehicle entirely. Or maybe Laming would have been a witness: *Pure chance, yeah. Rotten luck. Saw a sedan in the distance tearing away.*

Ray has to get out of the copshop. He goes to the main street, no place to go, just walking. Late afternoon sun mercilessly dazzles drivers heading west. A hazard for anyone heading that way, especially truckies who concede nothing to it. The oil drilling company bus pulls up. Jimmy and other workers emerge muddy and tired. They nod lazily.

In the beer garden at the rear of the pub, Ray sits at a table and pours beers as Jimmy joins him, washed and revived, wet hair stuck to his forehead. Jimmy downs his glass.

'How's your new life?'

Jimmy pulls a bored face. 'Lot like my old life. Bits good, bits shit. But I don't have to make so many decisions and I get paid.'

'How's Burt?'

'In another team. Won't see much of him for a while. Our shifts're out of sync. He's sick of it. Wants to go north.'

'And do what?'

'Work on a tropical island? Stare at chicks in bikinis all day? Live the dream.'

'You blokes're edging towards going your own ways?'

'Yep.' Jimmy looks sadly at his empty glass. Ray pushes the jug to him.

Jimmy pours another beer, tops up Ray's. 'Free piss from a copper's got to be sus. What'll this cost me?'

'I'm softening you up. Tell me all about duffing.'

'Why?'

Ray shrugs, not happy. 'The whole thing, the Randalls walking away, pisses me off.'

129

Jimmy snorts, mouth twisted. 'Duffers are bastards. Bring back fucking flogging, I say. What can I tell you?'

'I want to know about it. Can't be a dumb townie all my life.'

'Why not, heaps of dumb townies do it.' He smiles, gulps, and his beer and the smile drops. 'Okay, okay. Well, there are the small-timers, chancers, there's no knowing when or where they'll hit. Some just want a load of free meat to butcher at home. But the big-timers, they're serious. Send spies out as spotters, find a target, then the team comes in trucks they fill then sell by the load full. Take whatever's not nailed down. Your cattle, the best of them, your bikes, tools. Mate, they take your dog. You know what a working dog's worth—fucking fortune apart from how you love the bugger. Your dog! What's that tell you?'

Ray watches fascinated as Jimmy winds up.

'So maybe you hear they're around. You take a punt, you sit and wait with your rifle. But shit, where? You got thousands of acres, right? I had blokes working for me till I couldn't pay them but never enough to watch every bloody bull. It's not like a shepherd watching over a pissant flock. Stock's spread out, this paddock, that paddock. How do you pick where to put your ambush? You camp out and hide north, they hit the fucking south. And *when'll* they hit? You hide Monday, they come Sunday. Mug's game.'

'Did you try it anyway, waiting, trying to guess?'

'Fuck yeah. So full of hating them, the heat and cold and waiting and flies and snakes and fucking ants, nothing bothered me. But nah. Too many maybes.'

'There's nothing you can do?'

'Try listening for the trucks. Try patrolling huge areas, hope for lucky timing. We cornered a couple of bastards here in this carpark one time, heard whispers they were moon-lighting as drivers.'

'Not the Randalls?'

'Nah. Not that time.'

Maybe since Jimmy was away working his shift, he hasn't heard of the Randalls' attack, and its fatal consequences. Ray says nothing, thinks of the wife, now widow, and the two kids on their isolated bush block. Laming took the bad news there, says she's taking the kids to her brother, drives a taxi in Adelaide.

'These dickheads acted like we were joking so we damn near bloody killed them.' He laughs, a bitter sound, holds up a fist. 'Bit bloody. Bit pointless.'

Ray knows about blood from the ring. One time he saw the fight in the other bloke melt away and had to stop hitting him before he maimed or killed him. Not that stopping's always good. Who knows what the other bloke'll do if you ease up? Bastard might be foxing. It was a dead loss for his career. Hated being told he wasn't tough or hungry enough to be a pro. Hated it because it was true. Maybe he's not hard-headed or hungry enough for life in general. The army might've settled the question by sending him to Vietnam, to his war, so he could find out once and for all.

'We never proved they were duffers.' Jimmy rubs his eyes, shakes his head. 'Just made me a few more enemies I have to think about on dark nights.'

'You called Ian Taylor a duffer to his face.'

'And he laughed. Denied every-fucking-thing. Pissing in the wind, eh? The only way—catch them in the act. But it's not my problem anymore. Just yours.'

10

Ray enters Athos Café and is greeted by a smiling, aproned Nick, who indicates a table.

Nick says, 'You have had breakfast?'

'I have.'

'Coffee?'

'Mmm, please.'

Nick gestures to the middle-aged woman behind the counter who disappears into the kitchen. 'What does a boy from a cane farm like to eat? Do you cook?'

'Raised on steak and bacon and eggs. I cook a bit, look after myself.'

Ray savours posters of the Mediterranean on the wall. White houses against spectacular blue sea. Maybe a place his father offered his mother, once upon a time.

Nick brings coffees to a couple Ray recognises. He visited them on a domestic violence call. Their heads huddle close, serious talk going on. A boy and girl in typically ratty school uniforms slurp milkshakes at another table, with anxious eyes flitting to the adults. Sent away so the parents can talk? Ray sees an old cardboard suitcase held closed with a wide belt on the floor beside the man.

The woman serving reappears with baklava, goes back to the kitchen and returns with a pot of coffee and two small cups.

Nick joins him, pours thick, black coffees and leans back, arms folded over his apron. 'Enjoy.' Ray bites into the baklava and hums with delight. Nick congratulates him on his boxing gym. 'Kids hang around here, you know, talk about it, compare punching.'

Ray nods. 'Couldn't do it without Lord Billy's support.'

Nick says, 'He flew you out to stay at his home, I hear. A rare privilege.' He winks, intrigued.

'Don't know what I did to deserve it.' It's true. He's ready to joke about it but not reveal the vulnerability William let him see.

'Our mayor keeping his finger on the pulse. Checking out the new boy. I'm sure you'll get the job, whatever it is. How do you find him?'

Ray notes the word *job*. 'He feels strongly about the place.'

'For which we're grateful. Some mayors dress up in robes and mayoral chains, not Lord Billy. He's there to work in the corridors of power. He gets in and comes out with money for the shire. He operates on two principles, he says. One, every shire is at war with the state. The state government always thinks we're—you say, piss-ants?'

Ray laughs, the word odd in Nick's accent. 'Pissants.'

'So the only way shires get a fair deal is by force, trickery or theft. Lord Billy does all of that. On our behalf, fortunately.'

'Ian Taylor's the state MP. Isn't that his job?'

Nick pouts, dismissively. 'Useless man except to do whatever Lord Billy tells him. Principle two. Shires don't help other shires. Money for one shire is stolen from another. Dog eat dog.'

'So everyone's the enemy?'

'And Lord Billy outsmarts them all. Even uses his own money. He owns a large piece of most major properties in a two-hundred-mile radius and keeps them afloat. Creates jobs for locals, trying to stop the young all leaving for good. Imagine! Billy much loved and he's a Pom! Amazing.'

He and Ray laugh, sharing mock horror.

Ray goes fishing. 'He's no friend of Detective Kennedy.'

Nick's mouth twists. 'They work together as required, that's all.'

Ray drains his coffee. 'Wow, this coffee's got a kick.'

Nick preens. 'Bit strong for some.' He hesitates, which Ray notices. 'Now tell me, has anything come of Alice meeting Kennedy here? The day before her body was found and you arrived.'

'What?'

Ray's blank face provokes Nick into instant fury and he has to calm himself to speak. 'All this time I said nothing because Kennedy is your senior officer. How do you not know?'

'I don't know what you're talking about.'

'Please. Listen.' Ray, dismayed, watches Nick struggle to speak. 'The afternoon Alice went missing, she was here, working.'

'I know that.'

'But you know Kennedy came in?' He is close to whispering with rage, his hands busy. 'I saw Alice hover, then go to him. I heard nothing that was said. They went outside. I saw them through my window speaking, Alice mostly. She came back, agitated, positive, negative, I do not know. She asked to finish early. A little desperate perhaps. I agreed. She removed her apron and left.'

'With him?'

'With him. I never saw her again.'

'Did they leave in a vehicle?'

'In his own car. Not a police car. Took her bag. Put her bike in his boot I think. She didn't come back here.'

Ray squeezes both of Nick's hands, feels tremors pass through him. Anger.

———

At the copshop, Ray tells Kennedy to join him in the interrogation room. Kennedy is on the verge of dismissing him when Ray barks, 'Now.'

They stand each side of the room's only table, ignoring the chairs.

'What's up your nose?' Kennedy's stab at jocularity shrinks when he sees Ray has Alice's case folder.

Ray points to its single sheet of paper. 'Nothing in here about you meeting Alice the afternoon she went missing.'

'So, Sherlock?' His jaw is active.

'Account for it. Why it's not here. And what happened between you.'

'What're you accusing me of?'

'Not accusing. You know better than that.'

'She asked me if we found a bracelet belonging to the suicide.'

'Diah's? Took her months to ask that?'

'I didn't think we had it but said I'd take her to the copshop to see.'

'There is no bracelet. No record there ever was. Her parents never mentioned a bracelet. You sure this is what she wanted to know?'

'Careful, sonny. She asked. We checked. Nothing. She said okay. I dropped her home.'

'Witnesses? Anyone see you? What time? Why is there no record of this?'

'Because it was nothing. She got out. I left.'

'It's part of her timeline for the twenty-four hours before—'

'Yeah, yeah. Don't get knotted. All these details get entered when it matters. No sign it mattered at all.' He taps his temple, hard. 'It's all in here.'

'This report says she was abducted off her bike on her way home but you say you dropped her home? Her bike was found in a gutter, her bag in a gully down the road.'

'I dropped her home. She must've left her bag and bike at the café and went back to get them.'

Ray thinks about *must've*. Nick said Alice didn't return to the café. And she took her bike and bag. He drops the page and folder in front of Kennedy. 'Write it up. With times. Nick at the café is doing the same.'

Kennedy gives an extravagant shrug, doing Ray a favour. Ray stares at such elaborate nonchalance. A pose fed by rage at Ray's presumption? Or laziness? Or a half-baked cover-up? Looks like Kennedy's the last person to see Alice before she was abducted.

———

Arshag bails up Ray in the copshop carpark. 'It's fit to kill in there. Kennedy's on the warpath.' Arshag describes going to Alice's street. Met a neighbour who says she did see Kennedy's car then, which she knows of course, saw no one get in or out before it left.

Arshag holds fingers to his temples. 'What do we do with this?'

Ray shakes his head, excited but thwarted, all at once. 'I need to get out for a while.'

136

He drives out of Royalton under a cloudless sky, remembering times he thought an overcast sky was oppressive. Could do with a bit of that now. He drives and drives. Arshag has told him that until he learns to look properly, he'll see the same landscape everywhere. Ray manages a wry grin. He still isn't looking properly.

He finds a cleared space beside the narrow, sealed road and stops. Feels like the heat is beating a dull tattoo on the roof of the cabin. The previous week, two tourists broke down nearby and despite repeated warnings to stay with their vehicle, walked off to get help. One died, the other is still in hospital but expected to recover. Ray imagines walking away into the landscape. And walking and walking. He looks at his map of the area, then around at large patches of black clay amid the red-brown earth, sparse grasses and sturdy clumps of acacias. Not for the first time, he feels the land, the bush, is waiting somehow.

As a boy, he ran away one night from his parents' verbal brawls into the dark backyard and out the rear gate into the bush, where he hit darkness so total the entire world vanished. He waited in a kind of trance as blackness slowly dissolved, subverted by sly, gentle light from layer on layer of scintillating stars, becoming bright enough to reveal shapes, edges and objects.

When he could see again, he stole deeper into the bush, aiming to follow a straight line, easy to retrace, although he knew even then what everyone does is veer, left or right, in a curve too subtle to notice. He halted at a tree he knew, realised he was drifting right, and climbed up to perch well above the ground in a generous hollow where a large branch left the main trunk. He listened uneasily to rustling, snuffling, squeaking, stamping and grumbling in the dark all around.

At sun-up, he walked home, his porridge on the table as usual, nothing said. Maybe because both of his parents were cast out, or cast themselves out—it always was an Us, him and them, against the world. They had deep patience, time and space for him, despite their own corrosive, ravaging disappointments. The sickening unreality of the sudden shock of losing them stays with him.

He opens his window, leans out. Heat envelops his face like a hot towel, stinging his eyes, sucking them dry. He pulls back in. Whatever the bush is waiting for, it's nothing sentimental.

He checks the petrol gauge, two-thirds empty, and checks the map again. Puts a finger where he thinks he is, allowing for turnoffs that weren't there and others that shouldn't have been, estimating petrol needed to get to one of Taylor's northern properties. Berating himself for not checking petrol before leaving, not picking a point of no return and sticking to it. If he's where he thinks he is, Taylor's is close enough. He eyes the gauge again.

Shaming to have to ask for petrol but running out would be worse. How long would the copshop take to miss him? His trip book entry—*Heading north-west. Back today*—is typically cryptic, of limited use if he needs help. Kennedy and Laming would have no reason to dash to his aid. More likely they'd defer any search to make sure he suffered first. He shrugs that off as silly, then remembers the van bearing down on him.

He looks out at endless, gentle, almost rhythmical undulations in the surface of the land. Landscape as ocean. If he ran out of petrol he'd be becalmed. Like his stalled investigations. He mulls over the hostile, suspicious behaviour of Kennedy and Laming; the job offer from Lord Billy, if that's what it was; his growing but craven, covert estrangement from Stella's expectations; and oh yeah, an attempt on his life.

This last he hasn't even been able to announce, to make real. He imagined approaching the Inspector and Kennedy, even confronting Laming. 'You think Randall said what? Sounds like a joke gone too far. Randalls aren't the sharpest tools in the shed. If he even said it. Can't you take a joke?'

He drives on, boot light on the accelerator. Passes a low ridge on his left. A narrow dirt road not on his map. Or worse, it is and he isn't where he thinks he is. Words on a leaning, wooden signpost have weathered away. The road is gravel, ridges looking as hard as concrete but gouged. It's been used since the last rains, whenever the hell that was.

He wrenches the wheel, takes the turn. An act of faith. After an unnerving ten minutes, as the needle of the gauge sinks ever lower, he rattles over a cattle-grid in a rusty barbed-wire fence and curves right to a modest, single-storey house with insect-screen verandahs on the front and sides. Ray groans in noisy relief. Three large dogs, bull mastiffs, appear silently from under the house with ambiguous intent. He tosses them jerky he's learned to carry at all times, climbs out and is relieved when they respond enthusiastically to his pats. Starved for attention. No one responds to knocking or calling. The food and water bowls of the dogs link to stocked, auto-fill devices. They're cared for but no way to know if anyone was here recently.

He wanders to the rear of the house, the dogs happily tailing him. There are three wooden sheds, each single-car size, doors sagging. Timber grey, the sun is winning. One contains a pile of empty mesh cages, large and rigid enough to hold a medium-sized dog. A couple are longer. Ray thinks they're crocodile-sized, then dismisses the thought. As if you'd see a croc out here.

He walks past the sheds and stops in surprise at a plane, bigger than Lord Billy's. The decal on its side says *Cessna 210*. He opens a door. The smell inside is dense, animal.

As a kid, beyond excited, he'd visited circus tents that popped up magically in an open field. Large cages mounted on trailers. Heard his first roar of a real lion—the earth shook. Heavy, strong, rich smells, pure somehow. He was awestruck to see a lion, mane tufted and bedraggled. Two slinky, smooth leopards padding to and fro silently, ceaselessly. Elephants tethered in the field, swaying, swaying.

He sniffs the interior again. Yep, animal. Only the pilot's seat is still there, the rest of the cabin has been cleared. For cargo? Smuggling? Instinctively, he looks about, on alert. Bring in exotic animals, take out native lizards, snakes, birds. Lucrative. Which means high stakes. Which means danger.

He needs a camera. Like not checking his petrol, too bloody keen to get out of the copshop and away. And he hasn't even confirmed whose place this is. Notes the plane registration: GA-YSB. Memorises it as 'Go Away You Stupid Bastard.'

On the way back to his vehicle, he inspects the cages again. They can't be for crocs, he hopes. But why not? Stop off up north in the Territory on the way out. Fill 'er up and a big croc please, mate. A box contains maybe fifty cylinders, some aluminium, some cardboard, the kind used for mailing rolled-up magazines with diameters the size of his palm.

Watched lazily by the now bored dogs, he checks the front door. Locked. Who locks their doors? Nothing confirms this is one of Taylor's properties, but he decides to trust his navigation.

He drives to four large fuel tanks set away from the buildings. The first is avgas, for the plane. The second and third, diesel. The fourth, petrol. He taps the tank, it sounds full. Relieved, he fills up, writes an IOU on police notepaper and jams it under the front door. Then stops dead. If smugglers live here, leaving a note's a bit dumb. But taking petrol requires it. Courtesy wins. He pats the dogs, wondering what it would take to provoke real watchdog reactions. He labels the spot on the map as Taylor's. Tank full, he'll make it home fine. He'll have to explain his IOU but one step at a time. He'd check the mailbox if there was one.

Arriving back at the earlier T-junction, this time he turns left. Twenty-five miles later, he hits another T-junction and a wider road. After thinking, checking sun and shadows, he turns left. Another forty miles, his watch and the afternoon sun saying three o'clock, he re-enters Royalton.

As he parks in the copshop carpark, Laming returns too, in the other Land Rover, covered in orange dust. His stare is cold. Ray waits for him, undecided still on what to say, what to look for, even how to arrange his face. Decides to play it dumb, feed the bastard's natural arrogance. 'I went up to one of Taylor's north-west properties today.'

Laming snorts, watchful as ever, face blank. 'What the fuck you doing up there?'

'It's in our patrol area.' Ray remains blank too, thinking, *This piece of shit sent morons to kill me. One died.* With effort he controls tremors in his hands and arms and shoulders, wants to say, *Randall said you sent them. To kill me.*

Laming is still blank. Has the live Randall told him what was said? Did he say it or was it the dead Randall? Fuck. Does Laming give a shit who said what? Does he know

141

anything was said? Ray squints at an overbearing sky. What does Laming give a shit about?

Laming says, 'Our area's pushing two and half thousand square miles. You planning to visit everyone? We may never see you again.' He laughs. Too forced, the only sign of discomfort.

Ray comes to stand at Kennedy's desk. Laming hovers behind him, thumbs in belt loops. Ray shows his map to Kennedy who flicks a furtive glance to Laming, then Ray, who says, 'Found this place, one of Taylor's, I reckon.' He points to the marked spot.

Laming sniggers. 'Reckon? You don't know? You lost?'

'No one was home to ask. I knew where I was. All that army training, you know? Oh, hang on, you don't, do you.'

Laming gives him a get-fucked look as Ray feels Kennedy's hard stare.

Ray obliges, cocky. 'Found a plane. And animal cages. Wondered about animal smuggling.' As soon as he says it, Ray knows he's overstepped, and he tries to recover. 'We got a memo.'

'That right? Read memos, do you?' Kennedy leans back, sneers, dominant again.

Ray ploughs on. 'The place is worth checking again.'

'How come you were up there at all? You know he's the state member for this region? You got reason to poke around on his property?'

Ray laughs. 'I need a search warrant? You use them out here? No one even locks their doors. Except Taylor. I was looking round our patch, seeing how far I could go.' Lets that ambiguity sit there.

Kennedy manages another glance to Laming, which to Ray looks almost like a check for approval. 'Thought you were the rape and murder man. Given up on the poor girls, have you?'

Ray reddens and leans over the desk. 'It's tough stuck with incomplete case notes, 'specially when I'm sent chasing duffers and suicides and traffic accidents or whatever-the-fuck-else instead. Otherwise, I'm right on it. Maybe there's somewhere you think I ought to be looking? Someone I ought to chat to?' He half-turns to face both of them. 'Any fishing expedition you know'd help?'

Kennedy bounces to his feet and heads out of the office. 'Next time you go chasing fairy stories, put a proper note in the book so we know where to rescue you.' Laming, still impassive, hesitates, then follows Kennedy.

Ray stands there, angry, smelling blood in the water but staring at nothing. Is this how it feels to eyeball someone who wants you dead badly enough to have a go? What's the cop manual say about that? He looks around, the place is empty. Where is Arshag?

He phones the hospital. The surviving Randall is talking.

———

Randall lies alone in a four-bed room, bandages around his head and upper body. Seeing Ray gets him wriggling like a fish on a hook.

Ray takes his time. 'Well?'

'Well what?' Eyes wide, a dismal attempt at wide-eyed innocence.

Ray puffs his cheeks, slowly releases his breath. 'You remember what you said out there?'

'Said nothing.'

Ray snorts. A weirdness in being a copper: talking calmly to a prick who wants you dead and gave it a try. 'You know your brother's dead? You know that?'

143

Randall's face quivers, his mouth opens and closes, no sounds emerge.

Ray leans in. 'You worked it out yet? Doing someone's dirty work got him killed. Who sent you?'

Randall is in his late twenties but looks ten as he shakes his head vigorously, then has to stop, gasping in pain. 'Bad joke, that's all. That's it! Can't you take a fucking joke?'

'Your brother's dead. Ha ha ha.'

'Laming said it'd be a good joke. No harm done.'

'Your brother's dead. Am I getting through to you?'

Randall turns aside, sobs into his pillow. Ray leans in closer, sees colour in the bruises on his cheek and eye, then hears steps. He turns. Kennedy is close behind him, balanced on the balls of his feet. Had Ray not turned, would he have attacked?

'What the fuck're you doing? Harassing a bloke who just lost his brother?'

'Lost? Someone got his brother killed. Someone's gutless, dirty work.'

'Spare me.'

Ray stands his ground. Kennedy comes close enough for them to smell each other. Rum from Kennedy. Who knows what from Ray.

Kennedy says softly, with menace, 'Asked you the day I fucking met you, who wins, boxer or brawler? Think we know, eh?' He feints as if to throw a right.

Forewarned by his stiffening, Ray stays put, lifts no defence.

Kennedy laughs but knows he lost that one.

Ray turns to a staring Randall, and jerks his head at Kennedy. 'This the prick you're protecting? That how much you care about your brother?' Randall's trembling fear distorts his already mutilated face.

Ray walks past Kennedy who says, 'Anytime, anywhere.' Playground bullshit turned real.

The hospital is a low-set, rambling, converted home with a generous verandah on the front and sides. Ray sits on the front verandah, drinking a can of soft drink from a vending machine in the hall. Kennedy comes out, sees him, goes down-stairs, stops. He comes back and sits on the far end of the same bench.

He looks at Ray's drink. 'Shoulda got one of them.'

Ray drains the can.

Kennedy says, 'What's your version of who said what?'

'This an official interview?'

'Who said what's all I'm asking.'

Ray tilts his head back towards the building. 'He said Laming sent them.'

'Yahoo having a lend, got out of hand?'

'May be what he says now but it's not what happened.'

'You taking this seriously?'

'Bloke's dead for a joke.'

'People out here die for fucking less. You talk to Laming, you taint the investigation. My investigation, not yours.'

Ray laughs, sounding bitter even to himself. He sees Kennedy's hand is shaking and Kennedy sees that Ray has seen. It occurs to Ray that Kennedy came all the way over here to justify something. Not long ago his pride would never have let him. If he's worried about protecting Laming, he ought to be.

11

Ray brakes the Land Rover on the narrow, sealed road, surrounded by parched ironbark forest. He is beside a generous, fenced yard of startlingly green grass and a wooden house on high stilts, flowers in baskets hanging beneath it. Verandahs all around, of course. An open structure the size of a two-car garage covered in dark shade-cloth or canvas material, like he saw in Massacre Row, is a vegetable garden. In a corner, he recognises a sprawling Banksia rose bush. Two cattle dogs sit in the shade under the house, watching intently. Ray is about to get out when Arshag comes downstairs, in uniform and strapping on his handgun. He says something to the dogs then joins Ray.

Ray is sheepish, never thought to ask more about Arshag's life. 'You on your own?'

'Irene's a nurse, at work now.'

'My landlady's a nurse.'

'That'd be Dot.' Arshag laughs at Ray's bewildered expression. 'You're safe. Irene only tells me the good stuff. I checked on Peter, Paul and Mario being at that dance. There was a Tyborg dance then but ordinary Admit One tickets are used for every dance so having tickets is no alibi. The people running the dances know our boys. They cause trouble every time, drunk, stirring the locals, harassing women. They weren't there that night.'

'They're that sure?'

'Yep. And the Tyborg copper's happy to confirm those nights were peaceful. At least, no Royalton boys causing strife.'

'Good work. How can I meet Irene?'

'I hear something's being planned. Just a rumour.'

———

The relentless landscape rolls by but with the petrol tank full, and Arshag and a camera beside him, Ray feels less threatened today.

Arshag says, 'Thinking about the van nearly running you over, and whichever Randall saying Laming sent them. Why Laming, not Kennedy? Anything in that?'

Ray slowly shakes his head. 'I don't get those two. No love lost between them but they've got secrets.'

'Maybe the kind of secrets that mean no love lost. They know what we're doing today?'

'All in the trip book.'

'They think animal smuggling's a joke.'

'What if Taylor has a sideline in lizards and snakes and Kennedy didn't know?'

'Not sharing the loot?'

They drive in silence.

Arshag says, 'Irene saw you at the hospital.'

'With Randall?'

'And Kennedy.'

'Eyes and ears everywhere.'

'Thought it looked tense.'

'Kennedy ordered me out, then came over all friendly. Young Randall is a wreck. I'll try again when we get back.'

Arshag shakes his head. 'He's gone.'

Ray stares at him.

'Left this morning for his family place. Backwoods of Victoria somewhere.'

'He couldn't drive.'

'Took a train. Kennedy fixed it.'

'Shit! So that's that?'

Arshag points ahead as the entrance to Taylor's property comes into view. 'Kennedy will have rung Taylor too. If he's here today.'

Ray shrugs a shoulder, bumps over the grid into the yard. The same mastiffs trot out and he gives them jerky again.

A man appears at the front door. Ray recognises him from the day he fought in the boxing tent.

'G'day, I'm Ray Windsor. Royalton copshop. I owe you some petrol.'

Arshag starts to greet him but the man ignores him and approaches Ray at a calculatedly leisurely pace. In his late forties, thin-shouldered with close-cropped dark hair, so clean-shaven his face has a sheen. Newish slacks, short-sleeved shirt, pens in the pocket, shiny elastic-sided polished boots. A too neat, countrified package. Ray recalls Taylor is the local member of parliament. He doesn't offer a handshake and neither does Ray.

'You got an early start.'

'Early birds.' Ray grins, wants to add, 'caught the worm', because this is a bloke he'd enjoy annoying.

'You're the new bloke.'

Ray nods. 'And you'll be Ian Taylor.' He points to the fuel tanks. 'I was here before, got a refill.'

'Lucky I didn't need what you took.'

'I checked your level first, you were close to full.' There's silence as Ray pulls a can of petrol from the back of the Land Rover. The man stands in front of him, hands on hips, rising and falling as he lifts and lowers his heels.

Ray says, 'Can pay you now.' He puts the can down. 'Or have this. Bit extra and the can's free.' Enjoying being a pain in the arse.

The man says nothing. Lips taut. Working at control.

'What were you doing here, bit off the beaten track? You lost?'

'Everywhere out here's off the beaten track.' Ray notes Taylor's still given no sign he's even seen Arshag.

'This's my property. One of them. So why were you here—if you weren't lost?' His impatience is escaping now.

'Getting to know the area. People, like yourself. I saw all these cages. Wondering what they're for.' He points to the sheds and leads a move that way.

Taylor reluctantly follows, shiny boots gathering dust. Arshag stays back a little.

'Cages? For dingoes and ferals. Used to earn a bob or two for them. Not for years. Keep meaning to chuck them but the rubbish truck's not real reliable out this way.' He offers a sham grin. 'Look, I'm busy. Can't even offer you a coldie or a cuppa.' His tetchy mouth is tight.

'Your plane's impressive. You a pilot, Ian?'

Taylor considers Ray afresh, use of the first name grates, as Ray knew it would. 'Got a bloke for that. He's off visiting some mates today.' Waves vaguely and to Ray's eye, visibly puffs up. 'As local member in a big electorate, it's the only sensible way to get around. At my own expense. Also bring visitors here from up north and the coast.' He walks crisply ahead to the plane and opens its door. Ray peers inside, then stares. Four seats are now bolted in place, and the interior smells of cleaning agents.

He turns to Taylor who looks bored, and restless. 'Just had a clean?'

'Keep it presentable. For my constituents.' He nods at the seats and stares at Ray, daring him to ask.

Ray considers it, says, 'You spoken to Kennedy recently?'

'Couple of weeks ago? We don't chat much.'

'Right.' Ray sees Arshag has stayed back, looking at the flat plain beyond the fence, expectations low. Ray pauses, looks all around, feels Taylor's irritation beside him, then nods. 'Goodo.' He turns back towards the front of the house.

Taylor follows, rubbing his hands together. 'You're lucky you caught me. If I'd had more notice you were coming . . . You know, telephones, real easy to use.'

———

Arshag drives from the yard over the grid.

Ray says, 'Bastard had all the notice he needs. I knew, soon as I told Kennedy what I was thinking. Stupid. Guess I wanted to show off even if it was only empty cages.'

'Thick as thieves, Kennedy and Taylor, thick as thieves,' Arshag says. 'We can do another visit but I reckon this horse has bolted. Nice plane. I always thought being a pilot'd be great. Never occurred to me I could get a licence. After the war I had the money. Could've done it. Things you don't let yourself think.'

Ray stares at the landscape. Feels its endurance. Indifference. One day he'll be dirt himself. Likely never having become anything in the first place. Creeps like Kennedy, Laming, Taylor—they all have a clear sense of who they are. Crime can do that for you.

He says, mostly to himself. 'Kennedy's different lately. There's something.'

'We going to chat to the rape boys?'

'Tomorrow. Need a beer first. Taylor's got up my nose. Needs a slap around.' He grins.

'I love it when you say how you really feel. That the army influence?'

Ray drops Arshag at home to a dark house. Irene still at work. 'Looking forward to that event being planned.'

Arshag grimaces, puts a forefinger to his lips. Mum's the word.

———

The ancient, grandfather clock in the public bar is a six-foot-tall wind-up model, clicking and grinding its way to closing time. Ray slouches on a stool at the bar, worse for wear, too many beers. Three other drinkers huddle at a table near a window looking out to the dark main street. Barb dries glasses, stacks them, wipes surfaces, darts glances at those other drinkers. Ray talks on but she is barely listening.

'Year I was born, the Australian boxer Tommy Burns fought an American called Bell. Beat him in the eleventh. Heard men talk about it, wished like crazy I could've seen it. Tommy always felt like someone I knew. Early sixties, doing a promo tour, he came to my school. Catholic school, boxing, right? The school boxing ring was permanent, the way the Christian Brothers settled playground scuffles. Want a fight, eh? Well, get in the ring and do it like gentlemen. Being a gentleman was supposed to matter. Tommy patted me on the head, don't know why. But I was ten feet bloody tall. Told me to keep fighting.'

Arshag arrives in time to say, 'And you have.'

Barb lifts an eyebrow.

Ray realises she called Arshag, to save him from himself. Ray continues as if Arshag has been there all along.

'Tommy was a clean, honourable man. The rest of us try. He didn't seem to have the anger. Not like me. I could lash out anytime.' He chuckles, sort of. 'Kill some unlucky bastard one day.' Ray turns to Arshag. 'Want a beer?'

Ray sees Barb give Arshag a small head tilt at the other drinkers. Arshag nods, message received.

Ray turns and stares at them. 'What?'

One man, tanned and broad-shouldered in shorts and singlet, says, 'Got your mate to get you home? Put you to bed too? Kissy-kissy first?'

All three laugh.

Arshag keeps his attention on Ray, who slowly stands. 'Home. Now. Come on.' He's grinning tightly, keeping it light.

Ray puts a hand on Arshag's shoulder. 'You are my mate! You bloody are. Like it or bloody lump it!' He points at the three drinkers. 'Do I know you bastards?' He points at the man who spoke. 'I know you, motor-mouth. Where from?'

The man is angry, all pretence at jokes or teasing gone. 'Never seen you before. You're fucking nobody.'

One of his mates puts a warning hand on his arm. 'Wayne, don't.'

Ray says, 'No, no, let him come.' He stares. 'I fucking know you.' Holds his head trying to think, points again. 'Wayne!

The human bloody cyclone at the exhibition bout!' Ray whirls his arms around, leans into Arshag, laughing, thinking Wayne is enjoying it too.

Arshag propels Ray towards the door while Barb watches, distressed. She called a bloody cop. What else can she do?

Wayne crosses to Ray with the fixed gait of the angry drinker.

Ray laughs, pretending to shape up. 'You never laid a glove on me, the whole three minutes.' He sees Wayne winding up a punch, points to it, but Arshag pulls Ray aside and the man misses. Ray breaks free, faces Wayne, taunting, arms down, face set now, eyes cold. Happy.

Wayne swings a new one, Ray does a mocking skip away then steps in close, slaps him open-handed, left then right. Wayne staggers in shock. Some pain, mostly insult. Ray shapes up, feints with his right, then drives the left heel of his hand hard into Wayne's chest, yelling, 'Southpaw!'

Wayne staggers back and falls, the back of his head cracking onto the wooden floor. He rolls, groaning, curling up, sucking air. Arshag pulls Ray back and onto a stool as Wayne's friends advance, menacing.

Arshag holds up an open hand. 'Quit it now! Jeff!'

Jeff puts out an arm to slow his friend. They stop.

Arshag points at Wayne, still writhing, groaning. 'He's winded. He's fine. You saw him start it. Now it's finished.'

Barb calls out. 'Bar's closed. Go home all of you. Get!'

Arshag gets a quieter Ray outside where he slumps on a bench in the poorly lit street. The three drinkers emerge, Wayne's mates offering him unwelcome help as they stumble into the night. Arshag sits beside Ray, who is massaging his left wrist and breathing deeply, deliberately.

Arshag says, 'Barb called, reckons it's risky a copper out on his own, in no condition to look after himself. But I guess you were okay after all. Glad you didn't kill Wayne. You looked like that was on your mind.'

'I'll tell Barb thanks.'

'What brought this on?'

Ray crosses his arms. 'You ever tried on a straitjacket?'

Arshag half-laughs. 'Funnily enough, no.'

'I had to bring in this loony one night, in Brisbane. Crazy piece of shit. Thought he was Gandhi or someone. Took him to this asylum which you're not to call an asylum. He's like Wayne, threshing round, arms everywhere. So they put him in this straitjacket and take him away.

'I'm chatting to the nurse, big Islander bloke, and I ask him to show me how to put one on. The straitjacket. He thinks this's hilarious, says, "What if I can't undo it?" But he puts me in it. I'm standing there, tugging and pulling, no use. It's all fun, then I get worried. The nurse's looking at me funny, grinning a bit mean. Says his shift's over now, back tomorrow lunchtime. A new nurse comes out, another big Islander, they swap winks. First bloke nods at me, says to his mate, "Hey, need to lock this troublemaker up." They're laughing.

'They let me out but I remember how it felt. Not fucking good at all. Out in the carpark, I dry-chucked.' Ray leans back, sees the stars. 'This place, what we're doing, where we're at, the whole bloody thing, I'm back in that straitjacket.'

Arshag gets up. 'I'll drop you home.'

Ray gets up and Arshag points to his car across the street. They wait for two road-trains to roar past.

Arshag says, 'He'd have killed you with that punch.'

'Why'd he come after me anyway?'

'It's the sign you wear. Hit me. Love your fighting, don't you.'

'Keeps me going.' But something's missing. He hears himself saying, 'Lost without ever being found.' Shakes his head.

Arshag says, 'You a pub brawler now?'

Ray feels Arshag's disapproval. 'Used to be.' He makes a clumsy plea for reconciliation. 'You're a good man to have on my side, Arshag.'

'You are your own side.'

'I can walk home.'

'Get in the bloody car.'

'Shit. Did you just swear?'

'No fucking way.'

Ray drops awkwardly into the car. 'I'll thank Barb tomorrow. She's a wonderful woman.'

12

A dazzlingly bright morning under a cloudless sky, hot already. Arshag stops the Land Rover outside Ray's flat. Ray comes out buttoning his shirt, shielding his eyes from the harsh glare. He climbs in, looking pale.

Arshag grins. 'Well, look what the cat dragged in.'

'Where're we going?'

'Telling Peter and Mario their alibi doesn't work.'

'Where are they?'

'Fishing.'

'Ha. So are we.'

The radio buzzes, Louise's voice. 'Detective Windsor. Come in, Detective Windsor.'

Arshag grins.

Ray looks pained. 'Ray here.'

'Ray, good, car accident on Strathdees Road, a mile south past Robertson's. Single vehicle, driver believed dead. Identity unknown. No passengers. Ambos advised and on way. Over.'

'G'day, Louise. We'll take Stitts Road. ETA fifteen. Out.'

Ray says to Arshag, 'Let's go fishing another day.'

Arshag nods, does a U-turn and heads east. He turns at

the ever-hopeful INDUSTRIAL ESTATE signs and the few ware-houses of Stitts Road, accelerates past the water tower. The road is sealed and wide. They head south, most traffic heading into town. Friday is shopping day in Royalton. After ten more minutes, they see two parked cars ahead, one each side of the road. People interfering already. Arshag crunches to a halt.

Maybe eight yards off the road over flat ground on their left is wreckage of a third car, a Cortina GT curved around a large gum as if a giant hand contemptuous of human goods rammed it there. Ray tries to place seeing it before—every panel a different colour.

Ray says, 'Thorough.' No rubber on the road, no sign of braking. Ray still can't place the car, full of the usual dread of traffic accidents. Then he remembers, dismayed.

Arshag's face pales. He says something Ray misses, then, 'That's Benny Lee's car.'

Ray closes his eyes, recalls Benny behind the wheel, rolling by with a giant grin on his boyish face.

Arshag turns to speak but stops at Ray's shocked expression.

Ray feels his stare, waves as if from far away. 'Reminds me of something, another crash. Long ago.' Adds unconvincingly, 'I'm fine. Fine.'

He climbs from the police vehicle, lost in the day his mother was killed. He is with Mark, his best mate and about to become his brother. Both twelve, on battered bicycles enjoying another endless day, meandering through bush, whooping and tearing along cow tracks and narrow roads. Early after-noon, they emerge on a rise above a bush T-junction, noses filling with the stench of burnt rubber and petrol, seeing one car rammed into another. The second is broken in half by the force of the blow on its driver-side doors. Police and the local fire truck are there. Water, petrol and oil—and maybe blood, Ray recalls thinking—all over the road. The wail of an ambulance. Ray noting that the car that did the damage is like his mum's car. Mark kidding around, making crash noises. Ray joining in. A cop yelling at them to piss off or they'll be in bloody strife. Keeping on making their noises as they race back into the bush.

Home at dusk, sunburnt and hungry, pushing his bike. Noel, their neighbour, waiting for him, saying his mum has been in a car accident. Killed. The word like a punch. Noel's a dumpy, middle-aged man, usually an easy smiler but not smiling now, sitting there hunched, bare feet, washed-out navy-blue singlet and ragged shorts, drumming the top of the rickety verandah table. Saying the local cop was waiting but left.

Ray standing side-on, embarrassed to look at him as Noel asks if there's anywhere he can go, anyone to look after him.

Ray nodding. 'Sure, yeah, I'll head out to Mark's place. McDonald's farm.'

Noel getting up, relieved of his burden. 'Got your bike, so off you go, then. But listen, back in the morning, okay? Copper's coming round for a word, nothing to worry about.'

Ray remembering, *nothing to worry about.* Dumb thing to say. Remembers the dead weight of his bike, dragging it round to the way he came, riding, weaving to the end of the street in near darkness now, then stopping and walking back home. No lights. No noise. Sneaking back inside, opening a tin of something, eating it sitting on the floor of the verandah, no idea what's going in his mouth, no taste. Back against the wall, crying, rubbing his nose till it hurt, to get rid of the rubber and petrol stink, without success. Local copper next morning saying, *Come to the copshop, work out who's going to look after you now*. Ray never did. On his own now for real.

Ray makes himself face Benny's car, mechanically steps along the gouged wheel tracks towards it. Arshag shoos away a man and woman from each car, one woman crying. One man reeks of vomit, hands over the blue car's key. Puked, seeing the victim up close when he turned off the ignition. 'Thought it might bloody explode, eh, current still on.'

Ray knows them but their names won't come so he nods.

Arshag, upset, checks Benny for life. 'Benny, Benny!' Nothing.

He drags the buckled driver's door out of the way. The high-pitched, scraping sounds sting their ears. They falter at the dense, metallic smell of blood. Lots of it.

A man has stopped his tractor in the nearby field. Ray feels the man wondering, *How can anyone have an accident here?*

Arshag steps back, shivering, from the bloody, broken body. 'Stinks like a brewery. Lot smashed, can't tell if he's drunk any of it.' Tips his head towards the road. 'No sign of braking.'

'He loved this bomb of a car.'

Arshag shakes his head. 'Winter work Taylor gave him was over. But he was still splashing money around.'

'Didn't think Benny was flush.' Ray shifts his attention to the back seat. 'Jesus, look.'

Jammed every which way across the back seat and in foot wells are tangled barrels of handguns and rifles, and busted ammunition boxes, bullets loose. 'Make a quid from these, I reckon.' A siren is growing louder.

Arshag looks in. 'I don't even know what some of them are.'

Ray tries the door. No use but the window is smashed. He pushes out glass fragments, reaches in and starts to extract the weapons. The ambulance arrives behind him.

—

The morning sunlight is sharpening, hardening. Shadows retreat slyly across the ground to their owners. The man on his tractor is on the far side of his field now, driving along rows of young lucerne. Ray and Arshag order on the few passing cars. The ambulance has taken Benny's body. A man in overalls uses a crowbar to release a car part that's dug into the tree as his partner in a tow-truck gently pulls the whole vehicle away. The car makes another tired, high-pitched squeal as it comes free of the tree. The jaws of life have left the sedan a strange, crippled beast, bodywork crushed, dimpled and bent, doors out at odd angles.

Ray has seen too many traffic accidents, blocks images of his mother being removed from her car, inventing them because he never saw it.

The man with the crowbar walks around kicking the bent doors in, as closed as they'll ever be, then lifts an arm. The truck driver begins winching the car onto the tray of the truck. Ray and Arshag turn away.

The weapons and ammunition lie across a groundsheet on the grass beside the Land Rover.

Ray says, 'He was a happy-go-lucky bugger. Hard not to like. Came to the gym once or twice, strong as a bull, but always telegraphed his moves. Didn't telegraph this one.' Ray holds up the first weapon. 'Ingram Mac-ten.' A submachine gun, boxy, black and heavy.

'Ugly,' says Arshag.

Ray points at the groundsheet. 'Automatic pistol, American Special Forces.' He holds up a handgun. 'Luger. They're always in the movies. When I was a kid, I really, really wanted one.' It is grey, crosshatched handle, lots of scratches and indentations. 'Seen some action. German, of course. Popular with the Irish Republican Army.

'Ah, here's a favourite.' Ray sees Arshag grinning at his enthusiasm. A short-barrelled revolver now lies snug in Ray's hand. 'Colt Detective Special. Snub nose, thirty-eight. In the army, someone'd always try to trick you into finding the safety catch. Nice, good balance. Hey, a silencer.' It's a chunky, square handgun, a black cylinder on the end of the barrel.

Ray holds up a rifle. 'Shit, a Stoner sixty-three. US Navy SEALs and Marines. And this!' He squats and touches a rifle with a scope. 'Sniper's. Serious piece of kit, M-forty, I think. Remington. Expensive. Just what people need, a sniper's rifle.'

Arshag rolls his eyes at a dozen or so stapled, bloodsplashed foolscap sheets of poorly mimeographed tables of text. 'There're all here. And more. Kind of a catalogue.'

Ray says, 'Just what's here's worth a heap. Make someone rich. Better take them in.'

'Can't wait.'

———

Ray and Arshag spread the haul across Kennedy's desk. Laming is tense, open-mouthed, fixed on Kennedy's response as if for how to react. Kennedy's mouth works hard but no words come out, like he's deep in anger or shock. But at what? Ray thinks Kennedy wants to say something really fucking angry to Laming but can't.

Kennedy stabs the air. 'How drunk was he?'

'Don't know yet if he was drunk. Or sick. Or suicidal. Maybe he was celebrating. About to be rich.'

Kennedy says, 'Maybe just driving like an idiot. Bloody mug lair. Benny fucking Lee couldn't afford any of this.'

Ray lifts empty hands in query. 'Delivering them? Hawking them round? Or he stole them?'

No response. No one believes silly bloody Benny was up to stealing them. And where from anyway? Ray realises the room is deathly quiet. Arshag stares at the Luger, Laming the silenced handgun. Kennedy absently reaches out and touches the Remington M-forty, the sniper rifle, then in a cold lift of his eyes, looks directly at Ray. Ray feels a chill.

Kennedy says, 'Leave them with me.'

Ray looks at him, at Arshag, back at Kennedy. 'We haven't booked them in.'

'I'll fucking do it. Get back to whatever you were doing.'

Ray says, 'This's what we were doing.'

Laming stacks the weapons into a wooden crate and stands over it, arms folded.

Ray says, 'I counted them.'

Laming says, 'Bully for you. Bullets too?'

Kennedy leans back in his chair, hands behind his head. 'I'll take them to the Inspector. Chain of command, heard of that? If I need you, I'll whistle.'

Arshag and Ray emerge into the open at the front of the copshop.

Ray says, 'If Kennedy's talking chain of command, something's got to be real wrong.'

'Where're you going?'

'Fishing.'

'They still be there?'

'Get through the fishing to get to the drinking. Helps you recover from the fishing.'

—

The afternoon heat is losing its edge but still punishing. Shadows are lengthening as they sneak east. The stretch of creek is postcard beautiful. The water level is low, the creek about ten yards wide with steep sandy-clay sides. It looks at least three feet deep. Tall river gums have dropped bark into the water and on and around scrubby bushes. Peter, Paul and Mario have sagging, unattended lines out on rods rigged on forked sticks, and are lounging in folding chairs around an esky half-full of beer cans and cardboard carton near-full of empties. The heat of the day has curled leaves on a dehydrated bush lemon tree, and the trio look dehydrated too, despite their liquid refreshment.

Ray and Arshag are greeted with curses and heavy exhalations.

Peter sits up, stretches his legs over the esky. Getting none of his booze. 'Who told you we were here?'

Ray says, 'That's what parents are for.'

Peter glares at Paul and Mario. 'Not my fucking parents.'

Ray pushes Peter's legs off the esky and sits on it, cramping the space. Peter clearly wants to shift away but won't.

Arshag walks to the rods and a bucket of water containing a few yellow-bellies. 'Big fine, you ought to know, for under-size catch.'

Paul says, 'Bullshit.' Falls silent when Arshag stands beside him.

Ray pivots to each in turn: Paul, Mario, then Peter. 'Your ticket alibi is worthless. And people who know say you weren't at the dance that night.'

Peter's turn. 'Bullshit.'

Ray says, 'Hide nor hair. And it's important because Diah and Alice passed the service station on their way home from school on the days they were abducted. Right past Paul working on the semis. And Arshag has it on good authority from Paul's boss that during smoko in the arvo you used to set up boxes for seats and a table, and invite your mates to sit there too. To whistle and call rude words at any schoolgirls going by.'

Arshag says, 'You probably thought, because you're all heroes, they liked you giving them a hard time.'

Mario crushes his can and tosses it into the cardboard bin. Eyes the esky, folds his arms.

Ray says, 'I'm guessing sex is something you don't get a lot of. So these schoolgirls turned you on and, hey, being foreign, they were kind of available.'

Ray and Arshag let the silence grow. Ray hears tiny tinkles from water in the creek. The rods sway gently from the weak flow.

Paul shifts in his seat, half-reaches for the esky, stops, sits on his hands. 'This's bullshit.'

Ray ignores him. 'Here's what you have to think about. Two things.' He counts them on his fingers. 'One, the rapes. Who did them? Who held the girls down? Ripped their clothes off. And who took their knickers as souvenirs?'

He looks at each of them. Arshag slowly paces outside the circle, hands behind his back, jiggling the handcuffs on his belt.

Ray says, 'Two, suicide and murder. Heavy. What the rapists did to Diah was so ugly she decided she was better off dead. Can you imagine that? So her suicide is on the rapists. And who beat and strangled Alice and chucked her body in a gully like trash? Think about it. Everyone did different stuff but if we don't know what, everyone gets charged with everything. And if just one brave boy tells us everything, he might get to go home early. How the law works, got it?'

Ray stands, dusts himself off. 'Talk soon then.' He points to one rod that is bowing under a load. 'Who's the lucky boy?'

The three just stare at it as Ray and Arshag return to the Land Rover and leave.

Arshag says, 'You're an artist.'

'What do you reckon?'

'Paul'll buckle first, then Mario.'

'Peter'll hold out. And threaten them, which might work.'

Arshag says, 'They're not murderers. I don't think they're capable. Not even Peter.'

'So if you're right, and they couldn't do it, who else was there who could?'

'Where now?'

'Get grog. Go home. Drink grog. I've never asked you about your religious or other beliefs about life but you're welcome to join me even if you just want to watch.'

They go silent, watching the waiting landscape.

———

Crushed beer cans lie around a small bin next to the fridge. Harsh light, longer shadows and heat from the open, west-facing door make it mid-afternoon. At the table, Ray opens a new can. Arshag has one in front of him.

Ray says, 'How well did you know Benny?'

'Noisy. A loner, and lonely. Trying to be a hoon. Tough life, tough father. Biggest dream I reckon he ever had was owning an original Mustang. No prospects.'

'His back-seat armoury has to be the best prospect he'd ever have then.'

'The most Benny could be is delivery boy. No brains for more.'

Ray rubs his nose, smells petrol. He gets up to wash and dry his hands, again. The third time. He can't tell if Arshag's noticed. 'Thinking of those pages, the catalogue, how's a collection that big even get here? Why here? Got to be imports. And the ones in the list but not in the car—still out there somewhere. How'd they get to Royalton, or into the country at all? I reckon they'd be sold with no waiting, no delay, so the full load's maybe close.' He unfolds a map of Queensland. 'That catalogue's a serious weight. Bring them in by plane. Cheaper over distance.'

'And faster. And can land in uncheckable places.'

'Big enough to carry it all, small enough to slip by. A few remote stops to refuel. Maybe south of Darwin, west of Camooweal, north of Winton.' He points to roughly equidistant leaps across the map. 'Stop, fill up, flog a few.'

'You know your guns.'

'Hard not to in the army. Keeping up with Vietnam, just in case. That party's over but the guns never are. Yanks left them lying around like lollies. Got to go somewhere. Glut's not as bad as it was but it's still there. Guns and men.'

'Mercenaries?'

'Ex-soldiers're well-paid in some places. Hotspots, they like to call them on the news. Make wars sound neat and tidy. Got a call once about Mozambique. Had the whole package: insurance, expenses, overseas bank account. False ID if I wanted. But I have no overseas action, so lower pay.' Bleak grin.

'Tempted?'

'Nah. Proper war or none at all.' He goes to the door, leans on the doorjamb. Wispy clouds above are in long strings, the sky a flawless solid blue beyond. No wonder some ancients thought it was a dome. The Mozambique offer was serious. Some soldiers who never get to war feel a gap—all that training, nerving up. 'I met vets who tried it and swore never again. Dangerously muddy lines of command, too many cheap drugs, never sure who you were killing. And no why to it.

'Carrying that sort of load, plane'd be, what, six-seater?' says Ray.

'Like Taylor's Cessna.'

Ray growls, frustrated.

'I hate we handed the lot over,' Arshag says.

'Not much choice. Can't trust any of them, the Inspector either.'

Arshag says, 'You had any more head-ons with Kennedy about the Randalls?'

Ray shakes his head.

'But you don't think it was a joke?'

Ray considers it, shakes his head again. 'No. No joke.' He crushes his can, which isn't empty, and beer erupts all over him. 'Shit!' Ray wipes his face on his sleeve. 'What do you reckon I ought to do?'

Arshag gives a dead laugh. 'Hard to know the next move when someone tried to kill you but it didn't work and now you and this someone have to work together to find who tried to kill you, and you're both pretending it never happened?'

'Shit, Arshag.'

Arshag shrugs an unpersuasive apology. He lifts his eyebrows. 'You said you were sent out here because you refused a bad order?'

Ray sags. 'Those were the days.' The memory unwelcome, adding to the load.

'Tell me.'

Ray gets another can. 'I was new, a baby detective. Two long-timers, call them Abbott and Costello, took me to arrest a stirrer. Said he was blocking a crew trying to fix some major road. We go bush, end up on a two-rut track. No sign of a major road. Stop at this bush block piled with a wrecked big shed. Furniture smashed, fence chewed up and dumped on top. Someone's home, bulldozed.

'This sad bloke's there. The wrecked shed, everything was his. Screaming blue murder calling cops, politicians, reporters all thieves and thugs. Only road in sight's the two-rut track. While I'm saying, "What major road?" Costello heavies the bugger. Wades into him, hurts him. I get Costello to stop, I nearly get a kicking too. Abbott's like it's nothing, an ordinary day, hands in his pockets.

'They chuck him in a paddy wagon that came with us. Abbott's set to charge him—wait for it!—resisting arrest, assaulting police, public nuisance. The trifecta. Even considered foul language, for fuck's sake.

'Then through the bush on a rise I see this grand-looking house. New and exxy and, guess what, we're on the only track up to it. Abbott calls me a fuckwit cos I don't know it belongs to a government minister and he needs a road. The poor hero they beat up refused to sell his miserable block and there's soil and water runoff problems around so the road's got to go through there. Road's on the quiet. Naturally. So us guardians of the law, we sort him. They put all his bulldozed stuff on a semi that night, got rid of it.'

'In the dark?'

'Big lights like a movie, the full works.'

'Why take you along?'

'Testing me out. Job interview. I fucked up, refused to help. And here I am.'

Arshag pushes his hair back with both hands. 'What about the arrested bloke?'

'Released a week later, no charge. Guess he did the deal. Didn't have much choice.'

'And the road?'

'I went to Department of Main Roads. An upgrade for some road was official but no one from the department actually went out to look. Even better, the contract to build the road went to a private company which was already outed as co-owned by the minister who owned the house.'

'Got state funding to build his own road.'

'Sweet.'

Arshag looks uncomfortable. 'You were there, you could've spoken up.'

'Abbott falsified worksheets. Rubbity-dub.' Ray mimes an eraser action. 'Officially I was somewhere else. How can I know what's going on if I'm not even there? I spoke to reporters. Some've spent years chasing shit like this. Mostly they can't pin anything on anyone, these pricks all cover each other's arses. And I wanted to stay a copper.'

'Road got built?'

'Even as we speak.'

'Why stay a cop, with this going on?'

'Good question. It's like fighting, maybe. I'm good at it. Do what you're good at, eh? Maybe I keep hoping I'll do some good someday.' Thinks of Lord Billy, his noble aspirations.

Ray gets up, puts the remaining cans in the fridge. 'Come on. Enough time to write up talking to our three boyos. Got to do everything textbook.'

Arshag drives through empty streets, sun low, in their eyes. Looks at Ray tense, restless. 'You okay to be at work?'

'All I know how to do.'

Arshag parks at the copshop facing the street and goes inside. Ray stays, staring at the road. Trucks rumble, whine and growl by at deadly speeds. A tired, solitary tree on the footpath whips to and fro in their slipstream as if afraid. In the rear-view mirror, Ray sees Kennedy emerge from the copshop, head down, on a mission. He doesn't see Ray, heads across the road to the pub. Ray thinks about it, follows.

The bar is cool and dark as ever, lit by coloured glare from the red and green glass in the windows and door. The same lone drinker leans on a bench, watching what to Ray looks like the same horse race on the TV. Maybe the same beer. Ray nods to Barb, who pours him one. He takes it to Kennedy, alone at a corner table, and sits opposite. Kennedy jumps in surprise, for a moment like a guilty kid—even a dog expecting a kick—and stirs himself to leave.

Ray slumps in his chair, working at conveying no threat, tone calm, conversational. 'Who runs this shit show? You or Laming?'

Kennedy, taken aback, stares at him over what feels to Ray like an immense time and space that a punch could never reach across. If they're duelling, it's truce time.

Kennedy finally says, 'Your problem is you're too fucking thick to know you're not wanted.'

Ray sips his beer. Takes time to look around, sees Barb's eye on them. 'One thing to not want me. Another to want me dead.'

Kennedy shuffles his boots.

Ray says, 'Who's in charge? I just want to get it straight.'

'It's my fucking copshop.' Jabbing himself in the chest at each word.

'That's what I thought. At first.' Ray lifts and drops his shoulders exaggeratedly.

Kennedy seems ready to start the usual bluster then stifles a groan that could have been a sob. Ray, shocked, has no time to react further before Kennedy slams a fist on the table, mouth in a snarl.

Barb calls out, 'Hey! You alright over there?'

Kennedy's eyes are wild.

Shaken, Ray says, 'Try me. Spread the load.'

Kennedy stares into the outside brightness, then at Ray with eyes glazed by the glare. Ray watches in wonder as Kennedy's face slowly returns to its closed-off normal, then he examines his beer, drains it, hauls himself to his feet and walks out.

Ray swivels as if to follow, sees Barb's fierce look and stays put. What was that? A sob? The shame of that alone is enough for Kennedy to want him dead. Ray looks out through shimmering heat at the street. Shadow-boxing is as exhausting as the real thing. Except this is the real thing.

Ray returns to the copshop, meets Louise who tells him Paul, mate of Peter and Mario, has killed himself with his own twenty-two.

13

Ray sits on the same stretch of creek bank where he and Arshag met Peter, Paul and Mario fishing. Ray had told Mario to meet him at Petersens Dam but Mario insisted on here. He arrives barefoot on a squeaking bicycle that has seen better days. They sit on logs close to the eroding creek bank. Mario is drained, shaky. Ray lets the silence grow until Mario starts kicking the bank, making it crumble.

Ray says, 'What's wrong with Petersens Dam?'

Mario shrugs, bottom lip protruding, looks at Ray and holds his gaze. His shakiness leaves, surprising Ray.

Mario turns to stare into the creek. 'That chick killed herself.'

'Diah. Say her name.'

Mario's mouth trembles but Ray isn't letting him off. Wraps his arms around himself. 'Diah.'

Ray looks into Mario's eyes, which are red and puffy. 'What happened with Paul?'

Mario is silent.

'Why do you think he did it?'

Mario shakes his head, a sharp, intense action that might even hurt. Takes a deliberate breath, looks hard at Ray.

Ray says, 'He left you high and dry with the lot of it.'

Mario strains to speak. Ray leans in to hear. 'The girl—'

'Diah.'

Mario swallows. 'Diah.'

'What about her?'

'She'd come past the pipe shop, sometimes with Alice, or after Alice was at the café. Going home from school. I was mostly out bush laying pipes. I hardly saw her.'

'At the table and chairs outside the servo. You all saw her.'

'Few times. I can't take breaks from work like they can.' His voice alternates between strong and faltering. He stares at the water as if it revolts him, fixedly watching small whirls of current, the water today a pale blue-green with lots of busy water-spiders. Gasps, voice barely audible. 'I didn't kill no one. None of us did. It wasn't us. Peter or Paul or me.'

'Did you rape Alice?'

Shakes his head slowly, more a swaying motion. 'No, no. Couldn't. Not after, after Diah. We didn't know she'd do that. She didn't have to do that!'

Ray thinks about that, lets it go. 'Did you see Alice killed? Were you there when it happened?'

Shakes his head excessively again, and fast, whispers, 'Don't know nothing about Alice.'

'But you know who did it?'

More head shakes, tears flicking from his eyes.

'Why don't you know?'

'I heard it on the news. I wasn't there.'

Ray waves a dismissive hand, forcing it to stay open, not form a fist. 'If you don't tell me, you'll be as guilty and you'll cop jail for it.'

'I can't tell you who was there except it wasn't us.'

'Who organised the rapes? Who dumped Alice's body?'

'Not us! You're not letting me talk!' He holds out his hands, palms towards Ray.

Ray shuts up.

Mario looks up from under ragged eyebrows at him. 'Did Paul leave a note?'

Ray absorbs this. 'If he did, what would it say?'

Mario sighs, gapes around into the bush, screws his eyes tight. 'I never knew it'd be this bad. It was just sex!'

'You raped her. Don't you understand?'

Mario looks quickly at Ray again, then at the creek. 'I can't do anything now. Since Paul.' Tears run down his face which he wipes savagely to remove all trace of them. 'I told my mum what we did—what I did. To Diah.' He opens his eyes and sags, then again stares fixedly at the creek. Not crying anymore, or shaking. Exuding a calm Ray doesn't trust as Ray copes with his own shock at Mario's admission.

'Mum walked away. She isn't talking to me now.'

'What'd you say to her?'

'I had sex with, with . . . with the girl who died in the dam.' His voice blank, no emotion.

Ray finds his own voice needs forcing out. 'Why did you tell her? Why'd you do that?'

'I didn't think about the girl. Girls have sex all the time. Then she went in the dam.' He stares at the tops of the trees, forehead wrinkled, face troubled. 'I never thought, just from having sex.'

'Stop saying you had sex. What you did was rape, you hear me? Rape. Say it.'

'Rape.' As if testing the sound.

'Who was with you when you raped Diah?'

174

'Peter and Paul. Benny Lee could've come but didn't. He said not to do it.' He looks quizzically at Ray, as if for Ray's opinion about that. Ray feels relief for Benny, fucking futile as that is.

'Peter and Paul did it too?'

'Yeah.'

Ray pauses, then makes himself continue. 'When Diah was examined, she'd been hurt, torn up. Would've been blood.'

Mario gives a kind of shrug.

Ray takes a breath. 'You didn't think her bleeding was bad? And you ought to stop?'

'Women bleed. Don't know how. But every month. Normal. Isn't it?'

Ray pauses, looks at the creek. For help maybe. 'Petersens Dam's how far out of town? Seven miles? After the rape, you three drove back to town. How was Diah supposed to get home?'

'I was going to take her back to town. But we got into the beers. And then she was gone. Called her. Couldn't find her. So we pissed off. What else could we do?'

'This's when she was at the bottom of the dam, drowned.'

'We didn't know that. Didn't know she'd do that.'

Ray has to stop. When he was an apprentice, a surfie term for pack rape was 'stirring the porridge'. He's never understood how they got an erection. He looks around. Hears crickets, butcher birds. Hears the creek gurgling gently like it doesn't want to interrupt. Sees a family of ducks swimming. Smells sour mud. He picks up a small, fallen gum branch, crushes the leaves to smell the eucalyptus. On the far muddy bank, a white-faced heron steps delicately, hunting. Mario looks at the creek and has to turn away. Ray wonders if he sees Diah in the water.

'When she was dragged out of the dam, an article of her clothing was missing.'

'Peter. He took them.'

'The knickers.'

'Paul and me didn't know till he flashed them at us on the way home.'

Ray changes tack. 'Did you or your mother tell your father?' He wants to ask why he chose his mother first, although there's no real mystery there. Hasn't asked about the rape itself. He'll have to, not yet.

Mario nods again, wipes his face hard with the back of a hand. 'She did. He hit me. See?' He raises his shirt. He has an ugly welt on his chest and ribs. Done with a leather strap or something harder, an axe handle. Mario stares at it and says matter-of-factly, like a kid quoting a grown-up, 'Mum and Dad'll lose the farm now.'

'Why?'

'I'll be in jail and they can't work it on their own, too old.'

'How's the farm going?'

'Got debts, not our fault. Dad says it's god's will but I don't get that.' He pauses, squirms. 'Dad says they'll have to leave town now, from shame. Says I'm a weakling. Says me going to jail is right. Right and good. Even them losing the farm. Because he and mum raised me to be good and I haven't been. For the sex. The rape. Dad won't speak to me now. He says ever.'

Ray leans back. Mario is regressing, kid-like, as his defences fall away. The eye of the storm. Going to need help.

'We're going to the copshop now and you'll write everything down. Details. How you grabbed Diah. Where you took her. Who did what. All of it. The whole thing.'

Mario stoops, head bending forwards, nods.

'What about my bike?'

'I'll put your bloody bike in the back. Jesus!' Ray stops, takes a breath. 'Listen to me.' Mario looks up from under again as Ray says, 'If you know anyone else is involved in what happened to Diah and Alice, you have to tell me. Don't let anyone hide behind you.'

'I got nothing to do with Alice. Or Diah going in the dam. I don't know why she did that.'

'You don't know why?' For the first time, Ray seriously feels his control slip. Pain in his neck and shoulders and hands from wanting to belt the kid down. He gets up, out of range. 'You can't give me any names about Alice?'

Mario shakes his head.

'You'll be asked more questions about her because what happened to her looks like what happened to Diah. You understand that?'

Mario nods again.

Ray looks at the beauty of the creek, hears its tinkling this time. Hears the birds, breathes it in. He wants to tell Mario to soak it up, he won't see or hear or smell this for a long time, but says nothing. Jail will eat the bastard alive.

———

At the copshop, Ray escorts a mute Mario to a storeroom used for interrogations, bare except for table and chairs. Gives him pen and paper. Mario, cheeks blotchy, eyes red and swollen, stares at them, says, 'I'm not a good writer.'

Ray says, 'Take your time. Put down everything.' And leaves. Outside, he leans against the door, shaky.

Laming appears, angry, too close. 'What's all this about?'

'The kid says he was one of Diah's rapists.'

'And?'

'And bloody what?'

'The second girl? The murder?'

Ray shakes his head. 'That's it. Till I get his statement.' Wondering, *What's the problem?*

Laming steps towards the door as if he's going in and Ray puts out an arm to stop him. 'My bloody case. Where're you going?'

They're eye to eye as Ray realises he didn't get the case to solve it. He got it so he'd fail.

Laming stops, uncertain, as Kennedy appears at the end of the corridor, Arshag behind him. Laming fixes Kennedy with a look to melt metal, then turns back to Ray. 'Who else're you talking to?'

'Wait and bloody see. Why're you pushing me? You didn't give a shit all this fucking time and now you care?'

Laming freezes, says, 'This copshop's supposed to be a team, that's why.'

Ray is incredulous but before he can speak—or laugh— Kennedy approaches. Arshag stays back but in earshot.

Kennedy extends a mollifying hand. 'This Paul bloody shot himself. Jesus, you better've followed procedure. To the letter. No bloody harassment! And what about Peter?'

Ray snaps a look at Arshag who looks bewildered, knows his own face's got to be looking lost, but makes himself stay calm. 'He's my next stop.'

'The eyetie's copped for one rape, Diah. But not Alice, and not the murder. That it? So the job's a long way from done yet.'

'Mario's fucking Maltese, not Italian.'

Kennedy releases a shallow laugh. 'Write it up. All your shit.

Everything.' Kennedy sends another unreadable look to Laming, turns on his heel, brushes by Arshag and leaves. Laming hesitates then follows.

The corridor goes silent. Arshag checks they're alone.

Ray says, 'Mario might try to copy Paul. Need a watch on him.'

Arshag nods.

Ray says, 'Peter will run. I think he'll run.'

———

At Peter's property, brilliant shafts of afternoon sunlight slice through the trees, making walls of light. Arshag flanks Ray to knock on the door of Peter's shed. No dogs. The place not just empty—abandoned. He's gone.

Formal events are set in train. At the copshop, Mario is put in a cell under the building where the land falls away sharply, and the travelling magistrate is notified. Peter's details are circulated to other copshops. A warrant is issued for his arrest and planning begins to move the case to Tyborg. Louise reveals Mario's parents have advised her they will not visit him. Paul's body is in a freezer truck on its way to Tyborg, which has a morgue.

In a phone call from an angry Lord Billy, Ray discovers Paul's parents say Ray entered their house under false pretences, harassed their son at home and his work, and drove the boy to his death. Lord Billy says he refused to hear such accusations. He congratulates Ray, promises him any support that helps. The rapes and murder were a blight on all of Royalton.

———

In the early morning, at Petersens Dam, the sun is rising in a pale blue, cloudless sky, looming like the threat it is. Ray stands, trying to look into the water but it's too dazzling, too glittering, and he gives up.

Arshag sits on a log at its edge, under the grudging shade of a large scribbly gum. 'Paul did it out the back of their machinery shed. His dog was sitting next to the body when I got there.'

'Sooner you than me.'

'Kennedy meant to send you but the parents've barred you from the property.'

Ray kicks at weeds sprouting from gravel left from building the picnic shelters ages ago. Bark lies around, some with the mysterious pathways left by the scribula worm, looking like bad handwriting. As a boy, Ray was sure they were secret bush messages, if only he could decipher them. Paperbarks whisper behind them, water birds play and feast in front. Grass runs to the water's edge. The picnic area is less used since Diah's body was found. Ray selects flat stones from the gravel, takes them to the water's edge and throws, counting skips.

Arshag says, 'You believe Mario? They weren't involved with Alice?'

Ray comes to sit with him. 'Mario's beyond lying. Too much for any of them to do twice. I swear they only realised after Diah killed herself what a shit thing they did. *We're only having sex, what's the problem?* Jesus.'

'A copycat did Alice?'

Ray shrugs his maybe. That possibility too daunting yet.

Arshag kicks at an ant's nest and red ants pour out for war. Lifts his boots onto the log.

Ray shades his eyes from the stabbing sun, rubs them. 'I should've anticipated Paul. Knew he was weak.' He uses his boot to push walls of dirt around the nest, which does nothing to stop the angry flow and he lifts his boots too. 'We've got less than we thought for Alice. If we believe Mario, someone even more ruthless is out there.'

14

That evening, on Stella's verandah, the table cleared of dinner debris, Ray relaxes as Stella sits with a small pile of exercise books, marking student assignments. The stillness of a slowly cooling night, under very high, misty cloud. From deep in the bush beyond her back fence, a boobook owl is calling, almost like a cuckoo. Reminds Ray of night in the bush around the cane farm. A reassuring note. He describes visiting Intan and Fang Su, Diah's parents, to tell them about Mario's confession. Feeling their gratitude at the lifting of some of the load. In the light of Mario's statement, his trial at least will be over more quickly. Their refusal to attend any of it, long or short.

Stella's hand stays at her throat as Ray describes Mario's version of events. 'And Alice's parents?'

A brooding expression crosses his face. 'They'd hoped I had more about her. Of course. Not if we believe Mario, which I do, so far.'

'Intan and Fang Su would know Mario's parents?'

'Crossed paths, of course. Harry knows Mario, both in the water business. Asked me to pass on sympathy for them.'

182

Stella shudders. 'Imagine, out buying your groceries and the parents whose son raped your daughter turn up beside you at checkout. Ugly it's locals responsible. But a step towards not looking over my shoulder every time I go out. Lifts a bit of the fear and stain off the place.'

Ray recalls Lord Billy's similar comment, then feels uncomfortable that his next thought is that his success might cement his, or their, place in Royalton.

———

Ray, alone in the Land Rover, heads through dense ironbark forest so parched it looks as if he could snap off the trunks of the blackened trees. Bugger-all grass. The sun's dazzling flashes through the trees attack his eyes. Then the narrow, unsealed road leaves the ironbarks for fewer trees, open ground and low-rolling hills. A fire has been through recently, the earth still black with ash, green stubble starting. He's heading to Benny Lee's place to update his parents. All properly entered in the trip book.

Benny Lee's post-mortem revealed large quantities of alcohol in his system, offering some support for Arshag's theory that Benny had found a first-ever lucrative line of work and his new prospects overwhelmed him. Premature celebration. 'A deeply sad, sadly common result of intoxication. Benny was a popular young man, we'll miss his jokes and happy spirit.' Ray rolls the phrases around, practising them. He's met the father before, not the mother.

A small, starred hole in the windscreen appears, then the flat crack of what he slowly grasps is a rifle shot. His delayed response turns sharp at a second star and crack. He swerves left onto a rough shoulder that bounces him and the vehicle about. The windscreen shatters, glass fragments showering him, as his brain computes a thud as another bullet hits somewhere close. He swerves right then left again onto a flat stretch of ground, brakes in a flurry of dust and exits the vehicle, running low around its rear, then to acacias at a rocky outcrop. Handgun out, he tries to trace the shots back to an origin, picks a mound atop a hill across a gully, scarcely a hundred yards away. Forest open enough. Sniper rifle? Sure as shit not engaging that with a handgun.

Silence. Time slows. Dust and white cockatoos float to rest. He shifts elbows to avoid black ants, stinging bastards. It's bloody hot. Water's in the Land Rover. With the radio.

A strange, hollow silence. Sniper's pissed off. Or waiting for a cleaner shot. Ray recalls Kennedy tapping that Remington M-forty, like the solution to a problem. He hears the drone of an engine. An old ute appears on the road ahead. It pulls over to jam to a halt beside Ray's vehicle. Archie Lee, Benny's father, climbs out, no regard for cover, reaches into his cabin and comes out with a twenty-two rifle. 'Where are you?' Tops off his bravado by slamming the door like he hates it.

Ray searches for movement at the mound. None. 'Archie? It's Ray, Ray Windsor. West of you and getting up.' He stands, watching the mound, brushing off ants and debris. No movement. Nothing. He approaches Archie, handgun pointing skywards.

Archie is affronted. 'I heard the shots. Thought some bastard's having a go at my horses. Someone after you for god's sake or what?'

Ray leans into his cabin and uses his folding knife to dig out a flattened bullet from the seat. 'Hit the metal back.'

Archie says, 'That'll take a bit of identifying.' Looks around, nods at the mound. 'What do you reckon?'

'Yeah, the mound.'

'Not a bad shot, that range. Unless it's an expert, then it's a shit shot.' Winks at Ray who nods, gratitude for the concern.

Ray stares at the mound, lost in what he'd expect a copper to manage after years working with guns.

'Who'd you piss off?'

Ray laughs, pleased he can. 'Everyone, sooner or later.'

Archie manages a grin. 'Been shot at before?'

Ray shakes his head. 'Only in jest.' Which makes even dour Archie snort. 'You?'

Archie thinks about it. 'New Guinea. Strange feeling. Hits you later.'

———

Ray sits with Archie and Rose on their cool, shaded verandah above a gentle slope to a paddock where four horses stand under tall, silvery gums. Rose is in her late forties, stocky build, with brown hair cut short. Her brown eyes are busy, like her hands, which she puts to work pouring tea. Ray takes a fat biscuit but holds it, not eating.

Rose sits back, knits her fingers together to hold them still. 'Well, then.'

Ray says, 'The coroner'll say Benny was above the legal limit. Accidental death. We'll never know for sure but basically the finding'll say the crash was caused by alcohol.'

Silence, except for crows and magpies in the gums. Archie cracks large knuckles. He is stocky, broad. Maybe in his fifties. His eyes are a clear blue. Looking at Ray, maybe not seeing him. 'And them guns? Who give him the guns?'

Ray doesn't answer immediately, in case Archie has some idea, but he stays quiet. 'Might be some smuggling going on. We think Benny was delivering. Not a big wheel.' He shuts up.

One of the horses below breaks into an intense gallop, mane and tail streaming. Beautiful. Stops, flicking its head.

Rose tussles with herself to say, 'That's his horse. Pinto.'

Ray says, 'Benny was good in the gym. Good with the kids. We had fun in the ring, that exhibition bout.' Not true that last bit, but so be it. He thinks of Paul and his parents. Grateful he's out of that.

Tears roll down Rose's face, unheeded. Archie looks at her, down at the horses, back at her, puts his hand over hers, which she covers with her other hand. She nods.

Archie says, 'The bastards who give him the guns need flogging, then shooting somewhere that won't kill them, but'll hurt for a while. With the same guns. Don't care who hears me say it.' Rose pats his hand in half-hearted rebuke.

A police Land-Rover turns into the driveway, rattles over the grid and reaches the house. Arshag stops, waves from his window but stays put.

Rose waves to him. 'He got my call then.'

Rose holds up the teapot but Arshag smiles, shakes his head, and touches his watch.

Ray eases himself to his feet. 'Give us a call if I can help, anything.' Rose puts out a hand, not looking at him. He takes it and they exchange squeezes. He and Archie head to the Rover.

Archie shakes hands with Arshag, then Ray. 'Thanks for coming. Nearly got yourself killed too.'

Ray climbs into the Rover. 'Probably some idiot duck-shooter who got bored finding no ducks. Happened a couple of times on the farm I was dragged up on. Bullet through the living room once. Take care, you and Rose, eh?'

Archie lifts his chin, mouth firmly shut.

———

Arshag stops at Ray's vehicle and Ray points to the mound. They take out their handguns, check and load them, climb from the vehicle and do a calm pincer movement through the bush to the mound.

Arshag looks at the hollow behind it. 'Nothing.'

'No shells, no bootprints. Not even scuff marks.'

Arshag nods towards Ray's vehicle. 'Real dumb duck-shooters out where there's no water.'

He and Arshag exchange a grim look.

Arshag says, 'You okay to drive back?'

'Providing the bastard's gone home. Yeah, no worries. We need to check if that sniper rifle was in the bag sent to Brisbane.'

Arshag lifts his eyebrows. 'Maybe that horse's already bolted. You having fun yet? You been nearly run over and shot at. How's it feel?'

'Waiting for it to sneak up on me.' He feels like he's drowning in unknowables, unprovables. In filthy water from somewhere he can't see, flooding his mouth. Aching for solid ground, facts beyond hunches and fears, beyond knowing only in your gut, which can flip into knowing nothing at all. Wants enough to justify action. Justice.

———

Ray strides into the copshop on a mission. Arshag follows. Laming's desk is empty. Kennedy's is too but then he exits

187

the Inspector's office and shuts the door after him. Ray gets satisfaction that, upon seeing him, Kennedy tenses.

'What'd he say?'

'The guns? What do you think he said? Sent it all to Brisbane. Too big for you kiddies.' Kennedy drops into his chair as if carrying a weight.

Ray says, 'Serial numbers? Removed or registered as missing?'

'All the above. Usual.' He keeps a contemptuous grin but his eyes are shifty, maybe less smug than Ray would have expected for such a find. He recalls Kennedy's reaction with the duffers. Jesus, is he running guns too?

Ray holds his ground. 'Can I see the list of the weapons you sent?'

Kennedy pauses. 'Why?'

'Want to check something.' Nods inclusively to Arshag.

Kennedy holds up a typed version of the roughly mimeographed would-be catalogue.

Ray doesn't take it. 'Need to compare that with the original. Hate anything to be missed. Fall off the back of a truck.'

Kennedy relaxes. 'You accusing me of something?'

Ray leans over the desk. 'Some gutless wonder took a pot shot at me today. On the way to Benny Lee's parents.'

'Really?' Lazy, bored, as if Ray had kicked his toe, but Ray saw, the moment before, Kennedy's eyes widened and looked to Laming's empty desk. 'No blood. Guess they missed. Put it in the incident book. Get shells, footprints, anything?'

'That's it? I get shot at and that's it?'

'Get off your high horse, Windsor. You important enough to shoot? We get shooters all the time, don't know which end of the weapon the bullet comes out. As you know, for Christ's sake.' A tremor in his voice feeds into his eyes, makes them flicker.

Ray straightens.

Kennedy grins. 'Maybe you're just too bloody unpopular. No bastard's taken pot shots at me. Even Shaggers here doesn't get shot at.'

'Could've been a sniper rifle. Like from Benny's back seat.'

'Then I guess it'd be missing from the list, wouldn't it.' He holds it out, and grins.

Like a fucking wolf, Ray thinks as he takes it. Runs down it. Finds the rifle. His mouth tightens in anger even as a tiny voice in his head says that would've been too easy. Wants to say, *Could be on the list but never made it into the box with the rest of the batch.* Bloody box hasn't even gone yet, for fuck's sake. Trying to think who'll check the box in Brisbane. Anyone he can trust? No. Kennedy's fucking grin gets all his attention. Smack the bastard in the mouth. Demand where the fuck Laming is. But says nothing. Knows, right now, he can't cope with another bullshit answer.

Kennedy says, 'Shooting at you could've been a lot of things. Maybe get some evidence? Like real coppers? Anyway, haven't you got another rape and a murder to solve?'

Ray's vision frames in angry red, since Kennedy's right.

'All you've done is nab Mario, who handed himself in anyway, and you get big-headed.'

Ray leaves, every word of Kennedy's making his head feel like exploding. He strides across the wide street, between semis, and enters the hotel. At the bar, Ray signals for a beer, then another for Arshag, who appears beside him. Arshag holds up a tiny space between thumb and forefinger to Barb. A small beer comes for him.

Arshag says, 'Phoney war gets a bloke down.'

'Too much war and too much phoney.' Ray scrapes his keys on the wooden bar as if to leave his initials next to those already there. 'So we're looking at stock shunted on back-roads. Guns coming in. Lizard, snakes, cockatoos going out.' He looks at Arshag and they both laugh.

Arshag toasts. 'Saving lizards, snakes and cockatoos.' They laugh again.

Ray holds his head. 'Kennedy says, solve a murder I can't get a move on, while criminal shit's pumping along, always over the horizon, and I can't get a handle on any of it either.'

Barb approaches polishing a beer glass. 'Lizards, snakes and cockatoos? You blokes okay?'

Ray says, 'Animal smugglers. Big money overseas for critters we just get shitty with. Hard to believe round here but true. Getting them out alive's the trick. They whack them in cages, stuff them in cylinders. Fly some out. Send some poor buggers in the mail.'

'You're kidding me. Cruel! How do they shut them up? Snakes're pretty quiet but cockatoos?'

Ray drains his beer, signals for more. 'Get them drunk. Works on me.'

He turns to Arshag. 'You know, where I'm from, near a river, locals know whose boat's chugging by just from the motor, day or night. Don't have to see it. Surely people hear these planes? Planes are loud.'

'More space out here, bigger than a river,' says Arshag. 'And there're planes doing normal stuff. Guns're normal too. Even Lord Billy has a Mauser Karabiner 98-K. From Angola. I know from checking his licences. All of which are in order.' Sips his beer with a wrinkled nose.

Ray breathes out from puffed cheeks. 'They flood in after wars. Armies give them out, can't get them back. After nineteen-eighteen, and after forty-five. Yanks in Vietnam passed them out like toys. Hopeless trying to stop it.'

'We do the best we can.'

'Keeping the pressure on.' Taps a finger on the bar, then the side of his nose.

Arshag rolls his eyes. 'Uh oh.' Manages a grin.

———

Ray stands at the rear of Taylor's house where the plane was parked but no longer. He kicks at tyre tracks in what soft earth there is. He turns to look south from the house. A baked, dirt road broad enough to be a passable runway climbs to a slight rise three hundred yards away. A gust of wind blows, stirring dust that adds to layers already coating the house. Ray turns away, then stops at a foul smell on the wind. Thinks about it, then walks up the road. Hears Arshag follow in the Land Rover.

At the top of the rise, on his left in front of a clump of trees, a shed the size of a double garage squats back from the road, in the rear of an abandoned yard. A rectangle of several short, thick stumps mark out the shape of the house. Long dead garden beds and a rusty, caved-in water tank. Wind puffs erratically around him. Ray pulls his shirt up to cover his face. Christ, the smell is strong, and bloody awful. He and Arshag approach the shed's closed doors, faces set against the thickening, enveloping stink.

Arshag says, 'This'll be one of those search warrant situations Kennedy once warned me about.'

'Let's go back, get one. Inspector'll race it through for us.'

Dead branches sit roughly stacked against a shed wall. Arshag points to shallow marks in the dirt. The doors were recently hauled opened but are bolted with an old padlock. Ray pulls a steel bar from a pile of rusty machinery, watching for snakes, and wrenches the whole bolt off the door, splintering the grey, desiccated wood. They drag the doors open, releasing the full onslaught of evil odour. They turn away, dry-retching, fighting for breath.

The shed is packed with stacked cages of putrefying snakes, birds, lizards and what's left of baby wallabies and roos. And maggots and dense clouds of flies.

Ray and Arshag collapse on logs upwind.

'Someone pissed off too quick to finish the job,' Ray says, pointing to the stacked branches against the walls. 'Meant to burn the whole ugly thing.'

Arshag photographs the stacks of cages until he has to retreat, and Ray takes over.

Ray says, 'Got to take something back with us. Stronger evidence.' He grins humourlessly.

'How're we going to cope with it in the car?'

Ray goes back into the shed, picks up an aluminium cylinder capped at each end. Removes a cap, screws up his face, peers inside at arm's length, and shivers. 'Reckon this used to be a sulphur-crested. By the feathers.' Puts the cap back on and holds the cylinder away from his body as dark liquid drips from its lower end.

They drive away, leaving the shed as is but doors open. The cylinder is rolled inside layers of a groundsheet in the back of the vehicle. Arshag rolls down his window. 'Gee, what reaction will we get? Nice pat on the back?'

—

Arshag, Ray and Laming watch an irritated Kennedy unroll the groundsheet on his desk, revealing the cylinder, releasing the stench. Kennedy and Laming jump back and cry out in shock and disgust.

Kennedy yells, 'Jesus fucking Christ, get that out of here!'

Ray picks it up between finger and thumb, avoiding the liquid. 'Evidence.'

'Fucking outside now. Then I'll listen. Jesus.'

Ray takes the cylinder outside, arm out from his body, and leans it against the acacia tree in the carpark. Sees Kennedy through his grimy window waving sheets of paper to clear the smell.

Ray returns. Kennedy stares fixedly at Arshag, who looks impassively back at him. Laming's expression screams disbelief, then he shakes his head, returns to his own desk, shuffles paperwork. Mask restored.

Kennedy says, 'Jesus spare me, you're the lizard and cockatoo cops now, are you?'

Ray crosses to the official noticeboard, unpins a page, brings it to Kennedy, who rolls his eyes.

Ray reads, '*Action to stop animal smuggling. Australia signed a multilateral treaty last year, the Convention on International Trade in Endangered Species of Wild Fauna and Flora, nineteen-seventy-five. Animal smuggling is already an illegal, multimillion dollar industry. Be alert for smuggling where large distances and small populations make fertile ground for smugglers.*' He looks at Kennedy, points out at the cylinder. 'Found that at Taylor's. Shed full of it. Got it all on film.'

Kennedy massages his temples, eyes closed, then glances towards Laming before staring into space, mouth fixed. Ray sees his anger is more intense now, even as he tries for ridicule.

'Even you—*even you*—can't seriously say selling birds and lizards is a crime. Endangered? Fuck me. We got snakes and lizards and screeching cockatoos all over. What is this hippy shit?'

Ray can't shut up. 'You're not worried about people flying planes in and out, however they want?'

'What else is fucking new? It's what happens out here.'

'Carrying whatever? How would we ever know? What we found is a *fact*.' Doesn't say, *Or is Taylor too good a mate?*

Kennedy worries at it, face working. Then he speaks softly. 'Go, develop your fucking photos. Write your goody-two-shoes report. I'll send it to Brisbane to prove we take lizard nicking seriously. And that'll be the end of it. Now piss off, I've got real police work to do. And so the fuck have you.'

In the newsagency, Arshag stands at the counter under a sign, YOUR PRECIOUS PHOTOS DEVELOPED HERE! He hands the camera to the newsagent and rejoins Ray in the shade of an awning on the main street. 'Takes three days.'

Ray blows a hard breath into an elaborate cobweb hanging from the awning, sending it spinning, tearing, folding in on itself. 'The Great Animal Smuggler Hunt, dead before it was born. We're going to get laughed at in the pub.'

Arshag looks at the large spider rushing to retrieve prey wrapped in silk cocoons. 'We're strange about native animals. Hardly anyone eats them. Hardly anyone knows much about them. Maybe because they're native. Meaning unimportant.'

Ray looks at him, hadn't thought about it. 'Anyone deliberately cruel to animals is sick in the head. I'd flog them.'

'We're not leaving it alone?'

'We know who owns the property. We've seen the equipment, even if he's moved it. Shed's full of evidence. But, and it's a big fucking but, the plane's gone and maybe he's away enough to claim anyone could be using those sheds, or he never goes up that hill anyway. That's if it doesn't all mysteriously burn down while we fart about here.' He shakes all over, violently. 'Bridge gone. No access. Fuck off. Trespassers shot.'

Ray walks away.

Arshag calls out. 'You're invited to a dinner.'

Ray turns back.

Arshag winks. 'Tonight. Bring a friend.'

15

Ray and Stella step from under the weight of a hot late-afternoon sun into a cool structure the size of a large garage, a steel skeleton covered with dark green material that's near transparent. Along each inner wall are garden beds, in the ground or built up on metal trestle tables, full of healthy plants laden with vegetables. Hoses are strung along the roof in a basic irrigation system, now off. The centre of the space is cleared, with a trestle table set for a dozen diners.

Stella claps in admiration. 'I buy their vegies but I've never seen where they do it.'

The canvas flap over the entrance lifts, admitting Harry and Li, Intan and Fang Su, and Arshag with a tall, olive-skinned woman his age. Her long jet-black hair with greying streaks falls to her shoulders. Warm welcomes are exchanged as Ray realises Stella knows everyone.

Arshag approaches Ray and introduces Irene. Irene puts out a hand and Ray, smiling, squeezes it.

Irene says to Ray and Stella, 'You're good friends of Dot's.'

Ray winces. 'What's she told you? No, don't tell me. She's a lot of fun.'

Stella speaks to Irene, pretending Ray is not there. 'She's privileged. He doesn't like anyone much.'

Irene gives her a theatrical wink. 'He doesn't know if he likes me yet.'

Ray says to Arshag behind his hand. 'Conspirators.'

Arshag grins. 'You don't know the half of it.' It's a joke but Ray feels a familiar constriction. Enmeshed.

He shakes hands with Harry, then Li. Sees a small brooch on Li's blouse with a photo of Alice smiling. Feels a blow to his chest he hopes he hides. Badly wants to say something but nothing comes.

He approaches Intan and Fang Su, all three self-consciously aware of their last meeting when he told them about Mario. They squeeze their six hands together, silent acknowledgement of what they cannot say aloud, until Fang Su, indicating the air around them, says, 'Diah is with us. She visits whoever we visit.' Stella joins them and Intan and Fang Su shake her hand warmly.

Nick enters, supporting a tiny woman his age, each using a walking stick. Ray sees the rest of the party gently applaud their entrance, especially the woman's. Nick leads her to Ray and Stella, every step deliberate. 'I am honoured to present my wife, Aminta.'

Aminta bows slightly. 'Pleased to meet you.' She has a throaty voice at odds with her slight appearance.

Everyone finds their seat. Children of various ages up to mid-teens enter with plates of food. Stella proudly tells Ray they're from her classes. 'My Domestic Science future chefs.' She adds that Fang Su and Li lead some classes. The children excitedly distribute Chinese, Greek and Indonesian dishes with delighted claims of who cooked what. Guided by their hosts, Ray and Stella sample it all. Home-made fruit wines too, amid warnings of their potency.

Aminta explains she is from Greek Cyprus and not supposed to befriend a Turkish Cypriot like Irene. Ray looks at Arshag. His wife is of Turkish origin.

Irene speaks in measured, accented English, 'I am just returning from Cyprus to visit my mother who is too ill to travel and must stay there in the fighting. Do you know it?'

Ray shakes his head as Stella says, 'My colleague's brother is a policeman, serving there for a year as a United Nations peacekeeper. He loves swimming in the Mediterranean but sees the sadness. And the fighting.'

Ray says, 'The country is different from here?'

'Different but not always.' Irene says, 'You are from the coast, yes? I take Arshag to the coast every few years, see the turtles come across the sand to lay, the young ones struggling back. Same as beaches at home.'

Aminta says, 'Even on Greek Cyprus beaches. Turtles and the wind don't care about borders. Once upon a time no such borders.'

Irene nods emphatically. 'No solution yet. Maybe never. Too many stupid leaders.'

Aminta claps in agreement. 'Stupid men!' She lifts her arms to embrace the table. 'You men, okay. So far.' They all laugh.

Irene looks wistful. 'Those beaches of home. Once upon a time.'

Ray echoes, 'Once upon a time.' Looks to Arshag. 'Do you say *once upon a time* in Armenian?'

Arshag thinks about it, says, 'In Armenian we say, *There was and there was not.*'

Nick lifts a glass of wine. 'We asked you to be our guests to show our respect for your work here. In school, the gym. But in the law, necessary for life at all.' Everyone toasts Ray and Stella, who acknowledge the compliment shyly.

Ray looks to Arshag for help. 'Doing what we can.'

Nick shakes a cautionary finger. 'We know your difficulties. All alone, no one can change much. Sometimes a bad system destroys itself, crushes under its own weight.'

Ray is reminded of Lord Billy's rages.

Aminta flicks her hair back, defiant. 'What we hope for. The wheel turns.'

Harry points to Ray, 'Be in the right place at the right time. As you will be. For justice for our Alice. Finally.' Ray feels a hot flush envelop his face, and knows it's shame.

Nick climbs to his feet, reaches for Aminta. 'Now we go.' The gathering ends, everyone rises and moves about.

Harry addresses Ray alone. 'Final justice may not be the law's justice, but true justice. We hope for either.' Again Ray is struck by the similarity with what Lord Billy has said. The need to take justice into your own hands. Whatever that means. He nods to Harry, supportive but troubled.

Harry says, '*Píngshēng bú zuò kuīxīnshì, bànyè qiāomén xīn bù jīng.*' He nudges Li who nods too and says to Ray, 'Clear conscience never fears midnight knocking.'

Ray, baffled, realises everyone is silent. Harry smiles, wipes his brow to brush away all worry. Stella stares at Ray who looks at Arshag again. An odd, stalled moment. Easy farewells follow, promises to meet again soon.

On the footpath outside, Ray approaches Arshag. 'Midnight knocking?'

'No shame in doing whatever brings justice for Alice. If the law fails.'

Ray remembers complaining to a seasoned copper when the lone man was beaten for fighting against the politician's new road. The veteran gave him a pityingly look. 'It doesn't matter what happened. They'll sit at their typewriters and make it up. Why've I got to tell you this?'

Arshag turns to go.

Ray grabs his sleeve. 'Final justice?'

Arshag carefully frees his sleeve. 'You think I don't want it? But I'm a cop. I swore an oath to official justice. So did you.'

Ray and Stella arrive at her house, drop their helmets on the table at the back door. The sky is lit with the silver glow of an almost-full moon.

Stella kisses him, says, 'They were honouring you. Do you feel honoured?' She taps her knuckles on his chest. 'And what's the secret man-talk about midnight knocking?' He shrugs to dismiss it but she sounds a warning. 'Tell me.'

'They're afraid we'll find evidence to show who's guilty, but Kennedy won't act or we'll never convince a court. Then I should sort it out with a clear conscience. They've all lived through corruption and murder right in front of them. Shocking. Life here's supposed to be different.'

'They're like any parents. Dreadful things happened to their kids and they think the world's ignored it. I think so too. *Are* things different here? You don't sound sure.'

He wants to believe we've got better solutions. Wants to say it's why he's a cop. Instead he wonders if it's why he's not a good cop. If it's why he has trouble living with what being a cop now means. If it is that simple, he'll quit.

Stella is looking at him. 'Penny for your thoughts?'

He shrugs, which doesn't help.

———

Early next morning, bulging, dark clouds hug the northern horizon and a crisp chill is about as the sun emerges. Ray is running, labouring to match his breathing to his pace. Too angry. Well, fuck yeah, wondering if he'll get shot today, which he didn't mention to Stella, let Royalton Radio take care of that. His breathing loosens, rhythm returns, yielding to the strength in the routine. Unlike being a cop, where he has no routine and his best is not appearing at all. Needs a new approach. Kennedy's a lost cause. Alright, Laming. Who the fuck is Laming?

———

Ray has advance warning of the Royalton Show from posters on walls, fences, cars, telegraph poles and excited comments but is still startled when Stella pokes him awake Saturday morning to say they're going. No need for breakfast.

Large marquees stand on an empty paddock near the town centre. Ray and Stella join a queue to sample cakes, biscuits, preserves, bread and sausages. Luxuriating in the guilty pleasures of waffles, fairy-floss and hot-dogs, they stroll by displays of gardening prowess, a media and photographic exhibition by Stella's school, woodwork and blacksmithing products, everything proudly, locally made. Prizes awarded for each category, a process fraught with risk of abuse and even fisticuffs. Even over best flower arrangement.

Ian Taylor is busy everywhere, nattily dressed, his Akubra hat-band announcing him as the local MP. Greeting everyone like long-lost friends, even cooing over the odd baby. Ray avoids him.

He and Stella perch on temporary grandstands above an oval with a grassy centre and dirt track around its edge. They watch a parade of enormous but docile stud cattle, each led by young, serious children wearing their Sunday best. The immense prize-winning beasts amble placidly on the churned ground, impervious, or seeing it as their due, wearing award ribbons that will end up framed in the family home.

Horsemanship displays follow, tricks and skills of daring and close bonds and love of their horses. A booming, fuzzy public address system drones on with what Ray assumes is commentary but he can't make out a word.

A truck drives around the track at the edge of the ring, carrying three young women on its flatbed wearing sashes for Miss Royalton Show Girl 1976, first, second and third. Much whistling and catcalls, not all complimentary. The women stand, weaving with the truck's motion, hanging on to an unstable podium shaped like a white picket fence, waving free hands, smiling fixedly.

Ray nudges Stella. 'You should go in that. You'd win.' Gives her a stage-wink.

She shakes her head. 'Too old, eighteen to twenty-five only. Can't have an old woman flaunting her tits like that.'

Ray laughs but a middle-aged woman below turns to stare coldly at them.

Stella whispers, 'Damn. I said tits.' Pokes him with one of her own.

The ring empties as young men and women climb into it through and over the fence.

Ray laughs, disbelieving. 'Not the Greasy Pig?'

The crowd cheers as two small greased pigs explode into the ring, dodging and dashing amid hilarious near-misses, collisions and falls. The pigs win every encounter until one young man grabs a pair of hind legs, covering himself with mud and grease as the pig twists and bucks, squirms and squeals, nothing dampening the youth's gap-toothed smile of triumph.

Again the ring clears, followed by an ominous roar. Garishly painted, modified cars, utes, tractors and motorbikes burst in, tearing up the ground, doing wild U-turns that spray barrages of dirt over spectators on lower benches, some of whom, prepared, hold up sheets of newspaper for protection.

Leaving the action, Ray and Stella wander down a short side-show alley. Ray fails to win a giant teddy-bear in the shooting gallery. Stella inserts ping-pong balls into the mouths of rotating clown-heads to score a fairy on a stick, which she gives to a passing toddler. Then Ray has had enough.

In the garden behind the pub, he gets a beer and gin-and-tonic. He and Stella respond to friendly greetings but sit alone.

Ray teases, 'What sort of show is it without Sharman's boxing tent? Like a circus without lions and lion tamer.' He notices her grin. 'What? What did I do?'

'We're sitting on our own.'

'You want to join someone? Fine with me.'

She gives him a brusque, 'No.'

He lifts his shoulders, baffled.

She says, 'We must be getting serious. That's what they'll say. Couples sit apart when they're getting serious.'

He sips his beer. 'Serious about leaving.' He winks. 'I've seen the Royalton Show. What else is left?'

Stella says, 'I like it.'

'I like it too. But I don't want to be here liking it next year and the year after that.'

She looks away.

Their time together is lately more unsettled than easy-going.

Laming pops up on the edge of the area, looking lost, looking for someone, then leaves as abruptly. Ray and Stella share raised eyebrows.

She says, 'Looking for his invisible wife.'

'A wife? As well as a kid.'

'You work with him!'

'No one works *with* Laming. How come you know?'

She rolls her eyes and looks at him, making sure he's listening. 'Out here, it's hard to *avoid* knowing people. People share. But not you, you're a mud skipper, staying on the surface of things. Or in some invisible cocoon.'

He knows she's teasing, but right. And she doesn't understand it, or trust it.

'Tell me about his invisible wife.'

Stella laughs bleakly. 'It goes back before our time. Don't know her name. She never goes out.'

'Sounds like Kennedy's mother. Laming's wife hasn't got a gun too, has she?'

Stella laughs, but shakes her head at the sadness surrounding both women. 'He brought her here from Tassie one high summer over ten years ago. The story is, when she felt the heat here, she climbed into the water tank in their backyard and refused to come out, said she was staying till the world cooled down. Came out wrinkled like a prune and never went outside again. He shops, does the errands. The story's over the top for sure but, you know, with a mystery like that, people fill in the blanks, don't they.'

He gets the jibe. And the warning too. Nature abhors a vacuum and so do people.

He pictures Laming shopping for ordinary groceries. Imagines a woman's indistinct face staring from a closed window. 'Does he lock her in?'

Stella shivers. 'Not what I hear. Who knows what she does all day. They have a son, so there's that. The poor boy can't do straight schoolwork and his left leg is withered.'

A prolonged silence, which Ray notes is not their first. Time passes. They sporadically comment on people around them, slowly finish their drinks.

—

Ray wakes alone and startled in Stella's grand, brass bed. Hears her slightly raised voice.

'Come on, you can't stay there.'

He goes into the kitchen. Stella is calmly wielding a straw broom to coax a large python out of her walk-in larder.

Ray feels his blood drain.

She says, 'Six-footer, I'd say. Doesn't want to go.'

The snake is shiny, alert, beautiful, with coloured-diamond patterns along its back, its head raised and swaying, mouth opening and closing. A good yard is out in the kitchen, the rest still in the larder.

Ray stays back. 'Doesn't look upset yet but keep harassing it that broom and it might get cranky.' He takes a breath, braced. 'You need me to get it out?'

'Don't need a man to save me from a snake. Grab the rake, end of the verandah?'

He finds it, an ordinary metal garden rake, takes it to her. 'You're not going to stab it, are you?'

'Course not!' She laughs, then looks at him. 'What's wrong?'

He says, 'Nothing!' Too quickly. Feels her reading him.

The snake lies quietly on the floor. Considering its options, Ray figures. Stella carefully lowers the rake onto it so a pair of tines sit neatly across its body, a foot from its head.

She gently turns the rake so more tines engage its body, pinning it. The snake squirms, its head searching, but the trapped coils hold, without harming it. Moving slowly but firmly, Stella lifts those coils a few inches off the floor, and pulls all of the snake's six-foot length into the light.

Ray backs away, opens his mouth as if to offer help but thinks better of it. The snake stiffens, head waving more as Stella drags it, quickly now, to the verandah and over the edge, uncoiling the rake to free it. She leaves the rake and comes back inside closing the door behind her. Just another snake.

Ray, impressed, exhales in relief. 'Nicely done.'

'You okay?'

'Not keen on snakes.'

'Could've fooled me. You know pythons are harmless?' She laughs. 'Unless they strangle you.'

He offers raised eyebrows. 'How'd it get in?'

'Careless. Must've left the door open. Hope it didn't leave any babies in there.' She laughs as his eyes widen, and kisses his cheek. 'What's for breakfast?'

'Could've had snake.'

'Tastes like chicken.'

'You fit right in here, don't you?'

'Funny how you make that sound suss.'

'Don't mean to.'

———

It's dusk. Ray sits dripping with sweat in running shorts and singlet at the iron garden table on Dot's lawn, a six-pack close to hand. The sun is a flat sliver of gold between opposite houses, going, going, gone in a minute. Sulphur-crested cockatoos and crows fly raucously overhead.

Ray now sees his street differently. As Archie warned, it hits you later. He sees himself as a target, of another distant rifle, another malicious car. Even, his most colourful image, burnt to death by a Molotov cocktail hurled through the only door to his enclosed flat. The extremism of that at least makes him smile. Opens another beer.

'Got one for me?' Dot appears barefoot in a loose, cotton, long-sleeved top and long pants, hair in a functional bun.

'Reckon.' He opens another beer.

'Had to get out for a rest.' She winks. The cheerful lewdness she brings to everything gives him a full smile.

'How's the athlete?'

She chortles. 'You can talk, you and your pretty lady.' She laughs, wheezing like a lifelong smoker. 'He's good, we're good, which round here these days is good going.'

He lifts his stubby in toast. 'You're mates with Irene, wife of my esteemed colleague, Arshag.'

'A wonderful mate she is, too. Us nurses stick together. She reckons you and Arsh are busy boys. First of all, and I mean this, well done nicking the rapist. Shame about the one doing himself in, but bugger him, I say. No sign of the third one yet?'

'Over the border, Arshag thinks. His old man's got a property down there. If he goes there, local coppers'll grab him.'

Dot holds up a finger for each area of action. 'So there's that. Then duffers in semis, for god's sake.'

Ray wonders if she also knows he beat up the Randalls that day. Probably. Royalton Radio.

She goes on, 'Then poor Benny and those guns. And an exotic animals racket. Takes imagination to see a screeching cockatoo as desirable. Who wants one of them in a cage in the corner? Madness.'

'Popular when I was a kid. Good mimics, you can teach them to talk.'

'You worked out who's running this crime wave? Who's Mister Big?'

'We'll get there. Or put a big enough spoke in the wheel so that he goes elsewhere. Planes and trucks must be going arsehole to breakfast but no one comes and tells me.'

He feels her looking at him, thinking. She turns back to look upstairs, into darkness. 'Lover boy still out to it.' She looks at Ray again. 'Look, you know things in town aren't good. People leaving, kids into mischief, hooning, fighting. No work, no jobs, right? Your Stella knows there's nothing here for these kids when they leave school. As a copper, you could rethink all these capers you're dragging out into the light. Even the bloody duffing. Though everyone says they hate the duffers.' She waits, seeing if he gets it.

Ray shrugs. 'Giving people jobs?' Struggling with it.

She points at him. 'Without giving too much away, I'd say duffing worked better when it was happening elsewhere. Which it used to.'

'Whoa. Callous.'

'Look at Benny Lee. Sad, sad shock. Poor bugger gets so drunk with joy after earning a quid, he ends up killing himself. You know what I'm saying. Lock people up for breaking the law, you cripple the only economy we got still working. Every shift at work I see the pain and slow deaths happening to people with no job, no money, or prospects. Stinks, how we run our world. Jesus, you better give me another beer.'

Ray hears his phone, goes in to answer it, comes back in jeans, T-shirt and boots to tell Dot he has to go. 'Finish the beers. Grass fire, south fringe in Bell's paddock.'

'What'd start a fire there?'

'Kids maybe. They might need an extra pair of hands on the pumps.'

'They will. Kenny Strathdee's in the squad but he's still coming in for treatment on his feet, so he won't be there.'

Ray grins. Information flows around here like water. He recalls Stella's rebuke. What sort of copper doesn't heed what's going on around him? But what sort of copper is he?

16

The fire is burning westward in a neat line over almost the whole empty block. Low, lazy, crackling flames, not much smoke as the parched grass virtually explodes and vanishes. The larger menace is the cloud of glittering sparks dancing above, ever closer to tinder-dry wooden homes across the road.

Ray does have to step in for Kenny. 'What happened to him?'

Laurie, a man Ray knows from touch football, is uncoiling a hose. 'He'd been burning stumps. He's walking round, thinking they're all done. Steps on what he thinks is solid ground but it's a stump covered over, still burning. Went down a hole full of burning coals up to his knee. Silly bastard was barefoot.'

Ray winces, pumps more water as darkness deepens. In a lull, he looks around the clutch of concerned locals come to watch, and help, if asked. Amid them is a slim, middle-aged man with a boy of maybe eight years on his shoulders. The man automatically gives the awkwardly sitting boy extra support. Ray can see the boy's protruding eyes flash as they reflect the flames. He is moaning but in delight at the excitement, mouth lolling open, not fully controlled. The man is Laming.

Ray turns to town-side of the street, the nearest house. Sees the shape of a woman sitting on the steps of the unlit front porch. Too dark for details but something tells him it's Laming's house, and his reclusive wife. In public, almost.

He turns back to Laming, sees him start a swaying action, helping the boy sway in time, and the boy hums and squeals with joy. Father–son communion. At that moment, the fire is judged extinguished. People clap, cheer, turn to leave. Laming walks to the fire truck, his boy still swaying on his shoulders. He shakes hands, thanking the team. If the fire had jumped the road, his house would've been gone. He sees the next hand in line is Ray's, and jolts with shock, embarrassment, shame maybe. Hard to tell in torchlight. Because of the boy? Then the quick anger Ray sees so often. Their hand grip is shaky, Laming's swiftly withdrawn.

The boy changes tone, starts whimpering, bare heels kicking his dad in the chest, hands clamping hard on Laming's face. Laming turns on his heel, heads to the house. The woman on the porch slips inside as he reaches his front gate. The boy grunts and kicks erratically, droning, wordless all the way. At the porch, Laming lifts the boy down to the ground. The boy makes his disjointed way up the steps and inside. Laming follows.

Ray turns back as a water truck rolls by, spraying water across what didn't burn, across the dead leading edge of the fire over the paddock. Its lights turn the spray into a glittering fountain.

Ray recalls when farmers still burnt their fields of cane before harvest. Dry cane erupted into tall flames higher than houses, embers whirling even higher, which kids and crazy dogs tried to catch as they fell spinning to earth, already cold, black, burnt-out. Wildlife dashed underfoot to safety, oblivious to people and dogs. These days, tightly controlled, often only done for tourists. A source of mirth for those who knew the real thing.

He turns back to Laming's house. No lights. No sounds. Windows and door closed.

———

Next day, Ray approaches Arshag who is washing police vehicles with a bucket of soapy water and sponge. Ray starts to say it's easier if you use a hose but stops in time. No one wastes water like that. He gets his own bucket of soapy water and sponge and joins in. The red dust wipes off easily. Black clay not so much. He moves on to cleaning massed insect bodies from the windscreen.

Ray says, 'Ever play Chinese whispers out here?'

'Which is?'

'Invent a rumour. Tell one person. See how long it takes to get back to you from around the community. And how much it's changed.'

Arshag grins. 'Sounds like Royalton Radio.'

Ray says, 'You never told me Laming's married. Wife lives like a prisoner.'

'So they say.'

'Lash out, tell me more. I know nothing so I don't know what to ask.'

'Never stops anyone else. Okay, here's a nice story. One day, Laming comes to work all excited. His kid, four then, had come hobbling into the house screaming about water pouring from the sky. First time the little bugger ever saw rain.'

Ray laughs in wonder.

Arshag says, 'I remember it cos Laming looked happy. He must've realised it too cos he shut up.'

'He's been here a while?'

'Royalton's first detective. Back then, the only one.'

'See him now, hard to know how he ever made detective.'

'Before Kennedy he was fine. Then Kennedy swaggers in, stomps all over Laming's higher seniority. Sort of thing you get away with in out-of-the-way places.'

'Kennedy had dirt on him, or what?'

Arshag shrugs. 'Laming gutted himself, didn't fight back. Not long after, the Inspector came and let Kennedy expand his power however he wanted. How it looked, anyway.'

'Laming's boy stays home, same as the mother?'

'He can't do school. Doesn't go.'

Ray stares into his water, surface full of bits of insects, thinking of the boy and mother cut-off from the world. Laming too, in his way. What's that do to them? 'No wonder he's such a grim bastard.'

Arshag says, 'No one visits. Front door stays shut and there's a high metal fence round their backyard. Doesn't want to be part of anything.'

Ray scrubs some more. Hears again Stella's pointed words on Laming's closed family life, *'Fancy cutting yourself off like that! Make you a grim bugger. Some people like it like that. Go out of their way to get it. Others are grim from the start.'* Aimed at himself too when he talked about not wanting to be part of the place, stay in Royalton at all.

—

Ray squints out a window of the dusty, dented Land Rover, roasting in full sun, parked beside a hut of corrugated-iron scorching enough to blister skin. He's about twelve miles north-west of Royalton, facing sparse, limp vegetation sagging on glowing red dirt under a pitiless, blue sky. Tall white gums tremble as their branches shimmer.

He hunches in the front passenger seat in the glare and burning oven of another desert day. Out here, his eyeballs could boil in their own juices.

Where's this bastard plane?

He looks through an arc of windscreen cleared by the swinging wiper-blade, rimmed by caked, red dust and shrivelled insects. Out there is a corrugated-iron hut that a rusting sign shot through with bullet holes calls an amenities block. Pull your dick out in there, you deserve all the wildlife you get. Running past the front of the hut is a baked, red-earth landing strip, iron-hard, just wider than a local road. Its north end is lost in what looks like glittering flame against distant purple hills. Its near south end halts nearby at misshapen, defiant mulga trees, waiting like a threat, their trunks black. Thinks of that song by Frankie Laine about cool, clear water, the singer yearning for water in a desert. Then his ears fill with the sound of water, in gentle waves hissing onto shore.

He recalls when he was maybe eight, on an uncommon outing with his father in an old dinghy gliding around at high tide, outside the river mouth in a large, mangrove forest. On one side the muddy shore, on the other, glimpses of glittering ocean. His father rowing, a soft, rhythmic sound, while Ray sat in front, pushing branches aside or manoeuvring the dinghy around them. The air itself with a green tinge, blocking most of the intense sun.

214

Ray wide-eyed, leaned forward whispering, 'So quiet. Isn't it quiet?'

Saw his father's rare smile. 'Like in a church. A cocoon.'

His father pulled in the oars and they coasted. Ray felt the silence compound, grow heavier. He wanted to speak but couldn't break the spell of drifting, the soft splash of a negligible bow-wave, the popping of bubbles and clicking of crabs around the mangrove roots.

It was peaceful till his father's smile faded, replaced with a sudden, dark intensity. 'Listen to me. Look at me.' Shaking a warning finger. 'This's one of those rare times, rare, rare times, when it's okay to drift.' He put a hand in the water as small currents slowly started to rotate the dinghy. 'But too much drifting, that's a kind of dying.' His hands back on the oars, knuckles white. 'Come out here to take time, find out what your life is for? Sure. But living your life, you must commit! The only thing that makes it worth breathing at all.'

Ray recalls his confusion. You commit to a job or a promise but you can also commit a crime. Or be a loony like Aunty Barb and get committed. His father's face was tense, hard. Is committing what his dad did night after night at the table on the back verandah with exercise books and biro? Scribbling, his mother called it. Writing and writing, pulling out pages, tearing them up. Taking them to the incinerator at the bottom of the yard to watch them burn. Next night, doing it again. No one, including his wife, ever read what he wrote, which only made her yell at him more over what a waste of time his stupid scribblings were. Then came the unravelling of his job.

When he and his new wife came to Brisbane from out west, he became a reporter on a Brisbane paper for a time but there was some political strife over something he wrote, which cost him that job. He worked on an agricultural magazine for farmers he used to half-laughingly call 'Pig News' but lost that job too. In the end, his novel was abandoned, which he tried to joke about with self-slashing sarcasm. Even Ray the boy could see that.

Ray only knew this much about his dad because after his death, his mum talked about hopes they'd once had. His dad was supposed to become a famous writer. His mum didn't seem to have a plan apart from being in the whirl that came with famous writers.

He can see his father's hand over the edge of the dinghy, trailing in the green-blue water, twirling grass around his fingers. Sees his dad sit up, slapping the water with the oars to turn to the open sea. Ray ducking branches as they plough on, bursting from the forest into blinding sunlight on a flat ocean. Not a breath of wind.

So real, even now Ray feels the jerking to and fro of his father rowing on and on, farther and farther out, till he had to stop, panting. Directly under them, through clear water, small fish and a miniature forest of swaying sea grass, of uncertain depth.

Ray pointing. 'Shark! Dad, shark?'

'Bull shark, young one.' The shark, three feet or so nose to tail, moving lazily above the sea grass.

'It's ignoring us.'

'Good.'

'Do sharks attack boats?'

'Hungry sharks attack anything.'

Its languid movement merging it into the gloom of deeper water until it vanishes. The incoming tide gently but persistently lifting them, carrying them. A blur in the air then a gleaming splash as a shag dives underwater.

Ray laughs. 'Bird turning into a fish. See?'

His father slid out the oars. 'Time to go.'

Ray grinned, said like a grown-up, 'Home James and don't spare the horses.'

His father half-smiled. 'Home James and the fire's out.'

Ray's bare elbow touches the sun-exposed, metal sill of the Land Rover door and the burn snaps him back to the present. From his senses full of water everywhere to this parched spareness. Under one of the mulga trees is what could be fallen branches or an animal's whitened skeleton.

He gave Kennedy a report on what they'd found, potentially a base of exotic animals smuggling, without knowing what else to do, since he hardly expects it to go anywhere.

How did he end up here? His too-frequent thought. These days he feels he put a gun to his own head, common enough for real in this part of the world. Wipes sweat from his neck, hand dripping. The heat is a live thing pitted against the cabin and any fool who thinks he's safe inside.

Approaching the end of 1976. 'Nineteen-seventy-six!' Says it aloud as if to force a human scale onto the landscape, make it less lethal. Words here are noise, no grip. Like Stella's French.

Sick of waiting, he kicks his boots against the footwell in a wasted effort to stretch his long legs, and thrashes his shoulders to and fro, arms up in boxing crouch. Sweat flows down his spine. He arrived in Royalton in the middle of last summer, and soon'll come into the next. Months feel like years, carrying an echo of Arshag's warning. Stay too long, you never leave. He sees it in the hooded eyes of those addicted. A different idea of what you can love insinuates itself. What was shockingly featureless, even alien, transforms into a powerful beauty. The very idea of leaving turns shameful. Thinks of Stella.

A soft drone, at last. A silver gleam appears in the sky to the north. It floats over the hills, down onto the far end of the strip, bounces and heads closer on the ground, forming into the expected plane. All the makings of a drug-drop in a movie, except out there to meet the plane is Ray's Inspector, his fish-eyes dead, all done up in his dress uniform, stifling and cumbersome and too fucking weird out here. Who's visiting, for fuck's sake, the Queen?

Ray's fingers tap tattoos on his uniformed knees. Told to stay put and doing what he's told. He punches the dusty buttons of the clogged cooling fans. Empty drink cans and food wrappings litter the floor under his boots, invisible to the finicky Inspector, who, even after four years here, never drives himself or sits up front.

The plane rumbles up to the wall of bush and halts in a swirl of clattering props and dust. Alongside, only feet away, is the legal edge of the strip, marked by a waist-high cyclone-wire fence, six yards long with a rusted gate midway, too bent to close. Ray peers across at the plane through the window of the driver's seat, past the sweat-soaked back of Arshag, who is leaning on the fence facing the strip, lazily swatting flies with a switch of leaves, looking up from under his regulation, broad-brimmed hat, his expression unimpressed, eyes slitted against the glare. He's looking at the man coming down the unfurled steps. Ray hates waiting but Arshag exudes boundless patience. Or perhaps contempt.

The plane sits, outstaring the bush, props finally at rest. Beside it in the dazzling light stand two men, making no move to find shade, their shadows under their feet. The older man, from the plane, is grey-haired, wears a grey suit and blue tie, which looks eccentric here. The suit is attracting splotches of agitated dust. As he talks, he jabs a finger at the Inspector, who is taller but folded forwards, nodding, nodding, hands clasped at his chest. The shoes of the visitor and boots of the Inspector are sinking into the soft, shifting, scorching dust.

The man speaking looks in charge. What's drawn him way out here to stand in the heat and red dust? His manner says he is robustly instructing the Inspector in a matter of importance. From where Ray sits, the Inspector's long, narrow face, his half-closed eyes and distrustful mouth are blank, as usual. The men shake hands in spiritless fashion, avoiding each other's eyes. Getting through whatever it is. Then the man from the plane taps dust off his shoes against the plane's steel ladder, climbs up inside and snaps the door shut. Someone else is in there but they're a blur. Bloody short chat for a long trip. The Inspector backs off, back to Arshag. The engines cough then erupt in a belligerent whine and snarl. The props whip up huge spirals of dust. The plane shudders right around to face north and the quivering haze waiting to absorb it. The throttle opens with a painful roar.

The Inspector, thin lips pursed, holds his peaked cap on his regulation haircut with one hand, gives a kind of salute with the other and turns away. Ray grins, knowing the whipped dirt is attacking his eyes and nose. Arshag, at the fence, covers his face with his sweat-soaked hat.

The plane trundles off, ungainly, but swiftly picks up speed. It dissolves into the shimmering heat, reappears, hauls itself sluggishly upward, wings flashing, engines droning, fading.

The Inspector holds his pose, follows it until it disappears, then futilely stamps and shakes his boots. He turns enough for Ray to see him wipe his face, then stare at the bush. Like he's never seen it before, but then maybe he hasn't.

Ray stares at it too, feels familiar unease. Clumps of Mitchell grass and kangaroo grass hold together small mounds of red soil. Flashes of purple and gold flowers mark a perennial grass the locals call hairy panic. Stunted, rough-barked acacia and desert poplar trees stand amid grey-barked turkey bush shrubs, all looking marginal but tougher than all of them. Arshag knows a lot of their names.

Silence, a void, then the ear-piercing shrill of crickets explodes. The Inspector bashes his peaked cap against his leg, dust puffing, a violent act, and Ray is startled to see a stab of passion distort his whole face. Mouth pulled down, eyes narrowed, hard. It's hate. Hating this whole place, maybe even more than the corruption charges he came here to evade. Ray sees him wink humourlessly at Arshag, then facing him, unzip his fly, pull out his dick and piss on the dirt that hisses as it sucks away the wet. Arshag stays inert, surely gazing at the empty sky. Ray has to look away. Waits as the Inspector zips up, hears him crunch past Arshag, back to the Land Rover, flop heavily into the back seat and slam the door.

Ray watches Arshag take his time, then follow, folding into the driver's seat, impassively drive them away.

Glancing into the back, Ray notes his boss's smug air. Cat that got the cream. Did that grey-suited man fly who knows how far in his fancy plane to bring the Inspector a prez? What the fuck was that about? And in return, whatever the visitor wanted, gratefully received and understood. Deal done.

Ray thinks of Lord Billy, so proud to play the government for funds and infrastructure for the Royalton region. Shouldn't a local mayor have been here to welcome an important guest?

Who knows how any of this really works? Ray feels the angry power and appeal of Billy's grand words about making the region his fiefdom. A bulwark against vile corruption from outside.

The tortured trees flash by.

Ray feels a sharp tap on his shoulder and twists to look. The Inspector yells over the engine and wind rushing from the open windows. 'How long have you been here?'

Ray shrugs. 'Coming up to a year.'

'You miss the Big Smoke?'

Ray hesitates. Never thought of Brisbane as a Big Anything. 'Sure. Pizzas and bars.'

'Well,' says the Inspector, making noises like chuckles. 'Served my time. I'm off back there. Not before time. All things come, eh? Why don't I see you out of this godforsaken hole too. What do you reckon?'

Ray gives him a nod and the tongue-click of approval he gave his horse on the farm as a kid, but has to resist squirming at this tight-arsed gush of levity. So that's the deal. Lord Billy said the Inspector was biding his time here till he got the nod to return. Ray shifts in his seat, wary of why it includes himself. He feels complicit, co-conspirator in something he knows nothing about.

Back to Brisbane? Really? Time for a change? Again? He stares at a landscape that makes the whole idea of change seem irrelevant. If he doesn't want it, now's the time to say so. Speak up, say no before it gets official, set in concrete. He says nothing. Sneaks a look at Arshag, who of course gives no sign.

17

At the copshop, the Inspector climbs out before the vehicle fully stops, leaves his door open and struts into the station. Arshag parks in the only shaded spot in the carpark with space for the open door. He and Ray stay put.

Ray says, 'He pissing off, you reckon? Bet you'll miss him.'

Arshag punches the fan buttons, waste of time, and snorts. 'Sounds like you too. Like doing you a favour. Why's he thinking that?'

Ray grimaces. 'Buggered if I know. Can't remember the last time he even spoke to me.' Thinking, people call getting out a favour. Is it?

'We should've asked if he's seen any interesting guns lately.'

'I have. Asked him about Benny's list. He said matters before the copshop are in a holding pattern right now till certain larger issues were resolved.'

'No.'

'For real.'

'What did that mean?'

'Maybe he was hoping he was leaving and it's not his problem anymore?' Ray holds up his hands in mock-religious revelation. 'Boss Man came down from the sky to give him some larger duty. Scum floats up. He's probably already picked the new boy to take over here.'

Arshag takes his time. 'Kennedy.'

'Devil he knows.'

'I couldn't do it.'

Ray looks at him. 'You'd quit?'

Arshag shakes his head.

A slow-moving sedan topped with a sign saying OVERSIZE passes, heading west, hazard lights flashing. Shortly after, a road train thunders by, engine roaring in a lower gear, pulling a giant bulldozer on a wide tray taking up more than one lane, forcing cars coming the other way to pull over and stop to avoid it. In its wake, whirling dust and short-lived silence.

Ray says, 'This place needs a picture theatre. I miss movies. There was this shoebox place in Brisbane that showed foreign movies. It was great. Cheap too.'

'You'll go back there then.'

'Can't. A government politician decided all movies with subtitles were porn. Got the place closed down.' Ray shakes his head, at sea. 'To go or not to go.' The set of his jaw says it's not decided.

Arshag fixes a hard look on him. 'You turn down his transfer, his gift'—he tilts his head at the copshop—'you can forget about any rising career as a copper.' Shifts in his seat as if hemmed in, opens his door with excessive force but stays put. 'Haven't even been here long enough to get a tan.'

Ray grins. 'Yeah, still pretty white.'

Wins a wry, rare grin from Arshag.

Ray looks out at a nearby patrol car covered in dust, at the red earth, bone-dry and compacted hard.

He says, 'If I am out of here, tell the kids to keep their guard up. Keep training. There's potential there.'

Arshag grins, 'Yeah, you done a bit of good.' The grin fades. Ray knows what's coming.

Arshag says, 'Who'll get Alice now? Who'll get the case?'

What he's really saying is, he knows he should get it but won't, and who mustn't.

———

In the cool of early evening, Ray stares at the walls of his flat thinking disconnected thoughts about Brisbane and leaving, about Stella and Arshag, and the gym. Interrupted by a call from Barb at the pub to break up a two-man brawl before it turns into six. He's buzzing before he even gets there. They're big but grogged up. One is Wayne again. There's ducking and weaving, which he enjoys, smiling at them both, teasing, followed by scornful, well-aimed shoves and the flailing duo come to rest in the grip of their mates far enough apart on the uneven wooden floor to quit with honour. The other brawler starts to yell, jabbing the air, but Ray's warning finger quietens everyone.

He points to unfinished beers. 'Kiss and make up, you bastards.'

Their mates laugh, push Wayne and the other brawler forward. Wayne is ready to hit out or march out but the other offers an outstretched hand. Right up to the moment of contact it could be a trap, then they shake and nod with faces averted and return to the bar, the merriment of their mates winning out.

Jimmy approaches from a separate table, shakes his hand. 'Nifty footwork, twinkle-toes.'

'Jimmy. Where's your shadow?'

'Sleeping it off.'

'What happened?' Pointing to the brawlers, who are still arguing but without the violence.

'Who knows? Someone's fence pushed over. Wayne started it. Bear with a sore head.'

'Still out of work?'

'His old man too, apparently. Mean shit, his old man. Their property's fucked, bore's drying up. Know how they feel. Going down the tubes here, mate. Fucking rodeo's cancelled. Lucky I got no cattle anymore or I'd be going a hundred mile to Tyborg to sell them. Footy club can't raise a local team no more. Cricket's dead and buried, same. No wonder bloody Wayne picks fights. We're fading away.'

Raised voices. Wayne is threatening another drinker.

Ray says, 'Duty calls.'

Without ceremony he pins Wayne's arms back and to loud cheers marches him out to the main street, scoring a relieved nod from Barb.

———

Ray drives the Land Rover, rattling along dark narrow roads, Wayne sulking beside him. Slows at an unsealed driveway where the headlights pick out a leaning, milk-can mailbox, DICKSON hand-painted on it. Ray turns into the drive. Three big dogs, ominously silent, stay back but keep watch. Wayne whistles and growls at them and they retreat.

Ray knocks at the closed front door of a long, low house and waits. Wayne hovers beside him, making a whistling noise through his teeth, hands in the pockets of his jeans, while an Alsatian cross at his side looks for attention. The front door cracks open and the dog retreats. A big, lean man in his fifties, barefooted, in shorts and singlet, steps out into the yellow porch light. Wayne visibly shrinks, face wrinkling in something like a series of tics.

Ray says, 'Bob Dickson.'

Bob turns from Ray to Wayne. 'What the fuck you done this time?'

Wayne tucks his head into his chest. 'Just having fun.'

Bob puts meaty hands on his hips. 'You cops got nothing better to do?'

'Picking fights. His third time.'

'I know how many times. You his taxi?'

'Way he's going, he's heading for assault charges. I'm trying to do you a favour.'

'You think this family needs charity?' Lifts a hand to Wayne as if to cuff him. 'Get your arse inside. Don't fucking talk.' Wayne takes his hands from his pockets, goes inside, hitting the door jamb in order to avoid his dad. The dog pushes in too, quick as a flash.

Bob Dickson shrugs at Ray. 'Happy now?'

Ray turns to leave.

Bob Dickson says, 'Kennedy know you're giving us a hard time?' Mumbles under his breath, sounding angry, abusive. Goes inside, slams the door.

———

Back at the copshop, black night outside, Ray phones Lord Billy. 'William, how are you?' Hears a deep exhale.

'The news about the rodeo,' Lord Billy says. 'It's hurting. I did my best, couldn't save it. The end of my stint as mayor may be rushing at me. Not that I'll miss all the mountains of money I never made doing this thankless task.'

'Come on. You won't quit.'

'All the cattle sales'll go with it. Those sales brought money into town. A pall is forming over us.'

Ray leaves a respectful space to acknowledge the pain. Then, 'I left you a message a while back. Came across this plane at one of Taylor's places. Cessna two-ten.'

'Ah. Sorry, forgot. Nice unit. Six-seater.' There's a pause long enough for Ray to notice, then William says, 'What were you doing way up there?'

'Finding my way round. Meeting people I never get to see. Showing my face.' Ray waits. And waits.

William says, 'You spoke to him?'

'Briefly. He didn't want to say much. You know what he'd use it for?'

Lord Billy sounds genuinely perplexed. 'I'm wondering why he wants anything that big. Mind you he does wing it off to Bangkok often enough.'

'He has a pile of those metal cages smugglers use for exotic animals.'

'Oh.'

Ray waits. 'Any thoughts?'

'About smuggler cages?'

'About the plane first.'

'Well now. What can I tell you?'

Ray waits. Not a speedy chat.

'It has a good range. Just a few legs'd probably cross Queensland north to south.'

Ray says, 'Useful I guess?'

Billy laughs, a tired sound.

Ray prompts, 'And animal smuggling?'

'Oh goodness me, out of my depth there, my friend.' He laughs again. 'Ian's a funny fellow. Has funny tastes.' Ray isn't sure if he hears a testy undercurrent there, aimed more at Taylor than himself.

Billy says, 'Well okay, very good, all a tad strange but must go. If I hear anything useful, you'll know all about it.'

Through his copshop window, Ray sees a road train rumble past, heading east, carrying cattle. Doesn't need to see to know urine and shit'll be pouring off it in waves, in sync with the swaying of the long, heavy, unstoppable, perilous trailer. Bad luck the passing driver caught in it.

———

Just past sunrise, Ray wakes in Stella's bed. Hears her in the kitchen, singing. He puts on civvies and boots from a collection of his gear in one end of her wardrobe and joins her. 'What's the song?'

She looks at him. 'You don't know? "You Can't Hurry Love". The Supremes.'

They sit down to bacon and eggs on her verandah overlooking her backyard. The above-ground pool sparkles in glittering blue.

'Did I tell you, one of the two new mums in our a capella group has to leave? Says there's no way her hubby can cope with the baby alone one night a week. One night! Pathetic.' He knows she's watching him. 'What are you doing today?'

He says, 'How did you end up here?'

'At this table? Bought it at the fete. Under this roof? Bought it from the Averalls and moved in. In this life in general? Well, that's a toughie this early in the day. Why?'

'Feeling stuck.' The Inspector's offer is a lump in his chest like food stuck in his windpipe.

She pauses. 'With me?'

He gives her a chiding look. 'It's all shit at work and I don't know what to do.'

'Try teaching, you get used to that. Community night at school last week was unusual. Alice and Diah were mentioned.'

'Did you know them?'

'Too briefly. For young teenagers, they definitely knew what they wanted. Diah wanted to make movies. Alice wanted to be a pilot. Wonderfully and wildly impractical. Maybe. I think Alice just wanted to get away, escape to else-where. You'd know about that. Diah had a box brownie, loved photography.'

'What was the mood at the community group?'

'Unhappy. All biting our tongues, scared to say what we think.'

'Which is?'

'We know about Diah now, which is a relief, but it makes us feel it's more likely locals murdered Alice. Murderers among us.' She shudders. 'Like being infected with something ugly. Don't know what it is or who's got it or how to cure it.'

It won't be his problem soon. Mister No-Commitment. He can skip over the surface. Even being shot at and nearly run over already feels like it happened to someone else.

Better tell Stella soon or Royalton Radio will do it for him. But not today.

———

Ray leans against the back wall as Kennedy briefs combined Royalton and Tyborg copshops. Roads over a huge area marked on a map are to be staked out overnight with mobile shifts. First of what may be a number of snap, mobile traps to catch outback travelling salesmen peddling guns.

Ray wasn't going to speak but his mouth does anyway. 'We only thinking local delivery? What about planes?'

Kennedy's face is blank but hairs rise on the back of Ray's neck.

Kennedy says, 'Shaggers!'

Arshag looks up from under a closed brow.

'Take this townie out to Two Mile junction. If he breathes too loud, shoot him. You're covered.' Kennedy laughs, flicks a fuck-you glance at Ray. Some others also laugh but Kennedy's tone is odd. As a joke it doesn't work. Arshag stays impassive. Kennedy's last words as they all leave are, 'So watch it. Blokes selling guns might be more likely to shoot you than, say, blokes smuggling cockatoos and lizards.'

That does get a laugh, not from Ray.

———

The night is cold. The silent waiting lets chill creep into their bones. The Land Rover is immersed in black emptiness at the first X on Kennedy's map. No lights outside in any direction, except up.

Ray shivers. 'All looks black to me.' He rolls down his window, leans out. The gleaming sky is dense with so many points of light, they fuse as giant, shining clusters.

Arshag, behind the wheel, is only partly visible in the weak, green dash lights. 'Cold. Shut your window.'

Even in the dark, Ray can tell something is going on. Rolls up the window.

Arshag says, 'Laming shoved a piece of paper under my nose today. Said it was your transfer. He was crowing. *We got rid of the prick!* So, the Inspector's done it. You're out of here. It made Kennedy's day.' Arshag hears Ray's silence and has to ask, 'Did you know?'

Ray is thinking about how information moves in a shady copshop. 'Laming got advance notice, great.' More silence, then Ray gives a mirthless chuckle. 'The Brisbane bastard who sent me out here got it done quickly too.'

He's angry. He hadn't expected to be, but here he is, angry. Doesn't know what he's angry about most. 'Never overstay my welcome, that's me.'

More time drifts by, measurable only by absences. Lack of light, lack of movement, of external sound.

'Told Stella yet?'

Ray says nothing.

Arshag shakes his head. 'Better watch out. Kaye'll beat you to it.'

Ray curses himself. Hadn't thought of Kaye. An alternative Royalton Radio all by herself. He looks through the windscreen at the heavens. 'We've been here long enough to see the stars turn.' Points at the sky. 'That lot there were over here. Everything's rolling around. Makes me feel numb thinking about it.' He taps a tattoo on the dash. 'Stupid of me, eh, unpacking anywhere. Laming say where I'm going?'

'Brisbane north.'

Ray closes his eyes. Which achieves little. 'Some people back there'll shit nails.' He can't see Arshag's expression. 'You shitty?'

Arshag takes his time. 'I was hoping, with the Inspector gone, and a new boss, the copshop might strike it lucky, make a new start. Was hoping.'

Ray squirms. He feels guilty but also a familiar excitement at a new start elsewhere. 'When I was growing up, I thought everything happened elsewhere. I was determined to find it.' On the road again. 'I used to hitch-hike a lot, take rides going wherever.'

'Surprise, surprise.'

'Put your hand up for Alice's case.'

'That'd be a real surprise. Putting my hand up or getting it.'

They look out at nothingness. Let it go, let it go, let it go.

Ray says, 'Like Kennedy said, blokes selling guns are more likely to shoot us than blokes selling lizards.'

Arshag's voice sounds like it's coming from far off. 'I've seen three killings. My mother. My father. My aunt. Shot in front of me, then over and over, making sure. At our home in Marash.' He savours the name. 'They tossed their bodies into our house and set fire to it. My uncle and me watched from a nearby hill, him crying. My aunty was his sister. To protect me, he couldn't do anything but watch.'

'You said the man who brought you here was your father.'

'My uncle had attacked some Turks, they were hunting him. Wanted man. Taking my father's name got him out, me hanging on his hand. It was nineteen-twenty, I was two. After the killings, he carried me on his back in a sack with holes cut for my legs, head sticking out the top. Walked for god knows how far, how many miles. He told me later there were bodies on the road. An ugly, thick, sticky kind of smell. Clung to you, he said.' There's a tremor in Arshag's voice. 'Those killers just drove away, no justice.' Ray hears the sound of clothing as if Arshag is shifting around. 'Could I kill?'

'You ever?'

'No.'

Ray shakes his head too. A heavy pause. 'Once heard this cop saying how he'd shot and killed a crazy coming at him with a knife, his first. He joked that calling it his first made it sound like sex. It did fuck him up.' He peers into the dark, opens the leather cover on his luminous watch. 'Time's up.

This is dumb. If there were any guns on offer, Kennedy's probably bought them by now.' Joking but irritated.

'Good cover eh, send everyone out on a fool's errand.'

'Should've checked roads not marked with an X. Like with the duffers. Take me home.'

As Arshag drives, the headlights create a shining tunnel ahead through the dark. In intense bush blackness, Ray believed it was a magic space, the lights holding back the mysterious dark.

He thinks about Kennedy, the limits of what he might really be up to, to no avail.

—

Next morning, in the copshop, Ray knocks on the Inspector's closed door. Nothing. Waits, knocks again.

'Yes!' Peremptory voice.

Ray enters an almost bare office, devoid of personal references, some files already boxed. The view from the solitary window shows the rear verandah of the copshop and a slice of blue sky. The Inspector is at his desk, reading something official. He gives Ray an irritated glance. Ray feels hostile resistance to his being there. None of the vague goodwill from the aerodrome.

'I wanted to ask about the Alice case.'

'Alice? What about it? You been on it long enough. Why? You're leaving.'

The door opens behind Ray, and Kennedy enters with a wink. The Inspector ignores him, like the breezy entrance is normal. Kennedy leans against the wall beside Ray.

Ray considers asking to continue without Kennedy but it won't happen. 'When I'm gone, Arshag ought to get Alice. He's got the experience—'

Kennedy snorts. 'Listen. Everyone thinks Arshag's a native of this wide, brown land, right? And natives trying to be real cops chasing other natives is bad enough. But going after a white man? Joke. Nasty joke. Thought you two were mates.' Another cold wink.

Ray says, 'He's as good as any of us. Maybe better, if he got a go.' Ray has to avoid Kennedy's sneer or punch it.

Kennedy tut-tuts, like admonishing a child. 'Cos we keep him in his limits. A good boss does that. Something you don't get—knowing your limits.' He and Ray look to the Inspector, who has returned to his reading.

Ray says, 'Whoever gets it has to follow up on Alice's knickers. It's the only clothing missing. Might be a trophy.'

'Still on about that?' With a hollow laugh, hard to listen to.

Ray says, 'Basic detective work.'

The Inspector looks exasperated. 'Whoever takes over from you, Kennedy'll fill him in. And maybe explain why the case is still bloody open. That's the end of it.' He flaps a hand in dismissal.

Kennedy winks at Ray and bows for him to exit first.

———

Ray hunts Arshag down in the armoury, cleaning and oiling handguns. Arshag's Beretta semi-automatic pistol is on the bench, done to a dull gleam. Arshag reads Ray's face, starts dismantling his own handgun. Ray drops onto a stool opposite. The room's enclosed space and muffled sounds create a closed, meditative quality.

Ray picks up the Beretta, does a safety check. 'How old's this?'

'Nineteen-thirty-four.'

Ray tests its balance. 'Never fired in anger?'

'So my uncle said. Sent it from Italy during the war.'

'My old man gave me a sword. Genuine samurai, if you believe it. Got lost somewhere.' Ray aims the handgun at a target pinned to the wall, which is also a calendar with a photo of a naked woman. Arshag gently takes the Beretta and returns it to the bench.

'I like the Detective Special. I blame the movies.' He picks up a bullet. 'Mate of mine back in Caneville makes his own.'

'Case too?'

'Sure. And the cartridge, in brass.'

'An alloy, like you and me.'

'How's that?'

'Brass is an alloy, a mixture of stuff. That's us coppers, we're mixtures.'

Ray rolls his eyes. 'Not as shiny.'

'The more copper you put into an alloy, the better it resists corrosion. And corruption is corrosion.'

'The more copper, the less corruption. Yeah, right. Where do you get this shit?'

'My uncle the engineer. Knew his metals.'

'But not our coppers.'

Arshag continues cleaning.

'I told the Inspector to give you Alice.'

Arshag's eyebrows are eloquent. 'Went well, did it?'

Ray bows his head, lifts both hands, swings around to leave.

Arshag keeps cleaning. 'Something I need to know.' An edge in his voice.

Ray faces him as Arshag keeps oiling and wiping.

'After you leave, if you hear there's been a bit of bush

justice for Alice out here, you going to set the dogs on anyone?'

Ray takes a breath, holds it, exhales. 'Never dob you in. That what you're asking?'

Arshag feels resistance in the tone, lifts his eyebrows.

Ray says, 'I want something concrete tying Kennedy to it. Used to call it evidence. Once upon a time. Evidence enough for us anyway. I need it and I'll get it.'

'There was and there was not. You'll do this in the five minutes you've got left here? Stubborn bugger.'

'Not that you'd know anything about stubbornness.'

Arshag laughs quietly.

Ray says, 'You ever been back . . . where was it?'

'Marash?' Arshag keeps oiling. 'Long way to go for ashes.'

'You might run into your uncle. Wouldn't you like to see the place?'

'Yeah, I would. He'd be old now. Maybe eighty? Or dead.' Shrugs that off. 'How are you going to find anything before you go?'

Ray abruptly stands, mouth set.

Arshag, startled, says, 'What?' Then almost as a joke, 'You going now?'

Ray manages a wry grin. 'Something tougher. Much tougher.'

Arshag thinks about it, points at Ray, and grins cruelly. 'Stella. You haven't told her yet.'

'This is my moment.'

Louise appears, breathless and pale. 'Barry Slater might've shot his wife Betty and he's shooting his stock. His neighbour Terry just phoned.'

Ray gets up. 'Where're Kennedy and Laming?'

Louise shrugs, shakes her head. 'Don't know. But Barry's yelling he's going to kill Kennedy.'

Arshag stands too, winks at Ray. 'Not today, Stella. Maybe tomorrow.'

Ray winces.

18

Arshag drives Ray out of the carpark and turns onto the highway heading east.

Ray says, 'Barry the meat man. First time I met him I knew he was a loose cannon.'

'Your first lesson in the shadow job network.'

'Didn't you say he was having money troubles?'

'His place's only a hundred acres. Hasn't got enough of his own water these days. Bad times like now he has to buy it, get it trucked in.'

'Why would he want Kennedy dead?'

'A while ago Barry drove into town in a new ute.'

'With no visible means of support?'

'Except under-the-radar.'

'One of Kennedy's men?'

Arshag pulls a face. 'We'll see. About seven mile.'

They drive past the service station and out of town. Ray lost in fearful thinking about desperate parents, guns, and kids—a venomous mix. His own parents had the violence of toxic words, fed by their own disillusioned lives. But no guns. His parents've been on his mind lately, as disillusion comes for him too. Hoping Barry's kids are safe.

Arshag turns into a large, dusty front yard, bare dirt except for a narrow strip of green grass around the house. On their left, Ray shakes his head ruefully at a derelict tennis court, its surrounding ten-foot-high netting torn from leaning posts. The court needs weeding. No net. On their right are two car bodies on blocks. A barking brown dog strains at its leash, looking underfed.

Terry the neighbour, a bald, late middle-aged man in overalls stands at his fence, gesturing to the rear of Barry's house. Arshag goes to him. Ray heads around the tennis court side of the house. In the back corner, wheeled kids' toys lie abandoned in another bare earth yard. Beyond that is a stock pen with a dozen long-horned cattle, collapsed, motionless, blood pooling. One twitches and moans. Flies in hordes. No sign of a woman's body.

Arshag catches up, points to a barn across the yard. 'In the horse shed, they call it.'

'No horses now?'

'Relic of a past time. He's got his kids in there. Luke's six, Tammy's four.'

Ray closes his eyes. 'His wife?'

'Terry heard a scream and shots, all he knows. Barry shot at him so he pissed off.'

'Jesus, while he had kids with him? How well do you know Barry?'

'Not well. Always too angry to get to know. He's a happy clapper, not the sharpest tool in the shed.'

'They never are.'

A shot rings out and wood chips splinter into the air from the side of the house above their heads. Ray and Arshag duck back, Ray swearing.

A male voice comes from the partly open top of a half-door where a rifle barrel appears. 'Where's fucking Kennedy?'

Ray says, 'First things first, Barry. This's Ray Windsor here. Remember me? I'm the new boy who tried to knock off your load of meat.'

Silence.

'How's Luke? Okay? And Tammy?'

'With me and safe. Long as you don't do nothing stupid.'

'Betty in there too?'

'She fucking ran off like all fucking women do. Don't know where she went and she's not coming back.'

'Come on, Barry. That's the mother of your kids we're talking about. Can they hear what you're saying?'

'Better the kids know. Enough lies get told around here. Get Kennedy here. Not interested in you dickheads.'

'You need water in there? Bit hot.'

'Get Kennedy.' Another shot hits the wall of the house. 'Now.'

Ray and Arshag duck down.

Ray's cursing. *How the fuck do you negotiate?* He calls out, 'Alright! Hey! You promise you won't hurt those kids? Barry?'

Four or five quick shots smash into the house, shattering some windows.

Ray holds his hand over his mouth, almost gagging. Keep talking, no idea what else to do.

Barry's voice rises to a scream. 'Get him get him get him!'

'Okay! The copshop's radioed him. He's coming. He was out past Rochester's so he'll take twenty to thirty minutes. I'm not bullshitting you.'

Silence settles. A child's complaining voice is audible, not the words.

Ray shivers at images of horror in his head. Looks at Arshag. 'Kennedy'll make him worse. We've got to push this along. Who's best to keep him talking, you or me?'

Arshag steps out a little from the side of the house and waves. 'Barry? Arshag here. Long time, no talk. How'd this happen?'

A shot rings out and Arshag jumps back, gasping. 'Not me.'

Ray nods, calls out, 'Barry? You going to shoot me too? Better if you got me some meaty ribs.'

'Get Kennedy. Only Kennedy.'

'I promise, he's coming. But listen, are the kids hungry? I can get pies. A coke, lemonade?'

Silence.

'What sort of pie do the kids like?'

Silence.

'Giving a kid a pie can't hurt. What do they like?'

'Jesus fuck, I don't know.'

'Shepherd's pie. With the potato on top.' Ray smiles to hear a boy's voice. 'And Tammy likes pie with bacon. And two Fantas.'

'Good-o. We're not far from the servo. Tucker'll be here soon.'

Arshag says to Ray, 'I'll radio Kaye, get her to call the servo to bring it.' Arshag jogs back to the front yard.

Silence again.

Ray looks at his watch. Sweat streams down his face, his eyes sting from the salt. 'Hey Barry, how long you been living here? Must've been posh once, eh? Tennis and horses?'

Silence.

Ray tries again. 'I was brought up on a cane farm. Dragged up, we used to say. Nothing posh about a cane farm. Black ash and red dirt. Who'd you buy this place from?'

'From Kennedy. Me the mug.'

'You and Kennedy were mates, or what?'

'Your copshop's a fucking joke. He told me all about the joke youse are. Says he does his shit in plain view, you bastards never notice. Got so much on he has to keep records of where he's at or he can't keep up. Says he's got stuff in a filing cabinet that'd blow your minds. In a filing cabinet! You're all the same—jokes.'

Ray hears a different sound. Weeping, or moaning. Betty? No. From the shed, too full-throated for a kid. Jesus, it's Barry.

'Hey, Barry? You know, I haven't been in town long. If Kennedy's doing wrong, I need to know. Tell me. So I can do something about it.'

'Yeah? And get myself killed?'

'Tell me.'

'You hear what I just fucking said?'

'If Kennedy's into something, we need to bring him down.' Hoping his voice doesn't sound as hollow as it does to his own ears.

Barry gives an unnerving high-pitched laugh, awash with bitterness. 'Says the copper about the copper. You mob back each other up, no matter what.'

Ray calms his sharp breathing, keeps his voice even. 'What do you want from Kennedy? What happens when he gets here? Can I help sort this out?'

Silence, except for snuffling from the shed.

'Let me help you.'

Barry clears his throat. 'I want the money he owes me for jobs I've fucking done.'

'Okay! What jobs? Bit bloody stupid him not paying you.'

Silence, then Barry says, 'Keeps me on the never-never,

doesn't he. Duffing for him, meeting the odd plane. Wants me for his idiot delivery boy the rest of my bloody life.'

Ray stares into space, futilely tapping his pockets for pen and paper. 'Like Benny Lee?'

'Yeah. Poor dumb Benny and those guns. People say he was drunk cos he was happy to be making a quid. He wasn't fucking happy. He realised he was locked into working for Kennedy. Couldn't walk away, couldn't quit. No control even over his own life.'

'You reckon you're in control here?'

'I'm getting it back the only way I can, no fucking help from you. I know what I deserve and this's the only way I can collect. He promised me good money and gave me shit.'

Ray hears a kid squeal, then break into loud crying, calling for mummy. 'Shut the fuck up, Luke, or I'll do it for you.'

Ray hears the action of a rifle loading and his insides go cold. 'Hey, Barry!' Working to keep his voice flat. 'I think the pies're here. Want to let the kids come have them? Pretty rough for them in there.' He hears a kid squealing, wanting to go. 'Barry?'

'Go on, get the fuck out. You're the same as your useless mother.'

Ray sees the bottom half of the shed door scrape open. A girl appears, shoved out. She falls into the dirt but gets up and runs towards Ray, crying. He freezes as she darts across the open space, all knees and elbows and long, dark hair streaming behind her, painfully small and vulnerable, then she reaches him and he whisks her out of sight, holding her in a tight embrace, feeling the impossible slightness of her frame, close to tears himself.

'Barry, I got her. She's okay.'

He releases her, motions her to stay against the wall behind him. Musters the strength to continue.

'What about the boy, mate? Send Luke, too?'

'Get Kennedy here in five minutes or I shoot both of us, do us both a favour. Save my boy from a shit life, which right now's all I can offer him. Be fucking kindness to spare him that. You wouldn't fucking know.'

Arshag appears behind Ray carrying a tray with two pies in paper bags and two cans of Fanta.

'Barry? Tammy's got her pie. So you know, no one's shitting you here.'

Ray looks behind him. Tammy takes her food and drink and stands staring at him, light blue eyes dazed, dirt smeared across very pale hollow cheeks, holding the pie and drink at arm's length as if they are alien objects. Lost soul.

Arshag is bracing to carry the tray to the shed but Ray stops him. 'I'll do it. I've kept him talking, it's supposed to help. I hope.'

He calls to the shed. 'Barry? I got Luke's tucker. I'm bringing it. I'll put it outside the door. I'm not armed so don't bloody shoot me. All I've got is a pie and a drink. Coming out now.'

He steps into view with the tray, sways, lightheaded, finds his footing. Crunches across the open area as a rifle barrel protrudes from the shed. Not looking at it, Ray leaves the tray on the ground away from where the door will swing open, and backs away, hands in plain sight, till he is in the middle of the space, then stops.

'There you go. Shepherd's pie. Not trying to con you. I want this over, that's all. Especially for little Luke.'

The bottom half of the door swings partly open. Barry's head, neck and shoulder appear, arm reaching for the tray.

Two shots ring out.

Ray spins in shock and dashes for the side of the house, hears himself yell, not words, tortured noise. Then stares towards the front yard. Something was awry in the sound of the shots. They came from the front yard, not the shed.

He turns back to the shed. Barry is crumpled on the ground, blood running from his head and neck. Luke's frenzied screaming echoes inside the shed, and Ray's head.

Ray gapes at the front yard. Kennedy and Laming are walking towards him, both carrying rifles.

Ray holds up a fist. 'You fucking murderers.'

Kennedy stabs his finger into Ray's chest, managing to keep the barrel roughly pointing at Ray's head. 'I saved your fucking life, cunt.'

'You killed him to shut him up. What'd you do to drive him to this?'

Laming sneers like he's clearing his throat till Ray slaps him so fast Laming gets the pain but misses how it happened. Luke's crying becomes a deep rhythmic wail, guttural beyond his years.

Everyone turns towards the shed at movement along its side. A woman creeps into view. Betty, dishevelled, dirty, twigs and leaves stuck to her hair and clothes. She sees Barry's body, falters, then walks stiffly forward, head high, and steps over the body as if it were nothing. She wrenches the door fully open and goes inside.

'Luke, my little man! Luke, my little man!'

Scuffling, incoherent voices. A fraught silence. Betty reappears carrying Luke, covering his eyes so he can't see the body, which she steps over as before. She reaches Ray and the others, calling for Tammy in a harsh, cracked voice. Grabbing Tammy's hand, she vanishes round the front corner of the house with both kids.

Tammy's pie and drink lie on the ground, ants already approaching the pie, drink trickling from the can. A door slams. Ray figures they're all inside the house. He walks away to the front of the house too.

Kennedy's voice is thin, stressed. 'Get back here. What'd he tell you? Windsor!'

Arshag catches Ray in the front yard. 'What'd he say?'

'What we've known without knowing all along. Kennedy runs his own fucking crime ring here. And I've still got no idea how to prove any of it.'

'You look ready to do something stupid.'

'He was ready to kill his own family. Shoot his own bloody kids. Never been close to that before.' Ray hears a tremor in his voice, sees it in his hands, leans against the wall. Holds up his trembling hands to Arshag with a kind of wonder.

Arshag grabs them, squeezes them, presses them against Ray's chest.

Ray closes his eyes, tears coming out. Breathes deep and hard. Flashes of all four of his parents, no fucking difference between them, loved them all, loves them all. Laughs in relief.

Arshag releases Ray's hands, tilts his head to Kennedy. 'He say anything useful?'

'Kennedy runs everything. Leaves stuff under our noses. Something about a fucking filing cabinet.'

Arshag turns back towards Kennedy and Laming, who are standing over Barry's body. Ray straightens intently, turns away.

Arshag says to him. 'Where're you going?'

'Betty. Strike while the iron's hot.' He looks again at

Kennedy and Laming, at Barry's body. 'Call it in. Don't think they bothered.'

———

Ray knocks on the front door and waits. Watches Arshag work the vehicle radio. Hopes his trembling doesn't return. Never happened before. Betty snatches open the door, still pulling leaves and dirt from her hair, face wet with tears. She stares till a light in her eyes says she sees him. Her mouth works as if to speak but she can't find words. She walks back, into the house. He enters, closes the door.

The rooms are large, gloomy, virtually empty. Need a lot of furniture to fill this place. He enters a cavernous, bare kitchen, full of light from a line of windows. The kids are at a small table, eating bread and butter and vegemite. They don't acknowledge him. Barry shot out some of these windows, which everyone is ignoring.

Ray recognises from his own childhood the post-fight silence, the storm spent. Betty keeps brushing dirt off both kids, even where there is none. She looks at the kettle and for an awful moment Ray thinks she'll offer tea.

'Can we talk?'

She sniffs loudly, leads him back to the enclosed front verandah. Peers through a crudely installed, dusty louvre, maybe at Arshag in the Land Rover.

He joins her, relieved to see no one else in the yard. A wind is blowing dust and leaves.

'I have to ask some questions. I'm not supposed to say this but anything you say stops with me, I promise.' He realises he is holding out both arms. In collusion?

She turns to him, a scornful sneer forming. 'You're a cop, so you're with Kennedy.'

'I'm me. I'm not with anyone. Not in the club.'

She snorts in derision, tears brimming, looks away. 'My mum went to school with your mum. You're a Rogers, eh?'

He tries a smile. 'Guess everyone knows by now.'

'Why would you keep it secret?'

Silence.

'Did Barry give you any sign he'd do this?'

'Did I happen to notice he was angry enough to kill his own kids? And me? That what you mean?' She shoves tears off her face so hard she pulls at her whole cheek. 'What do you want me to say? He was a good bloke but, gee, times are tough and he meant well? Good family man? Well, he fucking wasn't. He punched me around and kicked any kid who come near him.'

'Where's Kennedy come in?'

She laughs, a spasmodic, disquieting noise.

'Barry did jobs for him and wasn't paid?'

Her large brown eyes are watery, cheeks flushed, long auburn hair straggly. She is worn out but Ray feels her defiance, full-blooded and growing, fists clenching, releasing.

'Yeah, but did he tell you I did, too? He tell you I was fucking Kennedy? Not that I wanted to. Any port in a storm. Figured it might've come in handy.'

Ray wants to say he's sorry, can feel his feet wanting to turn, walk away, but he makes them stay.

She spins to face him with a withering stare. 'I fucked Kennedy but I did none of his shithouse jobs okay? You get that?'

Ray holds up an open palm, holds his ground. 'It's Barry I want to know about. You've got kids to look after. No one's going to come after you.'

'What? Like I'm free?' She laughs in contempt. He watches her stare at him, then out the window, then look to the kitchen. She turns back to him, shakes her head like communication is impossible. 'Your mum's property was sold to Taylor. You met your cousin Jimmy?'

He grins, sort of. 'Yeah.'

'You know Taylor and Kennedy cheated Jimmy out of the place? With Barry's help. Cheated him, your family, took water and cattle? For years.'

Ray has no idea what his face is doing. 'How?'

'Bit of duffing. Made a game of it. Pinching stock here and there. Big joke, it was.'

'And his water?'

'You know the creek in old man Strathdee's place, next to Jimmy on the highway side? It runs into Jimmy's, tops up his dam, right?' She looks at him, realises he doesn't know. 'Anyway. Old man Strathdee's too old to get out and notice irrigation channels that never used to be there, running all the way into Taylor's. Guess Jimmy never noticed either.'

Ray knows Jimmy suspected at least but doesn't interrupt her.

Betty says, 'Mind you, he knew enough to know Kennedy was doing him somehow. Must've felt it in his bones.' She laughs at what must be Ray's expression of dismay. 'Got his finger in every pie, has Kennedy. And into as many cunts as he can too. Not anymore.' Betty looks to the kitchen, pauses, puts her hands on her hips in new resolve.

'Kennedy loves to chat after a fuck, as if you enjoy his company. Called Barry his delivery boy. Dumb-arse Barry'd come home parading pockets stuffed with cash, like he was rich for selling it all, then he'd have to hand it over to Kennedy so Kennedy could chuck him coins in return. Except, eventually he even stopped giving the coins. I mustn't have been fucking him hard enough.'

They peer through the louvres as Constable Baxter drives another police four-wheel drive into the yard, followed by the ambulance. Kennedy points to the backyard. He turns to the house and Ray is sure he sees them watching from behind the dusty, filmy curtains, but then turns away, looking unconcerned.

Ray says to Betty, 'You got anything to prove any of this?'

Her eyes widen at him. 'Like written down? This your first rodeo?'

Ray points at Kennedy, who is returning to the backyard. 'You need protection?'

She laughs unpleasantly. 'Everyone does. You think you don't?' More tears as the kids appear, faces besmirched with vegemite, and hug her legs. She holds them against her.

19

Ray joins Arshag at the Land Rover. 'She's leaving today, got a fire in her belly. Taking the kids to family out of town. Reckons Barry was the driver for whatever Kennedy was moving.'

'Any evidence? Smoking guns?' Knows the answer to that.

Ray shakes his head, nods towards Barry's body. 'Look what his smoking gun did here today.' Recalls that Brisbane cop, on evidence. 'You make it up as you go along.'

Arshag kicks at a low weed in the dusty earth. Severs its stalk and small branches, leaves the root. 'Ever verballed anyone?'

'No. You?'

'No. But it has its uses.' Arshag takes his time, stares at the sky. 'This whole place has done a deal with the devil. Used to be clean compared to the shit going on in other places. Now a local bloke's ready to shoot his kids? Dear god.' He has to pause. 'The place's eating itself alive.'

Ray hears an echo of Lord Billy. Just as vague, just as dire.

Barry's covered body is carried out on a stretcher. Kennedy looks hard at them as he passes, a flash of hard triumph in his eyes. Bastard's done some deal with the devil. Just as hard to get a grip on.

Ray puts out his hand and Arshag gives him the vehicle keys. 'Got to see a man about a dog.' Points to the other police vehicle. 'You go back with them?'

Arshag nods.

Ray says, 'Best I do this on my own.'

'Now?'

Ray kicks at the ground. 'No. Do that tough thing first.'

Arshag offers a sympathetic flinch.

———

Late afternoon, Ray rides into Dot's yard. Dot and Stella are examining the progress of the Banksia rose plants. He joins them, pecks Stella's cheek, notices a hesitation in her. He nods at the plant climbing the arch. 'Still alive?'

Dot scowls, and Ray feels some of its heat aimed at him, though she concentrates on the plant. 'The bloody metal frame gets so hot it cooks the plant.'

'Same with my bike seat. Burns my bum.' No responses. A failed attempt at levity.

Dot excuses herself. 'See you two later.'

Inside Ray's flat, he hugs Stella, face buried in her hair. When they release, she holds her gaze on him. Feeling furtive, he produces beer and white wine. They sit on the sun-warmed bench as the sun slips behind houses opposite.

He points his stubby at it. 'Go, damn you.'

'Where have you been today?'

'You know Barry? The meat man? He lost it. Threatened to shoot his kids and Betty.'

Stella pales, hand to her mouth.

Ray says, 'Betty and the kids're okay. Barry was shot dead by Kennedy or Laming. One of them. Or both. The body's gone to Tyborg for autopsy. Etcetera.'

She keeps her eyes closed. 'I know the kids. Never saw much of Betty.'

He recovers. 'Close to the bone. Something a lot of cops fear.' He loses his calm again, grips the stubby. 'My parents— all four of them—had their moments, but never that ... extreme. Different aggro, and frustrations. Yours?'

She laughs, squeezes his shoulder. 'Alive and kicking, sometimes each other, but after thirty years, they know how to dodge. Live in Brisbane. Still the same house. Eternally reliable.'

'Do you like them?'

'They're my parents. What's like got to do with it?'

He says nothing. Drains his beer, goes inside, returns with two.

He feels her examine him. Her eyes have a coolness he hasn't seen before.

She says, 'You're a restless soul. Not very eternally reliable.'

'If I stayed in the same place for thirty years, I'd be worried I was dead.' He looks at her in shock at saying it aloud. Now of all days.

'Well,' she says, 'imagine you thinking that.' Upset is hard in her eyes.

He starts to say he's sorry, then doesn't.

She says, 'Thing is, why do you think that?'

He shrugs.

'Not much for joining in, are you? You're good to be with, but always remote. Mixing's a bit of a burden.'

He says, 'You join in everything.'

'That's me. I love it.' Her seriousness is on full display. 'I don't know much about what you love. Maybe you don't love much. A cop trying to do good who doesn't believe in it?'

He looks into the night, away from her irritation. Shadow-boxing, and they'll keep doing it until he speaks up.

She fixes him with an intense stare. 'Do you reckon we can improve the world or is it a waste of time?'

'The world's not a waste of time. Trying to improve it is.'

'What a weird copper you are.'

'Trying to hold the line isn't bad.'

She waggles an empty glass, goes inside, turns on the light. He stays there.

She returns to the door. 'You cooking dinner tonight? What am I having?'

He stands up. Stalemate. He says, 'Spag bol?'

'If you've got enough garlic.'

He shakes his head, defensive, as if garlic were the worst of his problems.

She says, 'Who cooked when you were a kid?'

'Dad. Mum didn't like the kitchen. She murdered steaks.'

She scoops up her bag. 'My place! I've got everything we need.'

He pulls out his bike keys. 'I'll follow.'

He sees her absorb he's not staying over, then she passes him, heading for her car.

Ray leaves his bike outside her house and walks round to the backyard. Climbs to her verandah and perches on the edge of a chair. Watches clouds of insects whirl around the verandah light. The pool shimmers in the gathering dark. She emerges with beer, a bottle of gin, tonic and a glass with ice.

She hands him the beer without looking at him, starts to mix her drink, then erupts. 'So it's true. It's bloody true. You ever going to say it?' Her arm jumps like an independent limb and spills gin on the bench, missing her glass. She turns to him. Gin trickles to the bare timber floor of her open verandah.

'Who told you? Bloody Kaye?'

'What's that bloody matter?'

He realises. Dot. Royalton Radio. A voice in his head clearly tells him, 'Serves you right! What'd you expect?'

Heat still pumps down from the creaking iron roof but she is impervious. Ray notices at last she is wearing a shapeless shift the colour of her eyes and is barefoot. He recognises that what he originally saw as supple slenderness in her is now a steely leanness. Her hardened core becoming visible. He feels a sharp sadness he will never know more about that.

She faces him, agitated, feet shifting, a kind of stamping. 'Why? How? Did you request it? You in the shit again?'

Ray rises to get a cloth for the gin but she stands in front of him. He stops. 'I think it was meant as some sort of gift. From the Inspector. I didn't ask for it.' He shrugs, and sees this exasperates her almost beyond words.

'Did you ask why?'

'I don't know why he does anything. Never been any good asking him anything.' He goes to the railing, absent-mindedly straightens her towel and swimming costume draped there. She crosses to him and snatches them, shifts them out of reach down the railing. They stand side by side, not touching, facing her backyard. The glittering water of her pool reflects multiple flashes of the verandah lights. He can make out the green lawn around the pool, watered by splashing. Beyond that, the grass is burnt brown. They face each other.

Her mouth tightens. 'Why don't you have the balls to say you don't want to fuck me anymore?'

'I go where I'm sent. You're a teacher, you understand that.'

'Say no. You can say no, pick a new life. I thought that's what we were doing.'

'Stella!' Reduced to a whisper.

She looks at the gin on the floor, and nods slowly to no one. 'You don't want to say no.'

'We never made promises.'

'Just your bush fuck, was I? Lucky I'm not pregnant, what then?'

'Bloody hell, Stella.' But that stops him.

'Go. Christ, just go.'

'What'd you think we were doing here? You said you hated the place. I got sent here as punishment. What future would we have here?'

'How about a future somewhere else then? Can we do that?'

He swallows. 'We haven't got . . . enough.'

'Not enough what? Love? Guts?' She's shaking her head back, refusing to let tears flow. 'You have to give as well as take to know what you've got. If there was something you weren't getting, something you didn't want, you never said. Were you pretending all this time? Why didn't you say what you wanted? Do you even know?'

'What do *you* want? This?' His loose hand includes the house, backyard, town, everything.

'Maybe, yeah. You know what really pisses me off? I knew you'd do this but I couldn't accept it. See? I'm shitty with me as much as you.' She belts a fist against her own chest. 'What you are now is all you'll ever be. Spend your life going everywhere and getting nowhere. Piss off.'

He tramps downstairs, turns back.

She stares at him. 'Get, for god's sake. Get!'

He walks to his bike. Dried grass crunches underfoot.

—

Next morning, a Saturday, approaching midday, the sky empty of cloud, oppressively blue. The air is utterly dry, wrapping everything in scorching, suffocating heat. Ray rolls past the pub carpark on his motorbike. Kennedy's Sandman is there. Unmistakenly painted with scaly monsters and impossibly busty women. Ray exhales and accelerates away.

He parks at a chest-high, chain-wire fence around a modest, low-blocked wooden house. Wide verandahs, air-con box on the roof. The rusty shell of an EH Holden is sinking into long, brittle, brown grass in one front corner, a steel garden shed in the other. What Ray can see of the backyard is empty. He pushes the gate open. Two Staffies appear from under the house, growling, hugging the ground, parting for a pincer attack. He tosses jerky. They halt, swaying, then monster it, slavering, grunting, bickering.

He looks to the house. No sign of life. Where to find a filing cabinet. If Kennedy's doing half of what he's accused of, would he record it? Al Capone kept records, it got him jailed. Standing there with the munching dogs, Ray realises with stark, belated clarity that coming here like this concedes that he no longer trusts due process to bring Kennedy to justice. He's putting the trust in himself, more than ever before, trust he'll do this right. That he has to take what he needs. Use it to do what he has to do, and—face it—make up what fits.

Here we fucking are. In broad daylight, more crushing daylight than he's ever seen, and the only question is, house

or shed? Where would Kennedy store records, or incriminating trophies? The shed. Has to be. Crazy, pistol-packing
mumma's not going there. Too far, too hot. Ray prods himself
to move. Kennedy's demented mother gunning him down
mid-lawn would be too fucking shitty.

Shed's locked. He produces a collection of lock-picking
tools, tries one, no good. The next works. Inside, brain-
fogging heat descends in a cloak of musty air. A three-door
filing cabinet is neat amid a shamble of tools in dusty piles.
In plain sight. Also locked. Sick of it, he finds a tyre lever and
mangles the edge of the first drawer. Tears it open. Nothing.
Second, nothing.

In the bottom drawer, a bright blue bundle. It's what he
came for but it still shocks him into stillness. Imagines it in a
sealed, clear plastic bag on a courtroom table labelled 'Exhibit
A Item: Female briefs, blue. Size: S (Small).' Only one pair, so
Peter kept Diah's?

The force of his doing an illegal entry belatedly hits him—a
copper, doing this—followed immediately by knowing illegal
entry doesn't matter, not with these cops, in this world.

He braces, gingerly picks up the bundle, drops it into his
soft, grey plastic bag and shoves it in his pocket. Takes a
breath. So easy to find. Kennedy's gall? He looks for written
records of some kind. None. Kennedy stores all the details in
his head?

He slams the drawers closed, not caring to hide they've been
forced. He exits, pulls the door closed. Locks it. Tidy boy.

The dogs are waiting so he feeds them again. He reaches his
bike, grabs his helmet, then sees the Sandman approaching.
He makes it look as if he's just removed the helmet as Kennedy
crunches up to his gate in his Sandman, with Laming, and yells

out of his window at the dogs, who retreat. A bleary Laming climbs out, weaves to the gate, shoves it open and leans on it, ignoring Ray who is impressed Laming looks pissed already. Or maybe started that way. Kennedy also has the blank look of a drunk. Celebrating disposing of Barry? Then thinking, *If I'd killed a man yesterday, I'd get drunk too.*

Ray says, 'You want to watch out, mate. Cops'll do you for drunk driving.'

In the same tone he used for the dogs, Kennedy says, 'What the fuck're you doing here?'

'Wanted to ask you about the Alice case.'

Kennedy accelerates into the yard, scattering the dogs. Ray stays outside the fence. Laming hauls whisky and a carton of beer from the Sandman. Kennedy snaps the lid of his mailbox up, down, kicks the gate shut. Everything clipped, fierce. Laming reaches the verandah, drops into a deck chair, reaches into the already ripped open carton and starts on a can.

Kennedy turns to Ray. 'Still fucking here?'

'Thinking about Alice's knickers. Where they went.'

'Gets you hard, eh?' Kennedy points at him. 'Talk shop at the shop. Fuck off or I'll feed you to the dogs.' Walks away.

Ray looks across to Laming. 'Who shot Barry? You, or Laming?'

Kennedy turns back and points at Ray. 'Who saved your life, you mean? Laming's a better shot but I care more. You work it out.' Laughs, always something failing as a joke. Ray tosses his remaining jerky over the fence, detonating a vicious, spinning attack by the dogs on each other. Kennedy roars at them.

Ray leaves, wondering who to interview about poor delivery boy Barry. Not going to matter since the bastards won't let him near it.

He halts at the other end of town, at the boxing gym, stares at his hands. Shaking. Kennedy's inside his head. So is Laming, always the watcher.

The gym is oven-hot. Boys and girls spar in the rings or work on equipment. Arshag is showing one how to hold a stance. Ray waits. Arshag points the kid to a partner for a workout.

Ray palms him the grey plastic bag. Arshag feels its zero weight, shuts his eyes in realisation, pockets it. His face turns grey. 'In a filing cabinet?'

Ray nods. 'Keep it at the copshop. Maybe the new bloke . . .?' He lifts a pessimistic shoulder and meets Arshag's eyes, time slowing. Ray says, 'Not my copshop anymore.'

'Never been mine.' Taps the hidden bag. 'Getting this was a desperate act.'

'Better out of his grubby hands. But, no idea how to use it.'

'He'll know we've got it.'

Part of Ray, deep inside, gratefully acknowledges that *we*. 'Yeah. It was, I don't know . . . easy? But he's not used to pushback, is he?'

'You're busy for someone leaving. If you're actually leaving.' Arshag lifts his eyebrows.

Ray says, 'Yeah, yeah, I told Stella. She knew already. We're . . . not still friends.'

'You blaming the Inspector?'

Ray laughs, a self-deprecating sound. 'Nah. I could say no. Take the plunge, start a new life here. Fact is, I don't ever hang around much. You coming to my farewell fuck-off at the pub?'

Arshag grins. 'You know it'll piss people off if they wave you goodbye and you don't go?'

Ray chooses his words deliberately. 'I want a result for Alice. If not—' Lets that hang there. 'I won't go without it. But sticking to saying I'm going feels right.' Rolls his eyes to the sky. 'Christ, Stella'll be impressed if I stay, what do you reckon?'

Ray laughs at his own joke, just. Knows he badly wants to go. All it took was an opportunity to appear. Born with wheels on his bum, can't stay anywhere. Will that ever change?

He nods at Cassie attacking a punching bag. 'Getting into it.' She spots him, turns on a flurry of punches at the air and sparkles into a wonderful grin.

'Cassie's going to take on the whole world,' Arshag says. 'Have you told them? Want me to call them together?'

Ray swallows, shakes his head, takes a moment. He walks out, offering a clenched fist as they put on all sorts of fun boxing poses.

———

Ray parks at the copshop, stays sitting there, the bike radiating heat. Paralysis. Take the opportunity, escape? Or stay to fight? No way Arshag will get Alice's case.

A boisterous car horn shatters his deliberations. Jimmy in a ute does a neck-snapping dash across the whole main street, beating a thundering semi, its klaxon blaring. He grinds to a halt and yahoos through the open passenger window, shouting over a country blues cassette. 'Hey! Looking for you! Going out the old place. Wanna come?'

Ray drops into the ute beside him, adrenaline rising. 'Let's go!' Circuit breaker?

Jimmy yahoos again and plants his foot, his delight a tonic. They fishtail to the other side of the road and away, engine roaring, heavy metal objects in the tray behind rolling and crashing around. 'Can't get fucking booked, got my personal copper on board.'

Ray sinks back in the seat, making room for his boots amid crushed beer cans. Guitars are crying as town gives way to bush, more semis coming, shoving walls of air at the ute, highway stretching away. The song ends. Silence of a sort wraps around them.

'What are you picking up?'

'Fuck knows, I just threw stuff in boxes. Buggered if I know where I'll put it all. How much room've you got? Oh yeah, you're pissing off. Hey, when I drop into Brissy, I've got a place to stay, yeah?'

'Ah, sure.'

Jimmy laughs. 'Mate, your face!'

Ray twists his mouth into an apology.

Jimmy punches buttons, the cassette restarts. Time turns fluid.

———

Jimmy turns onto a narrow, sealed road, clunks too fast over the railway line at the train station Ray saw the day they met. Twenty minutes later, music roaring all the way, Jimmy trying to harmonise, they enter the large fenced yard of a long, low house that lies east–west. A generous, screened verandah runs across its width. 'Lots of Rogers have lived here. It had to keep growing so we'd fit. Everyone always did.'

The door is unlocked. Jimmy leads him into the stale smell of a house not lived in. Ray follows, alert, no idea for what. The empty rooms are not as large as he expected. Dark, exposed wood everywhere, tongue and groove.

'Auctioned off the furniture. Gave a lot away. What was I going to do with furniture? Here, your mum's old room.'

It's small, bare, with a dusty, saucer-shaped Bakelite lightshade, browned from the heat of too many bulbs. Bare French windows open onto the screened, western verandah. Faded pencil marks climbing one wall show her heights rising. Ray feels a rush of deep warmth for his mum that seals his throat. And takes him by surprise, as so much does these days.

Jimmy says, 'Dying of thirst. Esky in the ute,' and leaves.

Ray is wide-eyed, afraid he'll cry. He touches the pencil marks. His mother young, only this tall, shorter than him. Takes a deep breath, maybe to breathe her in, catch a sense of her.

Jimmy returns with cans and a black-and-white photo of two school-age kids laughing for the camera. 'My dad Gary and his little sister, my aunty, your mum.' Ann-Louise is shorter with an untidy ponytail. Ray laughs in wonder. The photo is creased. Box Brownie.

'You can have that one.' Indicating elsewhere with a lazy thumb. 'Before you piss off, go through the box, take what you want.'

The backyard rolls onto open paddocks, as at Lord Billy's. Two buckling tanks on wooden stands frame the rear corners of the house. Mint plants struggle under both. Clotheslines of sagging ropes on forked poles. A vegetable garden lost to weeds, inside torn netting. A mulberry tree in a car tyre. How'd a mulberry tree survive out here? Straggly citrus trees. He has that feeling again of supposedly inanimate things waiting.

His mother played on that swing—a piece of bum-sized wood on two ropes, one now broken, tied on a high branch of a tree he doesn't recognise. There are bulges in its bark, from carved names? The wreckage of a cubby made of odd pieces of timber. Kid's games conjuring up hopes and dreams. He thinks of his mother carrying these images in her head all those years. He's angry the place can be owned by anyone else. What will Taylor do with it? Don't ask, upset him and Jimmy both.

He'd felt shame, not coming earlier. Now, standing here, he knows why. He recalls a day, he was maybe ten, shaking, his mother dangerous and broken, face red and sweaty, crowding him, demanding he defend her against his dad, make him stop torturing her, destroying her life. While his dad sat on the back verandah, closed, head in his hands. Ray unable to move, terrified he was paralysed forever, terrified it proved he was weak, which is what she called him in rage or with contempt because he wouldn't *fight* for her. Until he broke out, and ran into the night to the bush behind their house. Get away, run away, get away. Remembers it now in his legs. Here at last, shaking again.

Jimmy nods at the desolate vegetable garden. 'Hard to grow shit here but Granny never quit trying.' Ray stares at the garden. Granny. Jimmy's giving him looks but Ray has no idea if he's behaving strangely.

'Can't see from here'—Jimmy points across the fruit trees and broken rear fence—'but the creek down there comes in from old man Strathdee's. It's dropped three feet in three years but it's permanent water. Though it was natural, you know? Dumb-fuck me. What Taylor wanted, the bastard. With what was left of our stock. Fucking duffers, kill them with my bare hands if I caught them. Word is local boys are doing it now.' Ray hears Lord Billy again, thinks about what Betty said. Best not mentioned now.

Jimmy's mouth makes a hard line. 'I tell you. Bloody thieves are a fucking problem but they're just fucking cabbies, eh? All they'll ever be. Who's paying them, they're the fucking animals.'

Ray shrugs. Who can disagree? 'You still doing the gas drilling?'

'Quit.' Stamps a boot on the ground. 'Took my know-how to Harry Cha, he gets a lot of water-drilling work. Hey, your motorbike, you taking it on the train with you?'

'Nope. You want it?'

'Shit yeah but I got no money, not even for a piece of crap like that.'

'It's yours. Gift for my long-lost cousin.'

'Ha, you're the one who was lost. You serious?'

'Done deal.'

20

Ray enters the copshop. On his desk is a long, brown, official envelope, like a threat. A week now till he's gone. If he goes. He encounters the Inspector leaving for somewhere. Ray knows he's meant to show gratitude for the transfer but can't get it out, which displeases the Inspector who surely hovers there for it. Ray found wanting, says the sour set of the man's mouth. Wasted largesse. Ray once again doesn't get the back-scratching trade-offs of how power works. Which is why he once more asks if Arshag can take over Alice's case. Futile, but he asks anyway.

The Inspector frowns, flicks a hand airily as he walks away. 'None of our business.'

Ray slumps at his desk, no one else around, trying to think it through. Piss off to Brisbane, be a cop who cut and ran? Or stay, fight for justice for Alice but effectively give up the Force? And then do what? No. Only solving Alice's case is a result to be proud of. Only that. His phone rings.

'Cuz?'

'Jimmy?'

'The duffers are back.'

'How do you know?'

'They're driving this dinged Chrysler Royal V8, you know with the big fins and—'

'I know a Chrysler Royal V8.'

'It's dark blue. Tinted windows. Venetian blind in the rear window.'

'A quiet little car no one'll notice, right?'

'Eh?'

'Go on.'

'I wouldn't have thought about it, but I was out at a well I'm drilling for Harry, bush-bashing down this track, and I catch a glimpse of this camp. Caravan, water tank, generator for fuck's sake. Soft bastards. And the Chrysler! Fuck, who goes off-road in a Chrysler Royal?'

'A recce?'

'Could be. Sheer luck I saw the camp. And it gets better. I reckon I saw a Sandman disappearing out a back way as I rolled by. Dragons and big tits all over it.'

'Kennedy.'

'Stupid, eh, like getting round with a big fucking neon sign on his hood. *Here I fucking am!*'

'Maybe he thinks it keeps him safe. Someone might've spotted you if you were that close?'

'No, mate, it's a funny thing. Maybe cos they're all over these days, no one notices company utes. Like Harry's, with writing on the sides. We're invisible, part of the landscape, like a postie.'

'Reckon?'

'Come on. Tell me. What's your postie look like? Young, old, black, white, brindle? Don't know, do you. No one knows their postie, just the bike or bulging bag. I wave to people when I'm driving, pricks never wave back. Never even see me.'

'Jimmy, are you winding me up to bust a bunch of duffers? You know more than you're saying, right?

'I can tell you're a copper. I wondered if you'd give a side-ways shit since you're pissing off.'

'Straight-up, clean police work'll go down just fine.'

'That's my cuz. Might even be a bit of biffo, eh?'

'We cherish it, mate. But hang on. Even if they're the who, what's the where and when? You taught me that.'

'Ha! Thought you'd stump me there, didn't you? I've got it figured. I reckon I know where this mob'll hit at least. So, how do you want to do this?'

—

Ray and Arshag wait in the police Land Rover deep in a sullen ironbark forest. The air is dry, sharp enough to cut the back of Ray's throat. A fire has recently raced through. Every tree is black. The earth is bare, with black patches. Tiny green shoots are on tree trunks and the ground. Ray stares, always astonished by the miracle. They are at the intersection of two bush tracks, weeds along the middle of each. On the other side of the intersection is the corner of a well-maintained, four-strand, barbed-wire fence.

A man on a stripped-down, army-green motorbike rides up inside the fence, no helmet, a large dog balanced on his tank, another on an improvised platform behind him. The bike stops, the dogs bound off and go snuffling. The man waits at the fence as a ute with Harry's company contact informa-tion on its doors drives up the track behind the Rover. Jimmy climbs out.

Jimmy says, 'Ray, meet Donnie Wexler, cattleman.' Ray shakes hands with Donnie across the fence. 'And Arshag, Ray's trusty duffer-smashing buddy, meet Donnie, Ray's other cousin.' Arshag and Donnie shake hands.

Ray says to Donnie, 'Cousins?'

Donnie winks. 'My granddad on my dad's side was the brother of your grandmum on her dad's side.'

Ray rolls his eyes at Jimmy, source of all confusion.

Jimmy says, 'No, no, the other way. Your maternal grand-dad and my paternal grandma.'

Ray closes his eyes. 'Pull the other one, you two, it's got bells on. Donnie, duffers are coming to hit you?'

'I reckon.' Donnie is tall, tanned, muscular, in shorts, sleeve-less shirt and boots. He pushes out a thick, pugnacious jaw and hooks long black hair behind his ears. His blue eyes flash anger as he points around. 'Jamieson's, north, have been hit. Sawyer's, east, the week after. Leaves me, pig in the middle. Had gear nicked, bloody exxy tools. They were checking me out, I'd say. And a week ago, some vehicle was making heavy weather of it over near Dog Creek on my eastern edge. There are good enough bush-roads through from Cotton Road they could use. It's how I'd do it. Can you help out?'

'For sure. We can stakeout wherever you want. But I'm obliged to tell you, serious violence can occur in appre-hending duffers, so only police can participate. No civilians.' He shakes a finger at Jimmy.

Jimmy looks at Donnie but dips his head at Ray. 'He's talking funny.'

Donnie grins. 'You can't stop me from being close by, can you? Starlight Hotel, on my own property.'

'Wouldn't dream of it.'

'Might even have a rifle with me, you know, for ferals.'

'But, no joke, you take a backseat if the shit hits the fan. This's a police operation.' Donnie and Jimmy nod very seriously to each other, then to Ray and Arshag, who nod back. Jimmy laughs, nodding wildly.

Ray shakes his head. 'Pigs in mud.'

Donnie says, 'Jimmy'll show you. See you there.' He swings onto his bike, kick-starts it and whistles. The dogs return and leap on, front and behind. Donnie weaves off quickly through the bush.

Jimmy rubs his hands together. 'Sweet. Fucking sweet.'

———

Dusk gathers over scattered clumps of paperbarks, mulga and ironbarks in a rough line running north–south beside a dry, eroded creek-bed on the edge of a plain. Ray and Arshag have small, dark-green tents among the trees. Jimmy has tied a khaki groundsheet to four trees for cover and spread another under it on the ground. He's in the creek bed, digging a fire-pit. Ray sits on a folding chair behind screening scrub, watching fifty or so Hereford cattle graze in the open. Huge, short-horned animals with massive brown bodies and curly white hair on their heads and chests. A hundred yards or so north of them is a half-empty dam ringed by cracked and drying mud. Two hundred yards east, a barbed-wire fence also runs north–south. Colours are fading, dark coming up out of the earth.

Jimmy walks by, pointing the shovel at the cattle. 'Enough dollars wandering around out there to put a kid through school, I reckon.'

Ray says, 'Speaking of kids, where's Burt?'

'I was going to break it to you gently. He's joined the army.'

Ray is shocked. 'I thought you cared for the boy. Does he know he'll get ordered around a lot by people he won't like much? What brought this on?'

'Trying to think up a fucking future. Reckons the army didn't do you much harm. Join the army, see the world, meet interesting people, then shoot them.'

'You don't always see the world. Will I see him before he goes?'

'Sure.'

'You'll miss him.'

'A man's gotta do what a man's gotta do.'

'You're not going to get pissed and join up too, are you?'

'Officer material, that's me.' Keeps walking. 'No, no.'

Opposite the campsite to the east, at a break in the fence, Donnie's motorbike appears on the ghost of a track and he rides quietly across to them, a twenty-two rifle and another of larger calibre crosswise on his back.

'Didn't bring the dogs. I'd never shut them up. They love a party.' He looks around and nods in approval. 'Nicely tucked away.'

Ray, Arshag and Donnie join Jimmy at the fire-pit, flames hidden in the hole. He's stirring a stew in a cast-iron pot over the fire, damper in coals to one side.

Sitting on logs round the fire, they eat in silence. Jimmy kicks sand over the fire as darkness falls out of a brilliantly glowing sky. No moon yet. Shifts organised, the others go to their sleeping bags.

Ray finishes his shift at dawn and lights the fire again. What a life. Cheeky being away from the copshop like this without authority but who at that copshop will lower the boom? Jimmy produces a vat of porridge to heat up. Arshag and Donnie appear, report no action last night. Donnie shares their breakfast then leaves for his working day. Jimmy departs for his shift with Harry.

The day meanders by. The heat builds pressure inside their heads. By mid-afternoon, the sky is turning white with thin, high cloud. Ray sleeps through the morning, Arshag in the afternoon.

Ray wakes in his tent, sees Arshag sitting against a large gum on the far side of the creek bed with what looks like a notebook and pencil. Ray joins him. 'Not sleeping?'

Arshag shakes his head. 'Too much excitement, eh?' He winks.

Ray sees the notebook is a sketchpad. Arshag draws with ordinary pencil in extraordinary detail. 'Landscapes. Never people.'

Ray gets comfortable beside him, looking at the creek bed and mulga trees between them and the cattle. They exchange comments about birds, shapes of trees. Nothing else comes up until their quiet stillness emboldens a dingo to inspect them, south along the creek bed. They have rifles to hand but neither moves. After a moment, the dingo trots calmly away into the bush.

Arshag says, 'If your other cousin Donnie keeps bringing food, we've got no reason to ever leave here.'

'Not my cousin.'

'You're not worried Donnie and Jimmy might be too enthusiastic? They've both got a bit of revenge to pay out.'

'Hope not. We need their manpower.'

'What'd you tell Kennedy?'

Ray says, 'We're being lizard police up around Taylor's. If Kennedy keeps thinking it's so stupid it's funny, he'll leave us alone.'

'He might've thought it was ridiculous at first but I reckon he was shocked at how much money it's worth. If he wasn't in it, and Taylor's doing it on the sly, could get nasty.'

'Hard to care about Taylor. Tomorrow I'll go in the copshop like normal, you go in the arvo. Then both of us back here overnight.'

Arshag laughs. 'How long can we pull that off?'

'Two more nights? Hoping the duffers don't take too long. Seems they might've been round here a while already. Luck of the draw.'

'Jimmy saw Kennedy's Sandman?'

'Leaving the duffer camp. If it's a duffer camp. I like conning Kennedy on this when it could be the job we get him on. Live in hope.'

Arshag nods at their rifles. 'How deadly, do you reckon?'

Ray's mouth forms a downturned-U. 'We'll meet the desperates, only in it for a quid. But if you're desperate, you can't afford to get caught either. If Kennedy turns up too, who knows? All bets off.'

Jimmy returns earlier than expected. Something in Harry's water drilling rig snapped. No work till it's fixed. He walks off with his rifle, looking for a swamp where he saw wild ducks. Brings back two and prepares them for dinner, duck stew on his mind.

Ray asks him how he learned to do it.

Jimmy says, 'Poverty.'

Dusk again softens the light, signals rising chill. Donnie returns and they eat together, share beer and rum. Donnie tells them he can't afford to lose his cattle to anyone. The sale of his stud bulls out there will tide him over for a year, and yeah, get his older kid through school.

Ray looks into the fire. Didn't think to ask him about family, never does.

Jimmy puts out the fire, they retreat to themselves, and their shifts. Donnie from nine to midnight, Arshag, midnight to three, Ray the graveyard, three to six.

Arshag wakes Ray just after three to a world filled with wondrous moonlight starkly tinging everything with silver. Ray carries his rifle slung over his shoulder as he walks around the inert cattle. About to do a loop to the fence and back, he hears an engine. He trots back to camp, finds the others checking weapons. Ray and Arshag take positions above the creek bed in the line of trees. Donnie and Jimmy head off to circle towards the gap in the fence, along with a reminder from Ray that this is a police operation. 'Sure!' they chorus. The moon near the horizon, soon be gone.

A ute, no lights, materialises at the break in the fence. Ray checks his watch to time how long it sits there, an ominous dark hulk, engine idling quietly. Can't see how many are in it. After an endless ten minutes, it slinks forward slowly into the field, south of the cattle, which ignore it. Another, more powerful engine is audible. A truck, at the same break in the fence. After two minutes it grinds into the field and turns to face the way it came. Two men with torches exit the ute with a dog, fan out in opposite directions around the cattle to drive them to the truck. Two men from the truck trot to its back, swing its rear open and start to assemble a ramp.

Ray and Arshag walk into the open, rifles at the ready. All four duffers are preoccupied with their work until one at the ramp freezes, a cry caught in his throat, a gun appearing in his hand.

Ray calls, 'Stop! Police! Drop the gun! Stay where you are!'

All four duffers act as one, two now with handguns, running for their vehicles. The pair running for the truck cabin meet Donnie, cold with anger, and stop at his deadly, silent smile. Aching to hurt them.

The pair at the ute meet a hyper Jimmy, voice cracking, jerking his rifle between the two of them. 'Fucking bastards! Go on, fucking try it! Come on, do it do it do it!'

One has a gun but holds it out from his body and drops it.

Jimmy yells, 'Here! Fucking here! Here!' They come closer, one trembling, then freeze, no closer.

Ray emerges from shock at all the guns, and nods in relief to Arshag. 'Too easy.'

Too soon.

Donnie walks to the one nearest him and swings his rifle butt at his head, smashing him to the ground. The man's dog runs and jumps at Donnie's head. Donnie falls backwards but gets off a shot. The dog whips away, thrashing, yelping at the wound, dying. Donnie scrambles back, staring at it, disbelieving.

The other duffer drags a gun from his pants and dashes for the gap in the fence, firing blindly back over his head, running close by Jimmy, who turns from the pair he's watching and aims at him.

Arshag yells, 'Stop!'

Ray yells, 'Jimmy, no!'

Jimmy fires. The man falls hard on his face, rolling and moaning, holding his lower leg. Jimmy howls with adrenaline and runs to him, reloading as he goes, leaving the two he was covering.

Arshag runs to them, holds them at gunpoint. 'Don't move.' He checks, no more guns. Looks at the nearest, recognises the younger Randall, and sighs.

Randall pulls a face. 'My brother's fucking dead thanks to you mob. Bloke's got to make a buck.'

Arshag handcuffs him, hands in front. The other aims a disgusted kick at Randall, forcing Arshag to yank him out of range. He looks closer at the kicker. In disbelief at who it is, but in total belief that he'd turn on his own partner. Cuffs him too but with his hands behind his back.

Ray runs to Jimmy and the shot man. 'Get his gun and cover him. Cover him!'

Jimmy stands over the man, points his rifle and yells unintelligibly as the man writhes, clutching his bleeding lower leg.

Ray grabs Jimmy's arm. 'Jimmy! Quit it! It's done. We've got them.' He slaps the barrel of Jimmy's rifle down to point at the ground then recognises the wounded man. 'Bob bloody Dickson? Big fucking surprise.' So where's bloody Wayne?

Dickson holds his wound. 'You fucking shot me! Which of you bastards fucking shot me? I'm bleeding to death.'

Jimmy hovers, panting, making himself breathe, weight shifting, one leg to the other.

Ray says to Dickson, 'Shut the fuck up!' And to Jimmy, 'You! Take it easy.'

Dickson twists and turns fiercely. 'You wait, you wait. Kennedy'll do you, you mug copper, he'll fucking do you.' He twists again, adding a larger rolling action to reach behind his back. Ray realises Jimmy, too jumpy, not thinking, didn't get Dickson's gun. The gun appears. Ray strains to pull his rifle around to hit Dickson's gun hand, sees Jimmy at the edge of his vision wrenching his rifle up one-handed at arm's length, aiming.

Ray yells, 'Jimmy!'

Dickson fires, hits no one, as Jimmy fires.

Ray again shoves the barrel down. 'Enough!'

Sees a bullet hole in Dickson's forehead.

He snatches Jimmy's rifle, a twenty-two, and tosses him his three-oh-three. 'This's yours. You used this one. This one!'

Jimmy, slack-mouthed, takes it.

Ray checks Dickson. Dead.

He grabs Jimmy's shirt, their faces close, points at Dickson. 'Listen! He disobeyed my direct order while armed. *He* fired first. I did what I had to do.' He pounds his fist on his own chest, sharply slaps him, glares at him, making sure the message is received. 'Get it?'

Jimmy stares at the body, nods over and over as his whole body ripples in extreme dry-retching. His first kill. Ray saw this reaction before in army training when a hapless soldier accidentally discharged his rifle into a mate at close range, exploding the man's chest.

Arshag calls Ray to the second duffer. Ray is incredulous. 'Fuck me. G'day Peter.' Peter, fugitive ex-mate of Paul and Mario, moans in quivering rage, kicking the ground.

Ray can't bear it, slaps him. 'Shut it. Fucking shut it.'

Peter wild-eyed, stops.

Ray bends in close. 'You came back? For this? Jesus Christ.' He holds up both hands, one with a torch, rifle in the other. It's beyond making sense.

Ray produces handcuffs, and checks the man Donnie hit, blood leaking through his basin-cut hair. The youth stares at him, eyes flickering in torch light. Ray steps back. 'Wayne? Wayne!'

Ray, on autopilot, turns to the formless lump of Bob Dickson's body, sprawled in the dark thirty yards away. Family fucking outing. He hauls Wayne to a sitting position to talk to him but Wayne emerges in a rush from whatever morass his head wound has taken him and gapes all around, moans to see his dog dead, twists and struggles to stand.

Ray pushes him back. 'Stay bloody still, we'll get you to hospital.'

Donnie drags the dog out of the torchlight.

Wayne says, 'Dad? Dad!' He backhands Ray and tries to crawl but flops down. Rolls over to stand but dizziness beats him and he lies still, breathing unevenly.

Ray doubts those glazed eyes even see what they're looking at.

Arshag says, 'Concussion.'

Donnie returns, stays back, head down. Sorry, or trying to be.

With the moon gone, stars cluster thick and glowing over the clearing. Ray follows the relaxed passage of a satellite. The silence is like a gap in time. Time for events to sink in. A death, Wayne's wound, so many fucking guns. Jimmy and Donnie involved in the worst way. Jimmy is covered if he can watch his mouth, but not Donnie. Maybe Wayne'll remember nothing and everyone can plead innocence. Except Ray himself for a fucked operation. Jesus, the fucking guns.

Arshag drives the Land Rover over, its headlights on the three duffers clumped on the ground, but not Bob Dickson's body. Makes calls on the radio. In a sudden release, Jimmy whoops and waves his new rifle in grim triumph. He prances around the captives in some parody of a movie war dance. Donnie joins in, then both turn to the cattle huddled in a dark silent mass at the far end of the clearing. Donnie puts on an apelike lope towards them, Jimmy does the same and the cattle toss their heads and lumber further into the darkness.

Ray grabs Peter's shirt. 'Who organised this? And don't waste my fucking time.'

Peter nods towards Bob Dickson's body. 'Him.'

Ray shakes Randall, who holds his knees to his chest against the cold. 'Who got you into this?'

Randall looks sideways at Wayne and with horror at the dead body. 'Them. Don't know anyone else.'

Ray sinks onto his haunches, leaning on the twenty-two. Bob Dickson dealt with whoever set it up but is dead. Ray looks at Wayne drifting in and out of mumbling, unsettled sleep. Did Wayne's father do it all? Probably. No one's left to tie Kennedy to the mess.

Randall hums, rocks, breaks into snatches of song. Wayne mumbles and snores. Peter stares mesmerised by the headlights. Adrenaline exhausted, Jimmy and Donnie return and slump to the grass. In a minute, they'll be fighting to stay awake. Ray grabs Donnie, forcefully tells him, whoever asks, he hit Wayne in self-defence. Reminds Jimmy about the swapped rifles.

Arshag and Ray patrol. The stars move.

21

Thirty minutes later, Kennedy arrives in a paddy wagon driven by Constable Baxter, followed by an ambulance. Ray watches Kennedy aggressively point a finger at Baxter, ordering him to stay in the vehicle.

Bypassing Ray, Kennedy orders Arshag to recount events. Dissatisfied with what he hears, or, Ray thinks, pretending to be, he questions Jimmy and Donnie.

Jimmy holds to his story and to Ray's eye, revels in it. Jimmy's hyperactive morale will plummet as he grapples with killing a man but, with luck, not in front of Kennedy.

Donnie says, 'Self-fucking-defence!' in answer to every question Kennedy puts to him, fiercely unrepentant, quick with accusations of being forced to fight duffers because Kennedy never does.

Kennedy's mood does not improve. When he turns to the duffers, it plummets. He freezes at seeing Peter, while Peter's outrage explodes at the sight of Kennedy.

He vibrates with anger, tears of frustration flooding his eyes. 'You promised me I'd be fine! You said!' Peter says.

Ray watches, fascinated by the intensity.

Kennedy turns away, trying for dismissive but shaken.

Peter is beyond indignation. 'Keep him away from me!'

Kennedy stands over Bob Dickson's body as it is readied for going to Royalton. After a concerned hesitation, the body is covered and loaded into the ambulance beside his groggy son. Ray and Arshag exchange a look.

Kennedy draws Ray aside. 'This's a fuck-up.'

Ray looks squarely at him. 'All round.' They hold each other's stare, Ray thinking neither of them knows anymore what the other knows. Stalemate? Kennedy holds up an open hand as if to make a point he hasn't found words for yet. Ray waits. In the headlight's glare, Ray sees what might be Kennedy's lip quivering.

In a voice low with menace, Kennedy says, 'Maybe you're too raw to understand, a bloke can get to a place'—pauses for breath—'and it hits him. If he loses what he's got, at this place, he'll never get back anything as good, again. Makes a bloke desperate to hang onto what he's got. Whatever the fuck it is.' A cold kind of laugh. 'Some'll even kill to keep it. So. If you're the one trying to take it away, it helps to know the scale of what you're doing.' He takes a breath. So many words.

Ray swallows, chilled. 'You warning me about something?'

Kennedy surveys the scene in the headlights. Says to Ray without looking at him, 'Pick a fight with a cunt who's got fuck-all to lose, deserve all you get.'

Kennedy steps back, orders Arshag and Ray to drive Jimmy and Donnie to the copshop to give a statement. He pauses, hating to say it, 'Then send the pricks home.'

Ray sees mutual silence will work with Kennedy, for now.

Randall climbs into the paddy wagon but Peter refuses to travel with Kennedy. He wrestles Ray and Arshag, yelling,

'Not with him! Keep him away. Not with him.' Kennedy stays back, rising on the balls of his feet, falling, rising again. Finally, Peter is put in the rear cage of their Land Rover. Kennedy's face is a mess of tics, anger. He turns on his heel, goes to the paddy wagon and leaves.

Ray turns to Arshag. 'They want each other dead. Peter's reaction surprised me but it shocked Kennedy.'

Arshag is as uncertain. 'A deal gone sour?'

Ray says, 'Putrid.'

Donnie returns from the dark, wiping away dirt, and tips his head back for a deep breath as if the air up there is better. 'Buried the dog. Can't just leave it out here.'

Ray nods, understands.

Donnie and Jimmy climb into the Land Rover back seat, aware of Peter huddled in the cage, occasionally moaning. Arshag drives them out of the clearing, stops for Donnie and Jimmy to improvise a barrier at the break in the fence. They halt at the duffer camp. What's left is the Chrysler, a smouldering fireplace, food refuse, cans and bottles. Donnie and Jimmy wait as Ray and Arshag prowl around the site. Peter makes no move, or sound.

Ray looks inside the Chrysler. 'Must be Randall's. The Dicksons own the truck, Peter the ute.' Jangly plastic animals and oddments hang from the rear-view mirror and any other protruding hook or button. 'He must be even younger than he looks.'

Arshag steps around a flattened clay surface where the tent was pitched.

Ray wrinkles his nose at the smell from the fireplace. 'What the hell were they burning?'

Arshag pokes at ashes with his boot. 'Nothing we can use.'

Ray clenches his fists. 'This's my god-awful fuck-up tonight. I should've known. All that rage boiling in Donnie and Jimmy. So desperate to fight back, take some revenge.' He drops his head. The urge to hit back. To retaliate hard. Urges he has no trouble recognising.

Arshag shrugs it off. 'I told Kennedy what happened near me. I didn't see what you and Jimmy were doing.'

Ray nods, not asking him to do more.

Arshag says, 'Will Jimmy hold out?'

Ray looks at him. 'I reckon his joy at having one over on Kennedy will make him strong.' Squeezes Arshag's shoulder. 'You did warn me about him and Donnie.'

'How could you stop them? Tell them to stay home, leave it to us? Bush justice, helps sometimes. Sometimes . . .' He wiggles a flat hand, expressing uncertainty.

'I know the risks you're taking. You're the one who lives here. I'm a tourist.'

Arshag manages a wry chuckle. 'Kennedy doesn't count me, hardly even sees me. But with what's between you and him, you can't keep sharing the same copshop. Or air.'

They exchange a look at the implication of that, which neither pursues.

Ray shrugs. 'He'll question me tonight but I should be interrogating him.' Indicates the Land Rover. 'Least I've got Peter, whatever good that counts for.' Wondering now about some double bluff from Kennedy.

'Whatever Peter's about,' Arshag says, 'Kennedy doesn't know what you've got, and what matters is he thinks you've got something. He must know by now what you took from his place.'

Unspoken is that they can't even prove whose knickers

they've got. The demands of the courtroom always receding from them.

Arshag punches the air, says, 'Did Peter have anything to do with Alice?'

Ray's eyes widen, hadn't thought of that. 'Mario said not. But . . .'

Arshag says, 'Maybe Mario knows less than he thinks.' He rocks back and forth on his heels. 'Kennedy tonight, stalking round, listening to no one. He didn't have to, he knew what was supposed to happen back there. And I reckon he thinks we *must* know. No wonder he wants to get rid of you.'

'He's got rid of me. I'm transferred.'

'I mean for good, for *his* good. To be safe he has to figure we're close to knowing as much as we need. Ignoring that is not a risk he'll take. We've got to stay awake to that. No dumb hero stuff.'

Ray laughs, sort of. 'We could push him to make a mistake. Bluff him into it.'

Arshag adopts a portentous tone. 'Time to kill the eagle with an arrow made of its own feathers.'

'You what?'

Arshag grins. 'Ancient Armenian saying. Us foreigners always have a deep proverb to light the way.'

'Give him enough rope to hang himself?'

'Close.'

Jimmy calls out, 'You two coming or what?'

At the highway, Arshag turns west. Dawn rushes up behind them, a radiant, yellow-red ribbon of light. Ray looks in the external mirror, looking for the morning star, astonished so much time has elapsed. Arshag watches for creatures keen to be roadkill, as if you can react fast enough to avoid them.

—

At the copshop, Ray enters the dim, poky, stale-smelling room that serves for interrogations and drops into one of two chairs at a bare metal table, cold to the touch. He looks at dusty walls, an indistinct pale brown. The sun struggles to force its way through a small, high set of venetians coated in dust and cobwebs. His entry enlivens dust motes to dance in any rare beam of sunlight.

Kennedy enters, slapping a manila folder against his leg. Grunts, 'Other chair.'

Ray moves. Kennedy takes the vacated chair, Ray facing the hazy window. Kennedy drops the folder on the table, then—everything a performance—a biro. 'As a courtesy to a fellow officer'—he pauses, like the words might make him throw up—'I'm not taking notes of this interview.' He takes out the copshop firearms book from the folder.

Ray works to control his face. No notes is no fucking courtesy. A dumb staring contest ensues till Kennedy leans back and rubs his eyes. Ray thinks about duels. Chuck two swords into the room. That'll fix this.

Kennedy says, 'You're a killer now? Congratulations.'

Killer. It's official. Ray stays immobile. He's genuinely lost as to how a killer's supposed to be since he didn't kill anyone.

Kennedy says, 'The poor bastard you shot was father of three teenagers. One with and two without.'

Ray looks blank.

Kennedy sighs. 'One male, two female. Wayne's all of nineteen. He'll go to jail, lucky him. All thanks to you.'

In the gym, Wayne would thrash a punching bag as if sheer violence substituted for skill, tears mixed with sweat, thinking no one noticed. A couple of times, his bruised face and arms had synced with his mum calling a neighbour for protection from his father. No charges laid.

Wayne in the exhibition bout was a windmill in a cyclone. Wayne in the boxing tent was bashed to the ground in thirty seconds. And there was Wayne at the pub, taking on all comers. Short-lived career all round. Your old man's dead, Wayne, be grateful for small mercies. Ray realises the room is silent.

'Didn't you hear me?' Kennedy says. 'Asked you a question.'

Ray is silent, his best weapon.

Kennedy leans in, speaks slowly as to a child. 'You shot Bob Dickson? You stand by that?'

'Course.' Has to clear his throat.

'You signed out the three-oh-three.' Kennedy opens the copshop firearms book to the page. Ray's signature is next to the three-oh-three box. 'Dickson's wounds're smaller than from a three-oh-three. Try a twenty-two. Like your cousin's.'

'As in my statement'—Ray nods to the folder—'Dickson disobeyed my order and ran. Rogers took a shot with his twenty-two, hit his leg, brought him down, tried to hold him, dropped his rifle. Dickson was overpowering him. I dropped my rifle, the three-oh-three, to assist. Dickson produced a handgun, fired at Jimmy, missed. I grabbed the nearest weapon, Jimmy's twenty-two. And shot Dickson at close range.'

'Amazing how closely your stories agree. Sadly, Donnie Wexler and Constable Shaggers missed everything.'

'They were subduing and guarding three other duffers.'

'Including Wayne, who was violently attacked by someone.'

Ray says nothing. Kennedy's next move will reveal if the lies have worked.

Kennedy leans as close to Ray as he can get. Taps the folder. 'Poor fucking Wayne. Must've fell and hit his stupid head.

Bad night out for the Dicksons. But you got it all sewn up. All in the family.'

Deep inside, Ray feels release he must not show. Kennedy's got nothing. Ray can't resist. Hears his own voice in a hoarse whisper. 'Feels like shit, eh? Know what's going on but can't prove jack-shit.'

Kennedy's breathing grows louder. He leans back, actually smiles. Ray goes rigid to keep from hitting him.

Kennedy says, 'Any cop worth his fucking salt knows more about what goes on than he can ever drag into the light and prove. Isn't that right? Secrets to the grave. Nice to know we speak the same language.' He consults his scribbled notes. 'Assuming shit happened like you say, you had no opportunity to interrogate Bob Dickson?'

Ray pretends to think about it. 'No opportunity.' His eyes and his smallest smile say the opposite. Letting Kennedy know it's a lie he has to accept. Knowing without knowing, it's every-fucking-where. Ray stares, working the bluff. The lie, the sins of omission.

Kennedy reads his notes again, taking his time, fingers in an erratic tattoo on the table. Then he looks up at Ray, mouth contemptuous, but he has to say it aloud, to show he knows. 'Know what I reckon? Your fuck-up cousin, Jimmy boy, shot the father in full view of his son. Wayne got to see his old man die. And, fucking impressive, big hero taking the blame, you set it up so your cousin gets away with it. How do you reckon Wayne feels about that, ace detective? You ask him? I did.'

'Wayne didn't witness his father's death. And for sure it would've been different if his father hadn't run. Hadn't deserted his son. Hadn't forced him into this dumb fuck-up to begin with. Or if the gutless bastard who set the whole disaster up hadn't done it. Maybe, maybe.' Ray stands, says, 'We finished?' He can't stay *and* control himself.

Kennedy is straining too, gripping his edge of the table. Ray can see him weighing it up. Recognises it: *Is doing the harm my hate wants worth it?*

Kennedy says, 'For now.'

Ray says, 'I'm interviewing Peter.'

'No, you're fucking not. I'm running this show.'

'Peter'll be charged with raping Diah. Different case, my case. You gave it to me, that's the end of it.' Ray flexes his legs to shove his chair back against the wall with a crash that startles them both. He bends slightly over the table at Kennedy, points at him. 'Any harm comes to him, it won't be hard to find who to blame.' And walks out.

In their empty office, Ray and Arshag quietly confer about protecting Peter. Ray is too tired to interrogate anyone now, ready to sleep around the clock, but Arshag can't stand guard that long. It has to be done now.

They return to the same interrogation room, nodding thanks to an uncomprehending and uninterested Baxter exiting from delivering Peter. Ray sits facing Peter, who is pale behind sparse ginger stubble, his lip in a contemptuous curl. Natural arrogance holding up well.

Ray says, 'You're charged with Diah's rape. Will you be contesting the charge?'

'I want to talk about the other one.'

'Alice?'

'You haven't got anyone for her.'

Ray's tiredness makes him giggle. 'Not like we're looking for a dance partner.' Arshag's quick glance warns him to stop. It's an effort, but he does. 'Okay. Alice. Was it you?'

'No. No way. But I know who. And who did what.' Ray waits. 'If I tell you all that, can I get off the Diah thing?'

'You just admitted to a police officer you raped Diah. What'd you do with her knickers?'

Peter blinks, tries to swallow, has to run his tongue around to wet his mouth. A chink in that arrogance. He nods sharply, decision made. 'I want to trade Diah for info about Alice.'

'Like in American movies?'

'Yeah.'

'Law's different here. Besides, Mario's told us about Diah.'

Peter's confidence dips, the curled lip quivers, then his confidence surges again. 'I know about Alice. You don't. And you won't ever.'

Ray rubs his eyes, leans forward, co-conspirator with a comforting tone. 'Tell you what, you tell me what you know and I'll see. Best I can do.' He whispers, 'This isn't a movie, okay?'

Ray watches him struggle with it. Still expecting the world to bend to him, despite his life being total fucking proof it won't. Here he is, impervious.

'Alright. But you've got to protect me. Not leave me here with them.'

'Who?'

'Kennedy and Laming.'

'I can drive you to Tyborg. Personally.' Not far enough but where would be?

'She went with Kennedy to find some bangle or something. He grabbed her, Laming joined in. They came and got me.'

Ray leans back, startled, tiredness banished. 'Why you?'

'They knew I did Diah. With Paul and Mario.'

'They knew?'

289

'Laming worked it out.'

'How?'

'He was at the servo one day and Paul and Mario and me were out the side where we used to sit. Teasing the chicks going past.' Ray's head whirls. Laming put it together, saw these pricks harassing Diah. Already had them in mind when Diah was found. Ace detective. He didn't need to talk to Barb or anyone.

Peter says, 'Him and Kennedy cornered me. Tricked me.' Resentful, aggrieved tone, that he allowed himself to be tricked.

'Why you and not Paul or Mario?'

'Laming called them chaff, said they'd blow away in the first gust of wind.'

Clever Laming.

'But they didn't arrest you.'

'They said a chick killing herself just for having sex was dumb, not my fault.' Ray bites his tongue. Peter taps the heels of his boots at the concrete floor. 'They said, let's do it again. Don't say shit to the others. I'd be in their team to get the next one. They had her locked up in one of Kennedy's pig hunt sheds. We all went there.'

'What do you mean *they*?' Ray has to jam his hands down on the table so they don't form fists.

There's a transformation in Peter, his breathing turning jagged. 'I didn't do it.' Part of Peter is getting the words out while part is trying to stop them. His eyes are looking inwards, seeing it all again.

'Explain.' Ray is almost whispering.

'I . . . I . . . I . . .' He makes a cackling noise that Ray realises is a word he can't say, then yells, 'I couldn't! I couldn't!' He slams his fists on the table. 'That first one's fault. Her dying.'

'You mean, physically, you couldn't do it?'

'No! Fucking satisfied?' Peter's face is distraught. His limp dick in hand in front of Kennedy and Laming. Ray stops himself asking what they did to him for that. This failure cuts Peter deeper than anything he did to Diah or Alice.

Peter breathes between clenched teeth, hissing, nodding furiously. 'Kennedy and Laming did it.'

'Then what?'

'Kennedy and me went for more grog. Laming said he'd look after her. I asked Kennedy what we'd do with her, to keep her quiet. He said we didn't have to do nothing, she'd be too embarrassed to talk. Might even invite us back. He said I ought to have another go fucking her. But we come back, she's not there. There was some blood, over where we had her. I got sick.'

'How much blood?'

'Shit don't ask me? Blood! Just blood. Fair bit. Not a heap. I don't know, do I?'

'You didn't see her murder? Or her body? And Kennedy was with you when she disappeared?'

'Yeah. She was just gone. None of us said nothing, it was like she'd never been there.'

'How was Laming when you got back?'

'Laming was Laming. Cranky mongrel, bit jumpy.'

Ray grabs Peter's hands and crashes them palms down on the table. 'You get a look at his hands? His knuckles?'

Peter yanks his hands away. 'Course not! What'm I going to do that for? Hold his hands, like I'm a fucking poofter?'

'And you're sure nothing was said about Alice? Where she was or what happened?'

'No! Nothing. Fuck all. Nothing.'

'What about between Laming and Kennedy by themselves?'

'Jesus, I got to keep fucking saying it? No. Nothing.'

'What happened next?'

'We sat around, it was just a booze up. They really got into drinking, made me drink too.'

'Made you?'

'Kennedy held me down and Laming poured whisky into me and down me, spilling it too. I flaked. Woke up there, them still drinking but going on about framing me. For everything. Saying they'd arrest me for the first one too so it'd be easy. Laming held up her knickers, said he'd plant them on me. I threw up, and they knew I probably heard them and they didn't give a shit and it made them laugh and laugh, me with vomit all over me. Then Kennedy took me back to my place.'

'But they didn't frame you. Why?'

'Fuck knows. Nothing happened, for ages. I figured I was okay, we were all okay, so I hung around as usual. Blokes who did it trying to find the blokes who did it seemed pretty safe to me. Till you fucked it all up.'

'Then you took off. Where to?'

'I was going home. Till I figured cops'd be watching the place.' Taps his forehead as if it proves his total brilliance. 'Then I run into Randall at the pub on the way. Only watering hole for miles. I'm broke and he tells me about the duffing. Why he was coming back.'

'So you came back too?'

'Easy bucks, old Dickson said. Stupid piece of shit.' Snorts at the injustice of that.

'Alice's knickers weren't with her body.'

'Laming took them. At the start. When he was ripping off her clothes.'

'You saw him do that or you think he did that?'

'Saw him.'

Ray thinks about what he's got. Has to ask. 'Diah's knickers. Tell me.'

'Burnt them. Not the same after she, you know . . .'

Ray puts fingertips to his temples. Enough.

———

Ray and Arshag sit in the Land Rover at Pioneer Creek, the creek's flow sluggish. Early afternoon in the meagre shade, windows down. Crickets making their white-noise buzzing. Mickey birds at war with everything. On the far bank, Ray watches a small landslip as more soil comes free around some tree roots, trickles away.

Ray says, 'Arresting two senior detectives? How're we going to do that?'

'Simple. Grab them. Cuff them. Put them in a cell.'

'Not in this police force. Kennedy's and Laming's word against Peter's. Nah.'

'And your train leaves tomorrow?'

'Don't think I'll be on it.' Ray notes that Arshag takes that in his stride.

'Obviously they know Peter's talked.'

Ray shakes his head. 'Won't worry them. His word's not enough. Him especially.'

'And the knickers? Which point to Kennedy?'

Ray closes his eyes, the light hurting them. 'In Peter's version, Laming must've put them there, covering his own arse. Like the true bastard he is.'

Arshag waves a warning finger. 'Or Peter's lying and *he* planted them there? Or they were at Kennedy's cos he did it.'

Ray manages a grim smile. 'Let's release Peter, tell each of them the other two're framing them. Send them all after each other. Do our job for us.'

The stab at humour lapses, replaced by a brooding silence.

Ray says, 'Peter's version doesn't settle who killed Alice. Still could be Laming took her away but he and Kennedy both killed her later. Or Kennedy did it himself.'

Arshag holds up empty hands. 'And Peter could be lying anyway.'

Ray rubs his eyes, shocked by his own tiredness. 'All we've ever known is she lay out there too long, exposed to the elements. Beaten then strangled. By person or persons unknown. Those sad blue briefs, size S, aren't enough, on their own. Dumb to think they ever could be.'

Arshag says, 'Peter's version rings true for me, as far as it goes.'

Ray nods. 'As far as.'

They fall into uneasy silence. Finally Arshag says, 'Is Peter safe?'

'So long as he's useful to them. They can still frame him. What are we missing?'

———

Ray enters the public bar and greets Barb, who points him to Jimmy's table. A jug of beer is there, a full glass in front of Jimmy, an empty for Ray. A third half-drunk. 'Where's Burt?'

'Told him you wanted to farewell him. Chickenshit ran away.'

'For real?'

'Got teary, lied about having a bus to catch, or a train or a hot-air balloon. Wished you well in defeating the forces of evil, and left.'

Ray sits, pours a beer, tastes it. Sighs, feels it flood through him like a heavy, clinging surge. 'I was looking forward to seeing him. You got an address?'

'Burt, Australian Army.'

Ray rolls his eyes. That'll work.

'You reckon he'll like army life?'

Ray warns, 'Not enough to follow him.'

'Okay, Dad.'

Ray grins. 'So you living here now?' Gestures to indicate the pub.

'Yep.'

Ray holds up his beer. 'Dangerous.'

'Yes, Dad.'

———

At the end of too long a day, Ray closes the door of his flat, turns his motorbike to ride out. Dot's door upstairs opens.

She leans over the railing. 'Hang on, you! You off to your farewell do?' She comes downstairs, barefoot, in her nurse's uniform.

Ray holds out both arms. 'Wow. You look neat.'

'Neat? That your best line?'

'Love a uniform.' They embrace warmly and hold it a moment longer than necessary.

She leans back, arms still around him and winks. 'My fella and I like to dress up sometimes.'

'What as?'

'Napoleon and Josephine? He read that Nappy wrote her a note on his way home from not conquering Russia or somewhere. Not just the costume, it's how to, you know, stage the encounter.'

'What'd his note say?'

'*Home in three days. Don't wash.*'

Ray feels his face go pink.

She laughs, letting him go, digging him in the ribs. 'Oh, you. Like your women clean, do you deary? I came down to tell you I have to work tonight. Tourist accident and I'm on so I'll miss your do. Just wanted to say, you know, I've enjoyed having you.'

'Me too. And, look . . .', he falters, his empty hand up facing her, 'this's not for Royalton Radio, but I mightn't go. There's stuff I'm still sorting out. Might need to stay a bit longer.'

She hugs him again, harder. 'Long as you like, love. You'll need a new girlfriend I hear.'

'One crisis at a time.'

'You still here tomorrow night, I'll shout you a drink. That do?'

'Deal. Say goodbye to Napoleon for me.'

'When he wakes up. Tough campaign. Endless demands made upon his person.' She grins and heads back upstairs, which lets Ray wipe away sudden, surprising tears of affection.

22

In the loosening cool of dusk, Ray parks behind the pub, looks to the back verandah. The farewell is in full swing already. Who are all these people? He feels a fraud, freezes. Can't face anyone. The bike's here, he could ride to Brisbane right now, tonight. It's his perpetual fantasy—get on the bike and ride. He makes himself breathe, takes measured steps.

Astonished, and showing it, he acknowledges clumsy cheers and joins the party. Sausage rolls and eskies. Parents of gym kids. Two teachers from Stella's school. No Stella, which saddens but hardly surprises him. There are people he helped with gun licences, victims of traffic accidents. He gets a fierce clinch of gratitude from a woman who now works in Nick's café, supporting her two young sons. Ray intervened, forcefully, against her man in their violent mess. The man left town to evade a restraining order that was never going to work anyway.

Ray in jeans, boots and T-shirt looks around at men in flares, women in jumpsuits or miniskirts. Awkwardness vanishes as drinks bite. He's surprised Lord Billy is not here. Someone asks after the Inspector but he left Royalton yesterday, which wins a cheer. Kaye stands by herself, rocking gently on her heels.

She raises a shy, or embarrassed, glass to him. Ray crosses to her, takes the liberty of kissing her gently on a cheek. She looks around then gently kisses him back. Ray thanks her for her help around the station. She says, 'I won't tell anyone about your family.'

Jimmy bursts in, greeting Ray with a fierce handshake that teeters on becoming a hug, getting clumsy, but Ray likes it. Kaye melts away. Ray considers giving Jimmy the bike keys on the spot, but the silly bugger's pissed and if Ray stays, he'll need it himself. He repeats the invite to come stay some time, hears himself doing it, amazed.

He's impressed as Harry and Li, and Intan and Fang Su arrive, welcomed by several guests. Ray hasn't told them, or anyone, about Peter. Intan bows, shakes Ray's hand, and presents him with a be-ribboned bottle of homemade liqueur. Harry silently gives Ray a parcel, shoebox size, wrapped in shiny, deep-red paper. Fang Su and Li each hold out a hand and Ray shakes them in turn. Nick is ill but sends his thanks. Job done, they leave as quietly as they came.

Ray scores boxing gloves, spirited pats on the back, and laboured jokes about how only weak-dicks piss off, which becomes *You'll be back!* which some mean sincerely. He puts his gifts on a small table that already has a small pile of good-wishes cards. The unexpected goodwill touches him.

Kennedy appears and offers his hand, ambushing Ray into taking it. He jerks Ray close, reeking of beer and roll-your-owns. 'Eat canvas, boxer boy!' He shoves Ray back and laughs as Ray almost falls, blindsided by the false affability. Does he know what Peter told him? Does he know Ray broke in? Or what he found? Does he even care? Ray watches for any sign, but it's impossible to tell.

Ray has to say, 'What are you doing here?'

'Cunt, for the sheer joy of knowing you're going. We never did go pig hunting. Shame you're pissing off, you could've come. If you were up to it.' He mimes a slashing action at Ray's throat, laughs, looks around for applause. Other guests force smiles, shake heads, raise eyebrows.

There's a vacuum until Laming steps up to Ray, hand extended. Ray holds up both hands instead and they shape up, mocking each other, making out they're joking. Jokes'll kill you one day.

Laming's lip curls as he leans in, voice low. 'I know what you took, softcock. What're you waiting for?'

Ray is desperate to say he knows Laming originally took them, but clamps his mouth shut. Laming releases braying laughter and heads off along the verandah. Ray sees Kennedy grab Laming's arm to whisper in his ear but Laming shoulders him away. Others who see it titter or shake their heads, embarrassed, turn away.

Ray holds his face in party mode as he struggles with Laming's jibe. He greets huddled groups, wondering why in a part of the world with space to burn, as it often does, people form such tight knots. Are they under siege?

Arshag arrives but Ray's delight dies at his glowering eyes. Arshag walks to an empty end of the verandah where Ray joins him.

Arshag speaks softly, urgently. 'Cassie's gone. Since last night. Her Uncle Don's just found out.'

'Gone? What's gone mean? Shuddup found out?'

'Didn't get home from the gym yesterday. Her drunken old man didn't notice. Shuddup found her bag and bracelet in the ditch beside Ruby Road where she runs home from the gym.'

Ray's mind races. He knows the road, only bush there, no houses. Laughter rolls down the verandah. He forces words out through numb lips, voice thin like from pre-fight nerves. 'Kennedy and Laming are here.'

Arshag's mouth and jaw lock, he flicks car keys against his trouser leg. 'If they've got her, they won't stay. And if they've got her, it's in a hideout.' He falters. 'Kennedy's got a pig-hunting shack off Bauldry's Road.'

'How do you know that?'

'Ages ago, one of his mates shot himself in the foot on one of the pig hunts and had to fill out the how, where and when in hospital. I went out, found the hut.'

'Was it where they had Alice?'

Arshag shrugs, shakes his head. Ray stares into the night, feels a breeze stroke his face. 'Kennedy was gloating about pig hunting before.'

Arshag's head juts out from his neck. 'They don't care, don't need to. I'm going to check it out now.'

A grating laugh disrupts the conversational hum. Laming.

'Why not flatten them here? Knock them down, make them talk?' Ray says.

He and Arshag lock eyes, wanting it, frustrated.

Ray says, 'We've got no way to make them tell us anything. We can follow them when they leave.'

'You're thinking like a townie. Out here there's no traffic, no other cars. We'll get sprung if we follow them. I can go there ahead of them. Right now.'

Ray grips his arm. 'If you find her, you can get her away. But what if she's not there? One of us has to stick with them. When they leave, I'll follow best I can. If she's not there, get back here.'

Arshag rubs his eyes. 'Can't we call anyone in to help?'

'Against these two? Who'd come? How cast-iron do you reckon we'd have to be? It'll be safer if you can just get Cassie away.'

Arshag says, 'You're in the patrol car?'

'Bike.'

Arshag holds up the Land Rover keys, and nods to inside the pub. 'Baxter's on duty a while longer. I'll radio him and he can call here, tell you what happens.'

Ray nods. 'Try, but I might be following them, god knows where. Fuck!' There's no time for a better plan.

A partygoer leaves, saying, 'See you, Ray. Look after yourself in the Big Smoke.'

'Thanks, Nev. Nice knowing you, mate.' Turns back to Arshag, who is anxiously stepping from one foot to the other, desperate to go, unsure what he needs to know first. 'Laming knows what I took from Kennedy's shed. Laming's more bloody sly than I thought possible. Must be from seeing me there the day I took the knickers. I thought he was pissed. I keep underestimating him. He had a go at me for doing nothing.'

'Laming?' Arshag growls his confusion, his face a tumult of fretting and anger. 'For doing nothing? And Kennedy's said nothing? Is this some trick? Dear god, I've got to go.'

Ray watches him stride downstairs and disappear. Another partygoer approaches, pumps Ray's hand, wishes him well, bobs his head happily, goes on his way. Ray kicks a calculated, gentle rhythm at the railing. Faces the night, desperate thoughts flooding through him. *What if Kennedy doesn't know about Cassie and it's all Laming's work? Fuck this, Cassie's what matters. Laming's thrown me completely.* He looks around urgently, hoping he's not speaking out loud. He grips the railing as if he might tear it off. Here he is, has evidence, an at least partly viable story, and culprits. Anywhere else, anyone else, it'd be enough. But here, now, it isn't. He shakes himself, recalling he has to watch Kennedy and Laming, not let them get away. He does his best to stroll among the guests, hounded by internal voices.

One says, '*You know, if we catch them, everyone'll say they knew all along.*'

He waves to the party, sucks in air as if from a physical hurt, sags, shakes himself, strains upright.

Another voice says, '*Kennedy doesn't care about evidence. Why should we?*'

Ray jams his eyes shut, hears his own voice say, '*If it comes to killing them, so be it.*' Has to pause, opens his eyes, gets another beer as he shudders even to talk about crossing that line. Silently answers himself, '*They might already figure killing us is worth it.*'

He hears what sounds like Kennedy guffawing at some remark. Still here. And that head over there looks like Laming's.

A departing partygoer shakes Ray's hand. 'Pleasure knowing you. When you leaving?'

'Tomorrow, yeah.'

'Don't miss your train!' Tramps down the stairs. Another punches his shoulder, more happy banter, wishes him well. Ray watches him become a dark smudge as he crosses the mostly unlit carpark.

Ray stares at the hand holding his beer. It is shaking. He puts down his beer, rubs his forehead with the fingers of each hand as if separating options, keeping them clear. Laming's

302

jeering again unsettles him. Would Laming betray Kennedy? Are they setting him, Ray, up? Kennedy said he would. It chills him. He joins a circle of guests, trying to look in party mood, still straining to find Kennedy and Laming.

He breaks away and approaches a huddle at the eskies. 'Anyone seen Kennedy?'

A man nods to the carpark. 'Just left with Laming. Pair of them pissed as farts as usual.' Nasty laughter. They have no friends here.

The man points at Ray. 'You been on one of his pig hunts? He doesn't shoot them, goes at them with a commando knife. Rather him than me! He hunts all over the place, got a few huts.'

Ray feels ill. A few huts? Cassie could be in any of them. He returns to the stairs to see Laming and Kennedy become part of the darkness, elbowing each other with rising force like a kid's game turning ugly.

The carpark is bounded by oleander bushes over six feet tall and spreading almost as wide. Ray runs as quietly as he can along a dimly lit dirt lane to where he guesses Kennedy and Laming will be. The lights are too weak to stop him stepping into an empty cardboard beer carton that he has to shake off like he's in a slapstick movie. He falls over a dumped bicycle, boot in the spokes, jarring a shoulder and scratching an ankle. He clamps his mouth shut to stop crying out in anger as much as pain, braced for Kennedy or Laming to burst through the bushes and attack him as they've wanted to since the day they met. Their voices, raised in a blazing argument, roll on unchanged.

He hobbles to a gap between trees, sees the shadowy figures of stocky Kennedy and stick-thin Laming between Kennedy's

Sandman and Laming's Monaro. Kennedy shoves Laming at the Monaro, their voices raw, words unclear. Laming opens his door and turns to speak as he stabs an accusing finger at Kennedy, who kicks the door shut and yells, 'Something's going on. Tell me or I'll thrash you, you bastard.'

Laming responds with an urgent cry, wields enough startling strength to jolt Kennedy hard against the Sandman, lifts a scrawny arm to punch him then stops, convulses, throws up on the ground. Kennedy jumps out of range, swearing, disgusted. Laming sways, spits in contempt and turns back to his car.

Kennedy comes after him growling like a dog. 'Answer me, fuck you. Are you at it again? If you fuck up again he'll fucking kill you this time, I'm telling you.' Who'll kill him? The Inspector's gone.

Laming wipes his mouth on his sleeve, says, 'Jealous, are you? Too gutless to do it yourself?'

'Jesus fuck.' He holds up open hands in defeat, says something Ray misses.

Laming clears his throat, spits again, drops into the Monaro, slams the door and rolls down his window. 'Don't even think about following me. Or go on, try it and prang it and fucking kill yourself. You don't know where I'm going. Last place's no good, tank's dry. This other place's fucking ace. Got grog, tucker. Good for days.'

Kennedy sighs noisily, stands straighter. 'You've been warned.'

Laming taps his forehead. 'Already got some other cunt to cop the blame. Who the fuck'll that be, eh?' He starts the engine. A deep, exhilarating rumble.

Kennedy abruptly looks like he loses all control. He stares all around as if for a weapon. Ray ducks back, afraid he'll be seen. Kennedy bends and grabs a handful of stones, futilely throws them at the Monaro and screams at Laming. 'I know what you did. Everything you did. You think you can drop me in it and walk away?'

Laming guns the engine harder and harder.

Ray dashes back down the lane, into the carpark and onto his piss-weak bike. It'll never keep up but he's got to try. Maybe forty yards away, under weak lights, he sees Kennedy cover his face against flying gravel as Laming wrenches the Monaro back in wild, dirt-splattering reverse and fishtails out to the street.

Ray snarls by on his bike, still righting it, into the street, no helmet, gloves or jacket, grimly relishing Kennedy yelling at him, garbled, angry, maybe even afraid. Ray feels the sting of rushing air, eyes watering, blurring his vision. His headlight is off to try to stay hidden. He guns the engine but speed for a chase was never built into this bike and Laming's tail-lights grow smaller as Laming surges north, away from the rear of the pub. The next intersection is crucial. Ray's throttle is open wide, his hand aching from his grip to stay at maximum power. The tail-lights way ahead turn left. Ray races to the corner, reaches the intersection, knows he's taking too long. As he feared, the tail-lights have disappeared.

Ray thumps the handlebar in frustration. Bloody insane. Laming siccing him on Kennedy, Kennedy attacking Laming. Dangerous, such bastards falling out.

The person most likely to get hurt is Cassie, and close second is Arshag, who may be heading into a trap or already there.

23

Ray rides under a limitless, starry sky. The moon is rising. He makes himself slow and halt. No sign of Laming for thirty minutes now. The bush is watching, waiting. He does a sharp U-turn, back to town.

Rides past Laming's house. All dark. Empty garage, doors open, swinging in a gentle breeze. Ray tries to think what he can say to anyone in that house that will help or make any sense. Rides on.

Lets himself into the copshop. Baxter is alone, asleep at the radio. Ray slumps at his desk. He phones anyone he reckons has hunted with Kennedy or Laming, asking about huts. Gets jokes, suspicion, lying denials, nothing useful. One copper asking about another when there's bad blood is a warning to shut up, not open up.

He phones Taylor, who insists he doesn't go pig-bloody-hunting with anyone anymore. 'Too long in the tooth for that.' Hangs up. Ray sits there, wondering if Taylor is now trying to phone Kennedy or Laming to warn them something's up. As if a pig-hunting shack would have a phone.

Rides to the pub, bangs on Jimmy's door. Jimmy opens

up half-dressed, mumbling he's had a skinful. Course he doesn't know where the fucking huts are. He's the last person who'd know.

'You know anyone who would?'

'Course fucking not. You fucking desperate or what?' Ray sinks onto a chair, doesn't bother to say yes of course he fucking is. As ready to curl up here on the ugly carpet as kill Kennedy or Laming. Shakes his head. Out of fucking ideas.

He rides past his own place. It's in darkness. He slows but keeps going out of town.

At an empty intersection of two narrow roads, he pulls off the road. Sits the bike on its stand, slumps on hard ground still warm from the day and leans against an unforgiving tree. He holds a shirt sleeve against his angry eyes. His bike ticks as if stretching from exertion. The road is black, empty. Sky aglow with starlight.

Ray bursts to his feet at the thought of Arshag. He can't stay here. Who knows what's happening or where, and look at him. He has to push back at the uselessness sapping his strength. Closes his eyes. He hears a sound, a *whoompf*, soft at the edges, hard in its centre. An explosion. A small orange glow is low in the sky to the north-east. Near Lenny Bauldry's all-night servo.

Ray hits the road, turns on his headlight, bends over the tank at full throttle, engine whining in complaint. Sees the servo lit up. Rides onto the cracked, uneven concrete apron. Lenny is standing there, looking north-east. Recognises Ray, points north with his left, then indicates a turn to the right with his other arm. 'Somewhere up there. Shack some blokes use for pig hunts.'

Ray readies to go, smells burnt tyre rubber. He looks to Lenny's wide-open, small, high-ceilinged lubritorium. One of those moments cops love but hate—someone caught doing wrong. Lenny winces, shrugs. The bastard's regrooving tyres. Dangerous and illegal. Ray shakes his head and rattles away, gut tight for Cassie.

He fishtails up a sandy track past straggly trees, skeletal in the flash of his headlight. Cuts the engine as he sees the glowing shell of a burning car, enough of it left to identify as Laming's Monaro. Ray turns away from an awful, stomach-churning smell but can't escape it. Never smelt it before but knows what it is. He halts out of range of the heat.

The fire is mostly done. Flames flicker here and there in what's left of the Monaro. A hunched black form that Ray guesses used to be Laming hangs from the half-open driver's door. Ray sidles closer, wary of another explosion, peers inside, dreading a smaller black lump in there. Closer. It's empty.

The roof has burst open to the sky, edges jagged and torn. The inside of the car is black, smouldering, seat frames twisted by whatever the hell blew up. Heat drives him back but he glimpses misshapen metal shapes in the footwells. Gas bottles? The fire crackles quietly, the dreadful stench.

He kicks the earth, walks about, stamping the ground as if to make it even harder. Feeling no sorrow. Shaking with frustrated anger that there isn't enough of Laming left to smash to the ground. Some night scuffles return. An owl screeches. Howl of a dingo or feral dog. Let them come.

He faces the open door of the dark shed. Has to do it. The shack's the size of a double-garage, window glass blown in, corrugated iron now slightly buckled, door hanging open.

'Cassie?'

Nothing. He steps up to the door. Black as pitch in there.

'Cassie?'

He returns to his bike, rummages in a side bag, finds a torch. Steps into the hut. The smell of gas inside is better than the stink outside. A gas cylinder is against the rear wall, a two-burner ring on top. Beside it, another cylinder bears a gas lamp. The two-ring burner is cold but the lamp is a little warm. He checks the knob. It's open but the cylinder is empty. Left on till it ran out. His torch reveals a wooden table, four rusty, folding metal chairs, a scuffed, metal ice-chest and a wooden sideboard, legs in dusty tin-lids, water long evaporated. The earthen floor smells dank. Folded stretchers lean against a wall. On an assembled stretcher are small pieces of rope, different sizes and lengths. Someone was tied up there. There's gaffer tape and a strip of dirty cloth, a gag? Out here? It was Laming who didn't want to hear her voice.

Ray swallows, sees another rope ending in a cut loop, long enough to reach from the post in the corner to the stretcher and a bucket. A neck rope, had to be. Whoever wore it is cut free, gone. Imagines Cassie on the couch, tied, gagged, gaping at him, mouth and jaw moving uselessly. The old ice-chest has beer, steaks, onions, sliced bread, butter.

On the table is a half-empty stubby of beer. An almost full open stubby sits on the floor next to the stretcher. Two people, or an absent-minded drinker, other things on his mind? He looks more closely at stains on the canvas of the stretcher. Black, dark red, crusty. He sniffs them. Blood. Cassie's? Too long for it to be Alice's? Or both.

The kitchen sideboard leans against the rear wall, almost as high. Leadlight doors over top shelves, drawers in the middle, doors over shelves below. On the earth floor in front of the sideboard are two table knives, a bread knife, more dried, black blood, and more rope pieces of odd lengths. Ray feels the edge of the table knives. Blunt. Blood stains on the rope pieces. Ray imagines Cassie trying different knives till the bread knife was sharp enough to cut herself free, cutting herself to do it. Or someone doing it to her till she bled.

He returns outside. In the moonlight the burnt car is splotchy, pale with black patches. Evil-smelling smoke issues from it. He will never forget the smell. That corpse is too big to be Cassie. Laming's car, has to be him. Did she do it somehow? Did she get away? The place sure as shit looks like a crime scene. Jesus, is any of the blood Arshag's? Where the hell is he? Was he here? The figure in the car? No, Even burnt, Arshag would be bigger. Surely. He backs away, leaves everything as it is. For now. Might need a revisit when he knows whose tracks he might have to hide. He turns at the rumble of an approaching car.

Lenny drives up slowly in what is basically half an FJ Holden. Only the front half still has panels, the rear only the exposed chassis. Lenny is open-mouthed, then covers his nose and mouth against the smell. 'Jesus. Didn't know if I ought to come. Fuck.'

'Go back, call the copshop. Tell them there's been an, ah, accident. Looks like Laming's gone and blown himself up with his gas bottles or something. Go.'

Lenny does a snarling U-turn and spins his wheels back down the track, Ray following at a safe distance. Lenny lives in a back room of the servo with a night bell rigged up for late customers. A trapped life. Ray rides on.

He parks at the pub. Kennedy's Sandman is gone. Ray checks with Barb at the bar. No message. She locks up in fifteen. The usual wink-wink back bar will be open for those in the know. Which Ray has to pretend he doesn't know.

Ray rides the broad, deserted main street, empty even of trucks. Crosses the bridge over Pioneer Creek at the western edge of town and catches a glint of metal on a dark shape in the park beside the creek. Kennedy's Sandman.

Ray turns off his engine, coasts to a halt behind it. His hand goes automatically to where he normally carries his gun. Lot of good that does. He sneaks up to the driver's door. A hunched shape is inside. Kennedy, slumped almost over the steering wheel, snoring. Ray hits the window with his keys. Kennedy jolts upright and twists to the window then grunts in anger. Ray steps back as Kennedy sprawls out, an open stubby falling out with him, splashing beer. Must have been sitting between his legs after he passed out. Beer all over his crotch.

Ray laughs with more gusto than it needs, considers saying what he's seen, returns instead to his bike and rides away.

Kennedy yells after the bike. 'Where the fuck're you going? What's going on, you bastard? Hey! Where the fuck's Laming? What've you done to him, eh?'

Ray hears *Laming* and stops, thinks about it. He turns the bike and returns to face Kennedy but stays on the bike. 'Tell me where Laming is? Where is he?'

Kennedy shouts, 'My fucking business! My business.' He waves dismissively and turns back to his car and rummages inside, looking like he's after another beer. Ray rides the bike closer, a few yards away. Kennedy straightens, a skinful of grog making it difficult, turns to face Ray, hate deforming his face. All the resentment and rage he has for the world there in the open, in his hand a pistol, which he aims at Ray.

'Attack me, you bastard? Attack me?'

He fires, misses, curses, aims again but Ray guns the bike right at him and crashes him against the car door. Kennedy doubles over, straddling the bike's front, slams his head into its headlight and slumps to the ground as Ray loses control and he, the bike and Kennedy start to slide, tangled, to the ground. The bike engine is dangerously hot. Ray contorts to force Kennedy back into the driver's seat and keep himself away from savage burns.

With Kennedy pushed back, Ray leaps off the bike and lets it fall to the ground. Kennedy stays still. Ray finds the bike ignition key, turns it off. The car door is bent forwards almost to the front mudguard. Kennedy's starting to snore. Ray retrieves the pistol, pockets it. He leans back against a tree, slides down to the sit on the bare ground. Closes his eyes.

He wakes with fright. Checks his watch. Maybe an hour later. He picks up the bike, grateful it's not larger, sees Kennedy stirring, decides the bastard will live and rides off, headlight askew.

He turns into Cassie's street, recalls dropping her off from the gym one day on the motorbike. Cassie being Cassie loved it, whooping all the way. Ahead on the right, isolated in an unkempt yard, is a high-set house. All its lights look to be on. Around it in the long grass are carcasses of cars and agricultural gear. A police Land Rover is parked outside and Shuddup's truck is in the drive.

Scarcely able to breathe, Ray walks through the decaying front fence to the front steps. A large lump there moves. Ray sees the gleam of a shotgun barrel. Shuddup. Confirming it, Mongrel emerges from under the stairs, barking.

'Mongrel! Gidowduvit or I'll bloody shoot you.'

Ray and Shuddup both register surprise as Mongrel retreats under the stairs, growling but not barking. Shuddup looks exhausted.

Ray points to the shotgun. 'No one's coming. Is she alright?'

Shuddup stands the shotgun against a railing, covers his face and sighs deeply before speaking. 'She is now. Come across her wandering down King's Road about ten or twenty minutes ago. Was out looking for her, saw this explosion. She'd been walking a bit. Not saying much. Something about gas bottles. Where's Laming? I'm going to kill him. And Kennedy. Touching Cassie. Don't care what you say.'

'Laming's dead. Burnt to death. Don't know what happened. Here to find out. Kennedy's drunk as a skunk.'

Shuddup absorbs this. Even in the poor light, Ray can see his face is drawn, unnaturally narrow. 'Okay.' Meaning, not okay, but he can wait.

Ray shrugs. He points upstairs. Shuddup moves aside to let him pass. Arshag appears on the verandah. Ray sees the butt of a handgun protruding from his side pocket. Arshag inclines his head to the dark end of the verandah. 'She's been asking for you. Didn't want to get cleaned or say nothing till you came.'

'Where's her old man?'

Arshag jerks a chin inside. 'Out to it, as usual.'

Ray walks to the dark corner. Cassie is in a deck chair. His throat closes at her roughed-up appearance. Recalls when he first met her, laughing because she'd made it to fourteen, with all the joy and spontaneity of a six year old. She is shaking slightly, hair lank, blouse dirty and torn, eyes staring. Face swollen, streaked with tears. She surprises him by struggling to her feet, grabbing him hard and holding him close, then just as abruptly she lets go and hunches back into the deck chair. He perches on the edge of a second chair. Silence. Time unreeling at star speed in slow motion overhead.

Cassie swallows, says in a tiny voice, 'I'm in trouble, eh?'

'You? No way.'

'You been there? See what I done?'

'The car. And the shack. Yep.'

She's staring at him. 'Killed him. Burnt him up. One less bad man, eh.' Grief and jauntiness and shame all colliding. Ray has no words.

Arshag brings tea in chipped mugs. 'Lot of sugar in the yellow one.' And leaves.

Cassie takes the yellow, both hands to hold it, shaking, wild-eyed, afraid. 'You two coppers, what're you going to do? That Kennedy's a bastard, he'll make you look after your mate. Your mate Crispy.' Consumed by fear, straining for hope.

He shakes his head. 'Not my mate. Not Arshag's mate. We're looking after you, Cassie. Top of the list.'

She talks on, mechanically. 'He put his thing in my mouth, right in my mouth, telling me to suck it, and he says Diah and Alice, hey, they loved it. But I didn't believe him.' She slaps hands hard over her face then yelps from the pain of the swellings. 'I chucked my guts, him shoving that in me. I feel like a dirty pig he touched me at all.'

'Not you, Cassie. Never you.'

Silence. Slurping her tea, touching her lips gently, grimacing. 'He hit me, the bastard. Tried to fuck me, shoved my legs apart.' She looks away as she shows him the tops of her legs, already bruising.

'Cassie, let me take you to the hospital, get you checked out.'

She shakes her head violently, clamps her legs together, arms around her chest. 'No. They mustn't know. No one!'

'How about if you told a nurse? I know a great nurse, she's a special friend.'

'Who?'

'Called Dot. She's a funny bugger, too. Bit like a big sister. She won't tell anyone.'

'Maybe.'

Ray nods, gently pats her arm, wonders at her amazingly small wrist, helps her calm a little as she yanks her skirt down.

'You're a bit like a big brother,' Cassie says.

Startled, Ray almost loses it, feels tears, mock-punches her on her shoulder, feels like an idiot. She pretends to block him, and shapes up while sitting.

She stifles a laugh, hand over her mouth. 'He was coming at me and I peed myself and couldn't stop it. Didn't even know till I smelt it. And he swore at me, pee all down me.' She hunches her shoulders defensively, wrings her hands. 'It stopped him, but it was a bit dirty of me.'

Ray can smell the urine, sees fear widen her eyes, his anger rising at it. 'No, no, you did nothing wrong, Cassie. You're all good.' He waits.

'He made me strip off. Grabbing at me, at me, at me. All over.' Squirming, sounding like that six year old again but without the joy. 'Says he has to fill up the gas bottles so we can stay in the shack for days, him doing me over. He makes me load the empties in his fancy car. Me in the raw. Him ordering me around. Dropping things then making me pick them up. Dropping them again. Saying he's going to fuck me because I'm a virgin.

'I smelt some gas in the bottles so I sneaked putting the windows all up and opened the bottles eh. I sneaked one in that still had gas in it but left it hardly hissing. He ties me up in the shack, still nothing on, eh. Goes out. I can still smell his stinking cigarette. Guess he got into the car. Lit up in there? I don't know. There's this boom.

'Did it to himself, I reckon. He was going to fuck me, shoved his knee into me, but I used our training eh, straight left, right cross, straight left, right uppercut.'

She swings with the punches.

'I smashed his shitty nose! Got him good. Blood everywhere.'

Ray remembers the stains on the table, the stretcher and the floor. 'Yeah, you got him good!' His fist up for emphasis.

He gently takes her arms, finds cuts up and down the inside of her wrists. She folds back deep into the deck chair, jiggling fiercely. Ray holds himself back from reaching out to her. 'You don't want anyone to know, right?'

'Right, right.'

Ray thinks on that. Have to go back. The blood and ropes still there have to go, burn the whole shed. 'How'd he get you into his car?'

'Me being stupid. He said there'd been this accident, my old man hit a tree. That's my old man alright, so I start to get in but I wasn't sure, never liked this cop. So I start to get out and he grabs me.' Holds up red wrists. 'Pulls me in and closes the door on my legs, which bloody hurt, and he biffed me on the head and my gym bag falls out. I'm wrestling him and I'm yelling and stopping him closing the door, but he must've hit me again, because I woke up in his stinking shed.'

She is staring at him but he can't tell what she sees. 'I'm bad. So bad. My old man says I got the devil in me. Reads some shit at me from his stupid bible about devils in pigs, says that's me.' She examines the cuts on her arms closely, makes a sound like sniggering. 'I cut myself free with his breadknife. People'll reckon I tried to top myself. That's what they'll think from scars there.'

'Nah, you won't get scars from those.'

She leans over crying, collapsing in his arms across the space between them.

Arshag appears. Cassie sits up, sighs, looks at them in turn. 'So what're you coppers going to do now? Coppers always look after coppers, my old man says.'

He wants to ask about her mother, where she might be. He looks at Arshag, then says, 'We're not going to do anything. If that's what you want, you don't have to do anything. I've been to the shack and there's no sign you were there, nothing.' He gives Arshag a look that says they have to talk, then turns back to Cassie. 'The car's burnt out, there's no sign you did anything. You're as free now as before all this. It's your secret forever. If you want.'

Arshag says, 'Idiot gets into a car full of gas, lights up a ciggy? What's he think's going to happen?'

Cassie hugs herself, speaks to herself. 'I don't want people making it a joke. None of their business.'

Ray and Arshag exchange a hard look. Saying nothing means Laming won't be held accountable for grabbing her, assaulting her, attempted rape and murder. But maybe, depending on Peter, and Kennedy, we can get him for Alice. For rape and murder. Enough. Bastard's dead anyway.

Ray says, 'All you've got to do is get better, okay? Get better.' But he's thinking, Kennedy knew. It's what he and Laming argued about behind the pub.

Arshag nods at the house. 'Maybe live somewhere else for a while? A safer place?'

She darts a look inside the house and shakes her head. 'Where would that be, eh?'

Arshag shrugs. 'You've already been cooking and washing yourself and your clothes for years. You just need a roof and you'll look after yourself fine.' He points a thumb at the stairs, to Shuddup. 'Don reckons it'll be okay.'

'I can live at his place?' She goes quiet.

Arshag says, 'You know the caravan he built, sitting in his back yard? He reckons he'll give you the house and he'll live in the van. It'll work out fine.'

Ray watches her nod, try for a smile.

'Old Uncle Don, Uncle Shuddup, the crazy bugger! He's already been keeping me safe from him'—she glances furtively at the house—'for years.'

Arshag says, 'Meanwhile, Ray and I'll make sure no one knows about Laming. You have nothing to worry about, ever.'

She nods, takes a breath, nods again, looks at them both with the openness of a child. Ray feels a stab of pain.

Arshag says, 'I got that hot bath for you, cooled down nice now. Got some clothes good for sleeping in. You can look after all that yourself in there, reckon?'

She climbs to her feet. 'Going to be a bit sore, eh?'

Shuddup appears at the top of the stairs. She joins him, moving gingerly, and he stands by the door looking a lot like a guard.

Ray and Arshag breathe large sighs.

Ray says, 'You should've had your own kids.'

Arshag looks at him. 'I'll check her old man's still out to it. Don't need him hanging round.'

Ray walks around the front yard at the edge of the light

from the house. The grass is long. He stares at a rusting car body as Arshag approaches.

Arshag nods at it. 'Thinking of making your own collection?'

'Yeah. Get a big yard, let the grass grow. Then sit some jalopies around, let them rust.'

Arshag says, 'Good for Joe Blakes.'

Ray takes a step back, looking around his feet.

Arshag says, 'I've had a go at a statement.' He reads from a sheet of paper.

'A Royalton detective died last night in an explosion believed caused by gas leaking from bottles in his vehicle, ignited by his cigarette. At this point the death is not considered suspicious. The Coroner has been advised. Relatives in the state's far north are being notified. Details soon.'

Ray's voice is a croak. 'Let the punishment fit the crime.'

'Perfect death,' says Arshag.

'If she made what happened to her official, she wouldn't be charged.'

'Not what she wants. That's good enough. It'll still be investigated.'

Ray says, 'Without her in it. Kennedy's case.' Deciding to say nothing about Kennedy firing at him. Sufficient unto the day.

Arshag taps the statement. 'I'll give this to Kennedy to send out officially in the morning. Soon as your train pulls out.' Manages a grin. 'He won't dare a real investigation. It's neat as is, especially cos Laming was known as a drunk.'

'We need Cassie to tell us if Laming told her what he did to Alice.'

'Some of which Kennedy would've done too. But she can't tell any of it without putting herself in the story. It comes down to Peter, or we've got nothing. And we need Kennedy to keep quiet about tonight.' He holds up crossed fingers.

Ray recalls Kennedy attacking Laming behind the pub. 'That shouldn't be a problem.' He paces about, awash with emotion, a flood rising. 'Peter, Peter, pumpkin-eater, need him to keep his fucking nerve. Prick thought he was a big man till he realised Laming and Kennedy included him so they could frame him for it later. He's after revenge.' Ray holds up empty hands. What will be will be.

Arshag's jaw sets. 'Kennedy deserves the same as Laming. Anything less isn't justice. But respecting Cassie, jail'll have to do. If it happens.' He shivers, forcing something deep inside himself.

Ray's head buzzes like a high-voltage cable at the very thought of Kennedy left to walk around free. And for Arshag, who would have to live with seeing him every day. Ray wears a tight, uncertain smile. 'Who'll tell Laming's wife?' Will the news be good or bad for her and the kid?

'Kennedy's investigation, he gets to tell her.'

Ray tries to think if he left any trace of himself in the pig-hunting shed or at Laming's car. Overseas, examining crime scenes is turning into an art form. And there's this new thing called D-N-A. But little of this has seriously, officially, reached Queensland yet. Lenny will say he was there, but after the explosion. So it doesn't matter. Anyway he touched nothing in the shed or Laming's car. No, he never leaves anything. The world closes over wherever he was, smooth as water filling a hole. 'So much has happened and we can't say a thing.'

Arshag says, 'What's left at the hut?'

Ray shakes his head. 'I could tell someone was tied up,

and there's blood. We want no questions asked, no mysteries, got to make the car fire spread further, into the hut. Turn the bastard into a charred shell. Think it can be done okay.'

'I'll have a look.'

Ray nods, relieved. 'That'd be good. I got Lenny at the servo to tell the copshop. They talked to you? What're they doing?'

Arshag says, 'I phoned Baxter when I got here. He rang Kennedy at home. Drunk as.'

Ray manages a laugh. 'Lucky he lives in a tiny town. Short drive home before he passes out.'

'Baxter's not sure what got through to him. He and Louise are waiting on me. I said I was looking for you but after your party, not sure where you ended up. I'll radio in, tell him I'm heading out there. Take it from there.'

The verandah lights cast long shadows. Ray turns to the house as Shuddup comes downstairs with a cleaned-up Cassie, carrying what she's taking with her in shopping bags. Shuddup and Cassie leave in his truck, Mongrel barking at the world from the tray.

Ray stares after them. 'Doesn't say much.'

Arshag smiles. 'Drives his dozer like it's a toy. He could sell tickets. He was married for a minute. Brand-new wife got electrocuted, live wires down after a storm. Broods too much, Cassie'll help him with that.'

'Any cop trouble?'

'One near G-B-H. Some moron picked him in the Tyborg pub. The bodily harm was grievous alright, but he got over it. Never went official. Why?'

Ray shrugs. 'Dark horse. That's all. Did you find the shed you went looking for? I was worried it could've been a trap.'

Arshag nods. 'It hasn't been used for a while. Tank busted, no water. I hung around, then, coming back, crossed paths with Shuddup. What time's your train tomorrow?'

'How can I go? If Peter reneges, we'll have more to do.'

'Trains run both ways.' Points a joking finger as if Ray needs reminding. Grabs Ray's shoulder. 'Go home. It's too late.'

'More ways than one.'

24

Ray sits at his kitchen table in the ambiguous dark of four a.m. Hasn't slept. Sees outside, still black but hints of colour emerging. Where'd the night go? He stares at the suitcase and canvas bag he came with, neatly packed. The train leaves at eight-thirty a.m. He can't sit here for another four fucking hours. The fridge is empty, the pub closed. Two voices yell in his brain: *Stay! Make Peter tell the truth about Alice. No! Go, you can't do any more here. No power over Peter or Kennedy. No! Stay. Arshag will be taken off any investigation. He'll be unprotected if he's left alone here.*

His phone rings.

Kennedy. 'Get your arse down the stock pen now. I'll tell you everything you want to know. And don't say you're already out of here. You've got bloody time.' He ends the call.

Ray notes the slurred voice. *Everything you want to know?* He looks at pale, pale light slyly entering his door. Can't be over. It can't be over because Kennedy rings up and says it is. A duel isn't over till it's over. He can't expect any fight with Kennedy to have rules. He looks at the gun he took from him. So be it. Kennedy will have another.

He steps out into the chilly last of the night. Dark is lingering. A pale yellow curve lies along the eastern horizon.

He walks with measured pace, takes a street on his left, which slopes down slightly to the police stock pen, about three or four hundred yards from the nearest houses. Hears ferocious barking. A big dog. Feral?

He stops dead. Sees flashes of a torch in the fading dark. Hears agitated cattle, lowing turning to grunting and bellowing. Thuds and crashing against the heavy timber planks of the pen walls. More bellowing. A human cry of pain. He doesn't move. His stomach clenches as he imagines horns and hooves ripping and stamping, clenches again as he recognises that voice. There's another cry, guttural and full of pain and fear under a rising mountain of bellowing. Is that a dog running from the back of the pen, and a ute parked down the road away from houses?

Ray cries out in anger and frustration, resenting being here, fearful too. He snaps into a fast trot towards the pen as that torch light flies into the air then disappears.

Ray braces at another roar of pain and fear, weaker this time. He reaches the pen, a mass of dark colliding shapes. At the external light box, he turns on the big lights, stares between the pen's horizontal, timber fence planks at an inert body being trampled and kicked around inside. The battered face is Kennedy's. Ray climbs the fence, stops astride the top plank to see people running from houses up the street calling out. 'What the hell's going on?'

A man shouts to Ray not to go in, it's bloody dangerous. Ray freezes. Kennedy lies still. The cattle are still barging and kicking but less now, the dog gone.

'Who is it?'

'Shit, Kennedy. It's Kennedy.'

'What's he doing in there? What the fuck happened?'

'There was a dog. I heard barking.'

'Yeah. Feral for sure.'

Ray makes sure someone's calling the ambos.

Recalls Arshag going out of his way to catch a dog loose on the street and return it to its grateful young owner. 'No one lets their dogs run loose. Loose dogs're likely to be feral. Ferals get shot.'

He shifts on the top rail. Takes deep breaths, waiting. The cattle are still agitated but exhausted. He is about to drop into the pen, climbs down slowly instead. Pushes through heaving bodies that now seem confused, lethargic. Avoids hooves and horns. The dust is cloying and dense, full of sweet and sour cattle stink. Reaches Kennedy, twisted, filthy, merging with the broken ground itself.

Near him, almost buried, a smashed, long torch and a handgun. The stench of shit and urine and fear is overpowering. He tries not to breathe. Elbowing cattle, shoving their massive hot bodies, he drags Kennedy to the gate where helpers haul them both out. Kennedy is bloody, crushed and broken, gored and trampled, bones out of his chest. He leaves a trail of blood but is breathing. His shattered jaw hangs open, he can't speak, but Ray feels a burning stare, the blackest judgement, from Kennedy's fading eyes.

Ray's mind jams, trying to figure it out. *Was it Mongrel? Would Shuddup do this for Cassie? On the stairs at her place, he said as much. Must've got Mongrel, gone hunting. Not a lot of places to look. Sees the Sandman. Lets Mongrel loose to lure the bastard out. But it was Kennedy who got me here. Shuddup didn't know I was coming. Christ I could've fucked it up, saved the bastard. Even grabbed Shuddup for doing it. Kennedy drunk. It was enough.*

The ambos arrive. Kennedy is dead. Ray leans back against the outside of the pen, stinking from blood and foul dirt, head still whirling. He looks back to where he froze. How long did he wait? Did it matter? Why was Kennedy in the pen? Too drunk to realise the danger? Why the gun? Not much use in a crowded pen. Was he setting an ambush? Knowing the rot had set in, that it was all falling apart. Got ambushed himself?

A large hand is on his shoulder. A man's voice cuts into his thoughts. 'You couldna done nothing, mate. Some of the stock's wounded themselves. Lucky no calves. You're a fucking hero going in there.'

Ray's gut lurches in disgust and he doubles up, dry-retching.

The man half-laughs, embarrassed. 'You did the right thing. To wait, let them settle.'

In pre-dawn light, darkness gone now, Ray straightens but holds onto the fence. Could he have got there? To do what? Get him out earlier. Hears in his head a priest, for fuck's sake, from when he was a kid, in confession, pressing him on sins of commission, sure, but sins of omission are sins too, my boy. Oh yes.

Ray phones Baxter from the office attached to the pen. Kennedy hadn't called him. Ray got the only invitation. Ray calls Arshag who says he's coming. Ray stands there, phone in hand, insides shaking. He wipes the Kennedy gun he brought clean, puts it on the desk.

Makes himself breathe. He can catch that train now.

He sees a notebook lying open on the desk but shoved aside. Written on its open page, two words: 'Mum, this—' Wallet, keys and coins are in a neat pile. Next to them a small key. Ray picks it up. Scans the spartan office. A filing cabinet, old, dinged, some rust.

The key opens it. The middle drawer contains thin files on loose sheets of paper. Single letters one side of the page, across from could-be numbers, maybe money amounts on the other. Some sort of code. Handwritten notes scrawled here and there, barely legible. Could be the records of the *everything you want to know* or ordinary but lousy records of the daily functioning of the pen. Stock in and out, costs, etc. Ray drops the file he's been examining on the desk. Leaves the key beside it. Lost interest.

He phones William, tells him that, as mayor, William's the only authority left to call, to report Kennedy is dead. After a pause, William says, 'Why not stay now? It'll be a brand new copshop.'

'My transfer means I've got to go. You've got to know when to go.'

William doesn't reply, hangs up. Ray does too, a little surprised.

He steps out into the street, avoiding looking at the pen. The ute that was down the road is gone. Daylight is here now. The crowd has dispersed save for two blokes standing in the middle of the road, smoking. Savouring the morning.

One is the man who warned Ray not to climb into the pen. 'There definitely was a dog. Barking, stirring everything up.'

The second man says, 'He stank like a brewery. Would've got in the pen through the door from the office. Chasing the dog. But why the gun? He'd be bloody lucky to stop a bull with that, just stir them up even more.'

Ray can't find a reply.

The first man says, 'Should've known better.'

Epitaph.

Ray walks off into the sounds of morning. A clash of crockery and cutlery spills out of one house. Another leaks smooth radio voices, Country and Western twangs. Kids squeal in games. Mismatched voices compete, sing, laugh. Someone's practising a guitar. The dogs know Ray, pay him no heed.

One more job to do but let the sun come up first.

———

Ray enters Kennedy's sunny front yard, distributing jerky to the dogs, who scrabble and brawl as before. Glances at the shed in the corner. Padlock gone and the door ajar.

A woman's high-pitched, scratchy voice startles him. 'He's not here.' Kennedy's mother is in her wheelchair in the deep shadow of the front verandah, blocking the top of the stairs.

Ray can't see a gun or holster. He stays where he is, in the sun. 'Mrs Kennedy?'

'I know who I am, sonny. And I know who you are. I saw you break into my son's shed. Took something away. I told my son you were here. What'd you pinch?'

Ray registers stark surprise too fast to stop it. 'Evidence in a case. If I'd known you were home—'

'—you'd have gone away and snuck back another day. You here to return what you stole?'

'I'm here about your son. Detective Kennedy.'

'You think I don't know who my son is? What's he done? Died in the line of duty? Like his useless old man?' Her face looks bent out of shape.

Ray searches for more words. 'You need someone with you?'

'Piss off, sonny. I've got me.'

'You don't want to know how or—'

'Leave me alone. How's the how or why matter? Go on, get.' Her face staying like an ugly mask, painted on.

Ray rides home, absorbing that Kennedy knew, all that time, that Ray stole from him, surely worked out what he took, and who planted it there so easy to find.

Maybe explains the hostility between him and Laming at the farewell party, and their argument afterwards. Maybe also explains Kennedy's speech when they caught the duffers, about someone so desperate to keep what they've got, they'd kill for it. His strange mix of despair and elation at Pioneer Creek after Ray told him Laming was dead. Piling pressure on Kennedy at the stock pen. And rage with Ray. What remains unknown is, if Kennedy realised Laming planted the briefs, why didn't he kill him for it?

25

Back in Dot's front yard, before the heat builds to smother all good intentions, Ray hugs her goodbye. Massed cockatoos whirl overhead with tormented screeches.

She says, 'You're off then. Did what you wanted to do.'

'Royalton Radio'll run versions and updates. If a Cassie comes to see you, look after her?'

She gives him a shrewd look.

He says, 'She'll tell you. She's a good kid.'

She points to the Banksia rose plants. 'You weren't even here long enough for the first bloom. Another month or so, my gardening book reckons. Going to press some of the flowers in a book.' Holds her hands flat, one on top of the other.

Ray grins. 'Damn. Missing another summer out here.'

She laughs.

As Arshag arrives, Ray gives her the motorbike keys. 'For Jimmy, he'll be around for them.'

At the train station, as he and Arshag climb from the Land Rover, a car Ray doesn't know stops nearby. Arshag gives Ray a look as a middle-aged woman emerges with a bag over her shoulder and a boy of about eight clinging to her with vacant eyes and sagging mouth. The woman, face averted, pulls the boy into the station. The car leaves. Ray already knows as Arshag says, 'Mrs Laming. And their kid.' Not waiting for any funeral. Is it the town she hates? Laming? The heat? Everything?

Arshag says, 'We never did her any favours.'

They enter the wide, dusty platform, Arshag carrying a small cane basket covered with a tea towel. Mrs Laming and the boy stand at one end of the platform. A family with three small kids is waiting too, the kids bored, pushing and shoving.

Standing apart is an older, gaunt man in a big, sweat-stained hat, faded button-down shirt, jeans held up on hollow hips by a broad, leather belt. Scuffed elastic-sided boots. A stuffed, ex-army kitbag leans on his leg. He has a defensive air. Perhaps none of this is what he expected at this stage of his life. He and Ray share nods. Ray cautioned him once, drunk and yelling in the main street. Nothing came of it. He is looking for work.

A distinct silence hangs over them all. The ambiguity of departures.

'You checked on Cassie?'

Arshag grins. 'Shuddup's getting her settled in. Left her old man to stew in his own juice. Queen of her new castle. Shuddup's in his van.'

'He really wants to live in a caravan? The heat. And the cold.'

'He's happy. Cassie says she'll do the cooking. They love a beef stew.'

'Lots of potatoes.'

'I reckon the van lets him feel free, think he can piss off at a moment's notice.'

They observe a short silence on that.

'She says she'll see you at the Olympics.'

They laugh, almost.

'Dot says she'll look her over if she comes in. Make sure she's okay,' Ray says.

Arshag hesitates, then says, 'Had a chinwag with Stella this morning. She'll give her extra attention too. Stella wishes you well but says not to call.'

Ray winces, stares at the empty paddock across from the station. 'Thinking about those two bastards. Burnt to death, gored and trampled to death.'

'Royalton Radio's getting bits of it right. I'm not saying a word.'

Ray feels a surge of sadness. 'I'll have to give evidence over Kennedy's death?'

Arshag shrugs. 'Doubt it. Death by drunken stupidity. Death by insanity. By suicide. Who'll care? Anyone asks, send them a letter.'

Ray hears defeat in his voice. shakes his head. So be it. 'What are you going to do?' Almost reaches out to touch Arshag's arm.

'Irene's got her eye on a place three klicks south. Forty acres. Garage and two sheds. We can live in the bigger one. Cattle yard. Black soil, permanent creek. Staying a cop doesn't have the pull it used to.'

They shake hands, then Arshag surprises Ray by stepping up to hug. 'Look after yourself,' Arshag says.

They hold there, Ray holding him too, then step back. Arshag hands over the basket.

'Find yourself in Brisbane, come see me.' Ray clambers aboard his carriage, mouth raw, sits by a window looking over a paddock, sun-battered and brown. Leafless balls

332

like tumbleweed lightly bounce across it at the mercy of a warming, erratic breeze. How'd he ever get here? His unceasing question.

A roaring engine announces William's plane swinging down to land on the nearby dusty field. William opens the passenger door, sits there, engine running. Ray grabs his bag, the basket and suitcase and jumps down from the train.

———

At the plane door, William signals him aboard. 'I'll take you. You'll be deaf for a day but you're welcome.'

'A round trip of six hundred and whatever mile just for me?'

'I'm picking up some milk.'

Ray settles into his seat, as William taxis the plane. They race back the way he came, engine deafening alright, bouncing till at last, a barbed wire fence in front looking too close, they lift into the air. Ray takes a breath, loves it. William banks the plane and they climb, heading east.

They soar above a receding Royalton. Already, Ray doesn't recognise terrain he has driven and ridden for over a year. He catches a hard, searching look from William, which promptly disappears. Avoiding Ray's eye.

The earth slips by beneath them, time vanishing.

William says, 'You're leaving for good.' His words are clipped as if he can't get enough air.

'Sure.' Ray sees William is angry. Because he's leaving? Ray starts to ask, when grating radio static fills the cockpit.

William flicks a switch.

'William? That you, William? Hello? This thing working?' It's a rough, rising voice, an older man under pressure.

'William here. Over.' Emotionless. Deliberate.

'William? Ian here, Taylor. Um, over.'

'Yes, Ian, I know it's you. Over.'

'Bloody hell, why aren't you here? Kennedy's been trampled to death in the fucking stock pen. Jesus Christ. First Laming, now Kennedy.'

'I know.'

'What? Well, what are we—? What the fuck are you doing?'

'Going shopping.'

Ray looks out the window, enjoying William baiting Taylor.

Taylor says, 'I've got a traffic jam building up here, mate. Bloody trucks lined up to hit Dooley's place and I need your word he's away like you said. And we need the go-ahead and dollars for the rest of them guns. We need you here, mate. That bastard Windsor's tangled up in Kennedy's death, fuck knows how, but it's a dead cert.'

'He's here with me. Ask him yourself.' Like a blade into soft flesh.

Taylor shouts, 'Jesus fuck!' The radio snaps into silence.

Ray stares at the slowly rolling earth, a hopeless distance below. A life-crushing distance. Sunlight flashes on what may be a distant windscreen. As bits and pieces of information slot into place, he slumps at his terrible mistake.

Hears a sardonic voice say, 'Should've taken the train. Fucked up again.' He looks at William but the voice was his own.

Ray looks around as if for signs to mark cardinal points. They seem to be heading east. 'Where are we going?' A slight tremor in his voice.

William says, 'I'd hoped you'd be returning to Royalton with me, but not so. In spite of everything we talked about.' His voice sour, accusing.

Ray, baffled, half-smiles. 'I was never going to stay.'

William offers a cold, cold smile. 'So it seems. I see now. I overestimated you.'

Ray looks at him, face blank.

'And underestimated. You know, I've needed Laming and Kennedy taken care of, oh dear, for months, and you managed both in one night.' He mimes doffing a hat.

Ray's turmoil stops him thinking, much less speaking.

William sighs. 'Poor Laming, dear me. He wasn't the sharpest knife in the drawer, as you people like to say. But deary me, to incinerate himself in a gas explosion? The carelessness. Perhaps you can fill me in on what really happened?'

Ray shrugs, hoping it looks casual. 'I was nowhere near whatever Laming was doing.' He feels like doubling over in rage at himself. *Cops are supposed to be good judges of character, isn't that what we say?* He looks out the window, then at William's hands controlling the plane. He wants to smash them away, and smash William too and shakes at the effort not to.

William sighs theatrically, a mocking, formal veneer over smouldering anger. And malice. 'It's no matter. Did you mean to save it up till the very end?'

He laughs grimly with what Ray is sure is appreciation. 'You see, when you cut loose that teacher slut I thought it was a sign you were preparing for a new start. We could be the team I wanted. Silly me. Instead, you dispose of Laming and Kennedy and try to run away.'

Ray absorbs the violence in the tone like lead entering his veins. 'I didn't kill anyone. And I was never staying. I'm not running away from anything.'

'Come now. Let's not turn my disappointment into contempt.'

Ray stares down at the earth, stunned. The land looks punishingly hot, red earth and scrubby trees with nothing to spare for humans. His gut contorts. William is running the guns, the duffing? Jesus, the snakes, lizards and birds too? Crime lord of the manor this whole time. Stella joked about William being a robber-baron. Ray trembles at being so fucking wrong. His fury, nowhere to go, turns back inside him, tearing his insides.

As if the radio call never happened, William says, 'They may close the copshop now. That'd be fatal for Royalton. We lose that, state government fools who've never set foot in the place will close the railway, then the school, the hospital. It'll kill a community that's gutted already. The knock-on effect spreads like a disease. Exactly what I've worked to prevent.'

'But all the stuff you're doing, the crime . . .'

'Some of it, yes, has rebounded on the community. Locals used to call the place an oasis free of that, when I had it all in order. I lost control. It's why I wanted you, damn it. Why can't you see? On the outside, one does whatever it takes. But inside, righteousness always. Why can't they see I'm here to protect the community?'

He's lost in a fucking fantasy, Ray thinks as he strives for calm, Billy's and his own. 'Legally, I had too little to charge Kennedy with. Or Laming. No one's going to listen to someone like Peter going up against those two. There would've been no convictions.'

William waves an empty hand. 'You killed them anyway.'

'I didn't kill anyone!'

'Of course not, dear boy. From my early inquiries, it's clear you didn't hold the match that lit the gas. You didn't goad the cattle. No, no. Laming's death, Kaye advises me, will be confirmed as self-inflicted. And not only were you not in the stock pen but you're acclaimed as a hero who tried to save Kennedy. What you did is give whoever did the deeds the hope and passion for their community to do it themselves. A community that strong is a community that can stand against the corrupting world outside. How can you not see value in that? It's your gift. And you leave?'

The plane grinds on in a cloudless, flawlessly blue sky. Ray tries to imagine escaping the plane, floating in that blue, sustained by its dense colour to land safely. The earth below keeps unravelling.

William says, 'The copshop has to stay. But run by people I can trust.' Ray notes *I*, not *we*, as William continues, unfazed. 'The Minister for Local Government is a fool, I'll push him on it. Taylor'll back me. As local MP, god help us, he's malleable. The only way the clod is useful. Good will come of this.'

Truths among William's tightly woven distortions sting Ray. His own need to physically fight, to hit and hurt, is enveloping his shoulders and arms, but thwarted. He stares down at indifferent country. A mass of moving dark dots could be kangaroos. Big reds are boxers too, till they sit on their tails and kick. The engine labours on. Wind whistles into the cabin from who knows where, the plane shaking as if having second thoughts.

Ray shifts his boots. It's a thin metal skin. He could kick it out.

'I trusted you,' William says. 'Eventually you could've run it all.'

Ray stifles a dismayed laugh at such craziness but it escapes him like a snigger. William reddens, snarls, shoves the stick forwards and the plane tips into a steep plunge towards earth.

Ray moans. 'William!'

Feels the lurch lasting longer than his life but it's seconds before William wrenches up the nose and level flight resumes. Wide-eyed, Ray dares a glance at William's twitching eyes, trembling mouth. Is he growling? The plane's racket makes it hard to know. Ray braces against the hard edges of the cockpit where he can and gulps fitful breaths. Not game to speak, he shakes his head, emerging from his panic to realise William is calm again, even chuckling.

Ray thinks of Taylor, of Jimmy's wondering how Taylor stays afloat with no income. Ray says, 'Did you give Taylor the money to buy my family's place?'

'The Rogers'? Of course, how else do I get to own every-where and everyone?'

Ray shakes his head at the ugly symmetry. 'Why didn't you let me take the train? I knew nothing about any of this.'

'Indeed. My mistake. Another one.' William gathers him-self, waggles a joking finger. 'I fooled you, what a clever fellow I am, but dear, oh dear, what have you done to me? You would have inherited my title, my estate. My enterprises. My aspirations.' He stares at Ray, needing him to know. 'I'm surrounded by dross! Thinking they're my kind of people.'

Ray feels the cloying grip of despair at his own blindness. Recalls Dot's joke that William saw Ray as a surrogate son. It seemed too silly, back then.

William's lips form a thin line, mouth whitening. 'In brief, since sadly you need clarification, Taylor, Kennedy, Laming . . . they all work for me. Or they do when they're alive. I fund them, command them. They're lost in debt to me, too greedy to resist. Pledged to me, do you see?' William's voice grates. 'You actually thought *them* capable of dreaming it all up? Doing it all?'

Ray is struck by an ugly thought so he says it aloud. 'What about the dead girls? You're lord of the manor, was that you too?'

'Ah, that. A blot on my copybook. But please, no! No part of my plans. Out of the blue, those pathetic boys raped that girl and I saw the attack for what it was, a threat to everything I was building. Luckily she killed herself, which drew a line under that. Or would have, until Laming and Kennedy, dear god, got ideas. These morons make a bit of money working for me, get a taste of power for the first time in their doltish lives and look what they do to me. At least Laming had the sense to finish what he'd started and silenced the girl. But Kennedy fell apart. Fell apart! As he did again last night. Eggshell man!'

'Last night?'

'Oh yes, he phoned me at some ungodly hour, ranting he was going to tell you everything, then kill you, then himself. Tell you, then kill you? For god's sake. Beyond reason.'

Ray considers present parallels but says nothing.

William wags an annoyed finger. 'He started raging at me again for making Laming top man. I hung up on him.' William looks exasperated. 'I had to do it. He couldn't take care of that girl and Laming stepped up. One works with what one's got.'

All this in an affectless tone. Like he's killed before. Mysteries surround this man. Wealth, Africa, his missing wife. A ruthlessness never held to account.

Ray struggles to imagine Kennedy falling apart, then recalls his sob in the pub, and that day outside the hospital, shaking. The neat pile of his wallet, keys, coins. All the signs.

William sighs at his own burdens. 'Kennedy going to water meant I had to deal with him too. Prop him up or get rid of him. Not as easy as killing some blasted girl. Laming couldn't figure out how. As if it's some deep problem. Dear me.' William shakes his head, which Ray reads as disgust.

'Kennedy and Laming were going to frame Peter for the murder of Alice. They would've gotten away with it too. Why didn't they?' Rays says.

'Too busy turning on each other. No trust left. Not a skerrick. Paralysis, yes? I was pushing Laming to act for both our sakes. Could feel the unravelling.' He whirls his fingers in the air. 'I certainly didn't expect he'd be so bold as to snatch yet another girl. What a hunger he must have. Or had.' A high-pitched laugh. 'Oh yes, Kennedy told me about her. He didn't know who she was.'

Ray struggles to keep his face still. *Cassie. Jesus, is she under threat? Think it through. William doesn't know who she is or what she did. Mustn't know. Say nothing.*

'Kennedy and Laming often lamented you arrived a day too late to blame you for the second girl. One of Kennedy's bad jokes to give you the case. Letting it all fade away made much more sense.'

'And your property grabs? With Taylor?'

William looks at him, eyebrows raised, mouth set. Ray feels that disgust shift onto him. 'Grabs? Hardly. Strategic investments. I control an area the size of small European countries. One property alone, north-west, is half the size of England.' He points airily. 'Even Taylor understands owning land. It's passing strange, the man's a neuter, at his best, yet people keep voting him in as their member of parliament. They're sheep. So I shear them.'

He sneers at a stupid world, boundless horizons laid out before them. He laughs as if he's above it all but there's pride there. He looks at Ray to join in.

'People know you're not a lord. Why pretend?'

William laughs. 'I don't wish to be insulting, I really don't, but I knew people would accord me more authority if I had a title. It's an Australian thing. It gave me clout. Even as a lie.'

Ray shakes his head, closes his eyes, lets the vibration and noise of the plane envelop him.

William clicks his tongue. 'My boy, I showed you a grand vista and, like the rest of them, all you see is the dirt in front of you.'

Ray swallows, throat raw, maybe from yelling over the engine, maybe from fear, but driven to know as much as possible. 'Why did Laming put the girl's underwear in Kennedy's shed? The murdered girl's.' Provoking, fishing.

'Oh, believe me, I roared at him for that.'

Ray stares at the sky. William confirming it.

William laughs. 'Know what he said? *There's more than one way to skin a cat!* What can you say to that? He wanted to frame Kennedy. They'd hated each other for years. I let him do it, it might even have sorted out the pair of them at each other's throats. Water under the bridge now. You fixed that double problem.' William savours that, holds out an empty hand, acknowledging him.

Ray stares at the sky, blue deep and forever, every direction. 'What happens next?'

'You can still choose. Even this late. With me or against me?' William is almost jaunty.

Ray, not fooled, sees the ugly resolve beneath. He stares at William. Where is that in his face? His eyes suggest shyness at first. Maybe the quick glances away and back shade into deviousness.

'Come, come, what's it to be?' Tense now, maybe sensing a late offer can only deliver humiliation. A shocking neediness emerges in a tremble in William's hands, his mouth. Vulnerable.

'What are my choices?' Ray's hostility is plain. Even his contempt.

William laughs, a thin sound, peers out of his window. 'I see. Well, I could kill us both. In despair, now you know all my sins.' He laughs again, points downwards. 'Spear us into the ground. Awful on the way but painless when we hit. Not my preference, you understand. Not after all the way I've come.'

He tilts up a defiant chin, presses buttons on the radio. Ray hears a burble like a bell.

It's Taylor again, this time more resigned. 'William?'

'Ian, my noble fellow. Remember all our jokes about plan B? Well, this is it. Execute plan B now. Tell me you understand, then set to.'

Static crackles in the cockpit.

Taylor sighs, 'Such a waste. Fine, plan B it is.' He's subdued, submissive, ends the call.

William says, waving flippantly. 'I could just drop you in Brisbane, then toddle off to my shopping. Luckily for me, your unhappy reputation with your colleagues is well documented. By the time you find a phone or a nice police officer or anyone at all to believe you, and by the time anyone out at Royalton gets off their bottom to go and look, plan B will have destroyed all evidence of wrongdoing. By me.'

He takes a deep breath, then, triumphantly, something decided, says, 'You're the misfit here, my boy. Not me. I'm the mayor. I lunch with ministers of the Crown and other powerful bags of shit and wind, pardon my French. I can let you walk away, watch you prove you're a fool no one believes, trusts or wants around. People want to believe the powerful, you see.'

Ray's anger rises, a swift tide. Stares at those hands flying the plane, wants to smash them aside, clenches his fists instead, fingernails cutting his palms.

William points a forefinger. 'You underestimate yourself, which suggests weakness. Deep faultlines.'

Ray shifts in his seat, despising that. Every part of him wants to lash out, crush William.

William shrugs. 'I saw your potential to remake yourself. I live a successful but isolated life. It would have been nice to share it with someone on my own level.'

'You had a wife.' Ray catches a glimpse of what may be furtiveness in William's eyes, gone in a flash.

'She was everyone's wife, in a way.' A weak effort to sound blasé but a raw, sharp anger erupts as a baleful, spiteful laugh. 'Same response to me as to a passing stockman. No discrimination. Humiliating. Unnatural.'

Ray thinks about it, finally says it. 'You said that garden bed at your place was your wife's. Your wife's what—grave? Her body's there, isn't it, what's left of it ... maybe still showing how you killed her.'

'Rubbish.'

But Ray sees his knuckles tighten, whiten. 'There's no way you would've told a slug like Taylor what you did to her. She's not in plan B, is she? She's there for the finding. Arshag will believe me. He'll dig her up.'

'I weary of this.' He points the nose of the plane down, this time more measuredly. Ray sees a long, grey-black ribbon snaking north–south across the red earth. A road. There's no sign of habitation. 'You'll be leaving this flight here.'

Ray swallows. Says, 'I'll die if you leave me out here.' Knowing full well, letting him walk away is not the plan.

26

They land on the road and roll to a halt. Ray sees by the plane's shadow that his window faces west. William leaves the engine running, the propellor flashing. Apart from a low range of hills on the western horizon, the landscape is identical on each side of the road, creating a strange mirror effect. Nasty joke if you're lost. There's a shallow ditch with a strip of sparse green grass fed by runoff from recent rain, then endless, hard, red-orange earth. Stunted, sparse trees. No apparent animal life, not even birds.

On his side of the road, a faint two-rut track branches off the bitumen. Some fifty yards along, a hunched, dark, alien shape. Twisted wreckage of a vehicle, ute maybe, once red, now brown with rust. Arse up not far from the track, cabin and front end crushed. The tray looks to be snapped, half broken off. Driver asleep at the wheel, or drunk. Ray, thinking like a cop, hopes no bodies are in it. He turns to find William has trained a Luger on him.

William cocks it, the jerky action betraying unfamiliarity. He laughs at the wreckage. 'Drive that home. You'll be right.'

Ray nods at the Luger. 'That was on Benny's back seat.'

'Something about a Luger, don't you think?'

Ray recalls saying something similar, which is distasteful. He looks around, transfixed by the familiar, endless, ruthless mulga and bare red earth, even at the point of a gun.

William looks at the infinite length of the road ahead, lifts the gun to Ray's face. 'Out. Get out.'

'Shoot me. May as fucking well.'

'Indeed. No one's watching.'

'How will you explain my disappearance?'

'I didn't have to explain my wife's disappearance. She was just—gone. I'll enjoy saying you got out in Brisbane, mouthing lies and nasty claims, and ran off who knows where. I have a friend there who'll swear to it. Out. No messy blood in my plane, thank you.'

'I'll be found.'

He taps the muzzle on Ray's temple, points his free thumb into the back of the plane where Ray sees a shovel held in a rack. 'You think this's the first time I've relieved myself of a fool?'

Ray opens his door, hesitates with mock concern. 'This ground's like iron. You sure you can dig a hole in it?'

William's face contorts with rage. 'Get out! Get out!' He fires a bullet past Ray's head. Deafened, Ray half-falls out into a silenced world. He climbs to his feet and turns to run— but where?

William is already scrambling across into the passenger seat, kicking the door fully open, Luger aimed. Ray elbows the door hard, jams it on William's outstretched leg, falls to the road, rolls under the plane. Burning, melted tar sears his bare skin. He gets up on the opposite side of the plane, ears still ringing.

Run, or use the plane? Running's crazy, nowhere to run to. William is out of the plane now, heading for its tail. Ray moves to the front, wary of the still spinning, shimmering, roaring propellor. William appears from behind the tail and shoots, too late. Ray is around the front.

William darts to the pilot's door but Ray is now outside the open passenger door. William yanks open the pilot's door as Ray slams his side. William growls in fury, detours wide around the propellor. Ray reaches the rear of the plane, ducks around the tail and sprints up the other side as William reaches the tail, firing uselessly at him as they cross.

They do the whole chase again. William is red-faced with frustration. He bends to fire under the plane, misses. But at this, Ray swears and takes off along the fading track. William comes around to that side of the plane and stumbles after him, struggling to aim and fire. Ray hears a bullet whistle by, pounds faster, trying to recall the size of the magazine, eight bullets? How many left? Can't count.

He darts from the track to the wrecked, broken-backed ute a dozen yards from the track. He ducks behind its front end. It's worse cover than the plane. William approaches panting, forced to slow.

Ray looks for a weapon. No stones. Handfuls of dirt he can never scrape up. He yanks at the bent, rusted, half-open passenger door, braced for a body, finds none but sees a pile of coiled rope inside. Better than nothing. He reaches in, grabs a coil as he sees a flash of movement, and pulls.

Jesus. He's grabbed a king brown, a hand-width from its head. By the coils, at least six feet long, in retreat there from the heat. And fuck, another one. A bloody nest. He gives a guttural yell but has the snake now, his hand locked rigid, and he hauls himself back, carrying it as if trapped with it, horrified by its thickness, its weight, the dry scales, the writhing beneath them. Hears his own voice, louder and louder, its strangled noises. Sees the snake's head trying to reach back, the tail whirling, reaching too. Glimpses William coming around the back of the vehicle, Luger pointed, making sure of the shot.

Ray cries in fear, steps back clumsily, pulling the snake free. Ray starts to turn, wailing, arm outstretched and whirling to try to stop it coiling on him, desperate to keep his footing on the uneven ground.

William is out from behind the wreck, gun down, open-mouthed, staring. Ray cries out in panic and revulsion and tries to hurl the snake at him but gets it wrong and flings it in the opposite direction, out into the desert, where it lands and slip-slides away.

William laughs wildly, points at Ray and weaves to and fro in a small parody of Ray's lunatic dance. He kicks the rusted rear of the ute in crazy victory, leans back against it, breathing hard to calm himself. Ray stands there, panting, exposed, waiting.

As William raises the Luger again, Ray sees a long, thin shape rise from the broken rear of the ute. Another king brown, its extraordinary strength holding it upright in space. Ray's turn to freeze, and stare.

It lunges at William's neck. He jolts, sees it, screams, his face ugly and twisted. He fires erratically as the snake strikes again and again at his neck, biting, biting, each hit a pounding impact that sends him reeling even as he keeps firing. Ray drops to the ground, curled up with no defence as bullets fly. The gun clicks empty. The snake falls over the edge of the ute.

William falls, too, and jerks about on the fiery, unyielding ground.

Ray stays motionless, face bloodless as the snake slinks past William and twists away, leaving a shallow, winding path in the dust. Ray recalls, as a kid, using the side of his cupped hands to make false but scary snake tracks across dirt pathways.

William reaches for him. 'Help me.' He convulses, vomits, scratches at his bleeding neck, shits his pants.

Ray watches to the end. No idea how long it takes.

27

Ray is in William's seat, plane engine off, cocooned in silence. The glowing orange sun is done with the day and fills a gap perfectly between two low, purple hills an unmeasurable distance away. The wide horizon is a paler orange. Something molten is leaking from the sun, flowing to fill all hollows. He's been here all day but time means little. He reaches for a drink but the plane's water bottles are empty.

Beside him is the cane basket Arshag gave him. Crumpled wrapping paper shows most items have been consumed. He explores for more.

Radio static signals a call. A bizarre sound here. Ray exhales, stares at the radio, unwilling to respond, then does.

'Ray Windsor.'

He hears a gentle laugh.

'You're supposed to say *over*. Over.'

'Arshag.'

'Taken a while. Sorry about that.'

'Thought you'd gone home. Couldn't find anyone who wanted to help.'

350

Arshag chuckles. 'It's fine. Helpers came out of the woodwork. And you're a lucky boy. Soon after I put the word out, a local flight saw your plane. So the cavalry's coming. Over.'

'Is it over? Really over? Over.' He laughs, wonders if it's sunstroke.

'I followed up at William's, what you said. Drove out this arvo. I'm here now.'

Through the odd burst of static, Ray hears Arshag pause, exhale, then continue. 'Like you thought. A body in the garden bed. The Baroness. Dressed up like she's off to meet the Queen. Over.'

'All dressed up and nowhere to go. And Taylor and the rest of the bad boys?'

'Taylor messed up plan B. Couldn't bear to destroy anything he thought he might make a quid from. There's evidence alright. And William?'

'Under the plane. Nothing I knew could help him. King brown.' Shudders.

'Deadly, them browns.' Arshag laughs at his own joke. 'You?'

'I'll have some scars. Even if they don't show.'

'You really picked up a six-foot king brown and threw it?'

'There'll be nightmares.'

'You expecting a big welcome home parade back in Brissy?'

'Ha. No, it's more of a bad penny thing.' He looks out at mulga trees, ageless earth, the sun halfway gone. He feels the pull of it. And loss.

He says, 'I'm going to get a new bike. Big bastard. Got my eye on a Ducati. Something special.'

There's a comfortable silence.
'Help'll be along soon,' Arshag says.
'No rush. I like it here.'
Arshag laughs. 'Told you.'

Acknowledgements

The settings for *Conviction* are invented, but stretch loosely across the Indigenous country of the Mandandanji and Barrunggam peoples.

I was raised near the mouth of the Burral Burral (Burnett) River and acknowledge the people of the Taribelang language, which connects the traditional custodians to the country where Bundaberg now sits.

Always was, always will be.

Conviction would not exist without the help of a small army. Thank you to my agent, Virginia Lloyd, a constant source of support and sound advice. Thank you to everyone at Allen & Unwin for your attention to detail and deep commitment to quality, particularly Jane Palfreyman, Angela Handley and Aziza Kuypers. And thank you to Rebecca Starford for her equally professional and useful structural edit. I have learned from each of you.

Even before I found an agent or publisher, I have had the formidable support of a team of doughty readers, particularly

Fran Ross, and also Margery Forde, Michael Richards and Ros McCulloch. A special thank you to the late Michael Forde, who took such time and care to offer wonderful insights and encouragement; parts of you are in this book.

Thank you to Melinda Holden for her unstinting advice on Indigenous references. Melinda's traditional connection is through her father's Taribelang (Bundaberg) and her mother's Warrgamayan (Ingham) heritage.

Last but never least, I am grateful to my wife, Julie, the wisest and most generous person I know. Your unfailing faith in this whole enterprise has made it possible.